W9-AFI-255

THE
World War II

100

A Ranking of the
Most Influential Figures
of the
Second World War

HOWARD J. LANGER

New Page Books
A Division of Career Press, Inc.
Franklin Lakes, NJ

THE WORLD WAR II 100
Edited by Dianna Walsh
Typeset by John J. O'Sullivan
Cover design by DesignConcept
Printed in the U.S.A. by Book-mart Press

To order this title, please call toll-free 1-800-CAREER-1 (NJ and Canada: 201-848-0310) to order using VISA or MasterCard, or for further information on books from Career Press.

The Career Press, Inc., 3 Tice Road, PO Box 687
Franklin Lakes, NJ 07417
www.careerpress.com
www.newpagebooks.com

Library of Congress Cataloging-in-Publication Data

Langer, Howard.
    The World War II 100 : a ranking of the most influential figures of the Second World War / by Howard Langer.
        p. cm.
    Includes index.
    ISBN 1-56414-506-9
        1. World War, 1939-1945--Biography. 2. Heads of state--Biography. 3. Generals--Biography. 4. Admirals--Biography. I. Title: World War Two 100. II. Title: World War Two One Hundred. III. Title: World War 2 100. IV. Title: World War 2 One Hundred. V. Title.

D736 .L36 2001
940.53'092'2--dc21   2001031540

Dedication

This book is dedicated to those anonymous influentials who fought the good fight, including—but certainly not limited to—the:

Marines at Tarawa,

sailors off Midway,

G.I.s in the Huertgen Forest,

airmen over the Ploesti oilfields,

submariners prowling the Pacific depths,

nurses on Bataan,

coast guardsmen along the Gulf of Mexico,

and merchant seamen braving the North Atlantic.

Acknowledgments

I would like to thank Bob Bly for thinking about me for this project, literary agents Marilyn Allen and Bob Diforio, and Career Press acquisitions editor Mike Lewis. As usual, I could not have done this without the enthusiastic support of my wife, Florence, friends, and family.

The staff of the New City (Rockland County, N.Y.) Public Library provided their usual cheerful assistance. Other county libraries that were helpful include Pearl River, Nanuet, Orangeburg, and the Finklestein Memorial Library in Spring Valley.

In addition to the books and authors listed in the bibliography, I made use of several encyclopedias, including the *World Book* and the *Encyclopedia Britannica*.

Other invaluable resources were *The New York Times, Current Biography*, and the *World Almanac*.

I shall always be indebted for an afternoon with the late William L. Shirer. His insights on Nazi Germany, Fascist Italy, the Soviet Union, and France were extremely valuable.

As every researcher has discovered through the years, the sources do not always agree. That goes not only for the factual material in this book, but for the value judgments as well. For all of these, I assume full responsibility.

Contents

Preface

"History," wrote Thomas Carlyle, "is the essence of innumerable biographies."

Surely innumerable men and women made the history we call World War II. Is it possible to limit those individuals and their accomplishments to a list of 100? The most bloody and devastating series of events in world history involved more than a billion people and dozens of countries, including the eight major powers of the time: the United States, Nazi Germany, the Soviet Union, the United Kingdom, Italy, France, China, and Japan. For reasons relating to the origins of the war, other countries that also significantly affected the conflict including Poland, Czechoslovakia, Ethiopia, and Spain.

As I saw it, the only way to create this list of individuals was to choose from the various groups involved, not only by nationality but by profession. That meant including not only the government leaders and the military, but the diplomats who made the deals, the scientists who designed the weapons, the intelligence people who broke the codes, the journalists who reported the war, and the warriors and the victims.

What we call World War II was basically three separate wars: the war in Europe, the war in the Pacific, and Hitler's war against the Jews. All three, I felt, had to be acknowledged.

Therefore, I deliberately avoided exclusively focusing on individuals commonly known as "great" or "important." Though a few of those selected for this book might be called such, many of the chosen are little known.

I selected individuals who were the most "influential." The dictionary defines influential as having the power to bring about change. In most cases, those profiled here *did* bring about change—for good or evil. In other cases, they tried to bring about change but failed. In a few cases, they had the power to bring about change but, for whatever reasons, chose not to do so.

Some of those who appear in this book are individuals representing a whole group of people. Douglas Bader, for example, represents the Royal Air Force, which saved Britain during Nazi Germany's blitzkreig. Three "first ladies" of their lands were selected to represent the multifaceted role of women in the war. Mordecai Anielewicz represents the Jews who fought back against the Nazi oppressors.

I elected to include some individuals whose influence was not felt until after the war: Anne Frank kept a diary, and Justice Robert Jackson was a prosecutor at Nuremberg.

Huge volumes of biography have been written about many of the individuals in this book. There are accounts in encyclopedias and other reference works that include far more information than could possibly be presented in the short chapters contained here. What I have tried to do is present a brief vignette about the person to identify him or her with a specific achievement or event: Heinz Guderian and the blitzkrieg, Isoruku Yamamoto and Pearl Harbor, C.A.F. Sprague and Leyte Gulf, and Albert Einstein and a letter to President Franklin D. Roosevelt.

I have included legends and apocryphal accounts because they added to an individual's influence. Sometimes I have described an event based on speculation: Joseph Goebbels awaiting the last letters from the trapped Germans at Stalingrad or Konstantin Rokossovsky being released from his cell following imprisonment for alleged treason.

Though there are 100 numbered rankings in the list, a few of these chapters include more than one individual. Husband E. Kimmel and Walter Short are together in the same chapter because they were the responsible naval and military commanders at Pearl Harbor. The Sullivan brothers and the four chaplains appear together because they served as extraordinary examples of heroism and sacrifice.

I can almost guarantee that every reader will search, in vain, for a specific name in the 100. Where, they will ask, are William H. Simpson, Marc Mitscher, Werner von Blomberg, Archibald Wavell, Claire Chennault, Curtis Lemay, James V. Forrestal, Wilhelm Canaris, and Oscar Schindler? These individuals are in Appendix A, with scores of other honorable mentions. There are also a number of "dishonorable" mentions, including Axis Sally, Tokyo Rose, and Joseph Mengele.

Some readers may object to the numerical rankings. Why is Isoruku Yamamoto ranked higher than Dwight D. Eisenhower and Douglas MacArthur? In each chapter, I give my reasons. I will listen to anybody who wants to argue the rankings from Number 9 down to Number 100, but I will defend to the death the choice of the top-ranking eight individuals.

Clearly, this list is purely subjective; there is nothing objective about it. As a child during the war, I recognized two groups of people: the good guys and the bad guys. We, the Americans, and our Allies, were the good guys.

But years later, when researching my books on World War II and the Holocaust, I discovered how simplistic that viewpoint was. The war was far more complicated.

I plead guilty to seeing things as an American. That is why there are more Americans represented in this book than any other single nationality (see Appendix C for the breakdown).

Now that you have been forewarned, meet the choices for the 100 most influential figures of World War II.

Introduction

A Brief History of World War II

Most historians date the start of World War II as September 3, 1939, when, following the German invasion of Poland, England and France declared war on Nazi Germany. However, the roots of the war are much deeper, going back to the Franco-Prussian War of 1870. After the defeat of France, Germany annexed Alsace-Lorraine. For more than 40 years afterward, whenever French officers met together, there was always the toast to "Revenge!" The implication of this was rarely spelled out. No comment was necessary, for every French officer knew exactly what the pledge meant.

A Changing Map

This is not the book to discuss the causes of World War I. Its consequences, however, directly affected not just the future of Europe but of the world.

The map of Europe was redrawn following World War I. France got back Alsace-Lorraine. The Austro-Hungarian Empire and former Imperial Russia were split up into a number of independent nations. Germany was held responsible for the war; it lost part of its European territory and all of its colonies overseas. Its military and naval forces were sharply limited.

One important outcome of World War I was the establishment of a League of Nations to settle international disputes. But, in a return to isolationism, the United States—the most powerful nation to emerge from the war—would not join the League, its Senate opposing U.S. participation.

The Rise of Hitler

Early in the 1920s, an Austrian who had fought in the German army as a corporal became the leader of a small new German political party. His name was Adolf Hitler (Number 1). The party, originally called the German Workers Party, became the National Socialist Party, or Nazi Party for short.

As the Nazi Party slowly expanded, a political party was taking shape in Italy. It was called the Fascist Party and was led by Benito Mussolini (Number 50). In 1922, Mussolini marched on Rome and was asked to form a new government.

In 1923, Hitler tried to copy Mussolini's example and take power in Munich by force, but his little band of revolutionaries was dispersed, and Hitler was arrested. He spent his prison time writing *Mein Kampf* ("My Struggle"), in which he set forth his ideas for a new Germany. He attacked the terms of the Treaty of Versailles, which had ended World War I; called for an expansionist Germany at the expense of its neighbors; and denounced Jews, not just in Germany but throughout the world.

During the next decade, Hitler built his political base. Joseph Goebbels (Number 44) became the Führer's propaganda chief. The Nazi Party proclaimed its own version of racial superiority. The true Germans were said to be Nordic supermen who should rule the world. "Sub-humans" were to be destroyed, and other undesirables would be allowed to become slaves of the super race.

On January 30, 1933, Hitler became Chancellor of a coalition government in Germany. He received the financial backing of the Krupp family (Number 68) and other important industrialists. The Führer proceeded to set up a one-party dictatorship, with an ultimate aim of ruling the world.

Prelude to War

The 1930s saw a series of missed opportunities to stop aggression. In 1931, Japan took over Manchuria. In 1935, Germany occupied the Rhineland and Mussolini invaded Ethiopia. Haile Selassie (Number 96) warned the League of Nations that it had to take action in the name of collective security, but the League backed down. In 1936, Francisco Franco (Number 75) set off the Spanish Civil War, lining up future players in the great war to come.

Nazi Germany illegally built up its armed forces. World War I air ace Hermann Goering (Number 43) was put in charge of a "commercial" airline, a front for the construction of bombers and fighters.

The year 1938 would become crucial for the Western democracies. Hitler had come to power in January 1933 and had spent the years building up the German army, navy, and air force. It was all contrary to the Treaty of Versailles, but Hitler had renounced that treaty long before.

Early in 1938, Hitler decided to take personal command of the armed forces of Germany. He named Wilhelm Keitel (Number 48) as his chief of staff. Hitler's plans to conquer Europe were underway.

Austria was occupied and incorporated into the Reich without firing a shot. Next, Hitler turned to Czechoslovakia and demanded the Sudetenland. A conference was held in Munich to discuss the matter. Taking part were Hitler, Mussolini, British Prime Minister Neville Chamberlain (Number 66), and French Premier Eduard Daladier. Conspicuously absent were Eduard Benes (Number 81) and other representatives of Czechoslovakia. They would later be advised that England and France had given away a piece of their country to Hitler.

Six weeks after their victory at Munich, the Nazis carried out a series of pogroms throughout Germany and Austria. During Kristalnacht, Jews were killed or rounded up and sent to concentration camps, synagogues were burned to the ground, and Jewish shops and businesses were sacked and put to the torch. The Nazis had previously enacted a series of laws denying Jews basic rights of citizenship, including the right to engage in certain professions. That November night in 1938, the Holocaust had begun.

War in the Pacific

While the attention of the world was focused on Europe, Japan was moving into China. Beginning in 1937, Japanese armies quickly seized Peking (now Beijing), Tientsin, and areas in the north of China. This was followed by a campaign against Shanghai, Soochow, and Nanking. Chiang Kai-shek (Number 87) set up a new capital in Chungking.

Following an orgy of rape and murder in Nanking, the League of Nations officially condemned Japanese aggression in China. But nothing else was done; the war went on.

The Pact That Shocked the World

The year 1939 would finally bring an end to appeasement. It began with Hitler taking over all of Czechoslovakia. He had promised Chamberlain at Munich that he had no further territorial demands in Europe. Now, it was clear that his promises were worthless. The German dictator started making demands on Poland. After World War I, East Prussia had been geographically separated from the rest of Germany by a large part of Poland. Hitler demanded this "Polish corridor." England and France had treaty obligations with Poland and indicated they would stand by those treaties if the Nazis invaded.

The world waited for bombshells to fall, but what came first was a political bombshell: a non-aggression pact between Nazi Germany and the Soviet Union.

Hitler had identifed the Soviet Union in his *Mein Kampf* as a target for German expansion. His political life had been devoted to fighting Communism. Several Russian generals had recognized the danger of a growing military threat in Nazi Germany and had recommended a preventive war before Germany got too strong. This had been countered by a crafty intelligence coup by Reinhard Heydrich (Number 25), who had framed Red Army officers and fooled Joseph Stalin (Number 4) into a purge of his army leadership.

But for now at least, Hitler and Stalin had made a deal not to go to war against each other. On August 23, 1939, German Foreign Minister Joachim von Ribbentrop (Number 52) and Soviet Foreign Minister Vyacheslav M. Molotov (Number 53) signed the Nazi-Soviet non-aggression pact. Under secret terms of that agreement, the two nations would divide up Poland between them. On September 1, Germany invaded Poland from the west. Two weeks later, the Soviet Union invaded from the east. Largely due to the blitzkrieg tactics of Heinz Guderian (Number 12), Poland was soon crushed.

As soon as the Nazi armies crossed the Polish frontier, England and France demanded that Germany withdraw its troops within 48 hours. When Hitler did not comply, the two Western allies declared war on Germany.

For six months after the fall of Poland, very little seemed to happen. Journalists began to call it a "phony war." But two things were overlooked.

First, the Soviet Union invaded Finland. The Soviets, deprived of much of its leadership in the Red Army purge, were badly mauled by the Finns until Semyon Timoshenko (Number 54) broke the Mannerheim Line. The Red Army began to rebuild its officer corps.

Second, during this period of relative "inactivity," Nazi Germany was methodically destroying small Jewish towns in Poland. Jewish ghettos were being created in or near major Polish cities.

Through the work of Polish intelligence officials, the British were now in possession of the secrets of Ultra, the German military code. Stewart Menzies (Number 15), head of British intelligence, was in charge of the operation that decoded the top-secret Nazi messages and saw that they were distributed to the appropriate political and military figures.

Hitler Strikes West

The blitzkrieg in the west came on April 9, 1940, with an invasion of Denmark and Norway. The following month, Hitler attacked Belgium, the Netherlands, and Luxembourg.

With disaster facing the Allied armies, Chamberlain resigned as British prime minister. He was replaced by Winston S. Churchill (Number 3).

Belgium was the key to reorganizing defense lines in France. As long as the Belgians held out for a while, the British and French could shore up new positions. But Leopold III (Number 95), King of the Belgians, capitulated too quickly, and Nazi armor poured into France.

Maurice Gamelin (Number 62) had sat behind the Maginot Line to await a direct assault by German forces. They failed to oblige, cutting through Belgium into the heart of France. The British Expeditionary Force, plus many French and other Allied troops, were trapped around Dunkirk. Under the direction of British Admiral Bertram Ramsay (Number 16), British and other Allied troops were evacuated by a fleet of small boats that took them back to England.

French Premier Paul Reynaud (Number 99) wanted to continue the fight from North Africa. He asked Marshal Henri Petain (Number 27) to return from his diplomatic post in Spain to help rally the French people.

From the beginning, Hitler had urged Mussolini to enter the war with him. The Duce had refused, saying that Italy was not ready. Now, with France tottering and England on the ropes, Mussolini declared war on Britain and France and invaded southern France.

Petain, seeing the situation as hopeless, favored an armistice. He replaced Reynaud as premier and asked Hitler for terms.

The armistice was signed on June 22, 1940, at Compiegne, France, in the same railway car where the Germans had surrendered in 1918.

In the United States, Americans heard the voice of radio correspondent William L. Shirer (Number 55) describe a contemptuous Hitler at the scene of his greatest triumph.

England Stands Alone

Many Frenchmen who wished to go on fighting the Germans left for England. Among them was General Charles De Gaulle (Number 51). He became a leader of a group called the Free French or Fighting French. There were also troops from Belgium, Holland, and Poland; even though their countries were occupied, they could continue the fight against Hitler. As a free, unoccupied nation, England stood alone against the Nazis. King George VI (Number 95) and Queen Elizabeth (Number 78) kept English morale high with their show of quiet courage.

In September 1940, representatives of Germany, Italy, and Japan signed the Tripartite Pact in Berlin.

President Franklin D. Roosevelt (Number 2) recognized the threat that Hitler posed to the world. FDR was facing an election for an unprecedented third term. The country was still isolationist, but American defenses had to be built up. The Democratic president called on two prominent Republicans to join his cabinet: Henry L. Stimson (Number 21) to head the War Department and Frank Knox (Number 60) to head the Navy Department.

Fortunately, America already had in place General George C. Marshall (Number 5) as Army chief of staff. He had started his duties on September 1, 1939, the same day Hitler had invaded Poland. Since then, Marshall had been hard at work building a combat-ready force.

Meanwhile, Great Britain braced itself for a German invasion. Most of its heavy guns had been left behind on the beaches of Dunkirk, and only America could help it rearm.

Also in 1940, the America First Committee had been formed in the United States to fight any involvement in the European war. Its chief spokesman was Charles A. Lindbergh, Jr. (Number 86).

As Hitler extended his sphere of influence all over Europe, Jews tried to reach haven in the United States. Many thousands were prevented from doing so through the efforts of State Department official Breckinridge Long (Number 73), who sent out orders to consular personnel in Europe to keep delaying the issuance of visas as long as possible.

Another controversial State Department official was U.S. ambassador to Britain Joseph P. Kennedy (Number 98), who made clear his feeling that Britain was going to lose the war against Hitler. Eventually, Kennedy was recalled to Washington.

Throughout 1940, the British, facing a Nazi invasion, were concerned that the powerful French fleet might fall into the hands of the Nazis. French naval commanders were asked by the British to sail their ships to French possessions in the Western hemisphere to prevent their seizure. When this request was ignored, British naval forces opened fire on units of the French fleet near Oran, North Africa. French losses were heavy, and a deep distrust formed between the two former allies.

Two major events took place in the latter part of 1940: Hitler's air blitz over England and the presidential election in the United States.

The British took a pounding and suffered significant civilian casualties. What kept Britain alive was its Royal Air Force, symbolized by such airmen as Douglas Bader (Number 10).

Across the Atlantic, Roosevelt walked a tightrope. He raised the issue of national defense while assuring voters that the United States would not enter any foreign wars. (The Democratic Party platform that year had used a similar phrase but added "unless we are attacked." Roosevelt was advised to include the phrase in his speeches, but he rejected the added note as being obvious.)

During the worst nights of the blitz, CBS radio correspondent Edward R. Murrow (Number 70) described the Nazi bombing raids, arousing sympathy in the United States.

In September, with the election campaign in full swing, the United States swapped overage destroyers in exchange for British bases in the Western hemisphere. The same month Congress passed the Selective Service Act. The course could not be clearer.

Aid for Britain

With the reelection of Roosevelt, the top priorities for the United States were national defense and aid for Britain. In the most daring use of analogy in American political history, Roosevelt compared the sending of arms to Britain with lending one's neighbor a garden hose if his house catches fire. Lend-lease became part of the national vocabulary.

The year 1941 began with Roosevelt's State of the Union address to Congress. In it, he enunciated "Four Freedoms" for the world: freedom of speech, freedom of religion, freedom from want, and freedom from fear. The traditional State of the Union address had become a State of the World.

The president sent his trusted aide, Harry L. Hopkins (Number 22), to meet with Churchill in London. American aid would be forthcoming.

That aid would come to Britain across the Atlantic in merchant ships. German U-boats under the command of Karl Doenitz (Number 64) prowled the sea lanes, sinking many British-bound ships. In order to protect these ships, American naval vessels accompanied ship convoys.

In April 1941, Germany invaded Yugoslavia and Greece. Later, the Nazis sent a glider force to capture the Greek island of Crete. Yugoslavia would prove a major sore point for Hitler throughout the rest of the war, as partisan guerrillas under Tito (Number 61) tied up huge German armies.

One of the strangest incidents of the war occurred in May 1941, when Rudolf Hess, Hitler's most trusted aide, parachuted into Scotland to offer Britain a peace plan: End the war and allow Germany a free hand on the European continent. Churchill refused.

Churchill knew of Hitler's next target: the Soviet Union. The breaking of Germany's Ultra code gave the British advance notice of the attack to come. The British tried to warn Stalin, but their warnings fell on deaf ears.

British intelligence impressed Roosevelt, who appointed William J. Donovan (Number 24) to set up America's own intelligence operation. With the help of William Stephenson (Number 23), the Canadian-born head of British intelligence in the Western hemisphere, Donovan began to set up what would become the Office of Strategic Services.

Invasion of the Soviet Union

On June 22, 1941, massive German armies rolled into the Soviet Union. Gerd von Rundstedt (Number 56) was in overall command; Russia's top commander was Georgi Zhukov (Number 17).

The Germans advanced quickly but were stopped by an early winter. The era of quick victory was over.

Meanwhile, back in Japan, a new premier had been selected in October 1941. His name was Hideki Tojo (Number 29). The Japanese government had decided to seize the territories of European powers too occupied with Hitler to defend their Pacific colonies. Only the United States Navy stood in the way. Admiral Isoruku Yamamoto (Number 6) was asked to plan a crippling blow on the U.S. Pacific Fleet at Pearl Harbor.

Attack in the Pacific

William Friedman (Number 40) had broken the Japanese code. From it, the United States had learned of Japanese interest in three specific areas: the Philippines, the Canal Zone, and Pearl Harbor. Area commanders were warned that a break in diplomatic relations was imminent. On December 7, 1941, a huge Japanese task force, including six aircraft carriers, attacked Pearl Harbor with devastating effect. Admiral Husband E. Kimmel (Number 19) and General Walter Short (Number 19), the top commanders in Hawaii, were relieved of their commands.

The Japanese quickly took Hong Kong and Wake. They attacked the Dutch East Indies in force. Tomoyuki Yamashita (Number 58) made his way through the Malayan jungles to seize Singapore. Masaharu Homma (Number 45) attacked the Philippines.

The U.S. Army Air Corps had been caught on the ground in the Philippines, and the island was open for invasion. The Japanese landed on Luzon and soon took Manila.

Douglas MacArthur (Number 8), commander of all U.S. forces in the Philippines, was ordered to Australia to take charge of all Allied forces in the Southwest Pacific. A doomed garrison was left behind under Jonathan Wainwright (Number 84). Bataan would fall in April and Corregidor in May 1942.

America at War

Following Pearl Harbor, Hitler made a fateful—and fatal—decision: He declared war on the United States. Italy and other Axis allies followed suit, including Hungary, Romania, and Bulgaria.

The United States and Britain decided to concentrate on defeating Hitler first, and then Japan.

Chester Nimitz (Number 18) was named head of the Pacific Fleet. Ernest J. King (Number 20) was chosen both the commander in chief of the U.S. Fleet as well as chief of naval operations.

Virtually the entire Pacific Fleet had to be replaced after the attack on Pearl Harbor, and many more ships would be needed in a multi-ocean war. The industrialists were called in, and shipbuilders such as Andrew Jackson Higgins (Number 69) and Henry J. Kaiser became household names.

Hitler's War against the Jews

Largely ignored in the midst of earth-shattering events was Hitler's war against the Jews. On the Führer's orders, a conference took place at Wannsee, a suburb of Berlin, in January 1942. Chaired by Heydrich and Adolf Eichmann (Number 91), it brought together the key German government officials to arrange the "Final Solution" of the Jewish problem. Jews would be transported to the east. There they would either be worked to death or killed outright. Death camp machinery was set in place, including gas chambers and crematoria. In the years to follow, many Christians would risk their lives to hide Jews or rescue them. Nearly the entire Jewish community of Denmark would be rescued by a massive effort on the part of the Danish people. The rescuers had been inspired by the courage of their king, Christian X (Number 95), who, it is said, was prepared to wear the first Star of David armband if the Nazis required Jews to display it on their clothing. The diary of Anne Frank (Number 90), a Jewish adolescent in hiding, would become an inspiration for the world when published after the war.

International reaction to the genocide of European Jewry was almost nonexistent. When the American vice-consul in Geneva got word of Nazi plans to slaughter Europe's Jews, he sent word to the State Department in Washington. An American envoy at the Vatican, going through traditional diplomatic channels, asked Pope Pius XII (Number 100) if he had heard of such reports and, if so, what could be done about them. The Holy See responded that they had heard similar reports that could not be verified. The Vatican had no practical suggestions to help the "non-Aryans."

The Allies Fight Back

After the attack on Pearl Harbor, it was important for the Japanese to believe that the United States still possessed some power in the Pacific. Jimmy Doolittle (Number 9) and a group of army pilots took off from the carrier *Hornet* to bomb Tokyo and other Japanese cities. The damage to the Japanese cities was minimal, but it accomplished two things. First, Japan had to hold back naval and air forces to protect the home islands. Second, it baited the Japanese to attempt to stage another Pearl Harbor victory at Midway. But this time the Americans were ready and badly defeated the superior Japanese naval force. Feisty American naval commanders, such as William F. Halsey, Jr. (Number 26) and Thomas Kinkaid (Number 35), shot up Japanese targets all over the Pacific at such a pace that the enemy thought the U.S. Pacific Fleet was much larger than it really was.

As battles raged in the Pacific, fighting in the Soviet Union continued to be fierce. Lavrenti Beria (Number 79) saw to it that any German gain on the ground would yield only scorched earth to the enemy. At home, Germany was forced to take defensive positions, as Arthur ("Bomber") Harris (Number 34) of the RAF began to send out 1,000-plane raids on Nazi targets.

In North Africa, Erwin Rommel (Number 39) led his Afrika Korps to initial victories. Harold Alexander (Number 76) was put in charge of British operations in North Africa. He sent Bernard Montgomery (Number 37) against Rommel, and the Afrika Korps was put to flight at El Alamein.

Dealing with the Vichy French

After the fall of France, Germany occupied northern and western sections of the country. The remainder of France was run from Vichy by Marshal Petain. The United States kept diplomatic relations with Vichy through an American envoy named Robert Murphy (Number 63). Using his contacts in France and North Africa, Murphy was able to gain French cooperation in allowing American forces to land in French North Africa with minimal resistance. The key French official in the operation was Jean Darlan (Number 59), who ordered a cease-fire.

As 1942 came to an end, it was clear that America had lost its innocence. U.S. troops were about to face German land forces for the first time in North Africa, American Marines were battling the Japanese in the Guadalcanal jungles, and a light cruiser named the *Juneau* went down in the Pacific with heavy loss of life. Among the casualties were all five Sullivan brothers (Number 85).

Russian forces, meanwhile, were slowly building a ring of steel around the German army at Stalingrad.

The Tide Turns

For the most part, the year 1943 would be the year of changing fortunes for the Allies and the Axis. It began in January with a meeting in Casablanca, North Africa, between Roosevelt and Churchill to plan military operations. It was here that Roosevelt announced to the press the need for "unconditional surrender" of the enemy.

Dwight D. Eisenhower (Number 7) was commander of American forces in North Africa, and it was clear that his prospects were excellent for future leadership.

Hitler had promoted Stalingrad commander Friedrich von Paulus (Number 57) to the rank of field marshal. Every officer in the German army knew that no field marshal had ever surrendered; the implied message to von Paulus was clear. But his men had run out of food, ammunition, and, most of all, their faith in the Führer. Caught in the steel trap of the Red Army's Vasily Chuikov (Number 42), von Paulus surrendered his 100,000 surviving troops. Only 10,000 would return after the war.

Another human tragedy, this one in the North Atlantic, became a symbol of what the war was all about: preserving human dignity and brotherhood in the midst of carnage and suffering. The *Dorchester*, an American troop transport, was torpedoed by a Nazi U-boat. There were not enough lifejackets to go around. Four chaplains (Number 85) gave up their lifejackets to four soldiers, locked arms, and went down with the ship.

In February 1943, American troops were bloodied in Tunisia at Kasserine Pass by the Germans; they would be whipped into shape by George S. Patton, Jr. (Number 11). When victory came to Tunisia and North Africa was secured, Patton and Montgomery would lead forces into Sicily.

The Italian Surrender

The Allied conquest of Sicily in July 1943 and the impending invasion of Italy itself led to the overthrow of Mussolini. The Duce was voted out of office by the Fascist Council; even his own son-in-law, Galeazzo Ciano (Number 80) voted against him. The Duce was deposed and held in detention. At the request of King Victor Emanuel, Pietro Badoglio (Number 74) was made new premier. His job: Get Italy out of the war.

Hitler sent the commando Otto Skorzeny to rescue Mussolini. The Duce was made head of northern Italy, which was occupied by the Germans at that time. But Italy surrendered to the Allies in September 1943 and a month later declared war on Germany.

Keeping Up the Fighting Spirit

Morale was extremely important for both civilians and the military. During a visit to army training camps, Marshall discovered that men on weekend pass wandered around nearby towns with nothing to do. He came up with the idea for the United Service Organizations (USO) shows to entertain the troops. Bob Hope and other performers made trips all over the world to the delight of American servicemen and servicewomen. A surprising favorite of G.I.s overseas was Eleanor Roosevelt (Number 78). The First Lady represented every G.I.'s mother looking in to see how things were going. She not only chatted about what was going on back home, but she was in a position to report back to the president on what was happening abroad.

Among newspaper favorites at home and abroad were correspondent Ernie Pyle (Number 71) and cartoonist Bill Mauldin (Number 72). Pyle told the story of individual warriors by name, home address, and family back home. Mauldin was the G.I.'s own editorial cartoonist, dealing with the realities of war with grim humor.

The War Rages on

As the Navy buildup continued in the Pacific, Marines and army forces struck one island after the other against tenacious Japanese resistance. MacArthur pushed for an early invasion of the Philippines.

In the United States, Madame Chiang Kai-shek (Number 78), in an address to Congress, pleaded for increased aid to China. Joseph W. Stilwell (Number 83) would be sent to China to see what could be done.

In Europe, German radio announced that the bodies of thousands of Polish army officers had been uncovered in mass graves in the Katyn forest, which had originally been occupied by the Red Army in its 1939 invasion of Poland. Goebbels said that the Soviets had murdered the officers; the Soviets blamed the Nazis. Wladyslaw Sikorski (Number 82), of the Polish government-in-exile, asked the Russians for an explanation. Then he died in a suspicious accident.

The Warsaw Ghetto Uprising

If the Nazis, with their modern equipment, struggled against the Red Army, they could at least show how easy it was to wipe out a ghetto of Jewish civilians in Warsaw. Heinrich Himmler (Number 65) gave instructions to destroy the ghetto completely; he wanted to make more living space available for Aryans. When the Nazis entered the Warsaw ghetto, they were fired on by a pitifully small and ill-equipped group of guerrilla fighters under Mordecai Anielewicz (Number 97). It took the Nazis a month to win the battle.

Prelude to the Atomic Age

Back in the United States, an officer in the Army Corps of Engineers named Leslie R. Groves (Number 32) was assembling what would prove to be the single most important, and certainly most expensive, project of the war: the Manhattan Project to produce an atomic bomb. In August 1939, Albert Einstein (Number 13) had written a letter to President Roosevelt suggesting the project. Physicist J. Robert Oppenheimer (Number 30) was chosen to direct the scientists at Los Alamos, New Mexico; other plants would be built in Tennessee and Washington state to produce the weapons.

The Nazis were working on an atomic bomb at the same time, but their efforts were concentrated on the construction of rockets under the guidance of Wernher von Braun (Number 31).

Crusade in Europe

Roosevelt and Churchill had conferred together many times. It was time to meet with Stalin, who had been pushing for a second front in Europe for more than two years. Following a meeting in Cairo with Chiang Kai-shek in November 1943, the two Western leaders met with the Communist dictator in Teheran. At that point, Stalin insisted that a commander be named to lead the invasion into northern France; it would be Eisenhower.

As invasion forces began concentrating in England, U.S. Army air chief Henry H. Arnold (Number 41) was assembling a powerful air force in support. In the months before the invasion, air fleets pulverized German cities, destroying railroad facilities and communications. Key players in the invasion would include Omar Bradley (Number 33), Patton, Montgomery, and Alan Brooke (Number 28), Churchill's chief of staff.

D-Day came on June 6, 1944. Rommel, who knew it was essential to stop the invasion on the beaches, urged Hitler to release forces being held in reserve. But Hitler believed that the Normandy invasion was only a feint, and that the real invasion would come across the Pas de Calais. He waited until it was too late. Once the beachhead had been secured, the Anglo-American forces were in Europe to stay.

Attempted Assassination

There had been an underground movement in Nazi Germany from the beginning of Hitler's reign. First civilians, then people in the government, and then members of the military believed Hitler would bring ruin on Germany. Several times Hitler had miraculously escaped plots against his life.

On July 20, 1944, Claus von Stauffenberg (Number 89) left a bomb in one of Hitler's headquarters. The bomb detonated, but the Führer escaped with wounds. Hitler's revenge was swift and terrible. Most of the accused plotters were executed; only Rommel was permitted to commit suicide and have his family and staff spared.

March across Europe

In rapid order, American forces broke out of the beachhead at St. Lo, liberated Paris, and launched a second major invasion in the south of France.

However, Operation Market-Garden, an attempt to seize major bridges in Holland, was hurled back by the Germans.

Hitler's secret weapons began to appear: rockets and ballistic missiles, snorkel submarines, and jet fighters. All were developed too late to change the direction of the war. In fact, the very factories needed to produce them in quantity had been largely destroyed.

The Soviet juggernaut smashed across Poland, with Konstantin Rokossovsky (Number 47) leading the way. As he approached Warsaw, the Soviet radio called on the Poles to rise up and help drive out the Nazis. Tadeusz Bor-Komorowski (Number 88) headed the underground Polish army and rallied for an uprising in the Polish capital. However, instead of moving into Warsaw, the Red Army waited on the Vistula until the Nazis had crushed all resistance.

The Crises of Leyte and the Bulge

Late in 1944, two battles created crises for American forces. One was a sea battle in the Pacific, the other a land battle in Europe.

In October, MacArthur finally saw his dream of returning to the Philippines fulfilled. His first objective was the island of Leyte. The Japanese succeeded in luring Halsey's fleet away from guarding the San Bernardino Strait, which led to the Leyte beaches. As a huge Japanese naval force under Takeo Kurita (Number 38) approached the strait, it was challenged by a tiny force of escort carriers and cruisers under C.A.F. Sprague (Number 36). The Americans put up such a bruising defense that Kurita withdrew.

The second crisis began in mid-December, when German forces under von Rundstedt broke through the Ardennes in a surprise offensive. Bastogne, a critical Belgian road center, was defended by U.S. forces under Anthony McAuliffe (Number 67). Patton's army relieved the garrison and saved the day. The Ardennes campaign would be known in military history as the Battle of the Bulge.

The Beginning of the End

As 1945 began, it was clear that Germany and Japan would be defeated. The Germans had tried a final offensive and lost. From east and west, their borders were under assault. The Japanese had no fleet left to speak of. Instead, they sent out suicide pilots to crash their planes on American ships. Still, the fighting raged on.

Even as the battles continued, plans were being drawn up for the post-war world. A plan envisioned by Treasury Secretary Henry Morgenthau, Jr. (Number 93) to turn industrial Germany into an agricultural country was rejected, but plans were made for occupation zones, with Berlin in the heart of the Soviet zone.

A Successor to the League of Nations

Guided by U.S. Secretary of State Cordell Hull (Number 94), the framework for a new international organization to succeed the League of Nations had been put together at Dumbarton Oaks in the summer of 1944. The new international organization, the United Nations, would be established at the San Francisco Conference in the summer of 1945.

The Final Act Begins

In February 1945, Roosevelt, Churchill, and Stalin met at Yalta in the Crimea. The Soviets promised to come into the war against Japan three months after Germany surrendered.

As American forces approached the Rhine, preparations were being made to cross that final barrier to the heart of the Reich. On March 7th, American infantrymen were astonished to find the bridge at Remagen still standing; explosive charges had failed to detonate. The G.I.s raced across the Rhine. Hitler ordered those responsible for blowing up the bridge to be executed.

In the Pacific, costly battles were fought on Iwo Jima and Okinawa, as the U.S. forces got closer and closer to the Japanese home islands.

The End

April 1945 brought the deaths and suicides of a number of war leaders. First came Roosevelt's death by a cerebral hemorrhage, which Hitler, in his underground Berlin bunker, thought was the miracle that would change his fortunes. Then came the report that Mussolini had been shot by Italian partisans, which was not a good sign. Hitler instructed Albert Speer (Number 77) to destroy all German infrastructure, stating that the German people were unworthy of him; Speer sabotaged the order so it would not be carried out. Hitler and Goebbels committed suicide as the Red Army stormed Berlin.

Doenitz, now in charge of the German government, sent Alfred Jodl (Number 46) to Reims to sign the unconditional surrender. It took effect on May 8, 1945.

Harry S Truman (Number 14), who had succeeded to the office of president on Roosevelt's death, met with Churchill and Stalin at Potsdam in July 1945. Midway through the meeting, Churchill would be replaced by Clement Attlee, head of the victorious Labor Party.

The successful explosion of an atomic device in New Mexico posed major political, as well as military, decisions for the United States. Should the bomb be used against Japan? Should a warning be given first? Told that an invasion of the Japanese home islands would lead to a million American casualties, Truman made the decision to drop the bomb. Hiroshima was hit on August 6, 1945, and Nagasaki on August 8, the day Russia entered the war against Japan.

The debate in Japan over whether to surrender was even more intense than the one in the United States over using the bomb. Emperor Hirohito (Number 49) made the final decision. Japan surrendered on September 2, 1945, on the U.S.S. *Missouri* in Tokyo Bay.

The Post-War World

The Nuremberg trials got under way at the end of 1945, with U.S. Supreme Court Associate Justice Robert Jackson (Number 92) as one of the prosecutors. The day of reckoning was at hand.

In the wake of World War II would come many changes. The fight for freedom would inspire colonies around the world to shake off their shackles for independence. African Americans would assert their full rights as citizens of the United States. Women would decide not to go back to being housewives; they would demand the economic and political opportunities available to men. And something called the G.I. Bill of Rights was about to launch tens of millions of Americans into a brand new, thriving middle class.

World War II had redefined civilization.

1 Adolf Hitler

Cruel and Cunning

NATIONAL ARCHIVES

Members of the German Reichstag "heil" Adolf Hitler as he announces that German troops have occupied the Rhineland.

Adolf Hitler may be considered the most evil human being in the history of the world. The single most influential figure of World War II, he planned it, prepared for it, and, when he was ready, launched it. His goal was to create a world ruled by a supreme Aryan race. Undesirables, those deemed "sub-humans," would be exterminated. Others would be allowed to live as slaves of their Nazi masters.

Today that sounds like the plot for a science-fiction movie, but in the late 1930s and early 1940s, it was all too real. Hitler's goal was a German Reich that would rule the earth and last for 1,000 years. In fact, it actually lasted only 12 years and three months, but it was long enough to bring civilization to the edge of destruction.

Calling himself Führer (German for "leader"), Hitler used brute force and psychological terror to bring his enemies to their knees. Tens of millions of innocents, including six million Jews, would die in the Holocaust. Others chosen for extermination included Slavs, gypsies, Jehovah's Witnesses, and homosexuals. Additionally, millions of soldiers would die on the battlefields of the war Adolf Hitler engineered.

Early Influences

Life began for Adolf Hitler in 1889 in Braunau, an Austrian town near the German border. As a young man, he wanted to be an artist, but he was refused entry into the Vienna Academy of Fine Arts.

In 1913, at age 24, Hitler moved to Munich, Germany. When World War I broke out a year later, he joined the German army. Gassed in combat, he was awarded the Iron Cross. Some theorize that Hitler chose poison gas to kill his victims because of this military experience, but that is by no means certain.

Following Germany's defeat in World War I, Hitler joined a fledgling political group that called itself the German Workers' Party. It later became the National Socialist German Workers' Party, or the Nazi Party for short. A spellbinding orator, Hitler quickly became leader of the Nazis. The Party called for a Germany in which only those of pure German blood would be German citizens; it required the elimination of those who contributed to a "degenerate" culture. Furthermore, the Nazis opposed the terms of the Versailles Treaty, which had ended World War I.

In 1923, the Nazis tried to seize power by force in Munich. The attempt failed, and Hitler was jailed for nine months. During this time in prison, he wrote *Mein Kampf* ("My Struggle"). The book's major themes include the unfairness of the Treaty of Versailles; the vision of a much larger Germany at the expense of its neighbors; the necessity for aggressive military action and the use of slave labor to achieve the ideal Germany; and a strong emphasis on anti-Semitism.

The origins of Hitler's anti-Semitism are unclear to biographers. It is possible that Hitler may have picked it up from Austrian rabble-rousers, who used anti-Semitic campaign speeches to win votes. In any case, *Mein Kampf* would become the bible of the Nazi Party and the Third Reich.

In the late 1920s and early 1930s, economic disaster hit Germany. High unemployment and a devastating inflation plagued the economy. In this politically volatile environment, a number of parties sought votes in the Reichstag (the German parliament), including the Nazis, the Social Democrats, the Centrists, the Communists, and numerous small parties. However, because of the multiparty system, no one party could get an absolute majority in the Reichstag to form a government. In January of 1933, after much political maneuvering, a coalition government was created, in which Adolf Hitler would become chancellor and other members of the Nazi Party would assume key government posts.

Hitler Takes Power

Once in power, Hitler proceeded to destroy his political opposition. Using his own private army to beat up opponents, trash their political headquarters, and physically prevent them from entering the Reichstag, Hitler created a rubber-stamp Reichstag. It passed legislation giving Hitler the power to rule by decree, outlawing other political parties, and utterly obliterating the rights of German Jews. Concentration camps were set up to imprison, terrorize, torture, and murder political enemies. In the beginning, Communists and trade unionists were targeted, but later, the list of political enemies expanded to include Jews, intellectuals, and clergymen who spoke out against Hitler.

The Führer began a military buildup. He tested the will of the Western powers by sending German troops to occupy the Rhineland, which violated the Treaty of Versailles. The German commander of the occupying army was under secret orders to withdraw immediately if there was any military move against him. When the Western forces failed to meet this military challenge, Hitler believed he could get away with anything. More importantly, he showed his military staff that bluffing could work. Hitler was on his way.

In 1938, using the threat of military action, he forced Austria to agree to incorporation into the German Reich. At a meeting in Munich in the fall of that year, Hitler demanded the Sudetenland, an important part of Czechoslovakia. British Prime Minister Neville Chamberlain (Number 66) and French Premier Eduard Daladier agreed to the takeover. Several months later, Hitler usurped all of Czechoslovakia. It was only the beginning.

Hitler's March through Europe

In August 1939, Hitler stunned the world by arranging a non-aggression pact between Nazi Germany and the Soviet Union. Hitler was preparing to invade Poland, and he knew that France and Britain had pledged to defend Poland. The German dictator agreed to split up Poland with Soviet dictator Joseph Stalin (Number 4). On September 1, 1939, German forces moved into Poland. Two days later, England and France declared war on Germany. World War II had officially begun.

The Soviet Union invaded Poland two weeks later, and the country was crushed by the two invading armies. Hitler turned with greedy eyes to the west, biding his time until the spring of 1940.

In April, German armies invaded Denmark and Norway. The following month, German troops invaded Belgium, the Netherlands, and Luxembourg. By May 12, 1940, German armies were crossing into France. The German *blitzkrieg* ("lightning war")—the use of armor and air power to support the infantry—crushed Allied armies. More than 338,000 English troops were trapped near the French port at Dunkirk but were successfully evacuated by a flotilla of large and small British ships. Then, on June 22, 1940, France signed an armistice with Nazi Germany.

Hitler hoped that England would make peace and give him a free hand on the European continent, but the new British Prime Minister, Winston S. Churchill (Number 3), refused, vowing that England would fight on. Despite an unrelenting air campaign against English cities, Great Britain would not surrender, bracing itself for a Nazi invasion that never came. Through the efforts of U.S. President Franklin D. Roosevelt (Number 2), England was resupplied with weapons to carry on the war.

In September 1940, Nazi Germany, Italy, and Japan signed the Tripartite Pact, linking the countries as allies for 10 years in a military and economic treaty.

In the spring of 1941, Hitler invaded Yugoslavia and Greece, then finally turned on the Soviet Union. On June 22, 1941, the Führer's armies struck deep into the heart of the Soviet Union, breaking Germany's non-aggression pact with Stalin. Within sight of Moscow, Hitler was stopped by an early Russian winter. The day of the quick victory was over.

Fighting on the Russian front was a long and bloody affair. For nearly four years, the armies battled back and forth along a huge front. Casualties on both sides were staggering. As Hitler's armies moved into newly conquered territories in the east, special German forces followed them, carrying out the massacres of Jews, Slavs, and other "undesirables."

A New Battle Front

The tide was turning. In the midst of Nazi Germany's seemingly unstoppable march through Europe, a new battle front was about to emerge. On December 7, 1941, the Japanese attacked Pearl Harbor. Hitler's Tripartite Pact with Italy and Japan required each to come to the assistance of any one of them that became involved in a war with the United States. On December 11, 1941—four days after the attack on Pearl Harbor—Hitler fulfilled his treaty obligation by declaring war on the United States. It would prove to be his most costly error of the war.

In November 1942, American and British forces landed in French North Africa to battle German armies retreating from Egypt. In mid-1943, American and British forces invaded Sicily and then the mainland of Italy, which soon surrendered.

The Fall of the Third Reich

On June 6, 1944—"D-Day"—Allied armies invaded Normandy in northern France. Once the beachheads had been secured, Nazi Germany was doomed. On July 20, 1944, a cadre of German officers tried to assassinate Hitler; it failed. In a last desperate throw of the dice, Hitler ordered a surprise assault into the Ardennes. It became known as the Battle of the Bulge. There were heavy losses suffered by both German and American armies; the Germans lost 120,000 soldiers, and the Americans suffered more than 76,000 casualties, but the Nazis were stopped and the German army destroyed.

With Russian forces closing in from the east and American and British forces from the west, Hitler awaited defeat in a Berlin bunker. At the end, he called in Albert Speer (Number 77) to give him his final order—an order Speer decided not to obey.

The Führer wanted Speer to have every German waterworks, power plant, bridge, tunnel, and major roadway destroyed. Hitler told Speer that the German people had failed him, were unworthy of him, and therefore should go down in destruction with him. That was what he had willed for the German people.

On April 30, 1945, after marrying his mistress, Eva Braun, Hitler (and Eva) committed suicide. A week later, Germany surrendered unconditionally. Hitler's war was over, but his legacy of hatred, death, and destruction lay amid the ashes of Europe.

2 Franklin D. Roosevelt

Risking Impeachment

COLLIER

No matter what the cost to his political future,
Franklin D. Roosevelt would not stand by and watch Britain go down.

When World War II erupted in the fall of 1939, U.S. President Franklin Delano Roosevelt was faced with a difficult dilemma. He believed that the threat of Nazism was a real one—and not just for Europe, but for the United States and the rest of the world. A majority of Americans, however, were isolationists, and they wanted nothing to do with any "foreign wars." However, when France surrendered to Germany in June 1940, Britain stood alone against Adolf Hitler (Number l). Roosevelt would not allow England to fall. He spoke of the United States becoming "the great arsenal of democracy." He compared giving military aid to Great Britain to someone lending his neighbor "a length of garden hose" to help put out a fire. When the fire was extinguished, the neighbor could return the hose. Thus was the idea of lend-lease presented to the American people. Who, after all, could be opposed to helping a neighbor put out a fire in his house?

Conferences were set up between American and British political and military officials. Roosevelt and British Prime Minister Winston Churchill (Number 3) even agreed on broad post-war goals in the Atlantic Charter. Announced in August 1941, it called for political freedom, a system of international security, and a reduction of armaments. All of this took place many months before the United States was officially in the war.

If President Roosevelt had yielded to the isolationists, Great Britain might not have been able to stand up against the Nazi juggernaut. Hitler would have had time to develop intercontinental missiles, and America's belief in the security of two great oceans might have proven as deceptive and illusory as the vaunted Maginot Line—the fixed French fortification between France and Germany— had been for France.

President Roosevelt risked impeachment to meet the menace of Hitler—and saved humankind from Nazi terror and slavery.

Early Political Success

Franklin D. Roosevelt was born with the proverbial silver spoon in his mouth at Hyde Park, New York, in 1882.

He attended all the best schools, from Groton to Harvard. His political rise was dramatic. He began in the New York State Senate, went on to become Assistant Secretary of the Navy in the Woodrow Wilson administration, and then ran for vice president on the losing Democratic ticket in 1920.

Tragedy struck when he contracted polio in April 1921 and was paralyzed from the waist down. Despite his handicap, he continued his political career and was elected governor of New York in 1928. Four years later, he was elected president of the United States.

The Depressions Ends as America Enters the War

Roosevelt took office as the country faced a grave economic crisis. Banks had failed, factories had closed, tens of millions were unemployed, and people starved while crops rotted in the fields. The Great Depression of the 1930s had begun. Promising the country a "New Deal," the Roosevelt administration set up a range of programs to get people back to work, support farm prices, institute a Social Security system, insure bank deposits, and build public works.

The economic crisis had not been restricted to the United States, however. It was worldwide and handled differently by each country. In Germany, for example, Hitler began building a powerful army and threatened his neighbors if they did not acquiesce to his demands.

When World War II erupted in 1939, Americans sympathized with England and France, but they generally opposed getting involved militarily.

In the presidential election of 1940, Roosevelt ran for an unprecedented third term in office. His campaign speeches emphasized that American men would not be sent to fight in any foreign wars. The Democratic Party platform had added the phrase "unless we are attacked," although Roosevelt thought that would be clearly understood.

The fall of France brought the crisis to a head. Roosevelt appointed two prominent Republicans to key posts in his cabinet: Henry L. Stimson (Number 21) as secretary of war and Frank Knox (Number 60) as secretary of the Navy. Together, Stimson and Knox developed strategies to support Great Britain and prepare the United States for the impending conflict. Supposedly outmoded military equipment was shipped to Britain; American destroyers were swapped for British military bases near American shores. The U.S. Navy helped convoy merchant ships carrying supplies to England. Finally, the United States instituted a military draft. When Nazi submarines began sinking American ships, Roosevelt ordered the U.S. Navy to shoot Nazi war vessels on sight.

Roosevelt was well aware that his political enemies would be searching for ways to discredit, or even impeach, him. Nonetheless he continued the course.

When Pearl Harbor was attacked by the Japanese and Hitler declared war on the United States, isolationism ended. "Now," said the president, "we are all in it, all the way."

The War Years

The strategy of the United States and Great Britain was to hold off the Japanese in the Pacific and defeat Hitler first. Well into 1942, the news in the Pacific was gloomy. The Philippines had fallen, along with Hong Kong, Singapore, and many other key American, British, and Dutch bases. But Japan was spreading its forces too thin throughout the Pacific. "Island-hopping"—attacking the most important islands and leaving the others to eventually run short of food, ammunition, and supplies—by the Allies would lead to many Japanese bases being left to rot on the vine.

The war in Europe was progressing. The Soviet Union had been double-crossed by Hitler and was fighting along a huge front. Joseph Stalin (Number 4) wanted a "second front" on the European continent to relieve pressure on the Soviets. The Western allies argued that the time was not ripe, that there were not enough landing craft, men, or equipment. The American military first saw action against the Nazis in North Africa in 1942, then in Sicily and on the Italian mainland in 1943. In September 1943, Italy surrendered to the Allies when its dictator, Benito Mussolini (Number 50), was overthrown.

At meetings of "the Big Three" (Roosevelt, Churchill, and Stalin), the Soviet dictator kept demanding a date and the naming of a commander for the second front. Dwight D. Eisenhower (Number 7) was chosen to lead the invasion. It came on June 6, 1944, with the invasion of Normandy. American, British, French, Canadian, and Polish troops waded ashore and secured a beachhead. Victory was only a matter of time.

In the Pacific, under the command of Chester Nimitz (Number 18), the U.S. Navy and Marines won major sea battles and took coral islands ("unsinkable aircraft carriers") with heavy loss of life. In the Southwest Pacific, Douglas MacArthur (Number 8) stopped the Japanese on New Guinea and then invaded other Japanese-held islands. He led American forces back to re-take the Philippines. Allied forces moved closer to the Japanese home islands.

Back in Europe, the Allies had withstood Hitler's Ardennes offensive in the Battle of the Bulge. The Allies seized a Rhine bridge at Remagen and swarmed into the Reich.

With victory in Europe imminent, Allied powers held conferences with the Soviets to bring them into the Pacific war. Stalin agreed to do so 90 days after the German surrender.

The Final Days of World War II

The spring of 1945 would bring peace closer and closer. And then, on April 12, 1945, Roosevelt told a friend in Warm Springs, Georgia, "I have a terrific headache." It was a cerebral hemorrhage; he never recovered. When Hitler heard the news of Roosevelt's death in his Berlin bunker, he was overjoyed. It was, he thought, the miracle he had been waiting for, but it made no difference. The war went on, and 18 days later, Hitler killed himself.

The war in Europe ended, but it looked as if the war against Japan would be a bloody one. However, years earlier Roosevelt had acted on a letter from Albert Einstein (Number 13) to win the race with the Nazis to build an atomic bomb. It would be used to end the war in the Pacific in August 1945.

Roosevelt's Legacy

Even after his death, Roosevelt influenced the process of world peace. The United States had chosen to stay out of the League of Nations following World War I. But discussions had taken place *during* World War II for a new international organization following the defeat of Germany and Japan. The new organization would be called the United Nations. Roosevelt made sure that both prominent Republicans and Democrats were included in the planning meetings. Bipartisanship would be as important in peace as it had been in war.

Roosevelt also left a uniquely American legacy. He had proposed the G.I. Bill of Rights in 1943. It was to provide for education, low-interest loans for housing, unemployment compensation, and a host of other benefits. That piece of legislation, passed in 1945, produced a new generation of college graduates, homeowners, and entrepreneurs. It also created the strongest and most prosperous middle class in the history of the world. Roosevelt did not want to see another time when veterans had to sell apples on street corners in order to survive, and he got his wish.

3 Winston S. Churchill

From Defeat, Defiance

NATIONAL ARCHIVES

Winston S. Churchill, sitting at left, attends the "Big Three" conference in
Yalta with President Roosevelt and Marshal Stalin.

Winston S. Churchill was one of the great orators of the 20th century, possessing an eloquence that inspired even amid crushing defeat. Anyone can stir passions by rejoicing in a triumph, but only a Churchill could lift spirits and inspire courage in the face of humiliating disaster.

On May 13, 1940, as British and French forces crumbled before the attacking German armies throughout Europe, Churchill, Britian's new prime minister, stood up in the House of Commons and declared, "I have nothing to offer but blood, toil, tears, and sweat."

He spelled out the goals of his government:

You ask, what is our policy? I will say it is to wage war, by sea, land, and air, with all our might and with all the strength that God can give us; to wage war against a monstrous tyranny, never surpassed in the dark, lamentable catalogue of human crime....

You ask, what is our aim? I can answer in one word: It is victory, victory at all costs, victory in spite of all terror, victory, however long and hard the road may be; for without victory there is no survival.

He used his words like warriors, sending them into battle against a brutish enemy.

His defiant "We shall never surrender!" roused his countrymen both at home and in the battlefield.

Britain held on, held out, and in the end, won.

Young Winston S. Churchill

The future British statesman was born in 1874 at Blenheim Palace, Oxfordshire. His father, Chancellor of the Exchequer, was English; his mother was a famous American beauty. Many years later, addressing Congress in Washington, Churchill mused that if it had been the other way around, and his father had been an American and his mother English, "I might have gotten here on my own." The congressmen loved it.

Young Churchill attended Harrow and Sandhurst, the British military academy. A budding journalist, he covered the Cuban rebellion against Spain in the late 1890s and the Boer War in South Africa from 1899 to 1902, where he was captured by the Boers, and later escaped. He served in the army, but turned to politics as his chosen career. He won a seat in parliament as a Conservative and held several government posts. During the early years of World War I, he was named First Lord of the Admiralty. Following the British military debacle at the Dardanelles (the strait between Europe and Asian Turkey), he was relieved of the Admiralty post. Later in the war he was Minister of Munitions. He held other government positions after the war.

War Comes to Europe

During the 1930s, Churchill viewed Adolf Hitler (Number 1) as a threat to European stability. He spoke out openly on the floor of Parliament, opposing appeasement of the Nazi dictator. "England," he warned after a perceived government sellout, "has had to choose between dishonor and war. She chose dishonor. She will get war." After the German invasion of Poland, Prime Minister Neville Chamberlain (Number 66) announced that England was at war with Germany. Churchill was again named First Lord of the Admiralty. The happy word went out to the British fleet around the world: Winnie's back.

In May 1940, following a series of British military defeats to the Germans, Chamberlain stepped down and Churchill succeeded him as prime minister. That same month, the German blitzkrieg struck deep into the heart of France, trapping more than 338,000 British forces around the port of Dunkirk. The troops were evacuated back to England, leaving most of their weapons behind on the French beaches. France fell and as Great Britain stood alone against the Nazi war machine, Churchill vowed to fight on.

Preparing to invade England, Hitler ordered his bombers to obliterate British cities. The British, valiantly defended by the Royal Air Force, would not yield, forcing Hitler to abandon any plans for invading England. Despite his countrymen's bravery, Churchill knew that the only hope for defeating Germany lay with America. He began corresponding with President Franklin D. Roosevelt (Number 2). The American leader, determined to help Great Britain prevail, sidestepped America's neutrality acts to provide military assistance to the British.

In 1941, a year after France fell, Hitler tore up an anti-aggression pact and attacked the Soviet Union. Churchill's decision was to provide Joseph Stalin (Number 4) with as much help as possible. The old Tory and the Communist dictator made strange bedfellows, but the war against Hitler came first. The Führer had once boasted that Germany could defeat any conceivable combination of powers, but the Churchill-Stalin duo was probably made a pair that Hitler could not have imagined.

England Gains an Ally as America Enters the War

As the year 1941 moved into autumn, relations between the United States and the Axis powers continued to deteriorate. In the Atlantic, American ships were being targeted and sunk by Nazi submarines. In the Pacific, relations between American and Japanese diplomats were on the verge of breaking down because of Japanese aggression in the area.

After the attack on Pearl Harbor, Hitler honored his pact with Japan and declared war on the United States. The deep friendship between America and Great Britain now became a strong and necessary military alliance.

Japan's sneak attack on Pearl Harbor was part of a broad strategy throughout the Pacific. Churchill looked on in horror as British military bases at Hong Kong and Singapore fell to the Japanese. He was concerned about Australia and New Zealand. But President Roosevelt ordered Douglas MacArthur (Number 8) to leave the doomed Philippines for Australia to take command of all Southwest Pacific forces. Japan had to be kept at bay while major efforts were directed against Hitler in Europe.

The Mediterranean region also troubled Churchill. The Suez Canal, Gibraltar, and North Africa were critically important to the Allies' strategies. But after British forces routed Germany's Afrika Korps at El Alamein, Egypt, American and British troops invaded French North Africa, trapping German forces and prompting their surrender.

After victory in North Africa, the Allies invaded Italy. Although Italy was on the European continent, this attack was not regarded as a true second front. That would come nine months later with the Normandy invasion.

As the war continued, problems arose between the Western Allies and the Soviets. Poland was of special concern to Churchill. It was the invasion of Poland that brought England and France into the war with Nazi Germany in the first place. Now came a whole host of issues: What was to be the nature of its government and its national army? When would free elections be held?

Churchill wanted to bring up these issues at Big Three conferences with Stalin, but Roosevelt preferred to wait until after the war to settle them. Besides, the Red Army was viewed as important in tying up Japanese forces during the forthcoming invasion of the Japanese home islands.

Churchill Exits as the Curtain Falls

In the spring and summer of 1945, the cast of characters among the Allied leaders changed dramatically. Roosevelt died, to be succeeded by Harry S Truman (Number 14). England voted out the Conservative Party of war leader Churchill, voting in the Labor Party of Clement Attlee. Of the original Big Three, only Stalin remained.

A year after the war ended, Churchill warned of an "Iron Curtain" drawn across the center of Europe by the Soviet Union. The Cold War had begun.

In 1950, Churchill became *Time* magazine's Man of the Half-Century. The following year, Churchill regained his position as prime minister. He wrote the multivolume history, *The Second World War*, and won the Nobel Prize in literature in 1953. He died in 1965, having served six British monarchs, from Queen Victoria to Queen Elizabeth II.

4 Joseph Stalin

Ruthless and Paranoid

NATIONAL ARCHIVES

Russian dictator Joseph Stalin (standing, second from right) appears to be thoroughly pleased with himself as Soviet Foreign Minister Molotov and German Foreign Minister von Ribbentrop sign the Nazi-Soviet Non-Aggression Pact.

There is an old saying that it is not *love* of the same thing that makes allies, but *hatred* for the same thing. And so it was in World War II. Joseph Stalin, a tyrannical dictator, would surely have been seen as the least likely person to be allied with Franklin D. Roosevelt (Number 2) and Winston Churchill (Number 3), the leaders of the Western world. Before the war, Stalin had been responsible for the deaths of millions of his own people. Churchill had once referred to him as "Genghis Khan with a telephone." Yet as part of the Allied forces, the Red Army and Russian partisans behind the lines fought with both courage and daring.

When the Nazis first invaded the Soviet Union, some peasants greeted the German conquerors with bread and salt, the traditional gifts of welcome. Then the Nazis began their mass executions, and Stalin appealed for the defense of Mother Russia. It was the intense hatred of Adolf Hitler (Number 1) and all he stood for that became the key issue for the Russian people, and the Anglo-American Allies.

The war on the Russian front was bloody and brutal. The Germans used Red Army prisoners as guinea pigs for medical experiments. On the other side, many Germans taken prisoner never survived the war.

Stalin's Red Army carried the brunt of the land war in Europe for nearly three years. The cost in Russian lives, both military and civilian, was staggering. The German army also suffered heavy losses.

Stalin's Rise to Power

The son of a shoemaker, Joseph Dzhugashvili was born in 1879 in Georgia, a province of southern Russia. He would later change his name to Stalin, "man of steel." Stalin studied for the priesthood at a seminary but was expelled for his radical views. He became a revolutionary, bent on overthrowing the czar. By 1901, Stalin was organizing street demonstrations; he was arrested and spent several years in exile in Siberia.

Following the Russian Revolution of 1917, Stalin worked his way up in the Communist Party hierarchy. Upon the death of Party Leader Nikolai Lenin in 1924, Stalin competed with other Communists for key leadership roles and emerged as absolute dictator of the Soviet Union. However, his economic policies proved disastrous. Millions of Russians starved while the Soviet Union exported wheat to the rest of the world. Independent landowners, called *kulaks*, were murdered by Stalin's forces because they were considered rich farmers whose land was valuable to the state.

Under Stalin's rule, Communist Party members who aroused any suspicion of disloyalty were put on trial and executed. This paranoia was successfully exploited by the Nazis in 1937 when German intelligence agents framed Russian army officers, leading to a bloody purge of the Red Army officer corps, supposedly for treason. Stalin could order murders at will. In 1940, from thousands of miles away, Stalin arranged the assassination of Communist rival Leon Trotsky in Mexico City long after Trotsky had been banished from the Soviet Union.

Late in 1938, Stalin brooded over the consequences of Adolf Hitler's meeting with England's Neville Chamberlain (Number 66) and France's Eduard Daladier in Munich. The two had agreed to hand over the Sudetenland, a piece of Czechoslovakia, to Hitler. Was it possible that they could help Hitler against Russia some time in the future? Stalin may have been unwilling to take the risk. Although it is not certain whether Russia or Germany made the first move, Stalin and Hitler shocked the world by making a non-aggression pact. In August 1939, the two dictators agreed to divide Poland. Germany attacked Poland from the west, and two weeks later, the Soviet Union did the same from the east. Each country's army occupied the specific territories that had been mapped out, and Germany found itself at war with England and France.

In 1940, as Hitler moved against Norway, Denmark, and the Low Countries (Belgium, Luxembourg, and the Netherlands), Stalin annexed the Baltic states of Estonia, Latvia, and Lithuania.

In the United States, the American Communist Party was taking its lead from Moscow and campaigning against any American involvement in the European war. Demonstrators in Communist marches chanted, "The Yanks are *not* coming!" That cry would change.

Hitler Betrays His Pact with Stalin

By the spring of 1941, Stalin had grown uneasy about a Nazi military buildup and airflights along Soviet borders. Then, on June 22, 1941, German armies launched a massive invasion. At first, Stalin was too stunned to issue orders for defense. His officers at the front waited for the signal to counterattack, but Stalin hesitated. He thought that there was some misunderstanding, but when Stalin recognized the truth, he called for all-out effort against the German invaders: "Not one step backward!"

The Russian winter came early, and German forces in front of Moscow were caught without winter clothing or equipment. Hitler would not move them back, fearing that any movement away from Moscow might bring comparisons with the retreat of Napoleon.

Stalin sought weapons and supplies from the West. After the United States entered the war, he wanted a second front in Europe to relieve the pressure on Soviet armies. The greatest sieges of the war took place at Leningrad and Stalingrad. In both cases, the cities held out; in Stalingrad, the German army was trapped and forced to surrender. The greatest tank battle in the history of the world was fought at Kursk.

Stalin ensured that his forces would not retreat by having bridges blown up and arranging for special forces stationed behind his armies to prevent retreats. But Stalin's main tactic was scorched earth. The Nazis would invade a village, town, or city, only to find it burned to the ground. Industry was shipped east of the Ural mountains, where it was safe from German bombing.

Despite his request for Allied assistance, Stalin would not permit American or British planes to land on Russian airfields following long aerial missions against German military installations. Thus, planes from the West often had to fight their way back to base without a stop to rest or refuel.

The Final Days

As the war in Europe began winding down, difficult decisions were being negotiated by Franklin D. Roosevelt, Winston Churchill, and Stalin about such things as borders, occupation zones in Germany, and the use of Russian forces against Japan. Stalin demanded and received a piece of Polish territory. Poland, in return, was to receive a piece of German territory. Russia's occupation zone would include Berlin, which was itself zoned. The Russians would enter the war against Japan 90 days after the war ended in Europe.

As the Red Army pursued the Germans, they occupied large areas of eastern Europe, which succumbed to Communist rule. When World War II finally ended, the Soviet Union dominated half of Europe.

Toward the end of his life, Stalin became ill and believed that he was being poisoned by his doctors. When he died in 1953, his body was first put on display with that of Lenin in Moscow's Red Square. But after his excesses were revealed by Nikita Khrushchev and others, the body was removed and placed elsewhere.

Could World War II have been won by the Western Allies alone, without the Soviet Union? Perhaps. But it would have taken much longer, been much bloodier, and probably involved a negotiated settlement rather than unconditional surrender. Stalin's role was crucial in the final outcome of the conflict.

5 George C. Marshall

First in War, First in Peace

U.S. ARMY

U.S. Army Chief of Staff George C. Marshall was the architect of American victory in World War II.

September 1, 1939, was a pivotal date in world history: Adolf Hitler (Number 1) invaded Poland, igniting World War II. It was also the date that George C. Marshall became U.S. Army Chief of Staff. At the time he took office, the U.S. Army ranked 19th in size among the world's armed forces, and that included its reserves. It had more men under arms than Bulgaria but fewer than Portugal. Before he was done, Marshall would build the U.S. armed forces to more than 8.5 million, fighting on many battlefields around the world.

Marshall's superb leadership, his absolute integrity, his dedication to the job at hand, his attention to detail, his ability to choose talented leaders for warriors, and his grasp of global strategy made him indispensable to the war effort. Ironically, that very set of skills may have cheated Marshall of the one thing he wanted most: to lead the Allied armies into battle on the continent of Europe.

Though no one man can be credited with winning victory in World War II, Marshall may have been the most influential. He was the architect of victory.

Early Military Career

Marshall was born in 1880 in Uniontown, Pennsylvania. He applied and was admitted to the Virginia Military Institute (V.M.I.). Why not West Point? Some observers have speculated that he might not have had the political connections for a Congressional appointment. His older brother, however, had gone to V.M.I., which might have been a factor in his decision.

Marshall graduated in 1901 and was commissioned a second lieutenant in the U.S. Army. He enjoyed his first command in Philippines; after returning home, he was given additional leadership training. He then became an instructor at the Army Staff College.

World War I began in Europe in 1914. By the time the United States entered the war in 1917, Marshall was a captain. In France, he successfully planned American troop movements prior to the Argonne offensive. By the time the war ended, he had become a trusted aide to General John J. Pershing and had attained the rank of colonel.

After World War I, Marshall served first in China and then at the Infantry School at Fort Benning, Georgia. It was an opportunity for him to spot the potential leaders for any future war.

In 1936, Marshall finally won his first star as brigadier general. In the early years of the Franklin D. Roosevelt (Number 2) administration, Marshall had caught the eye of the commander in chief and had been put in charge of Civilian Conservation Corps camps in several southern states.

In 1938, Marshall was appointed head of the War Plans Division, one of the most prestigious positions in the U.S. Army. He was now on the fast track. Soon after, he became the Army Deputy Chief of Staff. On one occasion, he was the only officer to oppose a suggestion by the president. He spoke out forthrightly, earning Roosevelt's respect. As war loomed in Europe, Marshall was chosen Army Chief of Staff. As Hitler's panzers smashed into Poland, Marshall assumed his new role, which was arguably Roosevelt's most critical appointment.

The War Years

It had taken Marshall 16 years to win his first star as a brigadier general. Now, after only three years, he was wearing four. A strong believer in air power, he lobbied for strengthening the Army Air Corps. In 1940, he began building the army using the Selective Service Act, but under that law, the draft was scheduled to expire in October of 1941. That summer, throughout the country, the letters O.H.I.O. were scrawled on the walls of many barracks. It stood for "Over the Hill in October." Yet war was imminent, and Marshall knew it. The draft act had to be extended. It appeared that the Senate would pass the extension, but there was concern about the House of Representatives. Marshall personally spoke to congressmen who were either opposed to or ambivalent toward the measure. As a result, the draft extension was approved in the House by a single vote, on which the fate of Western civilization may well have hinged.

As war approached, Marshall was involved in numerous issues, from national security to army morale. Roosevelt wanted England strengthened to defend itself against a German invasion. As the chief of staff, Marshall signed off on sending supposedly outmoded rifles to the beleaguered British at the same time some American servicemen were drilling with broomsticks. Upset at the sight of recruits wandering around the small towns near their training camps because they had nothing to do when off duty, Marshall came up with the idea of entertaining the troops; the United Service Organizations (USO) was born. Marshall reviewed the lists of his generals, choosing those for retirement so that younger men could step forward to command. Most importantly, Marshall met with his British counterparts to plan for future military operations.

War Comes to the United States

When Pearl Harbor was attacked, Marshall responded rapidly. Looking back to 1939, he commented, "Then we had the time, but no money. Now we have the money, but no time."

Marshall stressed the necessity of defeating Germany first, but he was at odds with Winston Churchill (Number 3) and the British on overall strategy in Europe. The English talked of hitting "the soft underbelly" of the enemy in southern Europe and the Mediterranean. Marshall wanted to go across the English Channel to northern France and then into the heartland of Nazi Germany. During the war, British and American political and military leaders often clashed.

The time came to select the overall commander to lead the Normandy invasion. Because the United States would play the major role in the invasion, the overall commander would have to be an American. Roosevelt would make that decision. Although it was common knowledge that he wanted the job, Marshall told President Roosevelt that he would do whatever the president wanted him to do. Although the commander in chief continued to press him, Marshall was adamant in his response. Reluctantly, Roosevelt made his decision; he needed Marshall in Washington. He chose Dwight D. Eisenhower (Number 7) to lead the invasion.

The End of the War and the Rebuilding of Europe

In September 1944, Marshall found himself in a terrible dilemma involving presidential politics. Roosevelt was running for a fourth term as president against Governor Thomas E. Dewey of New York. Marshall learned that Dewey had prepared a campaign speech that revealed that the United States had broken the Japanese code prior to the attack on Pearl Harbor. The implication was that the United States knew of the Pearl Harbor attack in advance and did nothing to prevent it. From Dewey's point of view, this information would be devastating to Roosevelt's reelection bid. However, it would be even more damaging to Allied intelligence. At that time, the Japanese still did not know that their code had been compromised. The continued monitoring of Japanese communications was vital in the Pacific, and Japanese messages to and from Berlin were helpful in fighting the war in Europe. Marshall wrote a letter to Dewey, advising him of the potential consequences to the war effort. Dewey decided not to use the disclosure in his speech.

Roosevelt died several weeks before Germany surrendered. The new president was Harry S Truman (Number 14). The former senator and vice president had long known of Marshall's abilities and brought him into his administration after the war. Marshall would go on to serve as secretary of state and secretary of defense. He would propose the Marshall Plan, which would provide billions of dollars from the United States for the purchase of food, raw materials, machinery, and equipment for 16 European countries, to help rebuild Europe.

In 1952, during the presidential election campaign, a few conservative Republicans denounced Marshall as "a living lie" and "a front man for traitors." Eisenhower, who was running for president, originally had inserted in a campaign speech a defense of his advocate and mentor. Fearing it would cost him votes, Eisenhower deleted it from his speech.

The following year, Marshall received the recognition he so richly deserved: He was awarded the Nobel Peace Prize for work on the Marshall Plan. He died in 1959.

6 Isoruku Yamamoto

Planning Pearl Harbor

NATIONAL ARCHIVES

This captured Japanese photo shows the action in Hawaii on December 7, 1941.
At bottom, U.S. ships under attack on Pearl Harbor. At top of photo,
in the distance, Hickam Field under assault.

In November 1941, nothing appeared amiss at the major Japanese seaports. Hundreds of Japanese sailors could be seen frequenting the usual bars and hangouts. At least they *looked* like sailors; actually, they were soldiers wearing naval uniforms. It was essential for foreign observers to see sailors walking around. Otherwise, they might wonder where all the sailors were, where their ships were, and what they were doing. In reality, Japan was getting ready to launch massive strikes by land, sea, and air throughout the Pacific.

Many of the sailors were already on ships in a task force in the Kurile Islands, north of Japan. That fleet was under the command of Vice Admiral Chuichi Nagumo, who waited anxiously for the signal to sail. His force consisted of two battleships, two cruisers, several destroyers and tankers, and, most importantly, six of Japan's largest aircraft carriers.

On November 26, 1941, the word came from Admiral Isoruku Yamamoto to proceed. Under strict radio silence, the task force sailed eastward. Its destination was Pearl Harbor.

Isoruku Yamamoto, the man who planned Pearl Harbor, had many misgivings about warring on the United States. But once assigned the task, he carefully mapped every detail of the daring and dangerous mission.

Yamamoto's Rise in the Japanese Navy

Yamamoto was born in Nagaoka, Japan, in 1884. Seeking a naval career, he attended the Naval Academy, graduating in 1904. He was commissioned an ensign and saw action in the Russo-Japanese War.

By the time World War I began, Yamamoto was a commander on duty at the Japanese Imperial Naval Headquarters in Tokyo. His superiors had high expectations for him, and he was sent to the United States to study at Harvard University. In his two years there, he acquired tastes for many American pastimes, from baseball to poker. He also became intrigued by the potential of aviation. After a stint back in Japan, he became naval attaché in Washington, D.C., a post he held from 1925 to 1927. During his tour of duty in America, Yamamoto became deeply impressed with America's industrial potential. It was, he believed, a vital element in any future war.

By the early 1930s, he was a rear admiral and a firm advocate for strengthening Japan's naval aviation. He had become a naval pilot. In the mid-1930s, the major powers, including Great Britain, France, Germany, Japan, and the United States, were attempting to set limits on armaments. Yamamoto, as head of the Japanese delegation attending these international meetings, announced that Japan could not accept unfair limitations on its military strength.

As Yamamoto rose through the ranks in the navy, he fought for more planes and carriers. In August 1939, he became commander of the entire Japanese fleet.

Planning the Attack on Pearl Harbor

When the Japanese government decided to conduct offensive operations throughout the Pacific, Yamamoto was assigned the task of taking on the American Pacific fleet. Although he personally felt that Japan would eventually be beaten in any war with the United States, Yamamoto dutifully prepared for the attack on Pearl Harbor.

Without any formal declaration of war, more than 350 Japanese planes would take off from carriers and attack specific ships at anchor in the naval base. Hickam Air Force Base and the Pearl Harbor Naval Air Station would also be bombed. In addition, a fleet of submarines would lie in wait off Oahu in case some ships tried to escape the trap.

The sneak attack on Pearl Harbor was successful beyond the dreams of the Japanese militarists: 19 American warships were sunk or damaged, and many American planes destroyed on the ground; 150 of the 200 naval aircraft were damaged. More than 2,500 men were killed. The Japanese losses totaled just 29 planes and 100 men.

After Pearl Harbor, Yamamoto would experience both successes and failures. He paved the way for Japan to overwhelm Malaysia and the Dutch East Indies. His troops would be turned back, however, at the Battle of the Coral Sea and decisively beaten at Midway.

Nevertheless, the United States was well aware of his skill and his potential for inflicting damage on Allied forces. The decision was made to assassinate him. Through official messages intercepted by American monitors, it was learned when and where Yamamoto would be inspecting Japanese installations in the South Pacific. On April 18, 1943, American planes shot down the Japanese bomber carrying Yamamoto. It was not until late May that Japan announced that he had been killed in action against the enemy.

The Legacy of Pearl Harbor

The Japanese attack on Pearl Harbor was crucial for three reasons:

1. It was one of the greatest victories (from the Japanese perspective) and one of the most humiliating defeats (from the American point of view) in the history of naval warfare.
2. It forced the United States into World War II, uniting people throughout the country behind the war effort.
3. It forced Adolf Hitler's (Number 1) hand. Under his pact with Japan, he was obligated to declare war on the United States, and he did so. The isolationists who had opposed getting into war with Hitler now had no other option. The declaration of war against Germany simply recognized the fait accompli. After President Roosevelt (Number 2) had signed off on it, he told the American people, "Now we are all in it, all the way."

Dwight D. Eisenhower

Leader of the Coalition

NATIONAL ARCHIVES

On the eve of D-Day, Dwight D. Eisenhower chats
with paratroopers preparing for the landings in Normandy.

There is a story about Dwight D. Eisenhower and his role as Supreme Commander in Europe that supposedly deals with an American officer who had gotten into a heated argument with a British counterpart. The scene is London circa 1943–1944, with the Normandy invasion still months away. A furious Eisenhower bawls out his subordinate in blunt language.

Finally he says, "If you had just called him a son of a bitch, that would have been okay. But you called him a *British* son of a bitch. For *that*, I am sending you home."

This insightful, almost apocryphal tale demonstrates Eisenhower's sensitivity about the coalition relationship. Even the closest of allies have different ideas about military operations, overall strategy, political problems, and post-war plans.

Eisenhower, affectionately known as "Ike," did everything possible to keep the coalition harmonious. The alliance held, and the war was won. The general's personality and his genuine friendship with key British figures carried the day.

A Rapid Rise through the Army Ranks

Dwight D. Eisenhower was born in Denison, Texas, in 1890. He was admitted to West Point in 1911. When he graduated four years later, he was commissioned a second lieutenant. World War I had begun less than a year earlier, but when the United States entered the war in 1917, Ike never made it overseas. Stationed in the States, he commanded something very new in the U.S. Army: a tank brigade. After the war, Eisenhower was promoted to major and served in Panama. From 1933 to 1939, he was on Douglas MacArthur's (Number 8) staff, first in Washington and then in the Philippines.

In the fall of 1941, army maneuvers were held in Louisiana. Ike was commander of the victorious army, catching the attention of Chief of Staff George Marshall (Number 5). Shortly after Pearl Harbor, Eisenhower was ordered to Washington to take over the War Plans Division. Promotions and responsibility came rapidly as the war intensified. By June 1942, Ike was in London to head the European Theater of Operations. By now he was a lieutenant general, with three stars. Two and a half years later, he would be wearing five.

Eisenhower and the North Africa Campaign

Ike's role was as political as it was military. He received his political trial-by-fire in charge of "Torch," the invasion of French North Africa. It was the fall of 1942, and Erwin Rommel (Number 39) was in full retreat from Egypt.

French North Africa was administered by Vichy France, the government of unoccupied France, whose capital was Vichy. Occupied France was under direct Nazi rule. The French government at Vichy was opposed to having its territory invaded by anybody, and here is where the politics came in.

To say there was bad blood between the French and their former allies, the British, is an understatement. When France surrendered in June 1940, its leaders firmly believed that England would "have its neck wrung like a chicken" and quit soon after. But England refused to fall to the Nazis, and that was a blow to French honor and dignity. What came shortly afterward was even worse.

Fearing that the French naval fleet might fall into Nazi hands, England had demanded that part of the French fleet at Oran either sail to the West Indies for safety or else scuttle its ships so the Nazis would not seize them. When the French refused, elements of the British navy attacked the French force, sinking several ships and killing 1,300 French sailors.

Amid this French and British animosity, the Allies were planning to invade French North Africa. The goal was to occupy the area with the least number of casualties, which could only be done if the operation was an "American" one. So American diplomatic and military staff secretly went ashore in North Africa prior to the invasion, hoping to gain French cooperation to ensure a relatively bloodless takeover through a quick cease-fire. The French were told it would be an American operation.

As it turned out, the British did supply air and naval support. A number of their troops also participated—but wore American uniforms.

Finally, Eisenhower—an American—was in command.

It was in North Africa that Eisenhower's troops got their first battle scars. In late 1943, Sicily and the Italian mainland were invaded. Benito Mussolini (Number 74) was overthrown and Italy surrendered.

The European Front

It was time to turn to Nazi Germany. In December 1943, Eisenhower was officially chosen to lead the Allied invasion of Europe. In the months prior to the Allied invasion of Normandy, D-Day, Eisenhower made it a priority to visit every camp, every airfield, every military hospital, every naval base, and every headquarters in England. He didn't just want to see *them*; he wanted the warriors to see *him*, to know that he was aware of who they were and what their jobs were. It was, he felt, an important morale booster.

The Normandy invasion—D-Day—was supposed to be on June 5, 1944. The weather was foul and the invasion was delayed. Weather, tides, and moonlight could have delayed it for weeks. Ike pressed the meteorologists. The ships were all loaded, and there was still the possibility for a surprise landing. What were the chances for the weather lifting? The meteorologists went back to their charts and reported that there was a chance that the weather would improve on June 6. Ike dragged on his cigarette and made his decision. It was a go.

As the operations proceeded, Eisenhower drafted a statement to be used if the troops had to withdraw from the beaches. In it, he took full responsibility for the failure and praised the men who had done everything that was humanly possible to make it succeed. The statement never had to be used. The landings succeeded and Hitler (Number 1) and his Nazi regime were doomed.

There would be many military and political decisions to come. Eisenhower wanted Harold Alexander (Number 76) to lead the British forces. It was not to be. Bernard Montgomery (Number 37) was chosen instead. The antagonism between Montgomery and his American counterparts was probably the worst-kept secret of the war.

Political and Military Decisions

Eisenhower's problems with Montgomery's failure to obey orders were legendary, but they weren't the only issues that needed to be resolved. Winston Churchill (Number 3) was pushing for an invasion through the Balkans instead of northern France. Charles De Gaulle (Number 51) held an inflated perception of what his role should be in the coming Normandy invasion. Joseph Stalin (Number 4) and the Allies were at odds regarding access to Russian airfields following long-range bombing raids by Allied planes. George S. Patton's (Number 11) had a penchant for public relations disasters, and Henry Morgenthau, Jr. (Number 93) had his own plan for post-war Germany.

There were still more questions: Should the Western Allies try to beat the Russians to Berlin? Should the Allies blow up the railroad lines to the death camps or the gas chambers and ovens being used by the Nazis? What was the best way to provide for displaced persons? Some of these were military problems, but all were political, as well. Eisenhower dealt with some, ignored others, and gave his opinions on still others. It was all part of running a coalition war. Some British historians have criticized Ike for being too involved in the political, but it all went with the territory.

When the European war ended in May of 1945, Eisenhower was an international hero. He came back to the United States and became Army Chief of Staff. He was chosen president of Columbia University, but went on leave to head the North Atlantic Treaty Organization. In 1952 he was nominated by the Republican Party for president. The Korean War had been going on for two years, and he promised to go to Korea and try to end the war. He won the presidency and four years later was reelected for a second term. Eisenhower died in 1969.

8 Douglas MacArthur

"I Shall Return."

NATIONAL ARCHIVES

Douglas MacArthur (front and center) splashes through the waters off Leyte Island as he fulfills a promise to liberate the Philippines.

In the months following Pearl Harbor, America's top military and naval leaders discussed priorities. It was clear that Adolf Hitler (Number 1) had to be defeated first. Japan would have its turn, but what should be done about the Pacific in the meantime? Which islands had to be held, and which could be sacrificed? Two of the main areas of concern were Australia and the Philippines. Ernest J. King (Number 20) told President Roosevelt (Number 2) that the key base should be Australia. Eisenhower (Number 7), who had only recently served in the Philippines, told Marshall (Number 5) the same thing. The Philippine garrison was to hold out as long as possible, but it could not be reinforced. Without such help, it would fall.

This was a bitter pill for Douglas MacArthur, the head of U.S. forces in the Far East. Headquartered in Manila, he had hoped that the Philippines could, with adequate supplies, be defended and held. MacArthur was ordered to leave the Philippines for Australia, where he would take command. Upon leaving the Philippines, he promised, "I shall return." It would take him two and a half years to get back.

During that interval, MacArthur would never give up his fight to keep a focus on the war in the Pacific. He was especially determined to make good on his pledge. From escaped prisoners of war he heard of the infamous Bataan Death March, when thousands of American and Filipino prisoners had been shot and bayoneted by Japanese troops. He also heard of horrendous conditions in the Japanese prison camps. These reports infuriated him and strengthened his resolve to return. It was not rhetoric, but a matter of honor.

Born to Serve His Country

Douglas MacArthur was born in Little Rock, Arkansas, in 1880. The son of General Arthur MacArthur, a decorated hero of the Civil War, Douglas attended West Point. He graduated at the top of his class in 1903. MacArthur was promoted rapidly, serving in the Philippines and Japan and as an aide to President Theodore Roosevelt. Before the United States entered World War I, he was on the general staff. In 1917, Colonel MacArthur served with the 42nd "Rainbow" Division, where he became chief of staff. As a brigadier general, he commanded his own battalion and was decorated many times for heroism in battle. By war's end, he was a major general. He became Superintendent of West Point and held other posts before his appointment to U.S. Army Chief of Staff in 1930, when the Great Depression was beginning.

In the summer of 1932, MacArthur was at the head of hundreds of infantry and cavalrymen ordered to disperse the "Bonus Army." The Bonus Army was a group of unemployed veterans of World War I who had come to Washington with their families to petition Congress for early payment of a promised bonus. Though the bonus was to be paid 10 years hence, they needed the money now. Some veterans squatted in unoccupied government buildings; others built shacks in Anacostia, in the southeast section of the District of Columbia. President Hoover ordered that the occupied government buildings be cleared. There is still debate on whether MacArthur went beyond his orders by tearing down and setting fire to the shacks in Anacostia, but the Bonus Army was dispersed.

A Pledge to Return

In 1935, MacArthur became High Commissioner of the Philippines. He also took on the post of military adviser to the Philippine government. In mid-1941, as tensions rose between the United States and Japan, the Philippine and American armies were combined into one, with MacArthur as its head.

Hours after Pearl Harbor was attacked, MacArthur's air force was virtually destroyed on the ground by the Japanese. With most of the American Pacific fleet crippled and its planes decimated, the Philippines were vulnerable to a Japanese invasion. It came in a matter of days. Within weeks, Manila would fall to the enemy. The situation was hopeless.

MacArthur was ordered to leave the islands for Australia to take command in the Southwest Pacific. It was on his arrival there in March 1942 that he pledged to return to the Philippines.

Some strategists were ready to concede part of northern Australia to the Japanese. MacArthur insisted on taking the offensive and achieved important victories on the island of New Guinea. MacArthur demonstrated what he could accomplish with the little he had. He knew that as long as he could achieve victories, he could keep alive the hope of liberating the Philippines.

At one point in the war, serious consideration was given to bypassing the Philippines and invading Formosa (Taiwan) instead. MacArthur lobbied Roosevelt as forcefully as he could for reconquest of the Philippines, and he won. In October 1944,

Americans went ashore on the island of Leyte. In a matter of months, most of the Philippine islands were set free.

The End of a War and the Beginning of the Nuclear Age

As the European war began winding down, more attention was focused on the Pacific. Supported by a naval fleet now in fighting form, the Allied forces and the Marines hopped from one island to the next, closing in on Japan.

The battle to take Okinawa was costly and bloody. It lasted from the beginning of April to the end of June 1945. More than 48,000 Americans were killed or wounded. The battle set the stage for the invasion of Japan. Then, on August 6, 1945, the first atomic bomb was dropped on Hiroshima. Two days later, Nagasaki became the second Japanese city to succumb to an atomic bomb. The war was over. On September 2, 1945, on the deck of the U.S.S. *Missouri*, Japanese officials signed the final surrender. Although the United States had originally called for "unconditional surrender," there was one important exception: Hirohito (Number 49) would remain as emperor, but subject to the orders of the Supreme Commander, MacArthur.

The five-star general would democratize Japan, bring the vote to its women, restore its industry, and lead it back to the community of nations.

But atrocities committed by Japanese forces in the Philippines would neither be forgiven nor forgotten. Masaharu Homma (Number 45) would be tried for the Bataan Death March and Tomoyuki Yamashita (Number 58) for massacres during the American re-taking of the Philippines. Both would be executed. In addition, not a single Japanese soldier would survive from the Japanese 16th Division, which had conducted the Death March.

The Question of Korea

The end of World War II saw many changes on the world map. Korea, which had been occupied by the Japanese for many years, was separated at the 38th parallel into a Communist North Korea and a democratic South Korea. In 1950, North Korea invaded South Korea. The United Nations raised an international force to stop the aggression. MacArthur was put in command of the operation. His brilliant performance, marked by the Inchon landings, stopped the North Korean forces. When the Chinese Communists entered the war in support of North Korea, MacArthur called for an expansion of the war to meet the new military situation.

In public statements and private letters made public, MacArthur took issue with the policies of President Truman (Number 14), his commander in chief. MacArthur was fired. It set off a political firestorm in the United States, and congressional hearings were held. MacArthur contended that the United Nations should deprive Red China of its "privileged sanctuary" and that "there is no substitute for victory." But Marshall would argue that a war on the Chinese mainland would be "the wrong war at the wrong time in the wrong place and against the wrong enemy." A truce between the two Koreas would result.

MacArthur retired, wrote his memoirs, and became a corporate executive. He died in 1964.

9 Jimmy Doolittle

The Raider from "Shangri-La"

NATIONAL ARCHIVES

Jimmy Doolittle takes off from the aircraft carrier *Hornet* to lead the bombing attack on Tokyo and other Japanese cities.

Shortly after Pearl Harbor, Roscoe Turner bumped into his old buddy, Jimmy Doolittle. In years past, when aviation was new and exciting, both men had been stunt fliers.

"Jimmy," Turner said, "you know we should try to do something to get even with the Japanese."

Doolittle poked his friend in the ribs.

"Look," he said, "that kind of stuff is for the young kids, not old geezers like us."

Turner agreed with Doolittle, who was then 45 years old.

Several months later, after the story broke that Doolittle had planned and led a surprise raid on Tokyo and other Japanese cities, the raid leader received this wire: "Dear Jimmy. You son of a bitch. Roscoe."

An Adventurous Spirit

From one point of view, Doolittle's raid could have been considered a disaster. The planes ran short of fuel and crashed. Damage to Japanese industry appeared to be

54

relatively light. Three American fliers who had been captured by the Japanese were executed. Even Doolittle thought it was a failure—until his commander in chief presented him with the Congressional Medal of Honor.

The raid had accomplished a great deal: It boosted American morale at possibly the lowest point of the war. It shook the morale of the Japanese, who had felt that their home islands were invulnerable to any enemy attack. Most important of all, it forced the Japanese high command to pull planes and ships back from the war front to protect the Japanese mainland. Those weapons would not be available in critical battle areas of the Pacific.

Jimmy Doolittle had a distinguished career during the remainder of the war, but he is included here for this one deed. He and 80 other American airmen, flying 16 B-25 Mitchell bombers, completely turned the tables on the Japanese. There would still be defeats after this, but the Japanese dream of a quick victory vanished in the 30 seconds Doolittle flew across Tokyo.

What enables a man to possess such courage and assume such risk? Doolittle had been a former prizefighter and a daredevil stunt flier. Some of that adventurous spirit and willingness to gamble for big stakes against great odds may have come from his dad, who panned for gold in Alaska when Doolittle was a little boy.

Doolittle's Early Career

Doolittle was born in Alameda, California, in 1896. A year before the United States entered World War I, he enlisted in the army and became a pilot. He saw no combat duty during the war. After the war he was cited for distinguished flying, studied aeronautical engineering, and went into private industry for a while. However, he remained in the reserves. Doolittle was recalled to duty in 1940. In January 1942, following Pearl Harbor, he was promoted to lieutenant colonel and assigned to Washington.

A Bold Plan

Doolittle approached his superiors with an idea. Why not give the Japanese a taste of their own medicine? Send carrier-based planes to the Japanese mainland itself and get even for Pearl Harbor. Of course there were obvious differences. There would be only one carrier instead of six, and there would be no massive fleet to escort it. There would be only 16 planes instead of 350. Most importantly, the attack would take place many months after war had been declared.

The plan was bold, but it was also dangerous. First, there were few ships left in the U.S. Navy in the Pacific. Most of the Pacific fleet was being repaired. Only a handful of carriers was available, and only one could be risked. Army pilots would have to be trained to take off on a minimum of ground space, comparable to the length of a carrier's deck. Airfields in China would have to be prepared to receive the planes after they had carried out their mission.

Doolittle began by asking for volunteers to take part in a perilous secret mission. Many more responded than were needed. The training went well.

A small naval task force under William F. Halsey, Jr. (Number 26) accompanied the carrier *Hornet* on its journey to Japan. The mission was uneventful until the task force was about 650 miles from Japan. Then a Japanese vessel suddenly appeared. It was sunk immediately. Though it was not known if the ship had radioed a warning to Tokyo, the planes had to launch at once because Japanese planes and ships might be steaming toward the *Hornet*.

A Surprise Attack

On the morning of April 18, 1942, Doolittle and his raiders took off. They flew just above the water to avoid Japanese radar. When they reached Japan, the raiders headed for targets in Tokyo, Kobe, Nagoya, and Osaka. The fliers dropped bombs on factories, a ship under construction, and an aviation school. The Japanese reported that only schools and hospitals were bombed.

Because they had launched the mission early, the planes ran out of fuel. Most of the airmen bailed out over China, where they were hidden by the Chinese. One crew ended up in neutral Siberia and were interned for the remainder of the war.

The Japanese military was humiliated by the daring raid. One senior officer committed suicide. The High Command insisted steps had to be taken so Japan would not be caught off guard again. Certain resources intended for the battlefronts were now set aside for home defense.

When Roosevelt (Number 2) was asked by reporters where the planes had come from, he quipped, "Shangri-la," the fictional city in Tibet immortalized in the novel *Lost Horizon* by James Hilton.

Tokyo radio warned that any American pilots who would try it again would get "a one-way ticket to hell." It failed to deter anyone. The saturation bombings, the fire bombings, and the atomic bombings would come, following the flight path initiated by Jimmy Doolittle and his raiders.

In the war years that followed, Doolittle rose to the rank of lieutenant general. He commanded forces in both the European and Pacific theaters, including the 15th Air Force in Tunisia and Sicily and the 8th Air Force, first in Europe and later in Okinawa.

Nothing he did would ever be as important to the war effort as the raid. For Americans, it restored morale; for the Japanese, it was a portent of what was to come.

After the war, Doolittle became an executive with the Shell Oil Company. He died in 1993.

10 Douglas Bader

Legend of the RAF

NATIONAL ARCHIVES

Fire and smoke rise up around St. Paul's Cathedral during the London blitz.
Douglas Bader was one of the Royal Air Force pilots whose courage and sacrifice defeated the Nazi air force.

"Never in the field of human conflict," said Winston Churchill (Number 3), "was so much owed by so many to so few." The British prime minister was paying tribute to the Royal Air Force (RAF), a group of men who defended the British Isles during the blitz of the German Luftwaffe. Though Douglas Bader appears here as an individual, he represents the entire RAF, especially those who flew the Spitfires and the Hurricanes during the Battle of Britain.

That is not meant to imply that Bader somehow was an average RAF pilot, though such a designation would be praise enough for any man, for the fliers of the RAF displayed remarkable courage and tenacity in England's darkest hour. During the Battle of Britain, it was not uncommon for them to fight the Luftwaffe against overwhelming odds, return to base, refuel, load up again on ammunition, and return to the battle.

That small group of brave men prevented a German invasion of England when it was most vulnerable. They restored English confidence and destroyed the myth of the Nazi super race. They are all represented here in the person of Douglas Bader.

Fighting against Overwhelming Odds

Why choose Bader? He was one of the top flying aces of the RAF, for one thing. That is impressive enough. But he was also downed and captured by the Germans; he escaped, was recaptured, and was sent to Colditz prison camp for the rest of the war. He did all of this on a pair of artificial legs.

Courage, stamina, determination, and fighting against overwhelming odds embody Bader and the RAF. That is why he was chosen.

Bader was born in London in 1910. He competed successfully for admission to the Royal Air Force College at Cranwell. In 1930, Bader was commissioned into the RAF. He became a fighter pilot. Two years later Bader crashed, and both of his legs were amputated. In 1933, the RAF discharged him. His military career was obviously over, and he went to work for a private company. But in 1939, when war broke out, Bader returned to the RAF. England was badly in need of trained pilots, so Bader was taken on, artificial legs or not.

In May of 1940, during the Dunkirk evacuation, the RAF supported the operation. Bader shot down his first German planes.

Great Britain's Finest Hour

Following Dunkirk, the war continued to deteriorate for the Allies. On June 22, 1940, France signed an armistice with Hitler (Number 1). England stood alone. In the middle of July, the Führer offered to negotiate, saying, "I am not the vanquished seeking favors, but the victor speaking in the name of reason." Churchill scorned the offer. His defiance infuriated Hitler, who ordered a massive bombing campaign.

Thus began the Battle of Britain. Hitler intended for the campaign to soften up British defenses prior to an invasion. He expected Germany to begin by taking command of the air over Britain. To do that, it would have to destroy the Royal Air Force.

The Germans had thousands of planes available to do the job, including bombers, fighters, and reconnaissance aircraft. England had only a fraction of that number. Hitler believed the air campaign could be accomplished in a matter of weeks, but he did not count on the mettle of RAF pilots such as Douglas Bader. Nor did Hitler know yet of the role that radar would play in warning England of oncoming air strikes. In fact, he never found out that the British had broken his military code and knew in advance what was coming before his generals did. A combination of radar, a cracked code, and the RAF was about to tip the balance in the war.

In mid-August of 1940, the Luftwaffe sent a thousand planes to hit airfields and port installations. By the end of September, the RAF had destroyed more than 600 planes of that mighty German armada. Hitler decided to break the spirit of Britons by destroying their cities. But the RAF inflicted such heavy losses on his air armada the Führer decided to discontinue the massive raids. Thousands of civilians would die, but England never flinched.

An Ace Pilot

During the Battle of Britain, Bader had been put in charge of a Canadian air group, which he whipped into shape. He was as tough a fighter on the ground as he was in the air, demanding whatever technical support and administrative changes were necessary to get the job done. And he kept on flying combat missions.

By August 1941, Bader was ranked fifth among RAF aces, with 23 kills. That month, he went down over France. The war was over for him. Except for a brief time when he escaped, Bader spent the rest of the war in a prison camp.

A year after the war ended, Bader retired from the RAF. He went back into private industry and died in 1982.

George S. Patton, Jr.

The Fightingest Field Commander

At an awards ceremony after the war, George S. Patton, Jr., stands between his commander, General Eisenhower, and his commander in chief, President Truman.

His nickname was "Old Blood and Guts," a name he earned through his colorful pep talks to his men. These talks were filled with Patton's ideas about how men should behave in battle, what they should do to the enemy, why America had never lost a war, and why it was important for fighting men to procreate. The language was always blunt, unambiguous, and quite purple. But the message was always crystal clear: The most important thing was to *win*.

Patton is included here for one major achievement: the containment of German forces, coupled with the relief of Bastogne, during the Battle of the Bulge.

An Olympian and a Soldier

George S. Patton, Jr., was born in 1885 in San Gabriel, California. Despite the fact that he had dyslexia, or perhaps because of it, Patton excelled physically. He would later demonstrate his prowess at the 1912 Stockholm Olympics, where he placed fifth among 43 competitors in the modern pentathalon.

He graduated from West Point in 1909 and was commissioned a second lieutenant in the cavalry. During World War I, Captain Patton was given command of the U.S.

Army's first tank unit. He was wounded in action, but he had found his niche: tank warfare. After the war, the highly decorated officer commanded a tank center. There he met and befriended Dwight D. Eisenhower (Number 7).

In 1932, the two majors served under Douglas MacArthur (Number 8), then Army chief of staff. They took part in the routing of the Bonus Army from Washington, D.C.

Following the outbreak of World War II, the United States instituted a strong defense program. This involved a military draft and training maneuvers in the field. In mid-1941, the Louisiana maneuvers demonstrated the abilities of potential field commanders. Patton distinguished himself during an extraordinary night movement of his troops. Military observers split on their evaluation of his tactics. They were either daring or foolhardy. George C. Marshall (Number 5) put Patton on his short list for field command in any future conflict. Here, indeed, was a fighter who was capable of doing the improbable, maybe even the impossible, in a critical situation. At the very least, Patton could keep an enemy off balance and constantly guessing on what he would do next.

Bad Press for an Aggressive Commander

When war came in December 1941, Patton was considered as one of the top field commanders. The first American offensive would be at French North Africa. It is said that Patton looked at the invasion plans, declared that there was a better way to do it, and that that was the way he planned to do it. Marshall immediately cut new orders for him, sending him back to oblivion. Patton relented at once, saying of course he would carry out the mission exactly as planned. There was no way he was going to miss this war.

Patton's men won their objectives in Morocco. He then took over command in Tunisia and began to plan the invasion of Sicily. There, he and Bernard Montgomery (Number 37) competed for territory and the glory that went with it. Patton tended to be more aggressive; Montgomery was more cautious. Patton certainly won the battle of the headlines, in more ways than one.

While still in Sicily, Patton got into trouble by slapping a shell-shocked soldier in an army field hospital. War correspondents in Sicily sat on the story. It became public back in the States when it was reported by a Washington political commentator. Patton, in disgrace, was ordered by Eisenhower to apologize to those involved. There had been and would be other public relations disasters, but nothing as serious as this.

In any case, Patton was officially in the doghouse.

The common wisdom is that Eisenhower made the final decision to keep Patton a field commander. Actually, it was Marshall. As for the Germans, they believed that Patton was being kept under wraps for something special in the forthcoming invasion of France.

The Phantom Army

When D-Day came on June 6, 1944, Patton seemed to have disappeared. It was obvious, thought the Germans: Patton was still waiting in England with a huge invasion force, ready to cross the Pas de Calais and invade France. Erwin Rommel (Number 39) did not believe it. He felt strongly that Normandy *was* the main invasion and begged Adolf Hitler (Number 1) to release the German reserves and send them to Normandy, where they were badly needed. Hitler refused and waited for the phantom army that never came. The reserves were sent in too late. The Normandy beachhead was secured by virtue of the greatest military deception since the Trojan Horse.

Patton surfaced in northern France with his 3rd Army.

In August 1944 the Allies broke out of the beachhead. Patton's army raced eastward, faster than field maps could be printed. When his tanks ran short of fuel, it was not unusual for fuel supplies to disappear mysteriously from storage depots or for hijackers to make off with oil trucks on their way to other outfits. To Patton, these were not pranks but deadly serious business. If his men ran out of fuel, they became sitting ducks to Nazi armor. Patton was determined to keep his tanks moving.

The Battle of the Bulge

The most serious crisis for the U.S. Army in Europe came in December 1944. The German army came crashing through the Ardennes, creating a "bulge" in the American lines. The great concern was that the Germans would cross the Meuse, take Antwerp, and cut off Allied supplies. To stall that German drive, American paratroops had been dropped into the vital road center of Bastogne with orders to hold it until relieved. The weather was freezing cold and it was snowing. All planes were grounded.

Who could be relied on to get through and relieve the American garrison at Bastogne? Only Patton. He had been heading eastward toward Germany. Now he turned his army 90 degrees, heading north for Bastogne, 150 miles away. The sources differ on how long that drive took; estimates range from 19 hours to three days.

All the sources agree that Patton asked his chaplain to compose a prayer for good weather, and the weather cleared almost immediately. The good weather helped, but it was Patton and his men who carried the day. By relieving Bastogne, they turned the tide at the Battle of the Bulge. Four months later, Nazi Germany surrendered.

An Imperfect Hero

There are many legends that surround his name. It is said that he wrote poetry, that he believed in reincarnation, and that he believed he had fought in great battles of the past. He was certainly a strict disciplinarian, a fierce competitor, and outspoken to a fault.

Patton will be remembered for the Battle of the Bulge long after his gaffes and public relations disasters have vanished from the footnotes of the histories of World War II. Whatever Patton's idiosyncrasies, he was a warrior of enormous talents.

Early in December 1945 he was severely injured in an automobile accident and paralyzed from the neck down. He died two weeks later and was buried in the American military cemetery in Luxembourg, alongside his men.

12 Heinz Guderian

Master of the Blitzkrieg

NATIONAL ARCHIVES

Though other military leaders had theorized about the value of armored warfare, it was Heinz Guderian who carried it out in Poland, France, and elsewhere.

The word *blitzkrieg* (German for "lightning war") was reportedly coined during the American Civil War. A Prussian military observer was fascinated by Union Army tactics that advanced forces in a zigzag pattern instead of a relatively straight line. This prevented the Confederate defenders from determining the real objective of the Yankee drive until it was too late. The zigzag route resembled a bolt of lightning, hence the reference to "lightning war."

Today's dictionaries, however, identify the term as originating in 1939, the year Nazi Germany invaded Poland. That is when the word acquired a whole new meaning. When the German forces attacked, they combined armor and infantry, supported by airpower; the emphasis was on speed, mobility, and massive strength.

The Blitzkrieg Revolutionizes Modern Warfare

Guderian was largely responsible for the blitzkrieg in Poland. He appears here for two reasons: He revolutionized modern warfare, and his early victories came very close to winning the war in the west for Adolf Hitler (Number 1). Only the defiance of Winston

Churchill (Number 3) and his absolute refusal to come to terms with Hitler prevented an early victory for Nazi Germany.

Other military figures had studied and theorized about the possibilities inherent in combined units of armor and infantry as a way of avoiding the stalemate of trench warfare prevalent during World War I. But it was Guderian who put the idea into operation. His tactics in Poland, the Low Countries (Belgium, Luxembourg, and the Netherlands), and France won Hitler's admiration and support. The campaign in the Soviet Union would be a different story.

Leader of the Panzer Division

Heinz Guderian was born in 1888 in Kulm, Germany. A career officer, he served in World War I in both communications and infantry posts. Late in the war, he was assigned to the German general staff. Guderian studied motorized warfare, and in 1933, (the year Hitler came to power), he was promoted to colonel. Two years later, he was heading one of Germany's new armored divisions. The German military called them panzer divisions; a rough translation of panzer is armor-plating or coat of mail.

Following World War I, military planners among the major powers examined the role of the tank in that bloody clash of arms. In England, France, the United States, and Germany, they weighed new possibilities for using armor. As always, the younger officers would come into conflict with the old guard, who tended to think of fighting in terms of the last war rather than the next.

Early Success, Followed by a Russian Winter

In Germany, Guderian championed the use of armor and then went on to prove what could be done. His Polish Corridor campaign was so successful that Hitler met with him at his headquarters in the field. The Führer congratulated him, then asked about casualties. Guderian reported that in the four divisions under his command, 150 men were killed and 700 wounded. A division, which consists of three regiments, can contain between 10,000 to 20,000 men. Hitler was amazed and told his general that in World War I, his regiment alone had suffered 2,000 dead and wounded on the very first day they were in battle.

Guderian's success in Poland was matched in Belgium and France in the spring of 1940, when Allied armies were crushed in short order. So it was only natural that Guderian was one of the commanders chosen to take on the Soviet Union in June 1941. At first, the invasion went as planned. But when the Russian winter came early, Guderian wanted to withdraw somewhat to more defensible lines until spring. Hitler would not hear of it, and Guderian was relieved of his command and assigned elsewhere.

When spring finally arrived, German tanks and other armored vehicles were bogged down in the mud. In addition, Russian resistance was the fiercest ever encountered by the invaders. This battle would be different. Hitler called on Guderian to return to the Russian front, but Guderian still did not agree with Hitler's tactics. As with others before—and after—him, he was replaced.

When D-Day came in June 1944, American generals, notably George S. Patton (Number 11), used the same blitzkrieg tactics against the Germans with great success.

Judging Other Nazi Officers

On July 20, 1944, German army officers attempted to assassinate Hitler and bring an end to the war. The Führer was wounded but survived. He began rounding up generals by the hundreds. Many went on trial and were executed; others committed suicide. Guderian fell under suspicion. He was not only cleared, but chosen along with Gerd von Rundstedt (Number 56) and Wilhelm Keitel (Number 48) to judge some of the accused officers.

Guderian took on other assignments afterward but never again had the chance to do what he did best: lead men in battle.

After the war, he was a prisoner of the American army for almost three years. He died in 1954.

13 Albert Einstein

The Pacifist Who Won the War

Funk & Wagnalls Co.

When Albert Einstein heard that the Nazis were working on atomic weapons, he wrote a letter to the president of the United States.

There are some people whose very names have become part of the English vocabulary. We call someone who appears to get out of difficult situations "a real Houdini." Someone who practices financial chicanery is often said to have engineered "a real Ponzi scheme." And someone whose intelligence may border on genius we will surely label "another Einstein."

The super-brilliant physicist Albert Einstein is known for many groundbreaking scientific theories. His remarkable works on the relativity of matter, energy, gravity, time, space, and light are known throughout the world. His theories have revolutionized our ideas and understanding of the universe.

What is far less known is the role he played during the weeks preceding World War II. All he did was write a letter addressed to President Roosevelt (Number 2), making the case for developing an atomic bomb.

It is ironic that Einstein should be represented here among the top war-makers. He was an ardent pacifist, but one who feared that Adolf Hitler (Number 1) and his scientists might get the atomic bomb first. If that happened, Einstein knew, it would mean the end of Western civilization.

From Germany to America

Albert Einstein was born in Ulm, Germany, in 1879. At the turn of the century, he became a Swiss citizen and worked in the Bern patent office as an examiner. Interested in how things work, he studied physics at the local university. In 1905, he won acclaim for his special theory of relativity, and he was besieged with teaching offers by many universities. In 1909, Einstein chose the University of Bern. Four years later, he was offered the directorship of the practical physics program at the prestigious Kaiser Wilhelm Institute in Berlin. In 1921, Einstein won the Nobel Prize in physics.

In 1933, everything changed for Einstein, for Germany, and for the world. Hitler came to power. The Führer hated Einstein, who was a Jew and a pacifist. The physicist's works were publicly thrown into the bonfires and his property was seized. At the time, Einstein was lecturing in America. Instead of returning home, he joined the faculty of the Institute of Advanced Studies at Princeton.

A Race to the Atomic Age

Early in August 1939, it was clear that Hitler was saber-rattling once again. War in Europe appeared likely. Physicists in the United States were genuinely concerned that the Führer's scientists were hard at work on an atomic bomb. They believed that only Einstein, preeminent in the field, could convince the American political and military leaders to avert the potential threat. Einstein was persuaded to write a letter to the president. He wrote:

> *In the course of the last four months it has been made probable through the work of Joliot, Fermi, and Szilard in America that it may become possible to set up a nuclear chain reaction in a large mass of uranium, by which vast amounts of power and large quantities of new radium-like elements would be generated. Now it appears this could be achieved in the immediate future. This phenomenon would also lead to the construction of bombs, and it is conceivable, though much less certain that extremely powerful bombs of a new type may thus be constructed. A single bomb of this type, carried by boat and exploded in a port, might well destroy the whole port, together with some of the surrounding territory.*

The letter was dated August 2, 1939.

In 1940, Einstein became an American citizen. By that time, his letter to Roosevelt had set in motion the Manhattan Project to develop an atomic bomb. Einstein opposed using the bomb on Japan, but in August 1945 atomic bombs were dropped on Hiroshima and Nagasaki. Within a week, the Japanese sued for peace.

Albert Einstein died in 1955, still clinging to his pacifist convictions. He was surely the most unusual pacifist in living memory, having set in motion the conception, construction, and delivery of the deadliest weapon ever unleashed on humankind.

14 Harry S Truman

"The Buck Stops Here."

COLLIER

Following the death of Roosevelt, Harry S Truman is sworn in as president. One of his earliest and most controversial decisions will be whether or not to drop the atomic bomb on Japan.

Shortly after passage of the Selective Service Act in 1940, Senator Harry Truman dropped in to see Army Chief of Staff Marshall (Number 5). The Missouri senator had been in the field artillery during World War I, had kept up his service in the reserves, and now wanted to go back into the army to help train new recruits. Bemused, Marshall asked how old he was, and Truman told him he was 56. The Chief of Staff suggested that maybe Truman could be more useful on the home front.

Truman had great respect for Marshall and agreed he was probably right. But how could he be useful on the home front? Truman then thought about the billions being poured into what was still America's defense program. The idea came to him. Truman got into his beat-up old car and set out on a one-man inspection trip around the country to see for himself how money for defense preparation was being spent.

That trip would result in the creation of the Special Committee to Investigate the National Defense Program. It would later be known more simply as the Truman Committee. It investigated possible fraud, waste, mismanagement, and corruption in the defense industry and would result in saving hundreds of millions of dollars. It also resulted in Truman winning the respect of fellow senators on both sides of the aisle.

The Decision to Use the Atomic Bomb

Truman's contribution to the war effort, through his committee work, was most impressive. But that alone would probably not have been enough to justify his inclusion among the top 100 influentials of World War II.

Truman is here for one of the most significant decisions of the war. He made it less than four months after he took office as president: the decision to use the atomic bomb against Japan.

We know that approximately 103,000 Japanese lives were lost in the bombings at Hiroshima and Nagasaki. But we will never know how many lives were spared, not just among the Allies, but among the Japanese as well, by the swift end to this bloodiest of all wars.

Succeeding President Roosevelt

Harry S Truman was born in 1884 in Lamar, Missouri. During World War I, he commanded a field artillery unit of the Missouri National Guard in France. After the war, he and a partner set up a haberdashery shop, but it failed. Truman spent years paying off every penny that he owed.

Truman went into politics, serving several years as a judge in Jackson County, Missouri. In 1934, he was nominated for the U.S. Senate. Thanks to the support of Tom Prendergast, the Democratic Party boss in Kansas City, Truman was elected. In 1940, Truman ran successfully for reelection.

The year 1944 was a critical one in American history. Roosevelt was about to run for a fourth term, but many Democratic leaders feared that he was ill and might not complete his term. They mistrusted Vice President Henry Wallace, who they regarded as an extreme left-winger. The president wrote a letter to convention officials suggesting two alternatives: Supreme Court Justice William O. Douglas and Senator Harry Truman. It was the senator who got the final nod and became vice president. Less than three months after the inauguration, Roosevelt died of a cerebral hemorrhage and Truman became president.

The Manhattan Project

The new chief executive soon became privy to some of the most important secrets of the war. During his days heading the Truman Committee, he had been tipped off about some kind of suspicious activity in the states of Tennessee and Washington. It appeared that many materials were going *into* these new plants, but almost nothing was coming *out*. What was going on?

When Truman began looking into the matter, he was told by legislative leader Sam Rayburn, "Stay away from it, Harry." He trusted Rayburn and let it go. Now, as president, he understood Rayburn's warning. Oak Ridge, Tennessee, and Hanford, Washington, were involved in building a top-secret weapon: an atomic bomb.

Five weeks after Truman became president, Germany was defeated and lay in ruins. Only Japan continued to fight. Now the questions started coming:

- Was it really necessary to drop atomic bombs on Japan?
- Why not warn Japan first?
- Why not arrange for a demonstration to show the power of the weapon?
- Was the bomb so barbarous that it might cause the United States to lose its moral authority in the world?
- With the Soviet Union about to enter the war against Japan, might that be enough to bring the war to a successful conclusion without using the bomb?

Truman looked at the figures for the kamikaze suicide bombers, who crashed their explosive-laden planes into American naval ships. He considered the estimates of American casualties in the forthcoming invasion of the Japanese home islands. Then, as commander in chief, he made the decision to drop a bomb on Hiroshima on August 6, 1945. Two days later, a second bomb was dropped on Nagasaki. A week later, the Japanese agreed to surrender.

A Stunning Victory

With the war ended, Truman found himself facing Communist threats to western Europe and the Far East that seriously affected the implementation of the Marshall Plan, the North Atlantic Treaty Organization, and the Berlin Airlift, as well as the decision to help South Korea oppose North Korean aggression.

In 1948, Truman won a stunning upset victory over Republican Tom Dewey and Democrats Henry Wallace and Strom Thurmond. The election proved that a Democrat could win the White House without carrying the South.

In the earliest days of his presidency, Truman had placed a sign on his desk: "The Buck Stops Here." The man from Missouri who had never gone to college knew his American history; he knew that people from one state vote for officials in that state, but that *all* the people vote for president. It was the president who had to make the tough decisions, and Truman made them to the best of his ability.

Harry Truman, the 33rd president of the United States, died in 1972.

15 Stewart Menzies

Master of the Ultra Secret

NATIONAL SECURITY AGENCY

This is the Enigma machine that held the key to an "unbreakable" Nazi secret code. Stewart Menzies of British Intelligence was in charge of decoding and disseminating the critical German military messages.

The story goes that when potential staff members came to Bletchley Park, just outside of London, they were interviewed by a top member of British Intelligence. If the interviewer felt the applicant was right for the job, he would very carefully outline the position. Secrecy, it was explained, would be paramount. And then would come the clincher.

The interviewer, according to the story, would take out a pistol from a desk drawer and place it on the desk in front of him. He would then inform the candidate that he had been made privy to information vital to the security of Great Britain. He had been told the most sensitive secrets of the war.

Then the candidate was given the offer he could not refuse. Because of the seriousness of the matter, if the candidate turned down the job, he would be shot. Candidates invariably accepted.

It is hard to take this story literally, but as an apocryphal tale it certainly emphasizes the importance of absolute secrecy. Great Britain's very life as a nation hung in the balance.

What happened at Bletchley Park is one of the war's best-kept secrets, probably even more guarded than the atomic bomb project. It involved a German coding machine called Enigma, a German device that scrambled messages radioed to military and naval commanders into secret codes.

The deciphering of the German code was called Ultra by the British. Mathematicians, cryptanalysts, and intelligence officers participated in the task. Stewart Menzies has been selected to represent all of those involved in Ultra: not just the Englishmen trying to decipher the codes, but also the Poles who discovered Enigma and brought it to England.

Deciphering an Engima

Stewart Menzies was born in London in 1890. During World War I, he was decorated for bravery. He entered military intelligence, which quickly became his life's work.

World War II brought him to the very top of the intelligence community. In November 1939, Menzies became chief of the British Secret Intelligence Service. He was now in charge of the Ultra program. The war was already two months old, and Ultra was busy uncovering Adolf Hitler's (Number 1) military secrets. Menzies, now known as "C," would become the model for Ian Fleming's character "M" in the James Bond novels.

How did Ultra begin? Prior to 1939, German intelligence experts were working on a machine designed to foil code-breakers. The machine was Enigma, which created an almost infinite array of possible permutations and combinations of codes. The machines were produced in quantity in a German factory.

A Polish mechanic worked in the factory and had the notion that these machines might be signaling devices. He stole one and took it back to Poland. The Polish secret service made a replica and had it sent to England.

The machine had four rotating drums. Around the drums were letters of the alphabet. A typewriter would be hooked up to the machine and a secret message typed in. The machine scrambled the message into code.

When the machine arrived in England, Britain's Code and Cipher School was in Bletchley Park, and the building was used by the code-breakers. Mathematicians and cryptanalysts, using the earliest computer techniques, broke the code. When war came, England could read all the messages being sent in secret to Hitler's field commanders. Great pains had to be taken to prevent the Germans from discovering that their code had been compromised.

Keeping Secrets: Sacrificing Coventry

It was Menzies who was responsible for the very limited distribution of the decoded messages. Because the code breaking was called Ultra, every message coming from it was deemed an "Ultra message."

The task was difficult. What do you do when you intercept a message that the Germans are going to bomb Coventry, as British Intelligence did on November 14, 1940? If you suddenly deploy aircraft and anti-aircraft weapons to Coventry, you may well tip off the fact that the German code has been broken. So you take the hit; to do otherwise is to risk discovery and lose the advantage of knowing what the enemy is up to. Coventry was bombed in late November.

Ultra was invaluable to the Allies. It was used during the Battle of Britain to keep track of coming air raids. It was useful in North Africa both for Montgomery (Number 37) at El Alamein and the Americans landing in French North Africa. It was useful in the invasions of Sicily and Normandy. Not only did the Allies know what Hitler was going to do, but they knew when, where, how, and by whom.

Ultra was also essential in the battle against the menace of the U-boat wolf pack. It was so effective that German naval chief Karl Doenitz (Number 64) was quoted as complaining, "The enemy knows all our secrets, and we know none of his."

A Final Betrayal

Menzies continued his intelligence role after the war, retiring in 1952. A decade later, he was shocked to learn that one of his most trusted colleagues, Kim Philby, had been a "mole," spying for the Soviet Union. Philby had actually been in charge of countering Soviet espionage. It was Philby who was the so-called "third man" who had warned Soviet spies Anthony Burgess and Donald Maclean that they were about to be arrested for Soviet espionage. All three ended up living in Moscow for the rest of their lives.

The betrayal devastated Menzies. He died in 1968.

16 Bertram Ramsay

A Miracle at Dunkirk

COLLIER

British troops evacuate Dunkirk. Admiral Bertram Ramsay was the naval officer who brought together many hundreds of boats of all shapes and sizes to remove the troops from the beaches and shuttle them back to England.

When did Adolf Hitler (Number 1) lose the war? Was it at Stalingrad? Kursk? El Alamein? During the Battle of Britain? On the beaches of Normandy? The Battle of the Bulge? Was it his failure to invade Britain after the fall of France? Or was it his decision to declare war on the United States following Pearl Harbor?

Each one of these events has its advocates. But an argument can be made that Hitler lost the war during the evacuation at Dunkirk in the spring of 1940.

In addition to army and navy personnel, many hundreds of English civilians took part in the massive evacuation of the 338,226 Allied troops from the French beaches of Dunkirk. Despite the dangers, civilians joined the Royal Navy in ferrying British, French, Dutch, and Belgian troops across the English Channel to safety. Admiral Bertram Ramsay is the man who conducted the rescue operation, and he represents all those involved in the rescue.

Rescue on the Beach

Bertram Ramsay was born in London in 1883. He joined the Royal Navy at the age of 15. During the next 40 years, he continued rising in rank and responsibility. In 1938, at age 55, he retired and his naval career appeared to be at an end.

But when war broke out in 1939, Ramsay was back in uniform. The vice admiral was assigned the command of Dover. It would prove to be one of the most important commands of the war.

Disaster struck the Allies in May 1940. A German blitzkrieg tore into the Low Countries (Belgium, Luxembourg, and the Netherlands) and France. Allied forces found themselves trapped near the port of Dunkirk. The German panzers, supported by aircraft, were pounding the trapped soldiers and inflicting heavy casualties.

What lay ahead for the trapped forces was obliteration, surrender, or, if possible, evacuation. The British decided to evacuate as many troops as they could; initially, they hoped to get 45,000 men off the beaches.

A Call for Civilian Help

Ramsay came up with a dramatic plan. He called for civilians with motorized vessels to aid in the evacuation. And they came, assembling at the specified English ports. A ragtag flotilla of 800 vessels, large and small, made the run: naval warships, yachts, trawlers, fishing boats, tugs, steamships, ferries, and lifeboats. Under blistering enemy fire, they made their way across the Channel to Dunkirk. They arrived empty and left loaded.

Ramsay created "roads"—traffic lanes in the Channel for the various vessels coming and going. Each boat would pick up a load of men, take them to England, then return for another group.

Meanwhile, German aircraft would bomb and strafe the fleet of ships. The Royal Air Force fought the attacking German planes. But British ships were hit and sunk. There were many casualties, but the vast majority of the men were saved.

A Break in the German Onslaught

After the war, German generals complained that they had been ordered by Hitler to halt their panzer attack outside the port. According to some German sources, Hitler felt that the destruction of the trapped force at Dunkirk might make the proud British fight even harder. The Führer was said to have thought that a partial evacuation would enable the British to seek honorable terms. That is only a theory; but the fact is, there *was* a brief pause, and the British *were* able to take advantage of it.

This explanation for the pause has never been officially confirmed. But if it is so, then it was a decision that might well have lost the war for Hitler.

Between May 26 and June 3, 1940, more than 330,000 troops were withdrawn from the Dunkirk beaches. The Allied forces left behind all their heavy equipment, but the troops would be alive to fight another day.

A Final Return to the Beach

When the evacuation first began at Dunkirk, Winston Churchill (Number 3) set a date to speak before the House of Commons. When he appeared, he confessed that he had been fully prepared to announce the surrender of a major part of the British Expeditionary Force in France. Miraculously the flotilla of ships and small boats had brought out most of the army.

Two and a half years after Dunkirk, Ramsay was heading up the amphibious landings in French North Africa. In July 1943, he landed British troops in Sicily.

In a stunning reversal of fortune, he took command of the huge Allied fleet that returned to France on the Normandy beaches on June 6, 1944. Tragically, he did not live to see the end of the war. Early in January 1945, a plane carrying the admiral crashed on takeoff from a French airfield.

17 Georgi Zhukov

Stalin's Toughest General

NATIONAL ARCHIVES

Georgi Zhukov moved from one battlefield to the next to plug up holes in the Soviet lines and go on the offensive against the German invaders.

It was March 1945. As the Red Army closed in on Berlin, Marshal Zhukov put in a call to his friend, Nikita Khrushchev, then the Soviet commissar in Kiev.

"Soon," he told Khrushchev, "I'll have that slimy beast Adolf Hitler (Number 1) locked in a cage. And when I send him back to Moscow, I'll ship him by way of Kiev."

Hitler killed himself in his Berlin bunker. There is not a doubt in the world, however, that the Führer would have been exhibited like a freak in a sideshow if Zhukov had taken him alive.

Zhukov is recognized here as the tough-minded commander of the Red Army during World War II. It is difficult to say whether Joseph Stalin (Number 4) really ever trusted anybody, but if he did trust one man, it was Marshal Zhukov. During the war, Stalin listened to him, confided in him, and sometimes even changed his mind on the basis of what Zhukov told him. After the war was another story.

Distinguished Service in World War II

Zhukov was born in 1896 in Strelkovka, Russia. He was a cavalry officer for the czar in World War I. Following the Russian Revolution, he joined the Red Army and the Communist Party. He escaped with his life during the Red Army Purge Trials of 1937–1938. In 1939, Zhukov distinguished himself in an undeclared border war with the Japanese over Outer Mongolia. The following year, Zhukov took part in war games as the leader of an "enemy" force. His force won, proving that Moscow would be vulnerable in the event of war.

In June 1941, Hitler attacked the Soviet Union. Stalin soon found that Zhukov could be relied on to take on virtually any military problem and do what was necessary to solve it. Zhukov began on the Russian central front, defending Moscow. Then he was sent to Stalingrad, where he turned the tables on the Nazi armies and forced the Germans to surrender. He was involved in the battle for Kursk, where the Red Army fought and won the greatest tank battle in the history of warfare. He went into Leningrad and bolstered the defenses of that city. Finally, Zhukov planned and carried out the final assault on Berlin. The city fell to the Red Army, and what was left of Hitler was found in the ruins. The war was over.

A Cold-Blooded Mind-Set

When Dwight D. Eisenhower (Number 7) met Zhukov, the two men swapped stories about military tactics, especially how tank commanders deal with the problem of mine fields.

Zhukov told Eisenhower:

There are two kinds of mines; one is the personnel mine and the other is the vehicular mine. When we come to a mine field our infantry attacks exactly as if it were not there. The losses we get from personnel mines we consider only equal to those we would have gotten from machine guns and artillery if the Germans had chosen to defend that particular area with strong points of troops instead of with mine fields. The attacking infantry does not set off the vehicular mines, so after they have penetrated to the far side of the field they form a bridgehead, after which the engineers come up and dig out channels through which our vehicles can go.

Eisenhower was stunned by the cold-bloodedness of the approach. Americans, he knew, would never tolerate that kind of deliberate sacrifice of men. Zhukov never blinked an eye at doing what he thought was needed to defeat the Nazis.

Some historians have called Zhukov "Stalin's trouble-shooter." He was that and more. Cold, calculating, and sometimes cruel, Stalin's deputy supreme commander beat Hitler at his own game.

After the war, Stalin's paranoia overtook him. Zhukov was assigned insignificant military posts and stripped of any real power. Once Stalin was dead, Zhukov was brought back to Moscow, and he took part in rounding up the leaders of NKVD, the dreaded secret police. When Khrushchev came to power, Zhukov was named minister of defense.

As various Soviet leaders came and went, Zhukov would periodically find himself in and out of favor. When he died in 1974, however, he was honored with burial in the Kremlin wall.

18 Chester Nimitz

Up from the Canvas

NATIONAL GEOGRAPHIC SOCIETY

Chester W. Nimitz, at right, discusses coming battle plans in the Pacific with Secretary of the Navy Knox.

Chester Nimitz took over command of a battered Pacific Fleet shortly after the attack on Pearl Harbor. There was not much left to command: Only four carriers had escaped the Pearl Harbor raid because they had been at sea on maneuvers. Virtually every other ship at the naval base had been either sunk or damaged during the Japanese raid. In short, the Pacific Fleet was down for the count.

Yet in six months it would be a fighting force once again, bloodying the enemy at the Battle of Midway and preparing the path to Tokyo, with Nimitz leading the way.

A Series of Commands Leads to the Pacific Fleet

Chester Nimitz was born in 1885 in Fredericksburg, Texas. He graduated from Annapolis in 1905 and was commissioned an ensign. His first command was a former Spanish gunboat in the Philippines. In 1908, he commanded a destroyer that, unfortunately, became grounded. He was court-martialed, but because of an excellent record he was let off with a reprimanded.

Nimitz was assigned to the submarine service in 1909 and within three years was heading the submarine fleet in the Atlantic. It would be his sole assignment during World War I. After a number of commands and promotions, Nimitz became assistant chief of something called the Bureau of Navigation, which dealt with naval personnel.

In 1939, he was put in charge of the bureau. Two years later, following the attack on Pearl Harbor, the newly named admiral was chosen commander in chief of the crippled Pacific Fleet.

The Battles of the Coral Sea and Midway

Nimitz faced two daunting tasks. First, he had to rebuild, refit, and replace virtually the entire Pacific Fleet. Second, he had to find ways to keep the Japanese off balance with the limited resources he had at his command. Small task forces were sent out to the Marshalls, Gilberts, and other Japanese-held islands to hit and harass. Army Lieutenant-Colonel Jimmy Doolittle (Number 9) and his raiders were taken aboard carriers to within a few hundred miles of the Japanese home islands to bomb Tokyo and other cities. The damage caused by those raids was slight, but it dealt a psychological blow to the Japanese: The American fleet was still very much alive.

In May and June 1942, there were two major naval battles with the Japanese. One took place in the Coral Sea, and the other off Midway Island.

At this time, the United States held one huge advantage. It had broken the Japanese code so that planned enemy attacks were known in advance. Early in May, a Japanese force seized one of the Solomon Islands north of Australia. Nimitz learned that the immediate Japanese target was Port Moresby, New Guinea. The ultimate target was the island continent of Australia itself. A major sea battle took place in the Coral Sea off the Solomon Islands in May 1942. Each side had approximately 120 carrier-based planes. There were losses on both sides; the Japanese lost more than 1,000 men and the Americans approximately 300. But the bottom line was that the Japanese fleet had been repelled.

In June 1942, an even more important battle took place near the island of Midway. The Japanese plan was to fake a major attack on Dutch Harbor, Alaska, draw the American Pacific Fleet there, and then have the main Japanese force invade and occupy Midway Island. Nimitz, heavily outnumbered, knew of the attack plans because American intelligence had broken the Japanese code. Yet it was a savage battle, with dive bombers and torpedo planes versus the big battlewagons. When it was over, the Japanese had to withdraw, having lost all four of their aircraft carriers and other vessels, as well as 250 aircraft. The United States lost one carrier, a destroyer, and 147 airplanes. Thousands of lives were lost. But the superior Japanese navy had suffered its first decisive defeat of the war.

A Final Battle and Victory at Last

Nimitz, using Marine and Army forces, started island-hopping across the Pacific. He would avoid the most heavily fortified islands and attack those less well-defended. Cut off from provisions, the heavily defended strongholds were left to rot on the vine.

The last great naval battle took place in October 1944, when the Japanese attempted to stop the Allied landings at Leyte in the Philippines by using a diversionary force as bait. The ploy worked and drew away William Halsey (Number 26) and his forces. But the Navy put up such a good fight that the Japanese never followed up on getting into

Leyte and wiping out the troop transports. It was the last gasp of the Japanese navy. Savage fighting would go on for many months, but Japan's hopes for victory lay crushed amid the wreckage of rusting warships at the bottom of the Pacific.

The atomic bomb is often credited with the American victory in the Pacific. But it was Nimitz and his admirals who met, staved off, and overcame the Japanese navy. The war in the Pacific was won before the atomic bombs were dropped on Hiroshima and Nagasaki, even though the Japanese refused to surrender.

Chester Nimitz, along with Douglas MacArthur (Number 8), witnessed the surrender of Japan on board the U.S.S. *Missouri* in Tokyo Bay on September 2, 1945. The admiral died in 1966.

19 Husband E. Kimmel/Walter Short

Foul-Ups—or Fall Guys?

NATIONAL ARCHIVES

The burning *Arizona* sinks at Pearl Harbor. How responsible were commanders Husband E. Kimmel and Walter Short for the disaster?

"There is a lot of talk around town (Tokyo) to the effect that the Japanese, in case of a break with the United States, are planning to go all out in a surprise attack on Pearl Harbor. Of course I informed our government," wrote U.S. Ambassador Joseph C. Grew in his diary on January 27, 1941, 10 months before the attack on Pearl Harbor.

Yet that blow against the U.S. Pacific Fleet turned out to be a huge surprise—especially to the two American commanders of record in Hawaii: Rear Admiral Husband E. Kimmel and Major General Walter Short.

The two men had taken their assignments in Hawaii in February 1941, just a few weeks after Grew had conveyed his warning to officials in Washington.

Did government officials fail to notify the new Navy and Army commanders in Hawaii? Were Kimmel and Short too busy getting established to think about it? Or did they dismiss the very idea as emanating from the pipe dream of some cheeky Japanese admiral? In any event, Grew's warning about Pearl Harbor was ignored.

So it came to pass on December 7, 1941, that the Pacific Fleet, the pride of the American navy, was decimated by the Japanese attack.

Questions Surround the Pearl Harbor Attack

Kimmel and Short appear together here because they are inextricably linked. Together they share some responsibility for the single most devastating military disaster in American history. During World War II, their leadership, or lack of it, allowed the Japanese free rein in the Western Pacific. In a matter of months, the Japanese had taken the Philippines, the Dutch East Indies, Hong Kong, Malaya, and Singapore. There was no American fleet to oppose them. In effect, Pearl Harbor was the first domino to fall.

Were Kimmel and Short guilty of dereliction of duty? Were they scapegoats? Or was there another possible explanation somewhere in between?

There have been many reports about Pearl Harbor by both official and private agencies. Many books have been written about the disaster, and occasionally, a motion picture or television documentary tries to "shed new light" on the subject.

However, many decades after the event, the basic questions about Pearl Harbor still persist:

- What did government officials know about the Japanese intentions?
- What was learned from decoded Japanese secret military messages and when was that information obtained?
- What warnings were given to Kimmel and Short, and when were they given?
- How did the Hawaiian commanders prepare for what was coming?

Whatever data exist can be used by both supporters and detractors of the two commanders to make their cases.

A Rivalry between Two Commanders

Husband E. Kimmel was born in 1882 in Henderson, Kentucky. He graduated from the U.S. Naval Academy in 1904. His most auspicious assignment was budget officer for the navy, from 1937 through 1940, operating in Washington, D.C.

Walter Short was born in 1880 in Fillmore, Illinois. He never went to any of the military academies, but was commissioned an officer following his graduation from the University of Illinois. During World War I, he served in France. After the war, he was one of the top officers at Fort Benning, Georgia.

What happened after Kimmel and Short took their new, divided commands in Hawaii? The word divided is used deliberately, because in those days, there was great rivalry between the army and the navy, and not just in Hawaii. It was traditional, but it worked ultimately to the detriment of both services. Was there a communications gap between Kimmel and Short? Did one know what the other was doing?

Whatever the answers to those questions, it is clear that Japanese intelligence officers were keeping track of *exactly* where in Pearl Harbor every single U.S. Navy vessel was located. This was learned by American code-breakers, who decoded secret Japanese messages to and from Japanese consular officials in Honolulu shortly before Pearl Harbor.

The problem is that other intercepted Japanese messages during the same time also indicated an interest in the Philippines and the Canal Zone. As a matter of fact, fewer messages dealt with Hawaii than either of the other two American bases.

A Warning Is Ignored

There is no doubt, however, about the official war warning of November 27, 1941, 10 days before Pearl Harbor. It was transmitted from Washington to *all* the top army and navy commanders in Hawaii, the Philippines, the Canal Zone, and the Presidio:

> *Negotiations with Japan appear to be terminated.... Japanese future action unpredictable, but hostile action possible at any moment. If hostilities cannot, repeat cannot, be avoided, the United States desires that Japan commit the first overt act. This policy should not, repeat not, be construed as restricting you to a course of action that might jeopardize your defense.*

The meaning of this unambiguous message sent by Secretary of War Henry L. Stimson (Number 21) was clear: Take the first hit, but be prepared for what is coming and take defensive measures.

Pearl Harbor was asleep, literally as well as figuratively, that December Sunday morning. In the early months of 1942, there were cries for the court-martial of both Kimmel and Short; they were later allowed to retire. To the end, both Kimmel and Short argued that if they had had access to the decoded Japanese messages, that they would have been prepared. They blamed their ignominy on Washington officials seeking scapegoats for Pearl Harbor.

Questions Linger

Political enemies of Franklin D. Roosevelt (Number 2) hinted, or have said outright, that he knew an attack on Pearl Harbor was coming and had failed to notify the Hawaii command. This is hard to believe when considering several facts about Roosevelt and the U.S. Navy. Roosevelt's first government role was assistant secretary of the Navy in the Wilson administration. More importantly, as president, he was commander in chief of both the army and navy. Any damage to the armed forces would be a personal affront. Additionally, with war approaching, it is inconceivable that Roosevelt would put the Pacific Fleet in peril.

Several months after the Pearl Harbor attack, Kimmel and Short stood accused of dereliction of duty. The two officers, ready to face a court-martial, were prepared to say that they simply had not had access to the decoded messages that had been intercepted. Clearly any formal proceedings would have resulted in the Japanese learning that their code had been compromised. The officers were allowed to retire, and later investigations would conclude that the pair simply had used poor judgment. Short died in 1949 and Kimmel in 1968.

In the case of the attack on Pearl Harbor, one winds up with more questions than one began with. Perhaps there will never be a final resolution.

20 Ernest J. King

"No Fighter Ever Won by Covering Up."

VETERANS OF FOREIGN WARS

Ernest J. King was the first U.S. Navy officer to simultaneously hold the posts of commander in chief of the navy and chief of naval operations.

"When the going gets rough," Ernest J. King once remarked, "they call out the sons of bitches." He was speaking of his own appointment to command the entire U.S. Navy following the Pearl Harbor disaster. He had a fully justified reputation for being as demanding of his officers and men as he was of himself. When President Roosevelt (Number 2) had to decide which should be defended with the remains of the Pacific Fleet, he asked King for a brutally frank assessment of which positions should be held.

Once those decisions were made, it was King's job to rebuild the crippled U.S. Navy and prepare it to take the offensive.

An Education in Leadership

Ernest J. King was born in Lorain, Ohio, in 1878. At 18, he was admitted to the U.S. Naval Academy. A year later, the Spanish-American War broke out. King was put on temporary sea duty and had his baptism of fire in Havana harbor aboard the U.S.S. *San Francisco*, which was fired on by Spanish shore batteries. When the war ended, King returned to the Naval Academy and graduated in 1901, near the top of his class. In the years that followed, he won a series of promotions; when World War I broke out, he was put in command of a destroyer.

Newer and greater commands loomed, and King was assigned to the staff of Admiral Henry Mayo, commander of the Atlantic Fleet. King was now in a position to understudy a command that he would assume a quarter of a century later. He was to learn much more than naval tactics; his lessons would include command, responsibility, and assertiveness.

Early Lessons on Initiative and Risk-Taking

One of the first things King learned was the importance of initiative. Sometimes it meant speaking out to a superior about a proposed regulation. In one instance, King urged that Mayo rescind a proposed regulation regarding specific procedures of naval ships at sea. King felt that individual skippers were in the best position to weigh the various factors that might be involved in varied situations. He argued that the skippers would find better ways of carrying out their missions if they were not strait-jacketed by rigid procedures. Mayo thought it over, agreed, and rescinded his order. Years later, King would issue a special order urging the encouragement of greater initiative among junior officers.

King admired Mayo's quiet toughness and his willingness to take an aggressive stand, especially in the face of Allied hesitation. During World War I, Mayo confronted a top British naval officer who expressed caution about a potentially dangerous naval operation. Mayo, rooted in the values of the mid-19th century, drew on a folksy saying of the time to make his point: "You cannot make omelets without breaking eggs, and...war is made up of taking risks."

Years later, in another war, King would embrace the idea and explain his aggressive stance in a more salty way: "No fighter ever won by covering up by merely fending off the other fellow's blows. The winner hits and keeps on hitting even though he has to take some stiff blows in order to be able to keep on hitting."

The Student Becomes the Teacher

By the time World War I ended, King had been promoted to captain. Through most of the 1920s, King was involved in submarines, ending up in command of the submarine base at New London, Connecticut.

In 1927, King made a critical career decision: He won his wings as a naval flier. Navy aviation became his new passion. Two years later, he was put in charge of the U.S. Naval Air Squadron in Norfolk, Virginia. By 1930, he was commanding an aircraft carrier, the U.S.S. *Lexington*. He was promoted to rear admiral in 1933 and made head of the U.S. Navy Bureau of Aeronautics.

Early in 1941, he was named commander in chief of the Atlantic Fleet, the job that his old boss, Admiral Mayo, had held in World War I. In December 1941, after the Pearl Harbor disaster, he was named commander in chief of the entire U.S. fleet. Shortly thereafter, he was also assigned the post of chief of naval operations. It was the only time in U.S. naval history that one man held both top posts.

Allies Hold in the Pacific

The strategy of the Anglo-American coalition was to hold in the Pacific and attack in Europe. Roosevelt (Number 2) asked King to review the resources available in the Pacific and make recommendations. King said that Australia, New Zealand, Hawaii, Midway, and the points between the latter two should be held. Of course, that did not mean that he would stay on the defensive. Not King.

Ships were badly needed for both the war against the Nazis and the war against the Japanese. In the Atlantic, the United States faced battles against Nazi U-boats, as well as preparation for landings in North Africa and Europe. In the Pacific, the task was to rebuild the Pacific Fleet and add amphibious ships for use in island landings. King was in constant communication with shipbuilders Andrew J. Higgins (Number 69), Henry J. Kaiser, and others. There were issues of design and scheduling, differences of opinion with the Bureau of Ships, and other political matters that had to test the strength of even King's tough hide.

The first post-Pearl Harbor invasions began in 1942. In the Pacific, the Marines landed on Guadalcanal in the Solomon Islands. In the European theater of operations, landings were made in French North Africa. From that point on, the Allies continuously attacked. North Africa led to Sicily and then to Italy, which surrendered. Former Japanese strongholds were seized throughout the Pacific, often at heavy cost in human life.

On June 6, 1944, came the Normandy invasion. Once that beachhead was established, the Nazis were doomed.

In October 1944, the Allies invaded the Philippines and the battle of Leyte Gulf ensued. That victory confirmed that Japan's days were numbered.

The Final Days of War

The final months of the war would bring terrible casualties to the U.S. Navy in the Pacific. Japanese suicide planes called kamikazes crashed into American ships, at terrible cost. Both casualties and ship damage were horrendous; more than 165 ships were damaged and between 24 to 40 were sunk. Several thousand seamen were killed. But the U.S. Navy held firm.

The war in Europe, mainly a land war, ended in a schoolroom in Reims, France. The war in the Pacific, largely a sea war, ended on board an American battleship, the U.S.S. *Missouri*, in Tokyo harbor.

King became a five-star Fleet Admiral in December 1944. In 1956, Ernest J. King, the fighter who never "covered up," died.

21 Henry L. Stimson

Bipartisanship in Time of Peril

Henry L. Stimson had served two Republican presidents as secretary of state and secretary of war. He joined the Roosevelt cabinet after the fall of France.

It was June 1940. France had fallen to the Germans; Great Britain had evacuated its armies from Dunkirk and was prepared for a Nazi invasion. America, though uneasy at the growing strength of Adolf Hitler (Number 1), was nevertheless strongly isolationist and wanted to stay out of any European war.

President Roosevelt (Number 2) pondered his problems and his options. How could he build America's defenses in the face of the antiwar sentiment? How could he help Great Britain defend itself and survive? How could he get Congress to see defense as a bipartisan issue?

Roosevelt made his decision. He appointed two prominent Republicans to the most important cabinet posts in his administration: secretary of war and secretary of the navy. Then the issue of defense would no longer be a partisan one.

He chose well, naming Henry L. Stimson secretary of war and Frank Knox (Number 60) secretary of the navy.

A Cabinet Appointee of Four Presidents

Stimson may be considered the most important figure in Roosevelt's entire presidency. His service continued into the early months of the Truman (Number 14) administration, until the war ended.

Stimson had the credentials, the standing, the character—and the guts—to talk straight, stand up for what he believed was right, and make the tough decisions that had to be made. In short, he could put aside party labels and speak for the good of the country.

Henry L. Stimson was born in 1867 in New York City. He graduated first from Yale and then from Harvard Law School.

He was a partner in a private law firm and then became a federal attorney. He served as secretary of war in the administration of President William Howard Taft. During World War I, he went to France as a colonel, commanding a field artillery unit.

He was President Herbert Hoover's secretary of state from 1929 to 1933. During this time, Japan took over Manchuria.

Stimson wanted to take economic sanctions against the Japanese. When this failed, he announced what became known as the Stimson Doctrine: The United States would not recognize any territorial change that had come about through aggression. Stimson returned to private law practice following Hoover's failed reelection bid. When World War II broke out, Stimson recognized the danger of Hitler and spoke out against the Nazi regime. He called for the United States to aid Great Britain and France and for America to build up its own defenses. In June 1940, at the age of 73, Stimson became secretary of war.

The War Years

In his very first year as war secretary, Stimson would work vigorously to provide lend-lease aid for Britain, to pass the Selective Service Act to build an American fighting force, and to begin production of war materials. He pressed the country to take a stronger stand against both Nazi Germany and Japan.

In November 1941, it was made clear to the administration that the Japanese, who were well-known for making surprise attacks, were planning a move in the Pacific. The exact place for that attack was not known, but the key American military and naval commanders were told to be on guard. Because the United States was a peaceful country, it could not make the first move. These were dangerous times, but Stimson made it clear that Japan had to strike first before America could respond. On December 7, 1941, that attack came: Pearl Harbor.

America responded. Millions of men and women were sent all over the globe: western Europe, North Africa, the Mediterranean, China, Australia, and throughout the Pacific.

In the closing months of heading the War Department, Stimson had to make what was undoubtedly the most profound recommendation of his long and distinguished career. It was for President Truman, who had succeeded to the office after the death of Roosevelt: Should the United States use the atomic bomb against Japan? His recommendation was that it should; it was.

In an article published in *Harper's* 17 months after the war ended, Stimson summarized the thinking that went into that decision:

> *The face of war is the face of death; death is an inevitable part of every order that a wartime leader gives.... The decision to use the atomic bomb was a decision that brought death to over a hundred thousand Japanese. No explanation can change that fact and I do not wish to gloss it over. But this deliberate, premeditated destruction was our least abhorrent choice. The destruction of Hiroshima and Nagasaki put an end to the Japanese war. It stopped the fire raids, and the strangling blockade; it ended the ghastly specter of a clash of great land armies.*

When Stimson took over as secretary of war, there was partisan bickering between Democrats and Republicans over foreign policy. By the time the war had ended, and Stimson had completed his tenure, former isolationist members of Congress were actually supporting the new international organization known as the United Nations. This proves that although the major political parties may have differing points of view, from time to time they do try to present a united front to the rest of the world, especially in time of peril.

Henry L. Stimson died in 1950.

22 Harry L. Hopkins

"Lord Root-of-the-Matter"

DOUBLEDAY, DORAN & CO., INC.

Harry L. Hopkins (left) began working for Roosevelt (right) on social programs.
When war broke out, he became the president's personal representative overseas.

He was the most trusted adviser of President Roosevelt (Number 2). Historians say that Roosevelt went from "Dr. New Deal" in his first two terms to "Dr. Win-the-War" in his last two. The transition is clear, and Roosevelt could not have accomplished all that he did without the prodigious workload assumed by Harry L. Hopkins. The former social worker could take on any job assigned to him by the president and carry it out skillfully, whether he was involved with a local relief agency or the Kremlin.

A Master Administrator

Hopkins was born in 1890 in Sioux City, Iowa, and graduated from Grinnell University in 1912. He was interested in social work and was employed by several relief and welfare agencies, administering relief programs in several states. In 1932, the third year of the Great Depression, Hopkins became head of the New York State Temporary Relief Administration. Roosevelt was then-governor of New York, and Hopkins quickly became a confidante of the soon-to-be president.

In 1933, with FDR in the White House, Hopkins was put in charge of administering the Federal Emergency Relief Act. The social worker from Iowa was now doing welfare work on a nationwide basis. As different relief agencies were established, Hopkins would become involved, one way or the other. The most controversial of these was the Works Progress Administration (WPA). It put people to work on federal projects, including the building of airports, bridges, dams, roads, post offices, and government buildings, giving jobs to construction workers, carpenters, bricklayers, architects, draftsmen, plumbers, and day laborers. Hopkins, however, insisted on providing work for people in many other occupations, and the WPA provided jobs for writers, actors, artists, and researchers, as well as other white-collar workers. It aroused great controversy, but Hopkins took the heat for the president.

With the coming of war, the president's agenda changed. Roosevelt needed someone to talk to Winston Churchill (Number 3) and Joseph Stalin (Number 4). What were these two men like? What did they need? What was the best way of working with them?

From Social Welfare to Diplomacy

The man who was in charge of what critics of the New Deal called "leaf-raking projects" was now in charge of administering the lend-lease program. As American industry turned out the war material, there were intense struggles to see who got what. Would the new tanks off the assembly line go to Great Britain, the Soviet Union, or the American army at home? In short, the military decisions became political decisions, and Hopkins was in the middle of it.

The coordinator of many a social welfare meeting was now arranging the agendas for the Big Three (Roosevelt, Churchill, and Stalin), foreign ministers' meetings, and dozens of interagency conferences. When he attended a meeting that bogged down in minutiae or strayed from the subject, Hopkins would say, "If we get to the root of the matter, the matter will stick to the root." He said it so often that Churchill dubbed him "Lord Root-of-the-Matter."

The hours and days were so long that Hopkins moved into the White House. Despite his failing health, he traveled extensively for the president, defying all the dangers of wartime travel. Unfortunately, there are some dangers that cannot be avoided, especially to loved ones.

On February 1, 1944, the war came home to Harry Hopkins. Stephen, his 18-year-old son, was killed in action with the Marines on Kwajalein atoll in the Pacific. It had been Stephen's first day in combat. He was shot while carrying ammunition to machine gun units.

The war went on, and so did Harry Hopkins. There were breaks for hospital stays, but as the war ground down there were new problems to be faced in the post-war world.

Roosevelt died in April 1945. President Truman (Number 14), his successor, asked Hopkins to go to Moscow and talk to Stalin about important issues in eastern Europe. It was his last presidential mission. Hopkins died in January 1946.

23 William Stephenson

The Spy in Rockefeller Center

COLLIER

From one of the most famous landmarks in New York, William Stephenson carried out British intelligence work throughout the Western hemisphere.

Everybody knows that spies hang out in secret hideaways, isolated from the rest of the world. Not William Stephenson. This famous British spymaster, whose code name was "Intrepid," had his offices in a beautiful suite in Rockefeller Center, in the heart of New York City.

Stephenson is included in our 100 not merely for his work in British intelligence, but also for helping William J. Donovan (Number 24) organize the Office of Strategic Services (O.S.S.) and train its operatives.

Varied Interests

Stephenson was born in Winnipeg, Canada, in 1896. During World War I, he was an air ace of the British flying corps, with more than two dozen downed enemy planes to his credit. His feats won him British and French decorations. Shot down and made a prisoner of war, he escaped to fight another day. These were the kinds of experiences that would later inspire Winston Churchill (Number 3) to give him the code name "Intrepid."

Following World War I, Stephenson took on new roles, as both financier and inventor. He had investments in every major product of the time, from radios to airplanes, he was also a boxing champion.

Among his foreign business interests, Stephenson had holdings in Germany. This gave him the opportunity to keep track of what Adolf Hitler (Number 1) was doing to prepare for war. Stephenson sent the data along to Churchill, the future British prime minister. When Churchill finally took that office, he had plans for Stephenson.

A Spy by Any Other Name

In 1940, the Canadian financier was given the title of Passport Control Officer, conducting business in Rockefeller Center in midtown Manhattan. His real job was security coordinator in the Western hemisphere for British intelligence. He became one of Churchill's chief contacts with President Roosevelt (Number 2); some sources say that Intrepid was *the* major contact.

Stephenson ran a spy network throughout North and South America. There were Nazi agents throughout Latin America, and Stephenson made sure that the United States, not yet in the war and lacking a spy network of its own, received information vital to its interests. He was also aware of Nazi agents in the United States, which sometimes put him in conflict with J. Edgar Hoover of the Federal Bureau of Investigation. Turf would be a problem throughout the war as both Hoover and Stephenson went after the same Nazi spies.

Creating an American Spy Ring

Intrepid's major job was helping the United States to get the Office of Strategic Services off the ground. The most important aspects were recruitment and training. Stephenson gave Donovan tips on physical and psychological characteristics of potential agents. More importantly, he provided training areas in Canada, where agents were taught all the dirty tricks of spying and staying alive behind enemy lines, including tactics of assassination, sabotage, the use of weapons, and radio contact.

There is no doubt that one of Stephenson's tasks on behalf of Churchill was getting the United States into the war. After one conversation with President Roosevelt, Intrepid reported back to London that FDR did not want to face a war the way Woodrow Wilson did back in World War I. Roosevelt was determined that the country come in united, not divided.

The Thrill of the Chase

After the war, Stephenson was honored for his work by both Great Britain and the United States. He was knighted in 1946 by King George VI and given the Legion of Merit by the United States, the country's highest decoration for a foreigner. But Intrepid could not shake the thrill of the chase. He found himself involved in incidents involving the Soviet government. He helped the Canadian authorities track down the atomic spy Dr. Alan Nunn May and assisted the Soviet defector, Igor Gouzenko.

There were undoubtedly other ways that Intrepid served Great Britain, Canada, and the United States after World War II that are still secret. He did, after all, have more than 40 years to go in an extraordinarily event-filled life, and he would have found it difficult not to be involved.

William Stephenson died in 1989 at the age of 93.

William J. Donovan

American Spymaster

GROLIER

William J. Donovan won the nickname "Wild Bill" from his exploits in World War I.
Here, he is being decorated for valor by French General Gaucher.

On July 11, 1941, President Roosevelt (Number 2) issued an executive order creating the Office of Coordinator of Information. Its purposes were defined as follows:

> *...to collect and analyze all information and data which bear upon national security; to correlate such information and data and to make it available to such departments and officials of the Government as the President may determine.... [and to carry out] such supplementary activities as may facilitate the securing of information, important for national security.*

The official description may have sounded akin to the duties of a bunch of scholars locked up in a library. The tip-off was the man chosen for the job: not the Librarian of Congress, but "Wild Bill" Donovan.

Donovan won his nickname on the Columbia University gridiron and on the battlefields of France during World War I. For his valor in combat, Donovan was awarded the Congressional Medal of Honor, the Distinguished Service Cross, and three Purple Hearts. In short, he was not about to take charge of a new research library in Washington. Donovan was in the process of becoming America's first chief spymaster.

Donovan appears here as the father of the Office of Strategic Services (O.S.S.) and, in effect, the grandfather of the Central Intelligence Agency (C.I.A.), which succeeded the O.S.S.

The Beginnings of a Spymaster

William J. Donovan was born in 1883 in Buffalo, New York. He graduated from Columbia Law School and had a successful law practice. During World War I, he was the highly decorated colonel in command of New York's "Fighting 69th" infantry regiment.

After the war, he founded a law firm, dabbled in Republican politics, and served as assistant attorney general in the Coolidge administration. In 1932, he was the Republican candidate for governor of New York, but he lost out in the landslide that brought Roosevelt into the White House and gave the Democrats control of Congress.

The year 1940 was a critical year for Roosevelt. France had fallen, but Roosevelt faced a country still strongly isolationist. He looked for Republicans who shared his views on the danger of Hitler (Number 1) and the need for a strong national defense. In June of that year, he had chosen Republicans Stimson (Number 21) as secretary of war and Knox (Number 60) as secretary of the navy. In July, Roosevelt turned to Donovan for an extraordinary assignment: Donovan was to act as a confidential agent for the president, visiting areas of Europe and the Middle East and reporting back his findings directly to Roosevelt.

The president was apparently satisfied with the job Donovan had done, because a year later, in July 1941, "Wild Bill" was named coordinator of information, a post just created by the executive order previously mentioned.

The attack on Pearl Harbor was still five months away; the United States was not yet in the war and therefore not yet ready to establish a spy network—at least not officially. But Donovan was in communication with William Stephenson (Number 23), a top British intelligence officer.

The O.S.S. Is Created

In June 1942, the spy agency—the Office of Strategic Services—was officially established. It replaced the Office of Coordinator of Information; Donovan was appointed director.

The O.S.S. was unlike anything the United States had ever operated before. As far back as the American Revolution, spies had been used to gather information on enemy troop movements, reinforcements, and installations. But this was the first official organization set up by the U.S. government for purposes of intelligence-gathering and espionage.

Although most of the work of the O.S.S. is still shrouded in secrecy, it sent thousands of agents behind enemy lines—not just for ordinary espionage, but also to work with underground groups fighting the Nazis, supplying them with arms, carrying out sabotage, assassinations, and generally undermining enemy control of occupied areas. "Wild Bill" was running it all.

The media have painted a romanticized picture of the O.S.S. during the war. As with any secret government agency of this size and scope, its triumphs are better known to the world than its failures. The latter are usually buried—sometimes literally. This much is certain: O.S.S. agents paved the way for the invasions of French North Africa, Italy, and France. Most of those agents are anonymous.

Perhaps the least anonymous O.S.S. agent was Allen Dulles, who ran an office in Switzerland. He wrote numerous books on secret operations, including his work with the German underground and arranging the surrender of Italy.

A New "War" and a New Spy Agency

Under Donovan, the O.S.S. established a secret intelligence agency for use in time of war. Several weeks after the Japanese surrender, the O.S.S. was dismantled.

But the Cold War made a similar organization necessary in peacetime, and the C.I.A. was established in 1947 by President Truman (Number 14). Many O.S.S. operatives moved into the new agency; Dulles, for example, became its first deputy director. He then served as director of the C.I.A. from 1953 to 1961, throughout the Eisenhower administration.

Donovan returned to his law practice after the war. He served for two years as Eisenhower's ambassador to Thailand.

William J. Donovan, America's first spymaster, died in 1959.

25 Reinhard Heydrich

Plots and Paranoia

NATIONAL ARCHIVES

Reinhard Heydrich, who had tricked Stalin into purging the Red Army officer corps, was given the job of carrying out the Holocaust.

At the height of his power, Reinhard Heydrich was called "The Butcher of Prague," "The Hangman," and "The Man with the Iron Heart." He reveled in the notoriety.

It would be easy to classify Heydrich as just another Nazi murderer. But he was involved in plots that set him apart from all the other killers. Heydrich was a natural schemer.

He appears this high in our ranking because he is credited with engineering one of the most extraordinary intelligence coups of the war, ranking with "Enigma" (the cracking of the German secret code) and "Magic" (the cracking of the Japanese secret code). Heydrich did not break any codes; he broke the Red Army command, and he did it without firing a single shot. The plot hinged on the German belief that Joseph Stalin (Number 4) was paranoid. It involved a scenario that would have been turned down as a script for *Mission Impossible*. But it worked. Though it took place before World War II began, it influenced Soviet defenses.

Joining the Nazi Power Structure

Reinhard Heydrich was born in Halle, Germany, in 1904. As a young man, he joined the navy but was cashiered out. Sources do not agree on the reason; either he was suspected of homosexuality or he impregnated a girl and refused to marry her. Heydrich was also suspected of having Jewish blood. This is particularly interesting, because he would later be in charge of the Final Solution to exterminate, among others, Jews and homosexuals.

In 1931, Heydrich joined the Nazi Party. That year he met Heinrich Himmler (Number 65), who asked him to set up an intelligence unit.

Adolf Hitler (Number 1) came to power in January 1933, and, from that point on, there were a great deal of secret jobs for Heydrich. He was intimately involved with Himmler and others in the 1934 "Blood Purge" plot, during which a number of top Nazi officials were declared enemies of Hitler and murdered.

Framing a Russian Marshal

If the Führer had been worried about internal security in the Third Reich, the question of external security now became a matter of concern. In the Soviet Union, Hitler learned, a Red Army marshal named Mikhail Tuchachevsky had apparently read *Mein Kampf* and believed that Hitler would attack Russia when he was strong enough. Some Red Army officers supported launching a preventive strike against Nazi Germany before Hitler got too strong.

How should Germany handle this threat? Historians still argue about who did what to whom. Documents dating back to December 1936 credit Heydrich with the plot that succeeded. The idea was a frame-up, which only a paranoid such as Stalin would believe: forge papers to suggest that Tuchachevsky was dealing with the Germans in a plot to overthrow Stalin.

Here is how Heydrich explained it to his aides:

> *Photocopies of these documents will be sold to the Russians at a high price, and we will make it appear that they have been stolen from the files of the SD [Security Service of the Nazi Party]. We will also create the impression that we are investigating the German side of the conspiracy.... Stalin will break Tuchachevsky, because he will receive this dossier through his own Secret Service and will be convinced that it is authentic.*

The plan was successful beyond the wildest dreams of the plotters. For Stalin did more than just break Tuchachevsky. Between 1937 and 1938, thousands of senior Red Army officers were shot for treason following a wave of show trials. Tuchachevsky was executed in June 1937.

The intelligence coup did two things for Hitler. First, it averted the threat of a preventive war by the Soviet Union. Second, it crippled the Red Army until a new cadre of officers could be created.

Kristalnacht and the Final Solution

In November 1938, during a 24-hour period, the Nazis unleashed a wave of anti-Jewish pogroms throughout Germany and Austria that became known as Kristalnacht ("The Night of the Broken Glass"). Heydrich was in the middle of the chaos. A year later, following the Nazi invasion of Poland, he organized the destruction of Jewish communities and the extermination of Jews in Poland.

He ruthlessly Nazified Czechoslovakia, where he earned his reputation as "The Butcher of Prague," staging a police blitz in which Czech men, women, and children were killed in large-scale public executions.

So good a butcher was he that Hitler personally chose him to implement the Final Solution to the Jewish "problem" in Europe. He and Adolf Eichmann (Number 91) and assorted bureaucrats met in Wannsee on January 20, 1942, to plan for the rounding up, transporting, and killing of all European Jews.

However, Heydrich's time was running out. Although sources do not agree, at the request of either the Czech government-in-exile in England or English officials, British intelligence parachuted two agents into Czechoslovakia to assassinate Heydrich. He was ambushed outside of Prague and his car was bombed. Heydrich was critically wounded and died on June 4, 1942.

Hitler's response was savage. Some 800 young Czech men were rounded up and shot. Thousands of Jews were shipped out of the Resienstadt "model" concentration camp and shipped east to the death camps. The town of Lidice, where the assassins had been harbored, was wiped off the map: Its men and older boys were killed, its women and children sent to concentration camps. The town was burned to the ground. It was a terrible price for the Czech people to pay for the death of their tormenter. But the Czechs were aroused by the savagery of the Nazi oppressors, and a surge of resistance rose across the land. This resistance would continue and intensify throughout the rest of the war.

26 William F. Halsey, Jr.

The Navy's "Patton"

COLLIER

William F. Halsey, Jr., would never pass up a fight. The Japanese were therefore able to lure him away from guarding the San Bernardino Strait during the Leyte landings.

In October 1944, Admiral William F. Halsey fidgeted as his fleet stood guard at the San Bernardino Strait. The strait led to the beaches of Leyte, where MacArthur (Number 8) was landing ground forces to retake the Philippines. The U.S. Navy believed that the Japanese were about to make a last, desperate attempt to turn the war around. The Japanese knew they had no hope for victory anymore, but maybe they could strike a heavy blow against the American fleet, a defeat so surprising and devastating that a negotiated peace with reasonable terms for Japan would result.

Halsey was not good at sitting around and waiting for something to happen. So, when he received word that a huge Japanese carrier force had been approaching from the north, it is possible that he read his orders from Nimitz (Number 18) one more time before acting. This was the part he liked best:

"In case opportunity for destruction of major portion of the enemy fleet is offered or can be created, such destruction becomes the primary task."

Halsey may have rubbed his hands with glee before giving the orders to attack the oncoming Japanese fleet. What he didn't know was that he was being lured into a Japanese trap, one he fell right into. Halsey's fleet was being lured away from the San Bernardino Strait by a Japanese fleet far less powerful than it appeared from a distance. A more powerful Japanese fleet lay in waiting for the opportunity to steal into the strait and wipe out the American landing forces on the beaches of Leyte.

Halsey is included here as one of the outstanding U.S. naval commanders of the war. He was certainly the most aggressive, and, with the nickname of "Bull," he was absolutely the last commander one would have chosen to stand guard duty when a battle was in the offing. His actions in the San Bernardino Strait would be referred to by critics as "Bull's Run." Uncalled for and unfair, the criticism would cast a cloud on a very distinguished career, and today the controversy surrounding the incident continues among naval historians.

A Distinguished Career

William F. Halsey, Jr., was born in 1882 in Elizabeth, New Jersey. He graduated from the Naval Academy in 1904. During World War I, he commanded destroyer patrol forces in the Atlantic and won the Navy Cross.

After the war, he was a U.S. naval attaché in Germany and the Scandinavian countries.

His career in naval aviation began in 1935, when he won his wings as a naval pilot. In quick succession, he was assigned to the carrier *Saratoga*, ran the Pensacola naval station, and was put in charge of a carrier division. By 1938, he was training fliers for the carriers *Enterprise* and *Yorktown*.

Following the attack on Pearl Harbor, Halsey commanded the task force that escorted the *Hornet* into Japanese waters. The American carrier brought the Doolittle (Number 9) raiders to bomb the Japanese home islands, including Tokyo, for the first time.

Halsey continued to carry the war to the enemy. He raided Japanese bases in the Marshall and Gilbert islands. He took on the Japanese at Santa Cruz island. His force sank two dozen Japanese ships off Guadalcanal in the Solomons.

A Controversial Decision

In the fall 1944, Halsey's action became the subject of controversy. MacArthur was about to return to the Philippines by way of Leyte. A Japanese response was expected, and Halsey was ordered to guard the San Bernardino Strait to protect the landings on Leyte beach.

Two problems confronted Halsey. First, there was divided command. Admiral Halsey reported to Nimitz, and Admiral Kinkaid (Number 35) reported to MacArthur.

Second, Halsey's orders, as outlined previously, apparently gave him the option of pursuing a Japanese force. For Halsey, the opportunity to go after a major Japanese force was irresistible. He left the strait wide open and chased what was, in reality, a decoy fleet commanded by Japanese Admiral Ozawa. That action almost led to disaster at Leyte.

Weighing the Options

What did Halsey see as his options for the future? He could guard the strait with his entire fleet and wait for the advancing Japanese fleet to strike. Halsey rejected that idea.

He could use his Task Force 34 to guard the strait and take the rest of his fleet to attack the approaching Japanese fleet. This idea was also rejected.

The option he chose was to leave the strait unguarded and use his entire fleet to confront what he believed to be the major Japanese fleet.

Japanese Admiral Kurita (Number 38) headed for the unguarded strait. A determined American naval force so bloodied him that he turned around and headed for home.

So, in the end, it all worked out for the Americans. The Japanese suffered enormous losses in the three Leyte Gulf sea battles, including all four of their carriers, most of their battleships, nine cruisers, and four submarines. From that point on, the Japanese would never again pose a naval threat in the Pacific.

Afterward, Halsey led successful raids on Formosa (Taiwan), the Ryukus, the Philippines, China, and the Dutch East Indies (Indonesia). Japan surrendered on Halsey's flagship, the *Missouri*, in September 1945.

Shortly after the war, he won promotion to Admiral of the Fleet. He retired in 1947 to work in the private sector, and he died in 1959.

27 Henri Petain

The Man from Vichy

QUARRIE CORP.

Henri Petain, head of the Vichy French government, shakes hands with Hitler.

The old man leaned forward in his seat. He cupped his hand behind his ear, straining to make out the words of the prosecutor.

Could it be so? Could it be true that Frenchmen would accuse him, Henri Petain, the hero of Verdun and a marshal of France, of dealing with the enemy, of acting against the security of France? That was close to treason! It was he who had headed the government when France was in deadly peril. It was he who had arranged the armistice with Adolf Hitler (Number 1). It was he who had saved France from chaos and civil war!

The 89-year-old soldier could not believe his ears. He was almost deaf, but the language was unmistakable.

Henri Petain is included here for several important reasons. He sought the armistice with Nazi Germany, agreed to the division of France into occupied and unoccupied zones, turned the French Republic into a fascist state, and decreed a whole new set of "Nuremberg laws" for French Jews. Despite these decisions, the United States maintained diplomatic relations with the Vichy government, a gamble for U.S. foreign policy that paid off.

A French Hero

Petain was born in 1856 near Arras, France. With the outbreak of World War I in 1914, Petain quickly advanced from colonel to full general, acquiring greater command of larger forces. He became commander in chief of all Allied forces on the Western front. Following a stunning victory at Verdun, he was named marshal. By the time World War I ended, Petain had become one of France's greatest heroes.

Between the wars, Petain served in a number of important military positions, including minister of war. As with many officers of World War I, Petain thought about any future war in terms of the last one. He was a staunch supporter of the Maginot Line as France's best defense, a strategy that would prove disastrous.

France Divided

Several months before war broke out in 1939, Petain was sent to Madrid as ambassador. After Hitler attacked in May 1940, Petain was recalled home to join the government as minister without portfolio. French government officials hoped that the return of the old war hero would rally the French people to resist. Petain thought that he was being brought back to bring about an end to the war.

Following a series of crushing German victories, the French cabinet split on whether to carry on the war. Premier Reynaud (Number 99) resigned, and Petain took over the government. He called for an armistice. It provided for a divided France. The northern part, including Paris, would be occupied by Nazi Germany. The southern part of France would be unoccupied, with the French capital shifted to Vichy. Petain would be in charge of the Vichy government.

The establishment of the Vichy regime marked the end of the French Republic. (The word *Republic* was, in fact, officially dropped.) The old French motto of "Liberty, Equality, Fraternity" was replaced by "Work, Family, Fatherland." The familiar freedoms of speech and the press went by the wayside. Petain ruled by decree.

Four months after the French surrender, the Vichy government, without any request from Berlin, issued its own set of laws depriving Jews of employment as teachers, in the military, or in government posts. This would later be followed by requiring all Jews to wear the yellow star. A Commissariat for Jewish Questions was set up. Tens of thousands of Jews were rounded up and shipped to death camps in eastern Europe.

Through all of this, Petain maintained that he was doing what was necessary to protect France. He believed that Hitler would win the war and that cooperation with the Führer was necessary.

The United States maintained diplomatic relations with the Vichy government. The military and political contacts were essential for the successful landings—that is, virtually uncontested by French forces—in French North Africa and Normandy.

Exile

In November 1942, upon the invasion of North Africa, Nazi forces occupied all of France. After the Allies landed in France, Petain was spirited away to Germany against his will. At the end of the war, Petain was arrested and tried for dealing with the enemy and crimes against the internal security of the state.

At his trial, Petain argued that he had spent his life in the service of France. How could anyone question his motives or believe these charges?

The verdict was guilty, and the sentence was death. But the new leader of France, Charles De Gaulle (Number 51), commuted the sentence to life imprisonment because of what Petain had done in the past for France. Henri Petain was confined on the island of Yeu in the Bay of Biscay. He died there in 1951 at the age of 95.

Churchill's "Marshall"

COLLIER

Alan Brooke, chief of the Imperial General Staff, reviews his troops.

In London, it is only a short walk from the houses of parliament to the Cabinet War Rooms. These underground facilities were constructed for the prime minister, key advisers, and support staff during the war. It was from these cramped quarters—conference room, map room, communications room, bunks, and washrooms—that the war was conducted seven days a week, 24 hours a day, from September 1939 to September 1945.

When touring these quarters today, an audiotape describes how each room was used and by whom. In addition, one hears firsthand accounts of what life was like in that underground world.

A Telling Exchange

The most fascinating account is one reenacting a conversation between Winston Churchill (Number 3) and Alan Brooke, his most trusted military adviser. Because the Cabinet War Rooms became a public museum only recently, long after both men had died, the dialogue is read by two professional actors.

Churchill is heard suggesting a military operation. Brooke says no. Churchill expands on it, as if he has been given a green light. Brooke says no. Churchill goes on, carried away by his own enthusiasm. This time Brooke says, quite firmly, "No, prime Minister." Churchill catches on. "No, eh?"

The museum's choice of this interchange represents the reality of the relationship between Brooke and Churchill. Throughout the war, every leader—Allied or Axis—had plenty of "yes" men surrounding him, telling him how wise and right he was.

Brooke, however, was one of the rare exceptions. He was a "no" man. Many times during the war, he had to listen patiently to a Churchill idea for some military operation and tell him point-blank that it would not work. When dealing with Churchill, whose experience, exuberance, and ego were unmatched, he had to be firm. More important, he had to have a thick skin, for Churchill did not take kindly to opposition. But the prime minister's respect for Brooke was genuine; and, no matter how hard he may have fought for a project, he always bowed to the wisdom and will of Brooke and the general staff.

Churchill's Top Aide

Brooke may be considered Churchill's George Marshall (Number 5). The similarities in the careers of Brooke and Marshall are striking. Both men held the top military posts of their respective countries, and both enjoyed the absolute confidence of their respective bosses, Churchill and Franklin D. Roosevelt (Number 2). Both generals dreamed of field commands. Both had been promised the command of all Allied forces in the invasion of northern Europe. Both accepted the less dramatic, but far more important, roles of planning the strategy of worldwide war.

Fighting in Two World Wars

Alan Brooke, the son of an Ulster family, was born in France in 1883. Descended from distinguished military ancestry, he attended the Royal Military Academy at Woolwich. In 1902 he joined the Royal Artillery. Throughout World War I, from 1914 to 1918, he fought in France.

At the outbreak of World War II, Brooke was given command of the Second Corps of the British Expeditionary Force in France. In 1940, when Hitler's (Number 1) panzers swept through France and trapped British forces at Dunkirk, it was Brooke who organized the defense and withdrawal of the British Expeditionary Force. Some historians credit Brooke with rescuing 150,000 troops who might otherwise have been captured. He did this by rejecting a proposed maneuver by the prime minister.

With Britain bracing for a Nazi invasion, Brooke was put in charge of the British home forces. England would not go down without a bloody fight. It is said that Britain was ready to go all out to fight for its freedom, including the use of poison gas if necessary, although that has never been verified. In any case, Hitler called off the invasion.

The "No" Man

In 1941, Brooke was named chief of the Imperial General Staff. The following year, Brooke faced the same kind of decision that Marshall would make. Brooke was offered command of all British forces in the Middle East. Brooke considered it and then turned it down. There is no doubt that he felt the country needed him more right there alongside Churchill, saying no whenever it was necessary.

Both Brooke and Marshall had been promised overall command of Allied forces in the invasion of northern France. Brooke was denied the post when it became clear that an American would be in supreme command. Marshall, too, would fail to have that honor, when Roosevelt kept him in Washington and Eisenhower (Number 7) got the appointment instead.

Brooke's role in World War II was enormously important for two reasons. During the war, it was well known that he was handling overall strategy for British and Commonwealth forces. Less well known was his handling of Churchill's role as a self-styled strategist and tactician. It was no mean feat. Brooke's diaries tell of Churchill's "imperious nature, his gambler's spirit, and his determination to follow his own selected path at all costs."

After the war, Brooke was knighted the Viscount Alanbrooke. He died in 1963.

29 Hideki Tojo

A Time for *Hara-Kiri*

NATIONAL ARCHIVES

When Hideki Tojo became premier of Japan, his government decided to go to war against the United States and Britain.

In past years, *hara-kiri*, ceremonial suicide, was part of traditional Japanese culture. Japanese in disgrace would commit *hara-kiri* to atone for sins that brought disgrace upon themselves or their families. Tradition called for a ceremonial knife or sword to be used to cut open the belly to show that one was pure inside.

Immediately after the Japanese surrender, a number of military and naval officers committed suicide for having lost the war. One notable exception was General Hideki Tojo, the former premier who had ordered the attack on Pearl Harbor and unleashed war throughout the Pacific.

Several days after the surrender ceremony on board the U.S.S. *Missouri*, American military police began rounding up suspected war criminals for questioning. That is when Tojo made his decision. On September 11, 1945, American soldiers pulled up in front of Tojo's house. The former premier looked out his window and said, "I am Tojo." Then he closed the window and disappeared inside the house. A shot was heard.

Hideki Tojo is one of World War II's most influential figures because he made the decision to initiate the war in the Pacific. Tojo was the chief symbol of Japanese militarism.

A Reputation as a Tough Officer

Tojo was born in 1884 in Tokyo, Japan. He graduated from the Military Staff College in 1915 and entered the army. He was a military observer in Switzerland and the Germany of the Weimar Republic.

By 1937, he had become a lieutenant general and chief of staff of the Japanese Army occupying China. Very quickly he acquired the reputation of being a tough officer, a firm believer in total war. Tojo was also credited with intelligence and perception, earning him the nickname "Razor Brain." In 1938, he became vice minister of war in the Konoye cabinet. Later that year, he rose to director of military aviation.

Expanding Japanese Power

In the late 1930s, Japanese officials began exploring ideas for expanding Japanese influence in the Pacific. Tojo proposed taking on the Soviet Union, but the idea was rebuffed. When war broke out in Europe in 1939, the subject of expansion became more compelling. In 1940, Tojo backed Japanese participation in the Tripartite Pact with Hitler (Number 1) and Mussolini (Number 50).

Upon the resignation of Premier Konoye's government in October 1941, Tojo became the new premier. The Tojo cabinet became the war cabinet. It decided to launch surprise attacks against major American, British, and Dutch bases in the Pacific. The key target was Pearl Harbor, where the U.S. fleet lay at anchor. If that fleet could be put out of action, Japan would have a free hand throughout the Pacific.

To make Japanese occupation more acceptable to the people of each East Asian nation they conquered, the Japanese introduced the idea of the Greater East Asia Co-Prosperity Sphere. It was an anticolonial slogan, supposedly offering freedom to those suffering under European colonialism. That worked for a while, until the Japanese began to oppress the very people they were supposed to be liberating.

Months before Pearl Harbor, Yamamoto (Number 6) had predicted that during the first six months of war, Japan would have it easy. After that, it would be very difficult. In June 1942—six months after the attack on Pearl Harbor—the Japanese fleet was bloodied at Midway, where it lost four carriers, 250 planes, and several thousand men. From that point on, it was all downhill for the Japanese. Island-hopping by American forces brought them closer and closer to air bases from which they could bomb the Japanese home islands.

Disgrace in the End

Following the attack on Pearl Harbor and a series of early Japanese victories, Tojo enjoyed the confidence and support of the Japanese people. But when things started going badly, his popularity plummeted.

In July 1944, Tojo resigned as premier. The war still had 14 months to run, and Japan would face firebombings and atomic attacks. The official surrender would come in September 1945.

The day that the American military police drove up to Tojo's house, the former premier knew his time had come. The Americans were rounding up war criminals. Tojo may have wondered if he had not led his country to a kind of national *hara-kiri*. It was time for his own. He drew out his pistol and pulled the trigger.

When the Americans rushed inside Tojo's house, they found him bleeding from a self-inflicted bullet wound in his chest. There were traditional *hara-kiri* knives nearby, but Tojo had used a pistol. Apparently he felt he did not have time to perform the traditional ceremonial act.

Why did he not shoot himself in the head, to ensure death? Tojo would later explain that he did not want to disfigure his face; he wanted his countrymen to know that he had carried out the traditions of his people. He wanted his death to be recognized. (There was still controversy, at the time, over whether Hitler had faked his suicide and fled Berlin.)

Tojo's suicide attempt failed. U.S. Army doctors patched him up and gave him some American blood plasma. Tojo would survive to face trial and execution for war crimes. He was hanged in 1948.

30 J. Robert Oppenheimer

"I Am Become Death...."

COLLIER

J. Robert Oppenheimer headed the group of scientists who worked
on the Manhattan Project and produced the atomic bomb.

As the blinding light of a thousand suns lit up the New Mexico desert that morning in July 1945, a line from the *Bhagavad Gita* flashed into the physicist's brain. It had been written in India 2,000 years earlier, but it seemed particularly significant now: "I am become death, The Scatterer of Worlds."

J. Robert Oppenheimer stared at the mushroom cloud rising over the desert where a huge steel tower had once stood. For more than two years, he and a staff of 4,500 scientists, engineers, and technicians had labored to reach this point. The United States had beaten Hitler (Number 1) to the atomic bomb. But what now? Hitler was dead and Nazi Germany had surrendered 10 weeks earlier. Would it be necessary to use the bomb against the Japanese? The forthcoming answer would haunt him for the rest of his life.

Building the Atomic Bomb

J. Robert Oppenheimer was born in 1904 in New York City. A graduate of Harvard, he went to Europe to study physics at Cambridge, Goettingen, Leyden, and Zurich. He then taught theoretical physics at the University of California and the

California Institute of Technology. His brilliant work in the fundamental particles of nuclear physics became well known throughout the scientific world.

Early in 1943, as the Manhattan Project (to build an atomic bomb) began, then-Colonel Leslie R. Groves (Number 32) tapped Oppenheimer to run the Los Alamos unit in New Mexico, where the scientists would work in virtual isolation. Their job was to design, construct, and then test an atomic bomb.

Years earlier, when Albert Einstein (Number 13) had first written to President Roosevelt (Number 2), the father of the relativity theory was not sure that an atomic bomb could be delivered by air. The scientists at Los Alamos had hundreds of details to work out—not merely the technical aspects of creating a critical mass, but also such issues as size, shape, and weight of the bomb, how it could be "armed," what altitude would be most useful for the greatest impact, how best to protect the bomber and its crew, and so on. And it all had to be done in the strictest secrecy.

Among the scientists working on the bomb were Edward Teller, Enrico Fermi, Nils Bohr, and Albrecht Bethe. Klaus Fuchs, a German-born scientist from Britain, also worked at Los Alamos; he turned out to be a Soviet spy who would provide atom bomb secrets to the Russians. At one point, Oppenheimer himself had been approached by Haakon Chevalier, a French Communist, to provide information to the Soviets. Oppenheimer responded, "But that would be treason." He never provided such information, but his casual relationships with people of all political persuasions would later lead to security questions.

The Atomic Age

The atomic age was born on July 16, 1945, at Alamagordo, New Mexico. An atomic "device" was set off. It had the power of about 20,000 tons of dynamite. The results were sent to President Truman (Number 14), then meeting in Potsdam with Churchill (Number 3) and Stalin (Number 4). Churchill knew all about it. Stalin, who said that he hoped the United States would use it, probably knew more about it than Truman did, thanks to Soviet spies.

The scientists at Los Alamos were divided on how and whether to use the bomb. Some wanted to warn the Japanese in advance. Others wanted to have some Japanese official witness an actual explosion. The decision was a military one: It would end the war and save more lives than would be killed by the bomb. Truman ordered that the bomb be used on Japan. On August 6, 1945, "Little Boy," a uranium bomb, was dropped on Hiroshima. "Fat Man," a more powerful plutonium bomb, was dropped on Nagasaki, on August 8, 1945. The Japanese surrendered.

After the war, Oppenheimer became director of the Institute for Advanced Studies at Princeton. An advisor to the Atomic Energy Commission and the U.S. Defense Department, Oppenheimer publicly opposed the building of a hydrogen bomb.

In 1954, he was accused of disloyalty to the United States. A three-man committee heard his case. It ended in a split decision. One committee member said he was loyal and should keep his security clearance. A second ruled that Oppenheimer was not loyal and should lose his security clearance. The third and deciding vote was that even though he was loyal, Oppenheimer was a security risk. His past associations had come back to plague him, and he was denied security clearance. Labeled a security risk, Oppenheimer's career was permanently crippled.

He died in 1967.

31 Wernher von Braun

Father of the V-2

V.F.W.

The V-2 rocket, which devastated London late in the war, was the brainchild of Wernher von Braun.

There are many legends about Wernher von Braun, probably because his renown or infamy lies strictly in the eye of the beholder. He was the father of the V-2 rocket, which killed thousands of innocent civilians in England, France, and Belgium. He was also a key figure in the American space program that landed a man on the moon.

Therefore the stories told of von Braun will vary widely. One story is that he intended to fly to England in the middle of the war to turn over to the Allies top-secret documents on German rocket research. Another story is that he had once explained why he became a member of the SS by saying, "It was just an honorary title—like being made a Kentucky colonel."

Portrayed as hero or villain, Wernher von Braun was one of the most brilliant scientists of the war. His work on the German rocket program revolutionized modern warfare.

Creating a New Weapon of War

Wernher von Braun was born in 1912 in Wirsitz, which was then a part of Germany. As a young engineering student, he became interested in the exploration of outer space. He met with other young Germans with similar interests. Many of them ended up doing research for the German military, and von Braun joined the ordinance department four months before Hitler (Number 1) came to power.

By 1937, von Braun was hard at work at Peenemuenden, developing new weapons. Hitler had a tendency to blow hot and cold on programs that temporarily caught his attention, and this was the case with the rocket program. But once the war broke out, Hitler became more concerned with what his troops were doing on the battlefield than what scientists were doing in the laboratory. In 1942, following a successful V-2 launching, the program received high priority.

When Hitler felt the program was not going fast enough, he assigned Himmler (Number 65) to take charge of it and increase weapon production. At this point von Braun, who refused to cooperate with Himmler, was arrested. Hitler rescinded Himmler's order and von Braun went back to work.

Rockets of Mass Destruction

The two weapons most associated with the young scientist are the V-1 and the V-2. (The "V" stood for "vengeance.")

The V-1 was basically an unpiloted jet plane filled with high explosives. Called a "buzz bomb," it was launched into flight with just enough fuel to reach the designated target. It would then fall to the earth and explode. The V-1 could be shot down before reaching its target, and about half of them *were* blasted out of the sky.

The V-2 was far more sophisticated. It was a ballistic missile, a rocket ship fueled with liquid oxygen. Because it flew at a high altitude, there was no defense against it once it was launched. The only way to fight it was to take out the launching pads.

The rockets were produced by slave labor in underground factories in the Harz mountains. Living conditions for the laborers were unbelievably horrible. They were undernourished, were brutally overworked, and lived in wretched slave quarters.

The V-2s were extremely effective in causing death and destruction, but their inventions came too late in the war to save Hitler.

New Allies

As the war wound down, von Braun and members of the scientific staff surrendered to the Western allies. The Soviets would acquire their own group of German scientists and engineers for their own weapons program.

After the war, Walter Dornberger, one of the top German scientists, was placed on a war criminals list. He was never tried, but he came to America to work for the U.S. Air Force.

Wernher von Braun was now at the start of a new career: working for the U.S. Army. He and his colleagues became part of an American missile program. Von Braun became a naturalized American citizen and a key figure in the space program for the National Aeronautics and Space Administration. He made major contributions to the successful moon landings.

He resigned from the government program in 1972 to work in private industry. He died in 1977.

32 Leslie R. Groves

Director of the Manhattan Project

CORBIS

Atomic bombs over Hiroshima and Nagasaki ended the war. Leslie R. Groves directed the Manhattan Project, which designed and produced the weapons.

From the earliest days of American history, the nation's leaders have turned to the military to carry out extraordinary missions involving threats to the national security or challenges to the national interest.

During the American Revolution, General George Washington was concerned about British naval power sailing up the Hudson River and cutting the colonies in two. So he ordered the forging of huge chains to be stretched across the river at West Point. The project was carried out under the supervision of the American military. To this day, links of that monstrous chain may be seen, most appropriately, at the U.S. Military Academy.

When President Thomas Jefferson wanted to explore the Louisiana Territory and seek a Northwest Passage to the Pacific, he sent an army expedition, under Meriwether Lewis and William Clark, to carry out the mission. Both were army officers. In addition, Lewis was Jefferson's private secretary. After several years of danger in the wilderness, the explorers returned to a heroes' welcome.

President Theodore Roosevelt called on Lieutenant-Colonel George Goethals to solve all the problems attending to the construction of a canal across the isthmus of Panama. The result was an engineering marvel, the envy of the world.

Taking Charge of the Manhattan Project

During World War II, the army was chosen once again to take on a multifaceted assignment: how to design, construct, test, and manufacture atomic bombs. And how to do it in absolute secrecy.

Leslie R. Groves was the army engineer who brought the people, places, and materials together. Under his direction, the job got done.

Groves was born in Albany, New York, in 1896. He studied at M.I.T. before entering West Point. Shortly before World War I ended, he graduated from West Point. Groves was involved in army supply services as well as engineering projects, including work on the Pentagon building.

On September 17, 1942, he received orders to take over a new project. The project would have its code name changed several times: the DSM project, Tube Alloys, Manhattan Engineering Project, Manhattan District Project, and, finally, just plain Manhattan Project.

A Race for the Atomic Bomb

The Colonel—he would eventually rise to lieutenant general—overcame many obstacles during the course of the war.

To begin with, he knew he was in a race against Nazi Germany to solve the riddle of the atomic bomb. It was no exaggeration to think that the outcome of the war depended on who would get the bomb first. The thought of such weapons in the hands of Hitler (Number 1) was the stuff of nightmares. So, as far as Groves was concerned, the clock was always ticking until Germany surrendered.

Secrecy was imperative, and the problem was not with the factory workers but with the scientists and engineers. The majority of workers were completely ignorant about what they were constructing. However, the scientists knew, and their normal instincts were to share what they had learned with others. This could be dangerous for security, and Groves had to impress on the scientific community to keep what they had learned within their own working groups. Some scientists could not take the security, the censored mail, and sometimes being shadowed by security officials. Several left the project before its completion.

Maintaining Absolute Secrecy

The Manhattan Project was divided into three parts: Los Alamos, New Mexico; Oak Ridge, Tennessee; and Richland, Washington. Facilities for the scientists were at Los Alamos, about 15 miles from Santa Fe. This was lonely desert country where they could work without being disturbed. The desert location was perfect for testing the first nuclear bomb.

Factories for producing nuclear weapons were located at Oak Ridge and at the Hanford Engineer Works at Richland.

It was Groves's job to see to it that housing and other needs were provided for the workers. Both transportation and communication back and forth among the three widely separated sites was not without difficulty.

Congressional investigators had to be shooed away as discreetly as possible, without tipping anybody off about what was going on.

There were spies to worry about, and not just from Germany or Japan. Though England was working with the United States on the bomb, the Soviet Union was out of the loop and apparently casting about for information.

There were always personnel problems. To begin with, there was J. Robert Oppenheimer (Number 30). The FBI suspected he might be a security risk because of his past left-wing associations. Groves, however, knew he was a brilliant scientist and insisted on keeping him.

The Atomic Age Begins

Groves was the one who had to arrange the testing of the first atomic device. Out there in the desert, in July 1945, Groves watched the great flash of light and realized that his job was almost over.

The Manhattan Project had taken nearly three years, had cost what was then a staggering $2 billion, and utilized more than 100,000 personnel. But in the end, the race against the Nazis had been won.

In August 1945, two bombs were dropped on Japan, and the war was over. Overnight, virtually all the secrets of the Manhattan Project were on the front pages of every newspaper in the world.

Leslie R. Groves performed his job during the war in complete anonymity. Though he became known after the war, he never received the recognition awarded to a George Goethals or a Lewis and Clark.

He deserved better. Groves died in 1970.

33 Omar Bradley

The G.I.'s General

NATIONAL ARCHIVES

Of all the American field commanders during the war, Omar Bradley was the most popular among his men.

"I don't believe I have ever known a person to be so unanimously loved and respected by the men around and under him."

That is not the kind of thing one usually finds written about a general. The writer was Ernie Pyle (Number 71), the war correspondent who was famous for writing about the enlisted men in the war. But Bradley was one "brass hat" he could not pass up.

Omar Bradley was one of the outstanding field commanders of the war. He is also credited with the most frank memoir of World War II. Beautifully written (and apparently with the help of a professional writer), *A Soldier's Story* offers Bradley's assessment of the key personalities, decisions, and battles in the European theater of operations. Although the ghost writer may have added a non-soldierly style, only Bradley could have provided the insight to interpret the strategies and describe the military and political figures of the war.

Rising through the Military Ranks

Omar Bradley was born near Clark, Missouri, in 1893. He attended West Point with Dwight D. Eisenhower (Number 7). Both graduated in time for World War I, but neither served overseas.

Bradley was spotted as a "comer" when he taught at the Infantry Training School at Fort Benning, Georgia. George C. Marshall (Number 5) directed the school and jotted down Bradley's name for future reference. When Marshall became Army chief of staff in 1939, he started examining his list of potential leaders. One of Bradley's first assignments was to head the Infantry Training School. After the United States entered the war in December 1941, Bradley was put in charge of the 82nd Division, followed by the 28th Division.

In November 1942, American troops got their first combat assignment of the war in the European/African theater: the invasion of French North Africa. Because a deal had been made with the French, the resistance was minimal. Real battle would come in Tunisia against the Germans.

In February 1943, at the Kasserine Pass, American units were mauled. Shortly afterward, Bradley was assigned to find out what went wrong. His investigation led to the assignment of Patton (Number 11) to take command of the demoralized 2nd Corps. In the summer of 1943, Patton was promoted. Bradley would assume command of the 2nd Corps, working under Patton in the campaign for Sicily. It was a military triumph for Patton, but he got into trouble for slapping a soldier. Patton was temporarily relieved of his command.

Securing the Beachhead at Normandy

Eisenhower picked Bradley to lead the 1st Army into France. The Americans would face fiercer resistance than any other unit taking part in the Normandy invasion. It was D-Day, June 6, 1944.

After the beachhead had been secured, the 3rd Army, led by Patton, became part of the 12th Army Group, under Bradley's overall command. This is the army group that set the pace for the Allied victory in Europe.

After establishing the beachhead at Normandy in June 1944, Bradley's army group broke out at St. Lo in July, freed Paris in August, and fought the Battle of the Bulge starting in December. In 1945, one of its units seized the Rhine bridge at Remagen in March and linked up with the Soviet army at Torgau on the Elbe in April. On May 8, 1945, 11 months after D-Day, Nazi Germany surrendered unconditionally.

A Conflict with an Ally

For Bradley, the war had its low points, as well as its high. The general's greatest crisis was the Battle of the Bulge in December 1944, when German forces cut through the Ardennes, thrusting deep into the heart of Belgium.

The American general faced two challenges: how to stop the German advance and how to get Montgomery (Number 37) to move his army to support the American counterattack. Montgomery not only dragged his feet during the battle but actually tried to take credit for containing the Germans. Rumors were rampant that Montgomery was about to be put in command of all the ground troops, including the Americans.

After hearing the rumor, Bradley told Eisenhower: "You must know after what has happened I cannot serve under Montgomery. If he is to be put in command of all ground forces, you must send me home, for if Montgomery goes in over me, I will have lost the confidence of my command."

Following this exchange, Churchill spelled out to Parliament the burden borne by the Americans during the Bulge. Any attempt to put Montgomery in command was scotched.

That remarkable statement by Bradley is from his war memoir, *A Soldier's Story*. The memoirs of important generals traditionally deal with their successes and honors, filled with false praise about those whom they may despise. But Bradley broke all the rules. His memoirs are blunt and honest about the events and personalities of the war.

Success after the War

After the war, no one was better qualified than Bradley to serve as administrator of veterans affairs, a post he held from 1945 to 1948. He succeeded Eisenhower in 1948 as Army chief of staff. The following year he became permanent chairman of the Joint Chiefs of Staff. In 1950 he was promoted to the five-star rank of General of the Army. He was the last man to hold that rank.

Upon retirement in 1953, Bradley became a corporate executive in private industry. He died in 1981.

34 Arthur Harris

The 1,000-Plane Raider

COLLIER

Arthur "Bomber" Harris sent out 1,000 bombers at a time to pulverize German cities.

When Dresden was firebombed in February 1945, one of the major transportation and communications centers of Germany was totally demolished. Many Germans died; thousands of them were incinerated immediately. They might have been the lucky ones. Others, according to writer Ruth Andreas-Friedrich, "ran like burning torches through the streets, [or] stuck fast in the red-hot asphalt, [or] flung themselves into the waters of the Elbe. They screamed for coolness; they screamed for mercy. Death is mercy."

Dresden was one of the last German cities to experience the 1,000-plane bombing raid.

Arthur Harris, who headed Britain's Bomber Command through most of the war, was the man who introduced 1,000-plane bombing in World War II. Cologne, Hamburg, and Dresden were Harris's major targets.

Becoming a Fighter Pilot

"Bomber" Harris was born in 1892 in Cheltenham, England. He worked in Rhodesia (now Zimbabwe) as a young man. When World War I broke out, Harris joined a Rhodesian regiment and saw action in German southwest Africa. Back in England, he joined the budding flying corps and became a fighter pilot. After the war, the Royal Air

Force was established, with Harris a squadron leader. Between the wars, he saw service in Iraq, Iran, and Turkey.

By 1933, he had risen to group captain. His next major assignment was in the Air Ministry as deputy director of plans. By the time World War II started, he had become air vice marshal.

In the early years of the war, Great Britain was hard hit by German bombers. The Nazis hoped that England would sue for peace before a risky invasion of the island was necessary. But Britain held firm and the invasion never came; Britain grew in strength and prepared to retaliate in kind.

A Better Way to Bomb

Sending a few hundred bombers over a target was not effective; Harris wondered if it might not be a better idea to send a thousand planes at one time against one city. Though Great Britain did not have the technology for true precision bombing, perhaps huge fleets of planes and plenty of bombs would do the trick. That many bombs were bound to hit the intended target and do a lot of other damage as well.

There were several different names given to this kind of bombing: saturation bombing, area bombing, and carpet bombing. Andy Rooney, then a reporter for *Stars and Stripes*, would later call it "close-your-eyes-and-bombs-away bombing."

The efficiency of this approach would ultimately be determined on the basis of losses. Would it prove too costly—in planes and lives—to sustain these super raids?

The trial run, the first 1,000-plane bombing of a German city in a single raid, was called Operation Millennium. Cologne, then the third largest city in Germany, lay in the Rhineland and was a major producer of machinery and chemicals. It was Cologne's bad luck to have good weather on the night of May 30–31, 1942. (Alternate target cities, which had bad weather that night, were bypassed.)

More than 1,000 RAF bombers dropped nearly 1,500 tons of explosives on the city. Of the 1,000 planes, about 900 targeted the city itself; the rest went after anti-aircraft installations and nearby German airfields.

Originally, the RAF had expected to lose as many as 100 aircraft; it lost fewer than 40. Equally important, the industrial damage to Germany was substantial.

The year of the Cologne raid, Harris was named commander in chief of the British Bomber Command.

The Firebombings Continue

Other massive raids followed Cologne. One of the fiercest was on Hamburg from July 24 through August 3, 1943. It included seven separate raids and involved nearly 2,400 British and American bombers dropping 9,000 tons of explosives. During that period of time, the fires in Hamburg never went out. A firestorm resulted, causing devastation beyond belief to the vital German port.

In the months just before and just after D-Day, Harris's Bomber Command was put under Eisenhower's (Number 7) direction. But once the Anglo-American forces were well established in France, Harris was put back in charge of the bomber group.

The massive raids continued, culminating in the firebombing of Dresden on the night of February 13–14, 1945. Before the war, the city had been known as "the Florence of Germany" for its architectural treasures and exquisite churches. These were gutted in the firebombing, along with rail lines and communications and industrial facilities.

A Questionable Approach?

The practice of saturation bombing has been criticized as excessive. But defenders of Harris's methods have recalled Hitler's (Number 1) bombing targets: Warsaw, London, Coventry, and Rotterdam—not to mention V-1 and V-2 rocket attacks against England. Nazi Germany, Harris's defenders said, had sowed the wind and reaped the whirlwind.

Arthur Harris died in 1984 at the age of 92.

35 Thomas Kinkaid

In the Spirit of John Paul Jones

Thomas Kinkaid, left, took on the Japanese navy all over the Pacific. His task forces engaged the enemy from the Aleutians in the north to the Solomons in the south.

I f one man could be chosen to represent the American naval war in the Pacific, Thomas Kinkaid would be that man. His task forces saw action throughout the Pacific—from the Aleutians in the north to the Solomons in the south. In all, Kinkaid and his sailors supported more than two dozen assaults during the Pacific war.

In the early days of the war, following the Pearl Harbor disaster, Kinkaid and his tiny task force saw so much action in so many places that the Japanese were led to believe that the United States had a much larger fleet roaming the Pacific than it actually did. Some naval observers have theorized that it might have been planned that way.

Distinguished Service in the Navy

Thomas Kinkaid was born in 1888 in Hanover, New Hampshire. The son of a rear admiral, he was appointed to the Naval Academy by President Theodore Roosevelt in 1904. The cadet was only 16.

Graduating in 1908, Kinkaid was assigned to the battleship *Nebraska* and then to the *Minnesota*. In 1913, he was selected to receive post-graduate instruction in ordnance.

During Pershing's military incursion into Mexico, Kinkaid was on duty in Mexican waters. When World War I heated up, he was assigned to the battleship *Pennsylvania.* After the war, he was serving on the *Arizona* when President Wilson sailed the ship to Europe. The president was on his way to the peace conference at Versailles.

The naval officer kept moving up the career ladder. He was assigned to the critically important U.S. Navy Bureau of Ordnance, and then as assistant chief of staff to an admiral.

Kinkaid received his first command in 1924: the U.S.S. *Sherwood.* Three years later, he was selected as gunnery officer to the commander in chief of the fleet. He won a plum spot at the Naval War College and then served as secretary to the naval panel, making recommendations on fleet disposition in the event of war. During 1932, Kinkaid was part of the American delegation attending the Naval Disarmament Conference in Geneva.

In 1937, Kinkaid was captain of the cruiser *Indianapolis.* Two years later, war broke out in Europe. Kinkaid became U.S. naval attaché in Rome.

A Game of Cat and Mouse

Six months before Pearl Harbor was attacked, Kinkaid was back at sea. The attack on Pearl Harbor would put him smack in the middle of the Pacific war. He was about to participate in the most extraordinary use of limited naval resources since John Paul Jones made do with what he had during the American Revolution. Kinkaid's initial battles with the Japanese were carried out with a small cruiser task force. His first assaults against the Japanese were raids on the Marshalls, the Gilberts, Wake, and Marcus; the battle of the Coral Sea; and the battle of Midway.

Two carriers—the *Enterprise* and the *Hornet*—joined his new task force. Kinkaid now engaged the Japanese more often and on a larger scale at Santa Cruz, Guadalcanal, and the Solomon Islands. All that was accomplished just in 1942. Every man on the carrier *Enterprise* would be honored with the unit citation.

In 1943, commanding joint American and Canadian naval forces, he wrested back two of the Aleutian Islands that had been seized by Japan the year before. The island of Attu was taken after fierce resistance by the Japanese that ended in mass suicide. The Japanese evacuated Kiska in one foggy night before Kinkaid could strike.

Closing in on the Victory

From the extreme northern Pacific, Kinkaid headed to the southwest to work with MacArthur (Number 8), island hopping closer and closer to the Philippines. The American fleet would land MacArthur's forces on the beaches, then support them with naval fire and air strikes.

Late in October 1944 came the Philippine landings. The initial target was Leyte. Kinkaid's force was in charge of landing the troops and getting them safely on shore.

The Japanese response came in three separate fleet movements. Though the Americans did not know it at the time, one of those fleets was assigned to lure Halsey (Number 26) away from guarding the San Bernardino Strait, which led to Leyte. Once Halsey was drawn away by the decoy, another fleet, under Japanese Admiral Kurita (Number 38), was to attack the landing forces and supplies on the Leyte beaches. But C.A.F. Sprague (Number 36), one of Kinkaid's captains, put up such fierce resistance with his tiny carrier escorts that Kurita turned around and headed for home. After Leyte came an attack on Luzon, the largest Philippine island, and then islands closer to the Japanese mainland.

Until the end of the war, the American fleet's biggest threat was from Japanese suicide planes called kamikazes. Japanese volunteers crashed their planes, filled with explosives, on American ships. The suicide missions were highly successful.

Witness to Surrender

The war ended in Tokyo Bay early in September 1945. Fittingly, Kinkaid was one of the witnesses to sign the Japanese surrender document. After the war, he was appointed commander of the reserve Atlantic Fleet.

Admiral Thomas Kinkaid died in 1972.

36 C.A.F. Sprague

"Combustible, Vulnerable, Expendable"

NATIONAL ARCHIVES

The hero of Leyte Gulf, C.A.F. Sprague took on an overwhelmingly superior Japanese force—and sent it scurrying home.

During the war, the letters CVE signified what the U.S. Navy officially called an escort carrier and unofficially called a baby flattop. But the sailors who manned the small aircraft carriers—with the grim humor they shared with one another—insisted that CVE really stood for "combustible, vulnerable, expendable." That is because the baby flattop did not have the armored protection or the firepower anywhere near that of the traditional carrier.

Under normal circumstances, the CVE would have been more than a nostalgic memory when the war ended. But Clifton Albert Frederick Sprague (he preferred C.A.F. Sprague) changed all that in the fall of 1944, when Douglas MacArthur (Number 8) began his campaign to liberate the Philippines. Sprague took half a dozen CVEs, numerous destroyers, and destroyer escorts, and he held off a huge Japanese fleet. This decisive battle took place in the Leyte Gulf during a few hours on the morning of October 25, 1944.

From Navy Pilot to Rear Admiral

C.A.F. Sprague was born in 1896 in Boston. He was graduated from Annapolis in 1917, and he became a navy pilot after World War I. Sprague was in command of a seaplane tender at Pearl Harbor the morning Japan attacked.

129

He undertook a number of key assignments early in World War II. He was involved in the defense of American shipping from U-boat attacks in the Gulf of Mexico. Sprague commanded Seattle's Naval Air Station and then was made skipper of the carrier *Wasp*. He saw action throughout the Pacific.

By October 1944, Sprague had risen to the rank of rear admiral, heading Escort Carrier Division 25. He was about to give the CVE a brand new image.

An Unexpected Battle

During the amphibious landings on the Philippine island of Leyte, his CVE unit supported the landing operations. As far as Sprague knew, the invasion seemed to be proceeding according to plan.

On the morning of October 25, 1944, Sprague received a report that enemy ships had been spotted near the San Bernardino Strait, about 20 miles away. That did not seem possible. Sprague knew that William F. Halsey (Number 26) was guarding the strait to prevent Japanese interference with the Leyte operation. If Halsey was not there, then only Sprague and his tiny CVE unit lay between Leyte and the Japanese. Sprague insisted on a confirmation of the sighting. The ships that were spotted had pagoda masts; they were Japanese.

The first thought that went through Sprague's head was probably, "Where the hell is Halsey?" Sprague would later find out that Halsey has been tricked by a Japanese decoy fleet of carriers.

Sprague, with six escort carriers, six destroyers, and several destroyer escorts, now had the responsibility of trying to hold off a massive Japanese fleet that included four battleships, eight cruisers, and 10 destroyers. The Japanese shells had up to 16-inch guns, and the American ships had only 5-inchers.

A Brilliant Deception

Sprague could not afford to have the Japanese discover how weak he was. The American ships let out a smoke screen. The escort carriers launched their planes carrying bombs that were not really effective against the heavily armored Japanese fleet. The destroyers closed in as best they could. The shorter the range, the more likely that they would do at least some damage, especially with torpedoes.

Sprague later described how he felt:

"Nothing like this had happened in history. I didn't think we'd last 15 minutes. What chance could we have—six slow, thin-skinned carriers, each armed with only one 5-inch peashooter, against the 16-, 14-, 8-, and 5-inch broadsides of the 22 warships bearing down on us at twice our top-speed."

But Sprague's tactics completely fooled the force under Japanese Admiral Kurita (Number 38).

"The failure of the enemy main body...to completely wipe out all vessels of the [CVE] Task Unit can be attributed to our successful smoke screen, our torpedo counterattack, continuous harassment of the enemy by bombs, torpedoes, and staging air attacks, timely maneuvers, and the definite partiality of Almighty God," Sprague concluded.

The uneven battle lasted more than two hours. Victory was in his grasp, but Kurita did not know it. He retired from the battle.

The End of the Japanese Navy

The American spirit of optimism and good humor is found in the anonymous sailor who, seeing the Japanese flee, mockingly complained, "They got away!"

Except for attacks by Japanese suicide planes (kamikazes), the Japanese navy was finished. Officially, however, the war would continue for another 10 months.

After the war, Sprague was in charge of navy operations at the atomic bomb tests at Bikini Island. Later, he was in charge of Carrier Division 6, the 17th Naval Division, and the Alaskan Sea Frontier.

C.A.F. Sprague died in 1955. He gave the initials CVE a whole new meaning: courageous, victorious, exemplary.

37 Bernard Montgomery

He Chased the Desert Fox

COLLIER

Bernard Montgomery, left, hero of El Alamein, would lead all
British military forces in the invasion of northern Europe.

The German officer put a finger into the bucket of water, then touched it to his tongue. Salty. One more well the British had gotten to. Not all were salted. Some had oil poured in, and others were just blown up. Armies may be able to survive on shorter rations and even on a careful use of limited ammunition, but fresh water was an absolute necessity. For the Afrika Korps, it was one more reason to break through El Alamein. Ahead lay Alexandria, less than 70 miles away.

It was late October 1942. German and Italian forces faced the British 8th Army at El Alamein in northwest Egypt. The commander of the Afrika Korps, Erwin Rommel (Number 39), had earned a reputation as "The Desert Fox," a skillful and aggressive desert fighter.

The commander of the British forces, Bernard Montgomery, was about to be tested in his first desert command. It became one of the major turning points of the war.

From India to Egypt

Bernard Montgomery was born in London in 1887. He graduated from Sandhurst in 1907 and spent five years with the British Army in India. When World War I began in 1914, he fought in France, where he was wounded in action. Between the wars, his army career was relatively uneventful. In 1938, he was stationed in Palestine, where his troops put down Arab unrest.

Just days before the invasion of Poland in 1939 and the start of World War II, Montgomery was assigned command of the 3rd Division. His outfit was part of the British Expeditionary Force that was sent to France. Following the German triumph in France, Montgomery and his men were among those evacuated at Dunkirk in June 1940.

After several commands, Montgomery was assigned to head the 8th Army, under Harold Alexander's (Number 76) overall command. In August 1942, Montgomery arrived in Egypt to assume his new responsibility. Two months later, his 8th Army faced the Afrika Korps.

The Battle for North Africa

As the battle of El Alamein began, the British had the advantage in manpower as well as in tanks. The Germans had the advantage of momentum and the most experienced desert fighter of the war. From Montgomery's viewpoint, Rommel's Afrika Korps was clearly threatening not only Alexandria but Suez. Rommel had to be stopped.

On October 23, 1942, the battle began with devastating British artillery fire. Then the British tanks moved in. The battle raged for nearly two weeks; on November 4, the British broke through. Short of tanks, short of supplies, and short of fresh water, the Afrika Korps was in full retreat.

Just days later, American forces would land in Algeria and French Morocco, squeezing the Afrika Korps between the British on the east and the Americans on the west. The battle for North Africa would end in Tunisia with Allied victory in May 1943.

Two months later, the Allies invaded Sicily. Montgomery led the British forces while George S. Patton (Number 11) led the Americans. The British and American armies continued into the mainland of Italy.

For the coming invasion of northern France, Montgomery was assigned command of all ground forces, with Dwight D. Eisenhower (Number 7) in supreme command.

Victory on D-Day

From this point on, the story of Montgomery is somewhat confusing. British military historians tend to picture Montgomery somewhat differently than their American counterparts. The field marshal, many British observers believe, faced the heaviest resistance on D-Day, was quick to obey the orders of his commanders, and was aggressive in the use of his army. The traditional American view is that the British commander had the weakest resistance on D-Day, that he did not always obey orders—at least not right away—and that he was timid, requiring neat lines before moving forward.

In August 1944, Montgomery was relieved of the responsibility for all ground forces. He retained command of the British forces in France, and Omar Bradley (Number 33) led the American forces.

In September, Montgomery's plan for Operation Market-Garden was launched. It involved the seizure of key points in Holland, followed by a sweep into Germany. Part of the problem might have been geography, trying to reach "a bridge too far." It might also have involved betrayal on the ground by a Dutch underground leader. In any case, the operation failed.

The Allies moved into Belgium. As December approached, Adolf Hitler (Number 1) was completing plans for his final gamble of the war. It would test the Anglo-American coalition as it had never been tested before.

The Battle of the Bulge

In mid-December, the Germans smashed into the Ardennes. The assault would forever be known as the Battle of the Bulge. It was an intelligence disaster and a communications nightmare. Two American armies, cut off from communication with Bradley's headquarters, were temporarily put under Montgomery's command.

According to the Americans, Montgomery would not move to help relieve the pressure on the critical Bastogne juncture. To make matters worse, the British commander then took the credit for stopping the Ardennes offensive. American commanders would regard that as insult added to injury.

The situation was so poisonous that Winston Churchill (Number 3) felt it necessary to set things straight. In a speech to the House of Commons, he let the statistics speak for themselves:

"The United States troops have done almost all the fighting and have suffered almost all the losses. They have suffered losses almost equal to those of both sides at the Battle of Gettysburg. The Americans have engaged 30 or 40 men for every one we have engaged and have lost 60 to 80 men to every one of ours.... Care must be taken in telling our proud tale not to claim for the British armies undue share of what is undoubtedly the greatest American battle of the war."

The year after the war ended, Queen Elizabeth II granted Montgomery a peerage. He became Viscount Montgomery of Alamein. He served two years as chief of the Imperial General Staff and then spent some time writing his memoirs.

Viscount Montgomery died in 1976.

A Sea Battle and an Election

U.S. NAVAL HISTORICAL CENTER

Takeo Kurita, who had victory in his grasp at Leyte, thought he was being led into a trap and withdrew.

The U.S. presidential election of 1944 was the first mid-war election for America since 1864, when Lincoln ran for reelection during the Civil War. The Great Emancipator's slogan had been, "Don't change horses in midstream." Though FDR did not use the phrase himself, many of his supporters did.

Nazi Germany was clearly on the ropes. Paris had long been liberated, and Anglo-American forces were battling into the homeland of the Reich itself.

The Japanese had suffered a number of stunning defeats, but the Pacific war still loomed.

From all indications, Roosevelt was about to win an unprecedented fourth term, though by a narrower margin than ever before.

It was late October. A major naval battle lay ahead in the Pacific, but only the Japanese knew it was coming. The battle would be of such scope and importance that it might not only affect the course of the war, but perhaps even swing the U.S. election the other way. And the key figure would not be an American politician, but a Japanese admiral.

The Battle That Could Have Been

Takeo Kurita was the naval officer who, at the Battle of Leyte Gulf, snatched defeat from the jaws of victory. His actions had the potential for major military and political ramifications.

Takeo Kurita was born in Japan in 1889. He was a career naval officer who took part in a number of important operations in the Pacific. Kurita had led an amphibious assault against the island of Java in the Dutch East Indies in early 1942. Several months later, he took part in the Battle of Midway (where he was assigned to support the landing of Japanese troops on the island), which was called off when Japanese naval forces were badly mauled. Kurita also saw action at Guadalcanal, where his force successfully shot up Henderson Field.

Kurita's role in World War II will forever be known in naval history as the battle he won and then threw away. It will be regarded as one of the great "what if?" debates of history.

Entering the San Bernardino Strait

In October 1944, the Japanese were told, apparently by the Soviet ambassador to Japan, that Douglas MacArthur (Number 8) was about to invade the Philippines.

The initial U.S. landings began on the island of Leyte on October 21, 1944. The Japanese strategy was to divide up their fleet into four separate forces, each with a specific route and mission.

Two forces, one under Vice-Admiral Ahoji Nishimura and a second under Vice-Admiral Kiyohide Shima, would take separate routes but meet to attack Leyte from the south.

The third force was led by Vice-Admiral Jisaburo Ozawa. He was the decoy, designed to offer a juicy target to the aggressive William F. Halsey (Number 26). The idea was to draw Halsey away from the San Bernardino Strait, which his fleet was guarding. Halsey was protecting the American amphibious forces landing troops on Leyte.

Kurita's fourth force was then to enter the strait and demolish the American landing forces at Leyte.

The deception worked. Halsey went for it hook, line, and sinker. He took off after Ozawa and the strait was wide open to Kurita. The original Japanese plan called for him to link up with Shima and Nishimura to wipe out the landing forces. But there was a lot of action along the way, and Shima and Nishimura never made it to their destination.

As part of the attack plan, the Japanese sent planes from land bases in the Philippines and carrier-based planes from Ozawa's carriers. Kamikazes (suicide planes) struck American ships; American carrier planes retaliated with their own firepower.

A Battle and a Final Retreat

The Pacific area around the Philippines was filled with battleships, cruisers, destroyers, and other ships of all sizes. The series of battles known collectively as the Battle of Leyte Gulf would be called the greatest sea battle in history, one that extended over an area of half-a-million square miles.

Before reaching the San Bernardino Strait, Kurita's force had run into trouble. First, his flagship was hit by U.S. submarines and sunk; he had to board another. Further along the way, his force was attacked by carrier planes, with additional losses. Though his fleet was damaged, it was still extremely powerful.

When he arrived at the San Bernardino Strait, it was wide open, because Halsey had gone after Ozawa. As Kurita sailed in, unidentified ships were spotted ahead. Kurita was not sure whether Ozawa had been successful in luring away Halsey. Could those unidentified ships be Halsey's fleet?

What Kurita did not know was that the American ships that lay ahead was a tiny group of escort carriers, destroyers, and destroyer escorts under C.A.F. Sprague (Number 36). The American ships had, at maximum, 5-inch guns compared to the Japanese 14-, 15-, and 16-inchers.

Sprague immediately set off a smoke screen and closed in. Luckily, a squall came up. Kurita had no idea what he was facing.

Hopelessly outnumbered and outgunned, the Americans fought so savagely that Kurita believed he was facing a major American force. After more than two hours of battle, he turned around and sailed home.

What if?

The Battle of Leyte Gulf officially ended on October 26, 1944. Back in America, Election Day was only a week away. Now comes the "what if?"

What if Kurita had sailed on, destroyed the American landing craft, and killed many U.S. troops on the Leyte beaches? Such a horrendous defeat might well have swung the balance in favor of New York Governor Thomas E. Dewey, the Republican candidate running against FDR.

A defeat in Leyte, plus a loss at the Battle of the Bulge two months later, might have been enough for a new administration to take a fresh look at "unconditional surrender." Might it have tried to offer terms? Would a United Nations have been formed based on the Dumbarton Oaks plan set up by Cordell Hull (Number 94)? It is all speculation; we shall never know.

Admiral Kurita, the man whose missed opportunity might have changed the shape of the post-war world, died in 1977.

39 Erwin Rommel

Destination: Suez?

NATIONAL ARCHIVES

Erwin Rommel, the "Desert Fox," inspects his Afrika Korps in North Africa.

In mid-November 1941, a small British commando group burst into what they believed to be Erwin Rommel's headquarters in a Libyan village. They sprayed the place with machine-gun fire, killing five Germans. Their objective was to kill Rommel, but he had moved his headquarters. Several commandos were killed in the attack; one escaped.

During the war it was rare to plot the assassination of an enemy officer, although there were exceptions. The Americans targeted Isoruku Yamamoto (Number 6) and the British did the same to Reinhard Heydrich (Number 25).

But Rommel was not that prominent a figure in the German Army hierarchy. He did enjoy a reputation as "The Desert Fox" and was regarded as the finest desert fighter of the war. His daring and tactical maneuvers were legendary, earning him the grudging respect of even his enemies.

A Daring Campaign

Why, then, an assassination attempt? His death would certainly have affected morale on both sides: a blow to the Germans and a boost for the British. But there had to be more to it than that.

It is possible that the answer lay in Rommel's campaign plan. His aim was to go across North Africa to the Suez Canal. Such a blow would have been devastating to Britain. Considering his daring in the past, it was not outside the realm of possibility.

He is considered an influential figure for a variety of reasons: his accomplishments in the battle of France, his command of the Afrika Korps, his work on the "Atlantic Wall," his analysis of "the longest day" of the war, and his death at the hands of Adolf Hitler (Number 1).

Early Success in Europe

Erwin Rommel was born in 1891 in Heidenheim, Germany. Interested in a military career, he attended the War Academy in Danzig and was a lieutenant when World War I broke out in 1914. He was wounded several times in action and decorated for bravery. Following a number of military exploits, he ended the war a captain.

Between the wars, Rommel taught at German war academies. He took part in the occupations of Austria and Czechoslovakia.

In the spring of 1940, his panzer unit struck out across the Meuse River in the campaign that would crush the Low Countries (Belgium, Luxembourg, and the Netherlands) and France.

Conquering the Desert

With continental Europe firmly in German control, Hitler turned to North Africa. Early in 1941, Rommel was named commander of the Afrika Korps. It was just in time, for Italian forces were being badly beaten by British troops under Archibald Wavell. Rommel used the same *blitzkrieg* tactics that had worked in France. British and German forces battled back and forth across North Africa. Rommel's major victories were the capture of Tobruk in June 1942 and his thrust to the border of Egypt.

But events elsewhere would affect what was happening in North Africa. Great battles were taking place all along the Russian front. German reinforcements would go there, not to North Africa. With the United States in the war, there was the possibility that American forces might get their first taste of battle in North Africa. Finally, a new British commander was taking over the British 8th Army. His name was Bernard Montgomery (Number 37).

A Final Defeat

In the fall of 1942, it all came together. On October 23rd, Montgomery began his attack on German positions at El Alamein. Rommel, ill in Europe at the time, was ordered back to North Africa. The worst was yet to come. On November 7th, American troops landed in French North Africa. The retreating Afrika Korps was now between the British 8th Army on the east and the Americans on the west. Battles would continue in

North Africa for another six months before the final surrender of German forces in Tunisia.

The Longest Day

After serving briefly in various posts, Rommel was put in charge of planning defenses for the "Atlantic Wall," a supposedly impregnable system of defenses against an Allied invasion along the French coast. Propaganda films were released showing huge fortifications being built in some unspecified area of western Europe. But the coastline of possible invasion places could not be protected at every point. Rommel did his best to build obstructions both in the water and on the land.

It was during one of his inspections of the coastline that he made the famous comment to his aide:

> *The war will be won or lost on the beaches. We'll have only one chance to stop the enemy and that is while he's in the water struggling to get ashore. Reserves [which Hitler planned to be located a hundred miles from key landing areas] will never get up to the point of attack and it's foolish even to consider them. The...[main line of resistance] will be here [pointing to the beaches].... Everything we have must be on the coast. Believe me, Lang, the first 24 hours of the invasion will be decisive.... For the Allies, as well as Germany, it will be the longest day.*

It was even worse than Rommel imagined. Hitler believed that the "real" invasion would come across the channel at the Pas de Calais. The reserves would not be made available for weeks, far too late to dislodge the Allies from Normandy.

Death by Poison

On July 20, 1944, a number of German officers set in motion a plan to kill Hitler and bring an end to the war. Hitler survived the assassination attempt and began rounding up the plotters, both real and imagined.

What did Rommel know of the conspiracy and did he actively participate in it? Most historians believe that he knew of the plot. There is disagreement over whether he was actually involved. His name may have appeared on a list of potential government officials following the overthrow of Hitler. In any case, two generals met with him in October 1944 with a message from the Führer: Commit suicide and save your family and staff, or face trial and put family and staff at risk. Rommel took poison.

Several months earlier, he had been wounded after his car was strafed by Allied planes. It was easy for the German radio to announce that he had died of his wounds. Rommel was lauded at a state funeral.

Shakespeare, Bacon, and the Purple Code

NATIONAL ARCHIVES

This machine was designed by Japanese intelligence experts to encode secret diplomatic and military messages. William Friedman and his team broke the secrets of the Japanese "Purple Code" machine.

Shortly after World War I began, William Friedman went to work for a private research company. Friedman's interest was genetics, and he was hired as director of the genetics department.

At work, he met a young lady who was in the ciphers department. She had a most intriguing project: to determine whether Francis Bacon was the real author of the works attributed to Shakespeare. Friedman became involved romantically and intellectually. He married the woman and became a cryptanalyst. It was a love match that would change history, for a quarter of a century later, Friedman would break the Japanese Purple Code.

Chief Cryptanalyst

William Friedman was born in 1891 in Kishenev, a town in Bessarabia, then part of Czarist Russia. He came to America when he was 2 years old. In 1914, he graduated from Cornell University, where he had majored in genetics. The following year, Friedman got a job with a research firm owned by one George Fabyan.

It was Fabyan who believed that Shakespeare did not write Shakespeare. What is more, Fabyan believed that this could be proved by cryptanalysis of the bard's works.

The young woman hired to prove Fabyan's theory got Friedman so fascinated by ciphers that he became a cryptographer himself. In a short time, Friedman was made head of the ciphers department.

During World War I, Fabyan offered the U.S. Army the use of his cipher department to train personnel in cryptanalysis. Friedman ran the operation. After the war, the Army Signal Corps offered Friedman a job, heading up its new Code and Cipher Section. In 1921, Friedman moved to Washington to start his new assignment.

Radio began to take on growing importance in government communications. So the Signal Intelligence Service was created, headed by Friedman. The new unit would intercept messages by radio as well as by wire.

In 1934, Friedman discovered that IBM was developing useful machines for mathematical analysis, and he snapped one up for use in the decoding process. Little did he dream of the future potential for computers in his work.

A year later, he was replaced as director of the unit but continued working as the chief cryptanalyst.

Unlocking the Japanese Secret

In the early 1930s, Nazi Germany was the potential threat. By the middle of that decade, Japan was a new power to be reckoned with. In 1937, Japan created a diplomatic code called Purple, using a machine with many switches and intricate wiring. Two typewriters were hooked in, one to feed messages in, the other to take messages out. A code book indicated which keys had to be pressed for use on a particular day. In addition, two codes were available each day, one for normal secret messages and the other for extremely important, super-secret messages. The system was so complex that the Japanese believed that it was unbreakable.

Friedman went to work to unlock the secrets of Purple. As day after frustrating day went by, the possibility of conflict in the Pacific became greater. Finally, on September 25, 1940, Friedman broke the Japanese Purple Code. Though it was used primarily for diplomatic messages, it transmitted valuable military and naval information as well.

A Source of Vital Information

Once the code was cracked, Operation Magic began. This involved not only decoding Japanese messages, but translating them into English, then distributing them to key civilian and military officials. All had to be done in the strictest secrecy.

Friedman had been working as a civilian, but he was also in the reserve. In 1943, he was put on active duty as a colonel. Magic was of obvious importance in the Pacific, but it was just as important in the European war. Before December 7, 1941, the U.S. Navy largely overlooked the Japanese interest in Pearl Harbor, but it did not make the same mistake during the war. Magic was vital in the Battle of Midway, clearly indicating the strategy of the Japanese fleet. It was also helpful in pinpointing the time and place where Admiral Yamamoto (Number 6) would be inspecting Japanese installations, which would cost the admiral his life. As far as Europe was concerned, the Axis partners exchanged information on both political and military affairs. Such data was of significant value to the Allies.

An Unlikely Hero

After the war, the great code-breaker continued doing cryptanalysis for new undercover government agencies.

When William Friedman died in 1969, there were no great public ceremonies in his honor. That quiet man who had worked so diligently at figuring out puzzles and ciphers and mysteries was as unlikely a hero as Shakespeare—or Bacon—could ever imagine. But he will go down in history as the man who broke Purple, one of the great victories of World War II.

41 Henry H. Arnold

Champion of Airpower

NATIONAL ARCHIVES

Henry H. Arnold, right, headed the Army Air Force. He made sure that American planes would dominate the skies over the battlefields of Europe and the Pacific.

In the early 1920s, an American brigadier general named Billy Mitchell tried to get the U.S. Army to put more men and resources into aviation. When he got nowhere, he went public and began criticizing superiors. He was court-martialed in 1926 and reduced in rank. His career had come to an end.

But Billy Mitchell's cry for airpower did not go unheard. Others saw the need and campaigned for the issue in less strident tones. One of those who did so was Henry H. Arnold.

Arnold's determination for airpower resulted in the most powerful force ever assembled: 95,000 planes and 2,500,000 men and women to fly them, service them, and maintain them.

An Aviation Pioneer

Henry H. Arnold was born in 1886 in Gladwyne, Pennsylvania. It has been reported that his first "flight" was off the family barn, using his mother's favorite parasol. He was graduated from West Point and became an infantry officer in 1907.

Four years later, he entered army aviation. He and another army officer became America's first army pilots. They took their first flying lessons from Orville and Wilbur Wright. In 1912, Arnold performed an unusual army surveillance. For the first time in American military history, he radioed from his plane a description of the disposition and movement of troops on the ground. A training school for army pilots was set up at College Park, Maryland, part of the Army Signal Corps.

During World War I, Arnold served as assistant director of military aeronautics. Though army aviation had demonstrated its worth during the war, many traditional army officers disdained an emphasis on airpower. As with armies all over the world, there was always competition for funding among the various branches. Arnold, as Mitchell did, strongly believed in airpower. As the debate raged, Arnold did his part to keep up public interest in aviation.

He set up airmail service linking Washington, Philadelphia, and New York. He started the Aerial Forest Service. He also developed a method for refueling aircraft while still in flight.

From 1935 to 1938 he was assistant chief of the Army Air Corps; he became chief in 1938.

The news from Europe was alarming at this time. Nazi Germany was rearming, with a strong emphasis on its air force, and was also threatening its neighbors. Arnold spoke to all the major American aircraft manufacturers, urging them to start designing new bombers and fighters and to begin mapping out future expansion.

In 1939, war broke out in Europe and George C. Marshall (Number 5) became Army chief of staff. The following year, he chose Arnold as his deputy chief of staff for air.

Creating the Most Powerful Air Force in History

Arnold threw himself into his work. It had been Marshall who commented, "Before, we had the time but not the money. Now we have the money but not the time." Obviously, planes were needed, but so were pilots, navigators, bombardiers, and maintenance crew. Training was needed and airfields had to be secured.

Before the war was over, Arnold was chief of the U.S. Army Air Forces throughout the world. In his capacity as a member of the American Joint Chiefs of Staff, and the Allied Combined Chiefs of Staff, General of the Army Arnold created the largest, most powerful air force ever. It was his army planes that took part in tens of thousands of missions all over the world. His planes took off from the carrier *Hornet* to bomb Tokyo, obliterated German warplants, flew supplies "over the Hump" from India to China, carried out the low-level bombing raids over the Ploesti oil fields, and dropped the atomic bombs over Hiroshima and Nagasaki to end the war.

He retired in 1946. But before he did so, he laid the groundwork for two new programs: the creation of a unified U.S. Air Force and the establishment of a National Air Museum as a part of the Smithsonian. The current Air and Space Museum in Washington is a direct result of his efforts.

Henry H. Arnold, the man who vindicated Billy Mitchell, died in 1950.

42 Vasily Chuikov

Hero of Stalingrad

COLLIER

The city of Stalingrad burns during the Nazi siege.
But Vasily Chuikov will trap the German army in a steel vise.

You may search a current map of Russia with a magnifying glass, but you will never find Stalingrad. During World War II, it was one of the world's most famous cities. You might conclude that it no longer exists. Where has it gone?

The city is there, all right, but it is now called Volgograd. After the death of Joseph Stalin (Number 4), the Russian people wanted to wipe out the memory of the Communist dictator.

It will remain Stalingrad in the history books, however, even if not in the geography books. There in Volgograd today stands the statue of Mother Russia with an upraised sword in her hand. The statue is taller than the Statue of Liberty and memorializes one of the most savage battles of the war. It was the furthest point that Adolf Hitler (Number 1) reached in his plan of conquest.

Leader of the Red Army

Vasily Chuikov is the man whom most historians credit as the hero of Stalingrad. He was born in 1900 in Serebryanye Prudy, Russia. Following the Russian Revolution during World War I, he first joined the Red Army and then the Communist Party. After serving several years as an officer, he entered a Russian military academy. He was assigned to China first in 1927 and then in 1929. These assignments led to his service for four years in the Far Eastern Army.

Following the Nazi-Soviet pact of 1939, he led a Red Army force in the invasion of Poland from the east, after the Nazis invaded from the west. He also led a force in the invasion of Finland in 1939. Though the Finns were badly outnumbered, they bloodied the Russians, exposing the Soviet Union's unreadiness for war. Soviet military capabilities were strengthened.

In 1940, he was sent to China as chief military advisor to Chiang Kai-shek (Number 87).

The Battle for Stalingrad

Hitler invaded the Soviet Union in June 1941, but Chuikov did not return to Russia from China until early 1942. In July 1942, Chuikov became temporary commander of the 64th Army at Stalingrad. As the Nazis advanced on Stalingrad and the battle heated up, Chuikov's general command was expanded. At one point, he declared that "we will either hold the city or die there." It was the kind of attitude that appealed to Stalin, who issued his Order of the Day: "Not one step backward!"

The battle for Stalingrad began on August 23, 1942, when German forces reached the Volga river, north of the city. It would end on January 31, 1943, when German Field Marshal Friedrich von Paulus (Number 57) surrendered to a Red Army lieutenant. During those five months, the battle raged around and inside that strategic city on the Volga river.

Military historians have written many volumes about the German and Russian armies locked in deadly combat in that beleaguered battleground. In many other cities throughout the world where hand-to-hand fighting was involved, one finds a familiar reference to fighting block by block. In Stalingrad, the fighting was not just building by building, but literally room by room. Factory workers, men and women, had taken up weapons. It was a prime example of what the Russians would refer to as the Great Patriotic War.

Stalin had deliberately blown up the ferries and other boats that might have been used to get across to the other side of the Volga from Stalingrad. The defenders of the city fought with their backs to the river. There would be no Dunkirk, and surrender was out of the question.

Fighting for Mother Russia

Chuikov had the personal daring and the military skill to take advantage of German military mistakes and Hitler's stubborn refusal to accept statistics that might interfere with his plans. Chuikov encouraged the fighting spirit of soldiers and civilians alike. The people were fighting not for Stalin or for Communism, but for Mother Russia. Stalin, himself, had emphasized that early in the war.

When the end came in Stalingrad, an estimated 100,000 Germans and their allies surrendered and were marched into captivity. Only 10,000 of the 100,000 prisoners would be repatriated after the war.

Chuikov led Red Army units across eastern Europe into Germany, and into Berlin itself. The German capital surrendered on May 2, 1945. It was two days after Hitler committed suicide. Chuikov would become commander in chief of Soviet forces in Germany. After the death of Stalin in 1953, Chuikov would be given many more honors and hold high defense posts, including deputy minister of defense and commander in chief of Soviet ground forces. His war memoirs were highly praised by both Soviet and Western scholars.

Vasily Chuikov, hero of the city once known as Stalingrad, died in 1982.

43 Hermann Goering

From Air Ace to War Criminal

NATIONAL ARCHIVES

Under the guise of developing commercial aviation in Germany, Hermann Goering developed a powerful military air force.

Following his war crimes trial at Nuremberg, Hermann Goering was sentenced to be hanged. Goering made no plea for mercy. He did request that he be shot by a firing squad. Hanging, he said, was for common criminals. His plea for a change in punishment was rejected, but the sentence was never carried out. The night before the scheduled execution, Goering took poison.

Thus ended the remarkable career of Hermann Goering: flying ace, Nazi politician, commander of the Luftwaffe (German air force), art connoisseur, art thief, drug addict, and convicted war criminal. It was truly a colorful life. Goering was Adolf Hitler's (Number 1) right-hand man up until the last days of the Führer's life.

Early Ties to Hitler

Goering was born in 1893 in Rosenheim, a town in Bavaria, Germany. He chose a military career and saw action as an officer during World War I. He became an air ace and even took over as leader of Baron von Richthofen's squadron following the baron's death.

After the war, Goering lived in Scandinavia for a while as a flier and salesman. In 1922, he met Hitler for the first time and immediately joined his ranks. The Nazi leader put Goering in charge of organizing the S.A., the "brownshirts" or storm troopers. The S.A. was a private army of thugs and hooligans who beat up political opponents and disrupted their rallies.

When the Nazi attempt in 1923 to seize power in Munich failed, Hitler was jailed, but Goering escaped to Austria. Several years later, when the heat was off, Goering returned to Germany and rejoined his old cronies. By this time, Goering had acquired a serious drug problem. It was an addiction that would stay with him the rest of his life.

The Nazis Take Power

Goering was backed by the Nazis for political office. In 1928, he was elected to the Reichstag (the German parliament). Four years later, he was elected Reichstag president. Following Hitler's rise to the chancellorship, Goering became a member of his cabinet. The former flying ace took on additional government responsibilities and started placing Nazis in critical police positions.

Early in 1933, a mysterious fire gutted the Reichstag building. A mentally disabled Dutch Communist was blamed for setting the fire, but scholars believe that Goering himself was responsible for the blaze. In any case, Goering used the incident as an excuse to set loose thugs not only on the Communists, but on other opponents of the Nazis.

Creating the Luftwaffe

As Hitler rose in rank and power in Nazi Germany, so did Goering. By 1935, the former air ace was heading the Luftwaffe. When war came in 1939, he had become heir apparent to the Führer.

The Luftwaffe provided the support in the air for the blitzkrieg on the ground. It helped capture Poland, Norway, Denmark, Belgium, Holland, Luxembourg, and France. In the Battle of Britain, however, the Royal Air Force prevailed.

With the invasion of the Soviet Union in 1941 and the fierce Soviet resistance, the blitzkrieg slowed down, and the Luftwaffe lost its punch. Once America was in the war, German industry was hard hit by air raids. Goering had once boasted that Germany was invulnerable to enemy bombing. In order to embarrass him, the RAF would find out when Goering was scheduled to deliver one of his speeches over Berlin radio. The British would then carry out air raids during those times. The air raid sirens would sound and Goering would be forced to interrupt his speech to seek a bomb shelter and shut down the radio signal.

It is ironic that the Luftwaffe developed the jet plane, far superior to any American or British aircraft, too late in the war for mass production.

Whether in victory or defeat, Goering took every opportunity to have valuable works of art stolen for him from both private and museum collections all over conquered

Europe. For many decades after the war, survivors would institute claims against private collectors and even well-known museums for works stolen by Goering.

From Trusted Advisor to Traitor

In April 1945, as the Russians closed in on Berlin, Hitler announced to the world that he would stay in Berlin to the end. Goering, located in an area of Germany still not in danger of capture, asked other Nazi leaders what the Führer's statement meant. Most told him that it looked like a transfer of power to Goering. Because he was not sure, Goering sent a message to Hitler:

"In view of your decision to remain in the fortress of Berlin, do you agree that I take over at once the leadership of the Reich, with full freedom at home and abroad as your deputy...?"

When Hitler received the message, he was apoplectic and denounced Goering as a traitor, read him out of the Party, and said that he should be shot.

Goering never took over. Following Hitler's suicide and the surrender of Germany, Goering was seized by the Allies, put on trial at Nuremberg, and sentenced to death. In 1946, on the night before he was to be executed, Goering cheated the hangman and swallowed poison.

44 Joseph Goebbels

Propagandist to the End

Joseph Goebbels, one of Hitler's closest aides, was chief propagandist for the Nazis.

Today they are called spin-meisters, public relations consultants, image creators, and public affairs specialists. But during World War II, they were called propagandists.

Some of them may have winced at the word, but not Joseph Goebbels. His official title was Minister of Public Enlightenment and Propaganda, and he loved it. His job was to buttress German morale at home and smear Jews, Bolsheviks, and the Treaty of Versailles abroad. The Germans, he maintained, were fighting in Europe to save the West from Communist slavery.

That is what he emphasized after the war began, particularly after Adolf Hitler (Number 1) invaded the Soviet Union.

In the years before World War II began, Goebbels concentrated on building the Nazi state, glorifying Hitler and Hitlerism, and extolling the theory of an Aryan "master race."

Wielding Absolute Control of the German Media

Given Goebbels's uninspiring physical appearance, one can only wonder how the Germans glorified his depiction of the tall, blond, blue-eyed, handsome pure-blooded

Aryan. A short, dark man with a leg brace, he would undoubtedly have been relegated directly to the gas chamber on stumbling off the cattle car at Auschwitz.

However, he was very good at what he did on the German home front. That is because he had complete control over German radio, newspapers, magazines, books, theater, and motion pictures. It was illegal for Germans to listen to foreign broadcasts over shortwave radios. This monopoly of the media enabled Goebbels to brainwash a nation during a 12-year period. There were dissidents and there was a German underground trying to fight Hitler. But the Nazi secret police kept anti-Hitler activities to a minimum, and those who were caught were severely punished.

Goebbels had only one client to please—first, last, and always: Adolf Hitler. The propaganda minister's loyalty was absolute to the very end. Who else would have had his six children murdered so that they could join Goebbels and his wife in death following Hitler's suicide in Berlin?

The Propaganda Campaign

Joseph Goebbels was born in 1897 in Rheydt, Germany. After graduating from Heidelberg with a Ph.D., he did some writing but was not particularly successful at it. His life changed when he heard Hitler speak at a rally during the 1920s. Goebbels was captivated by the Führer. He joined the Nazi Party and became editor of its newspaper. When Hitler rose to power in 1933, Goebbels became his propaganda chief.

He began by arranging for the public burning of books of so-called "degenerate" writers, including Thomas Mann, Erich Remarque, Jack London, Helen Keller, Albert Einstein, and Sigmund Freud. Goebbels continued with a major campaign against German Jews. Jewish businesses were boycotted, German Jews were beaten on the streets as police stood by, and they were subjected to vicious attacks in the media. The groundwork was being laid for the Holocaust to come.

In the blood purge of 1934, conducted against elements out of step with the rest of the Nazi Party, dozens of prominent Nazis were murdered at Hitler's behest. Goebbels, considered a left-winger and thus out of step, narrowly escaped death. It is possible that Hitler himself saved his propaganda chief.

Public Spectacle and the 1936 Berlin Olympics

Assured he was in the Führer's good graces, Goebbels went forward with his propaganda program for both domestic and foreign consumption. He staged huge Nazi Party rallies as ritual spectacles. He also prepared for the approaching Berlin Olympics of 1936. Goebbels wanted to show the international community how far Germany had progressed under Hitler. One of the things Goebbels did to improve the German image was to temporarily remove the signs in public places that read "No Dogs or Jews Allowed."

The Olympics were largely a public-relations success, as German athletes racked up the highest number of medals among the nations. There was, of course, the embarrassment of an African American named Jesse Owens, who easily outran the German athletes; Hitler had to "leave early" so he did not have to shake hands with Owens, a black man. But the situation was eased a bit when the American Olympics Committee removed Marty Glickman, a Jew, from a competition he was expected to win. The role of Goebbels in that international intrigue has never been established.

War-Time Propaganda

When war came in 1939, Goebbels set up his enemies list: Jews, the English, the French, the Poles, and international bankers. (Bolsheviks would be added in June 1941, when Hitler attacked the Soviet Union.) According to Goebbels, these were the enemies that the German people were fighting, and he used all the media at his command to inflame German passions against them.

In addition to manipulating media and finding scapegoats, Goebbels was shrewd at analyzing special situations.

Once he sent a camera crew to photograph what was going on inside a Jewish ghetto. He had expected to show people acting like animals. Instead, the photographs conveyed humaneness in the face of privation and danger. The pictures were suppressed, for Goebbels believed they would only evoke sympathy for those struggling to survive behind the ghetto walls. At the time of the German entrapment at Stalingrad, he ordered that the letters of German soldiers addressed to their families back home be sent to him first, for possible propaganda purposes. The letters were suppressed as defeatist and never delivered.

Goebbels was quick to seize on the discovery of the bodies of thousands of Polish army officers in the Katyn Forest of Poland in 1943. He maintained that they had been killed by the Soviets,; Joseph Stalin (Number 4) insisted that they had been killed by the Nazis. (Half a century later, the Russian government would confirm that the Soviets had indeed carried out the massacre.)

The last act of propagandist Goebbels was to die with his wife and children beside his beloved Führer. As the Russian forces approached Berlin, Hitler ordered Goebbels to leave the bunker with his family and save himself. The propaganda chief told Hitler that for the first time in his life, he would have to disobey him.

Hitler committed suicide on April 30, 1945. Goebbels, his wife, and all of his children joined him the following day.

45 Masaharu Homma

A Question of Responsibility

V.F.W.

American prisoners carry a fallen comrade during the Bataan Death March.
Masaharu Homma, who commanded the victorious Japanese forces in the Philippines,
would be held responsible for wartime atrocities.

On April 15, 1942, the American and Filipino soldiers who had surrendered at Bataan began their grueling march from Mariveles to San Fernando. The 65-mile death march would take six days. The sun was burning hot and the air stifling. Little food or water was available. And along the way, Japanese guards—part of Masaharu Homma's army—would bayonet stragglers, club or shoot other captives for sport, and bury alive some sick and wounded who were unable to walk.

An estimated 10,000 prisoners—2,500 Americans and 7,500 Filipinos—died on the forced march. It would forever be known as the Bataan Death March. Those who survived it were packed by Homma's troops into railroad boxcars that took them to the end of the line. They then walked another seven miles to reach their prison camp.

Douglas MacArthur (Number 8) heard about it months later, when escaped American prisoners told him of the terrible ordeal. The American general who had led forces in the Philippines bided his time. When the war was over, he would make his move.

Masaharu Homma, conqueror of the Philippines, whose troops were responsible for the atrocities, was arrested and charged with war crimes. Was Homma responsible for the actions of his troops? If so, what should the penalty be?

Military Achievements Lead to the Philippines

Homma was born on Sado Island, Japan, in 1888. After graduating from the Japanese war college, he was assigned to the Japanese general staff. During World War I, he was sent to France to see the British Army in action. When the war ended, he taught at the War College before being posted to India.

He served under several officers until 1927, when he became an aide to the younger brother of Emperor Hirohito (Number 49). By 1938, he had become a lieutenant general in command of the 27th Division at Tientsin, China.

In 1940, he commanded the army in Formosa (Taiwan). A month before Pearl Harbor was attacked, he received his orders for the coming war with the United States. His goal: the Philippines.

The Philippines Fall to the Japanese

Homma's force landed in northern Luzon island late in December 1941. A second force landed near Manila several days later. According to the timetable, Homma was supposed to have the entire Philippines in Japanese hands by the end of January 1942. Manila fell early, but American and Filipino forces withdrew to the Bataan peninsula. It was a good defensive position for a while, but attempts to resupply the besieged army failed.

In April 1942, the sick, starving Bataan garrison of 35,000 men—running out of ammunition and watching as the big Japanese guns were dragged closer and closer to vulnerable military hospitals—surrendered. It was one of the largest surrenders of personnel in American military history. Then the nightmare of the Bataan Death March began.

In May, just weeks after the fall of Bataan, Corregidor fell, and the entire Philippines were surrendered to a victorious Homma. By August 1942 he was back in Japan. The following year he became a government minister.

Homma Faces War Crimes

When Japan surrendered in September 1945, MacArthur ordered the arrest of Homma, who was taken back to the Philippines. In January 1946, he was put on trial in Manila.

Listening to the witnesses testify to the atrocities of the Bataan Death March, Homma insisted that he had been completely unaware of such events. But the prosecution argued that, as commanding officer, he was responsible for the actions of his troops.

Homma was found guilty and sentenced to death. It is reported that his wife personally appealed to MacArthur to spare her husband's life, but it was to no avail. He was shot by a firing squad in April 1946.

The trial and execution of Masaharu Homma introduced a new interpretation of the code of military justice. Commanding officers were now required to control the actions of their men or take responsibility for the consequences of those actions. Using this interpretation, the atrocities of the Bataan Death March became Homma's burden to bear, and he paid for it with his life.

46 Alfred Jodl

Unconditional Surrender

COLLIER

At the Reims surrender ceremony, the German delegation sits with its back to the camera. Alfred Jodl, in the foreground center, faces the victorious Allies.

P eace came to Europe quietly. It did not come on a mighty battleship in the enemy's harbor among thousands of spectators, but rather in a little school-house in Reims, France. The date was May 7, 1945.

Unconditional surrender (one that is absolute and unqualified) did not come easily. At the last minute, the German emissaries balked. Dwight D. Eisenhower (Number 7) said that if the surrender was not signed, he would shut down the Western front to fleeing Germans who wanted no part of a Red Army occupation. Accounts of Nazi atrocities in the Soviet Union had made their way back to Germany, and many Germans feared retribution.

Signing the Surrender

General Jodl, the chief German emissary, had communicated Eisenhower's threat to Karl Doenitz (Number 64), the new head of the German government. Jodl was instructed to proceed with the surrender.

The general signed. Then he put down the pen and addressed the victors.

"In this war," he said, "both [the German people and the German armed forces] have achieved and suffered more than perhaps any other people in the world. In this hour I can only express the hope that the victor will treat them with generosity."

This story is as much about "unconditional surrender" as it is about Jodl. The concept was extremely controversial among both the Allies and the Axis powers during the war. Its significance is examined here in correlation to Jodl not merely because he signed the surrender, but because of his standing in the German military hierarchy when he signed it.

One of Hitler's Most Trusted Advisors

Alfred Jodl was born in 1890 in Wuerzburg, Germany. After graduation from the War Academy and General Staff School, he became a field artillery officer. During World War I, he fought in both France and Russia and was wounded in action. After the war, he remained in the army and continued to rise in rank.

Hitler came to power in 1933. Two years later, Jodl became head of Germany's national defense section. By the time Hitler invaded Poland, Jodl was head of operations.

The Polish campaign gave Hitler and Jodl a chance to work closely together. They clearly respected each other: Jodl admired Hitler and Hitler admired Jodl for his judgment of character. Jodl became one of Hitler's most trusted advisers.

As the war went from victories to defeats, Hitler began replacing his generals. But Jodl hung on and became a trusted assistant to Wilhelm Keitel (Number 48). The two top German officers were there in the Berlin bunker when Hitler issued his last orders and turned the government over to Doenitz. When the surrender discussions were set in motion, Jodl was chosen to act on behalf of the Reich.

Why Require Unconditional Surrender?

The Allies were very clear. It would be "unconditional surrender." Such a surrender is rare in modern times. In the Civil War, General Ulysses S. Grant had insisted on it but had been generous with Confederate prisoners. Following the surrender at Appomattox Court House, they were given Union rations and many were permitted to keep horses or mules for spring plowing. Confederate officers were allowed to keep their horses and sidearms.

In World War II, the concept was raised at the Casablanca conference in January 1943. President Roosevelt (Number 2) announced the idea at a press conference there. Winston Churchill (Number 3) later told Parliament that he knew nothing about the call for unconditional surrender until the president had spoken to the press. Later, Churchill would concede that he had discussed it with the president beforehand.

Throughout the war, some American and British observers had commented that "unconditional surrender" would prolong the war. Nazi propaganda chief Joseph Goebbels (Number 44) used the issue to frighten Germans about the slavery that lay ahead for them if Germany ever accepted it.

Shadows of the Past World War

Why, then, was the United States so insistent on it? Part of the answer may lie with an old general from an old war. In 1931, General of the Armies John J. Pershing, who had led the American Expeditionary Force in World War I, published his memoirs. Not long after the Treaty of Versailles was signed, extremist parties in Germany were decrying the "stab in the back" by German politicians. These parties—notably the newly formed Nazi Party—were claiming that Germany had not lost World War I at all, but that the German military had been betrayed.

Pershing was certainly aware of this when he looked back on the mistakes of World War I and its aftermath:

"Instead of requiring the German forces to retire at once, leaving material, arms, and equipment behind, the Armistice terms [of 1918] permitted them to march back to their homeland with colors flying and bands playing, posing as the victims of political conditions. If unconditional surrender had been demanded, the Germans would, without doubt, have been compelled to yield, and their troops would have returned to Germany without arms, virtually as paroled prisoners of war. The surrender of the German armies would have been an advantage to the Allies in the enforcement of peace terms and would have been a greater deterrent against possible future German aggression."

Germany Accepts Unconditional Surrender

The United States was not going to make the same mistake again. So it came about that it was the German military that surrendered unconditionally in World War II. Doenitz, who had led the German navy, was the official government head who authorized the surrender. Jodl, one of the top officers of the German armed forces, signed it.

Jodl was arrested by the victorious Allies shortly after the war ended. Late in 1945, he was put on trial at Nuremberg for war crimes. In 1946, he was found guilty and hanged.

Most of the Nazi war criminals have already faded from memory, but Jodl will always be identified as the symbol of a once-powerful German military force that was forced to yield to unconditional surrender.

The Captive Hero

COLLIER

Konstantin Rokossovsky narrowly escaped death during the Red Army Purge.
He went from accused Soviet traitor to war hero.

The prisoner heard the sound of boots coming down the cellblock. Were they coming to beat him, or question him, or—more likely—both? It had been like that for more than two years now. Maybe this time it would be a bullet behind the ear. Rokossovsky stood up in his cell and waited.

This time it was different. These were not the bully boys with their special talents for causing pain. The same guard unlocked his cell but there was another man he had never seen before.

He wanted to ask what was going on, but he had learned, painfully, not to speak first. "You are being released," the stranger said.

Rokossovsky did not know what to say. He had been imprisoned for what seemed an eternity. Through the grapevine he had learned that many of his fellow officers had been shot during a purge of the Red Army and that a new war had started in Europe.

Rokossovsky still did not know why he had been imprisoned in the first place, why he was being released now, and what would happen to him once he was finally freed.

Konstantin Rokossovsky is the Red Army officer who was virtually pulled from the grave to become one of the foremost military tacticians of World War II. Rokossovsky would play a vital role in what Russians would forever call the Great Patriotic War.

A Student of Tank and Air Warfare

Konstantin Rokossovsky was born in 1896 in Velikiye Luki, then a part of imperial Russia. In 1914, he joined the czar's army and fought in World War I. After the Russian Revolution broke out, he joined the Red Guards and later the Communist Party. He took part in the civil war that followed and the wars in Poland.

Rokossovsky studied at Soviet military academies, most importantly the Frunze Academy, where he studied tank and air warfare. It could not have been better preparation for Adolf Hitler's (Number 1) coming war against the Soviet Union.

In 1929, Rokossovky served in the Far East along the China frontier. He became friends with Georgi Zhukov (Number 17) during this time as their career paths coincided. They enjoyed the camaraderie.

Imprisoned for Treason

In 1937, everything changed. Joseph Stalin (Number 4) began his purge of the Red Army officer corps. Shortly afterward, Rokossovsky was arrested and charged with being a counterrevolutionary. He was arrested, imprisoned, and brutalized, but he had always maintained his innocence.

What Rokossovsky did not know was that General Boris Shaposhnikov of the Red Army had requested that, because of Rokossovsky's military skills, he be released and allowed to return to duty. Sources differ on exactly when the Soviet dictator agreed to free the prisoner. It was either a number of months before or right after the German invasion of the Soviet Union.

Rokossovsky was back in command, first of a cavalry unit, then a mechanized unit. He was under Zhukov again, in the military district of Kiev.

The Nazi central attack in Russia was aimed directly at Moscow. Zhukov planned the defense of the capital, placing Rokossovsky in the Smolensk area. The tough Soviet resistance, coupled with an early, severe winter, stopped the German assault.

Hitler's hopes for a rapid victory flew away with the frigid winter winds. The era of trench warfare may have been long gone, but the era of enormous casualties was not. The German invaders were being destroyed by a combination of Soviet strength, partisan resistance behind the lines, and German resources stretched too thin.

"I fought against the fathers," Rokossovsky once said. "Now I am fighting the sons.... I do honestly think the fathers were better soldiers." The Germans knew him and feared him. As a psychological weapon, the Soviets often dropped leaflets over the German forces with the message, "Rokossovsky is coming!"

He rose rapidly in rank. Wounded and hospitalized, he insisted on returning to duty. He led Soviet armies in some of the greatest defensive battles of the war: the defense of Moscow, Stalingrad, and Kursk. Several months after the German surrender at Stalingrad, he was promoted to general of the army.

New Tactics for Winning the War

The Russians were now on the offensive. In June 1944—the month the Western Allies landed at Normandy—Rokossovsky was named a marshal of the Soviet Union. His army swept into Poland, rounding up and destroying trapped German forces.

When he reached the gates of Warsaw, Rokossovsky stopped at the Vistula River and paused to regroup. An uprising had started in Warsaw under Tadeusz Bor-Komorowski (Number 88). The idea was to help the Russian armies drive out the Germans. But the Russians waited until the Nazis had defeated the Poles. Then the Soviet army moved into the city. Apparently Stalin did not like the idea of an independent Polish army that was not under his control.

Rokossovsky rolled into East Prussia and Pomerania. He appeared to be aiming for Berlin, but Stalin saved that honor for Zhukov. The German capital fell in May 1945.

According to military historians, Rokossovsky had instituted tactics that had significantly helped win the war. His wide encirclements of Nazi forces trapped hundreds of thousands of Germans. He sometimes "buried" Soviet tanks, leaving only the turrets above the ground, so that they could act as fixed artillery when necessary. Another Rokossovsky tactic was to hold off his tanks while infantry and artillery fought the enemy. When the German tanks broke through, he would send the fresh Soviet tanks to finish them off.

After the war, Rokossovsky served as defense minister and in other military positions.

Konstantin Rokossovsky, who rose from political prisoner to hero field marshal, died in 1968.

48 Wilhelm Keitel

The Man Who Obeyed Orders

DOUBLEDAY, DORAN & CO., INC.

Wilhelm Keitel (left), Hitler's chief of staff, gets a briefing from military aides.

Wilhelm Keitel almost appears to be two different people. There is one Keitel as viewed in the summer of 1940, when he was made a field marshal. In the sources available at that time—probably from the Nazi propaganda ministry—he was a good soldier, a distinguished officer from a family of fine officers, dedicated to his job, and a brilliant tactician.

Sources published well after the war, however, portray a different man. Historians now see him as a farm boy who made good, if you can call working for Hitler good. He is pictured as an army bureaucrat who was no more than Adolf Hitler's (Number 1) "yes man." Obviously, the true picture is somewhere in between.

Wilhelm Keitel was Hitler's chief of staff. He advised Hitler on military matters, but his major function was to take orders from Hitler and then see that they were carried out. Unfortunately for Keitel, some of those orders were contrary to international law. Keitel would pay for his eager acquiescence with his life.

Carrying out Crimes against Humanity

Keitel's crime was that he passed along to the armed forces Hitler's edicts on the treatment of civilians. When those edicts were carried out, they constituted war crimes and crimes against humanity.

The edict on hostages was very simple. In order to insure good behavior in a town, a city, or an entire country, you selected a number of residents who were held hostage. If one of your soldiers or officials was attacked, the hostages were immediately executed.

During World War I, the Germans did this in Belgium. They would imprison the mayor of the town, the religious leader, the school principal, and seven other residents of the town. After a German soldier was shot and killed, all 10 of the hostages were lined up and shot by a firing squad. The lesson: You shoot one of ours, we shoot 10 of yours.

By World War II, the use of hostages was prohibited under international law. The Nazis, however, made their own laws.

A Rapid Ascent through the German Military Ranks

Keitel was born in 1882 in Helmscherode, Germany. He joined the army in 1901 and served in the field artillery. During World War I, he was on the general staff in the ministry of war. After the war, he was assigned to the field artillery section. During the 1920s, he was an instructor at the cavalry school and then assigned to the army ministry.

Keitel kept getting his promotions. The year after Hitler came to power, he was commanding an infantry division. From 1935 to 1938, Keitel was chief of the administrative department in the war ministry.

Early in 1938, Hitler decided he wanted to be the commander in chief of the armed forces. He chose Keitel as his chief of staff. From this point on, Keitel was at the Führer's side constantly. He was at Munich in 1938 when the Western Allies caved in to Hitler and gave up a piece of Czechoslovakia. When plans were made for the allocation of German resources, it was Keitel who pushed for an emphasis on airpower at the expense of the navy. When France surrendered at Compiegne, Keitel was present. When an attempt was made on Hitler's life in July 1944, Keitel was there and was wounded. When an army tribunal was set up to judge the accused army officers of plotting to kill Hitler, Keitel sat as a judge along with Gerd von Rundstedt (Number 56) and Heinz Guderian (Number 12).

Nazi Reprisals against Civilians

Keitel is one of the few German officers who opposed the invasion of the Soviet Union, and he put his reasons in writing. He made no such argument, however, in either the hostages order or the horrendous "Night and Fog" order.

On December 7, 1941, the Führer issued the *Nacht und Nebel Alas* ("Night and Fog Decree"). Any individual who endangered German security was not to be executed immediately, but was to be arrested late at night, taken into the "night and fog," and vanish without a trace. Neither family nor friends would be told of the arrested person's whereabouts or fate. No statistics exist anywhere on how many of those in occupied countries were disposed of in such fashion. The underground French, however, kept careful records and estimated that as many as 30,000 French men and women vanished in the night and fog.

The worst case of Nazi reprisals against civilians came after the assassination of Reinhard Heydrich (Number 25) in Czechoslovakia. The town of Lidice, where the assassins were alleged to have hidden, was totally destroyed. All its men and older boys were executed, its women shipped off to concentration camps. Some of its Nordic-looking children were shipped to Germany for adoption by good Nazi families.

Keitel may or may not have been appalled by these actions. But by passing the orders along without any dissent, he had made himself an accessory to murder.

Keitel Executed as a War Criminal

At the end of the war, Joseph Stalin (Number 4) insisted that Keitel take part in a separate surrender ceremony for the benefit of Soviet cameras. This took place a few days after the German surrender to Dwight D. Eisenhower (Number 7) at Reims.

Keitel was put on trial at Nuremberg for war crimes, crimes against peace, and crimes against humanity. He pleaded that he was only carrying out orders. After he was convicted, he admitted his guilt. In 1946, following the refusal of his plea for a firing squad, Keitel was hanged at Nuremberg.

49 Emperor Hirohito

The Last Word

NATIONAL ARCHIVES

The most tempestuous Japanese debate of the war would come in its final hours. Should Japan end the war and surrender? Hirohito would make the final decision.

If Japan had refused to surrender after the atomic bombings, there would have been an invasion of the Japanese home islands, a battle of unprecedented size and scope. Suicide attacks would have been launched against Allied naval vessels, including troop transports. Japanese resistance would have been fiercer than ever.

The casualties would have dwarfed anything ever experienced in any war ever fought. The official estimate of American casualties *alone* was one million men, including killed, wounded, and missing. Japanese casualties would have been in the many millions.

The decision of one man—Emperor Hirohito of Japan—prevented that bloodbath. He had approved many other military and diplomatic decisions during his reign, but this one distinguishes him as an influential figure.

The Royal Seal of Approval

Hirohito was born in 1901 in Tokyo. He became the 124th Japanese emperor in 1926.

As emperor, he held supreme executive powers, but most often signed off on the policies proposed by the government in power.

He was emperor during the Japanese occupation of Manchuria, in 1931, the war on China from 1937 to 1945, and the attack on Pearl Harbor and other Pacific targets. He had to approve each one of these major aggressive actions—and he did so.

Hirohito ruled Japan when the Japanese forces committed the so-called rape of Nanking, just prior to the outbreak of World War II. In December 1937, following the Japanese occupation of that city, an orgy of slaughter and rape swept through the Chinese capital. An estimated 260,000 Chinese were killed, many having been used for bayonet practice. Tens of thousands of Chinese women were raped. Hirohito received a full report of those atrocities—and did nothing. For a time during the war the name of Hirohito was listed as a possible war criminal. It was later dropped.

The Decision to Surrender

After the atomic bombing of Hiroshima and Nagasaki in 1945, a rift developed in the Japanese government and military hierarchy between those who wanted to surrender and those who wanted to fight on in the hopes of negotiating a better settlement.

Hirohito sided with those who wanted to surrender. His decision might have been influenced partially by a captured American pilot who told the Japanese that the next atomic bomb would be dropped on Tokyo itself. The pilot had no authority to make such a statement, and no such plan was in the works.

In any case, Hirohito made two separate recordings in which he announced the Japanese surrender. It was to be broadcast over Japanese radio. Those who opposed the surrender tried to seize the recordings in order to destroy them before they could be broadcast. The plot failed, and Japan surrendered. The only condition was that the emperor would remain on the throne.

Avoiding the Obliteration of Japan

On August 15, 1945, Hirohito made his first radio broadcast to his people:

> *"We have ordered Our Government to communicate to the Governments of the United States, Great Britain, China, and the Soviet Union that Our Empire accepts the provisions of their Joint Declaration [which had called on Japan to surrender]....*

> *"[T]he war has lasted for nearly four years. Despite the best that has been done by everyone—the gallant fighting of military and naval forces, the diligence and assiduity of Our servants of the State and the devoted service of Our one hundred million people—the war situation has developed not necessarily to Japan's advantage....*

> *"Moreover, the enemy has begun to employ a new and most cruel bomb, the power of which to do damage is indeed incalculable, taking the toll of many*

human lives. Should We continue to fight, it would not only result in an ultimate collapse and obliteration of the Japanese nation, but also it would lead to the total extinction of human civilization."

A New, Democratic Japan

The official surrender took place on September 2, 1945 on board the U.S.S. *Missouri* in Tokyo harbor. Douglas MacArthur (Number 8) became supreme commander to administer the conquered Japanese territory. Under MacArthur's guidance, Japan would attain true democracy. It would soon have a new constitution, allow women to vote, and eliminate the vast powers once held by the emperor. The very first signal of these new changes came about when Hirohito personally called on MacArthur. The event was photographed and appeared in newspapers around the world. From that point on, the Japanese looked at their emperor through new eyes.

During the time Hirohito had ruled Japan, he had made many decisions, often relying on the recommendations of government and military officials in carrying out his duties and approving government policies and programs. But when the time came to end the war, he never hesitated. In his own mind, he must have considered the possibility that he might be tried as a war criminal sometime in the future. There was always the possibility that the pro-war faction might try to have him assassinated or throw the country into civil war.

Nevertheless, Hirohito did not hesitate to make the decision. He had the last word, and he ended World War II.

Hirohito died in 1989, having outlived many of the major figures of World War II.

50 Benito Mussolini

Hitler's Junior Partner

DOUBLEDAY, DORAN & CO., INC.

Mussolini entered the war when he thought it was over.
His mistake would lead to his own overthrow and turn his country into a battleground.

He wanted to return Italy to the glory of ancient Rome, but he badly misjudged the way to do it.

Benito Mussolini set himself up as dictator, dreamed of expanding the borders of Italy, used poison gas to subdue African warriors who had little more than spears to defend themselves, allied himself with Adolf Hitler (Number 1), and stabbed France in the back when that nation lay crushed and bleeding.

At the end, he was mowed down by machine guns. Then, according to an Associated Press account, "Mussolini was beaten, kicked, trampled upon, riddled, hanged head downward, mutilated and spat upon, his head treated as less than carrion, his memory hideously reviled." That description of Mussolini's fate is literal, not figurative.

An Ally and a Burden for Hitler

Mussolini was Hitler's closest ally, but his influence on the war was relatively marginal. He had been built up by Hitler as an important world leader. Winston Churchill (Number 3), however, dismissed Mussolini, believing he would more likely be a burden on Nazi Germany. In fact, there is a story of Churchill meeting Joachim von Ribbentrop (Number 52) at a diplomatic function in London prior to World War II.

"My dear Churchill," von Ribbentrop is supposed to have said, "Just remember, if there is another war, this time Italy will be on *our* side."

"But that's only fair," Churchill puportedly responded, "*We* had them the *last* time."

Creating a Fascist State

Benito Mussolini was born in Dovis, Italy, in 1883. He fought in World War I, was wounded, and returned home to found his own newspaper. Beginning as a socialist, he decided to establish his own political organization, the Fascist Party.

In 1922, he led a march of his supporters through Rome. Shortly afterward, King Victor Emmanuel III asked him to form a government. By 1928, Mussolini had suppressed political opposition and ended parliamentary government. He was firmly in control as dictator.

In 1935, Mussolini's troops invaded Ethiopia, a nation helpless against the Italians' modern weaponry. Ethiopian Emperor Haile Selassie (Number 96) took his case to the League of Nations, asking for a system of collective security. The League, despite his pleas to stop the Italians from using poison gas against his people, did nothing. From that point on, the League was nothing more than a debating society. Hitler took note of that.

Mussolini sent modern military equipment to support Francisco Franco (Number 75) during the Spanish Civil War, which began in July 1936 and lasted nearly years.

Italy and Nazi Germany Become Military Allies

The year 1938 brought Mussolini his greatest prestige. Hitler invited him to Munich, along with Neville Chamberlain (Number 66) and Eduard Daladier to "solve" the Sudentenland crisis. The four men agreed to slice off a piece of Czechoslovakia for Nazi Germany. In exchange, Hitler promised he would make no more territorial demands in Europe.

In 1939, as Hitler was occupying the rest of Czechoslovakia, Mussolini was invading Albania. The Rome-Berlin Axis pact was signed, linking Nazi Germany and Fascist Italy militarily.

Late in the summer of 1939, as Hitler prepared to attack Poland, he urged Mussolini to join him in the war. The Duce felt that Italy was not yet ready to go to war. Yet nine months later, with France on the verge of surrender, Mussolini entered what he believed would be a relatively short and profitable war. It proved to be neither.

A Failed Invasion of Greece

Envious of Hitler's victories, Mussolini decided to invade Greece late in 1940. The Italians were badly bloodied, and Hitler had to bail them out. In April 1941, the Führer's troops pummeled the Greeks and forced the British to withdraw. But in doing so, Hitler fell behind in his scheduled attack on the Soviet Union. Outside of Moscow, his troops suddenly confronted an early Russian winter. From that point on, the day of blitzkrieg warfare would be over. Churchill had been right: Mussolini would be a costly partner.

Following Pearl Harbor, both Germany and Italy declared war on the United States. For Mussolini, it was all downhill from there. Allied victories in North Africa in 1942 and 1943 led to an invasion of Sicily in July 1943, and then the Italian mainland itself on September 3.

Mussolini's Violent Demise

Key members of the Italian government led by King Victor Emmanuel III and Foreign Minister Galeazzo Ciano (Number 80) realized it was all over for Italy. But they also knew that Mussolini would never step down from power voluntarily or quit the war. A false intelligence report was circulated that Mussolini was in danger and had to be protected. He was spirited away in an ambulance, then arrested and placed under guard by the new regime. Italy then surrendered to the Allies on September 8, 1943.

Hitler moved quickly. He sent a commando group to free Mussolini and set up a puppet government in northern Italy to carry on the war. The Nazis occupied a large part of Italy, which became a battleground for opposing German and Allied armies.

In April 1945, as German forces left Italy, Mussolini tried to make it to Switzerland. He, his mistress, and members of his puppet cabinet were seized by Italian partisans. They were lined up and shot.

A terrible fate was in store for the Duce and his mistress, Clara Petacci. After being shot, the bodies were publicly exposed for further mob violence. It was April 28, 1945. Two days later, Mussolini's senior partner, Adolf Hitler, would take his own life in a Berlin bunker.

Leader of Free France

COLLIER

Charles De Gaulle refused to recognize a French surrender to Hitler.
He made his way to London to lead a force of "Fighting French."

"During the course of this war," Winston Churchill (Number 3) once said, "I have had to bear many crosses. But the heaviest was the Cross of Lorraine." The Cross of Lorraine was the symbol of both Free France and of Charles De Gaulle himself.

Churchill had nobody but himself to blame. In June 1940, as France was about to quit the war, the British prime minister walked out of a meeting with French officials. Standing at the doorway was De Gaulle, looking very solemn. Churchill nudged him on the shoulder and murmured, "*L'homme du destin* (the man of destiny)."

The Self-Designated Leader of Free France

Whether De Gaulle thought that was a special summons to him, or whether he was planning to do it all along, the French general flew to London to continue the war against Nazi Germany. He would be court-martialed in absentia in France and condemned to death, but he would also become the head of what would be called Free

France. This was not exactly accurate, geographically speaking. The nation of France had been divided up between northern France, occupied by the Germans, and southern France, temporarily unoccupied. The unoccupied part was supposedly governed from Vichy and was dubbed Vichy France, constantly under Nazi scrutiny. It was headed by Henri Petain (Number 27), the great French hero of World War I.

De Gaulle's title as the leader of Free France was self-designated, but Frenchmen did rally to his cause.

Advocate of More Mobile War Tactics

Charles De Gaulle was born in 1890 in Lille, France. He studied for the military, and two years after graduation he was in charge of an infantry regiment fighting the Germans in World War I. He was wounded several times and captured. Released after the war, he took part in defending the newly independent nation of Poland against the Red Army.

In the mid-1920s, De Gaule was on Petain's staff. By the early 1930s, when most of the French military were calling for stronger fortification of the Maginot Line, De Gaulle was advocating a more mobile army based on tanks, armor, and airpower. In 1934, De Gaulle put his ideas into a book called *The Army of the Future*. For the most part, however, the French army was wed to the Maginot Line, the fixed fortification between France and Germany.

On the other side of the Maginot Line, the German military was undergoing similar debate. Its own version of armored warfare would be tried in the early stages of World War II. It would be dubbed blitzkrieg warfare.

The Leader of the True France

War came to Europe in the fall of 1939. After crushing Poland in September, the Germans waited until the spring of 1940 to attack in the west. They avoided the Maginot Line and swept through Belgium and Holland to overwhelm France. With an armistice imminent, De Gaulle flew to England to fight another day.

To say that De Gaulle did not get along with his Western allies would be an understatement. Members of Churchill's cabinet witnessed numerous incidents of the prime minister ranting and raving over the Frenchman's haughtiness and insolence. Nevertheless, tens of thousands of French colonial troops came under his flag, as did many naval vessels. De Gaulle was the self-proclaimed leader of all Frenchmen who wanted to continue the fight against Hitler. He brought together an army of 45,000 troops and a navy of some 20 ships.

De Gaulle was very jealous of his standing in the world as the leader of the true France. He objected to the fact that the United States kept up diplomatic relations with Vichy France, although that relationship allowed American soldiers to get ashore in French North Africa in an almost bloodless invasion. To do that, the United States had to make a deal with Jean Darlan (Number 59), who became high commissioner of French North Africa until his assassination. Attempts to choose other French military to work alongside De Gaulle and share leadership failed.

The Liberation of Paris

As D-Day approached, De Gaulle became more and more demanding. He wanted greater say in military, political, and economic decisions regarding France. The Allies needed him to make a radio appeal to the people of France, calling on them to overthrow the Nazis. Not until the final hour before the invasion did he agree to do the broadcast.

When American and French forces took Paris, he was right there for the liberation. He set up a provisional government.

After the war, when his old chief, Petain, was sentenced to death for crimes against the people of France, De Gaulle commuted the sentence to life imprisonment.

De Gaulle was chosen head of the provisional government of France, but soon afterward he resigned. Army generals are used to making decisions and having their orders carried out. Democratic politics don't work that way. So De Gaulle took time out to write his memoirs.

The President of France

In 1958, a crisis arose over the issue of a free Algeria. With France facing civil war, De Gaulle ran for president and was elected. He assumed strong executive powers. He championed the independence of Algeria as well as other French colonies in Africa. Many Frenchmen in Algeria would not give up the country without a fight, and four years of bloody war ensued.

De Gaulle's viewpoints were expressed without regard to diplomatic niceties. He advocated French development of atomic weapons, opposed British entry into the European Economic Community, and, while visiting Canada, publicly advocated the independence of Quebec.

During his term as president, he made it a point to call for a referendum of the people to back a particular government policy. When he lost just such a referendum in 1969, he resigned. He died the following year.

52 Joachim von Ribbentrop

The Role of the Deal-Maker

NATIONAL ARCHIVES

Joachim von Ribbentrop (standing) engineered Hitler's major pacts.

When Joachim von Ribbentrop appeared before King George VI (Number 95) as Germany's new ambassador, he played the role of loyal Nazi observing protocol. He bowed the required number of times, each time giving the Nazi salute. It did not endear him to the British audience, and he got nowhere in his attempt to bring about some kind of formal agreement with Great Britain.

Von Ribbentrop is recognized as influential because of the deals he *did* put together for Adolf Hitler (Number 1) with Italy, the Soviet Union, and Japan. Each pact, for very different reasons, had a significant effect on World War II.

From World War I Soldier to German Ambassador

Joachim von Ribbentrop was born in 1893 in Wesel, Germany. As a young man, he had a variety of jobs in Britain, Canada, and the United States. With the outbreak of World War I in 1914, he returned to Germany. He fought in the war, was wounded, and won the Iron Cross.

After the war, despite a struggling German economy, von Ribbentrop did quite well for himself selling wines, especially champagne. An unabashed social climber, von Ribbentop sought out ways to ingratiate himself with leaders in business and politics, which led to meeting Adolf Hitler in 1932. They hit it off; when Hitler came to power the following year, von Ribbentrop convinced Hitler that he was an expert in foreign affairs. He took on the role of roving ambassador and deal-maker, reporting directly to the Führer.

The Deal-Maker

In the summer of 1936, von Ribbentrop was named ambassador to Great Britain. Though his efforts to make a deal with the British never came to fruition, he was extremely successful in negotiating three of the most important pacts of the war. All were formalized during his early years as foreign minister, a post he achieved in February 1938.

As early as 1936, an agreement had been drawn up between Hitler and Benito Mussolini (Number 50). The Rome-Berlin pact was formalized in May 1939. The two dictators were officially in bed. It was their answer to the Anglo-French alliance, and it clearly defined who would side with whom in the coming war.

The pact between Nazi Germany and Fascist Italy came as no real surprise. The shocker was the Hitler-Stalin pact of August 23, 1939, a week before the scheduled invasion of Poland. Nazi Germany and the Soviet Union signed a non-aggression agreement and, in a secret protocol, split up Poland. With this deal, Hitler had secured his eastern frontier until he was ready to break the pact and strike at the Soviet Union. Von Ribbentrop himself signed the pact in Moscow, along with Soviet Foreign Minister Vyacheslav Molotov (Number 53).

The third deal negotiated by von Ribbentrop was the Rome-Berlin-Tokyo pact of September 27, 1940. Also known as the Tripartite Pact, it spelled out when and how the signatory powers would help each other in the event of future conflict. This could be regarded as the single most important alliance of the war, for it would lead to Hitler declaring war on the United States after Japan attacked Pearl Harbor. Once the United States was in the war, the Axis powers were doomed.

The Dedicated Nazi

With America a belligerent, the conflict became truly a world war. There was little need for Hitler to have a Foreign Minister. The Führer's interest was military, not diplomatic, but von Ribbentrop held on to the redundant job.

Von Ribbentrop was Hitler's foreign minister by the sufferance of the Führer, and the diplomat knew it. He became the biggest sycophant in Hitler's court, which was quite an accomplishment, considering the fierce competition. No one was a more dedicated Nazi; no one played a greater role in persuading Hitler's allies to round up their

Jews and deport them to the east for extermination. His enthusiasm would come back to haunt him at Nuremberg.

Guilty at Nuremberg

After the Nazis surrendered, von Ribbentrop was put on trial with other Nazi officials. After a lifetime of playing parts, von Ribbentrop tried some new roles.

He began as the reluctant Nazi who was being persecuted, literally crying before the tribunal that he was absolutely innocent of any wrongdoing. That didn't work.

Next he switched to being the defiant Nazi stalwart: "Even with all I know, if in this cell Hitler should come to me and say, 'Do this!' I would still do it." That didn't work either.

His final role was that of the martyred Nazi. On the gallows at Nuremberg, it is said that he looked upward, shook his head, and said, "Forgive them, for they know not what they do."

But they knew. They sprang the trap door. Von Ribbentrop's final curtain went down on October 16, 1946.

53 Vyacheslav M. Molotov

Man of the Hammer

NATIONAL ARCHIVES

Vyacheslav M. Molotov was Stalin's tough negotiator.

Vyacheslav M. Molotov lived to the age of 96, which is quite remarkable for a Russian Communist who spent so much of his life working for Joseph Stalin (Number 4). The Russian dictator dealt harshly with any perception—real or imagined—of disloyalty, and few of his commissars survived the various purges. Molotov, however, was one of the exceptions. To say that he merely carried out Stalin's wishes would be misleading. He did that, but he also had a razor-sharp mind and a strong will of his own. He was an excellent debater and a shrewd negotiator.

Molotov was one of the five individuals who ran the Russian war effort. The other four members of the State Defense Committee were Stalin, of course, Lavrenti Beria (Number 79), Georgi Malenkov, and Kliment Voroshilov.

An Early Revolutionary

He was born Vyacheslav M. Skriabin in 1890 in Kukarka province, now better known as the Kirov region of Russia. Later, as a young Communist revolutionary, he would adopt the name Molotov, which means "of the hammer."

At 15, he was a leader in the Marxist youth movement and took part in the abortive revolution of 1905. He was arrested and exiled to northern Russia. There he promptly organized the railroad workers. From this point on, he was in and out of jail. It was during this time that he took the name Molotov.

He attended a polytechnic institute in St. Petersburg and secretly organized students and workers. In 1912, he and another young Communist named Stalin founded the newspaper *Pravda*. He was expelled by the czar from Moscow and sent to Siberia in 1915. The following year, he escaped and became a member of the Communist Central Committee, which prepared for the Communist Revolution. It came in 1917, with the czar overthrown and the withdrawal of Russia from World War I. Molotov and Stalin together became members of the National Revolutionary Committee.

Rising in the Ranks of Stalin's Hierarchy

After Russian industry was nationalized, Molotov was appointed head of the People's Economy Council in 1918. From this point on, Molotov rose higher and higher in the Soviet hierarchy. In 1925, he became the youngest member of the powerful politburo. Following the death of Lenin, Molotov backed Stalin for the position of Soviet leader. Five years later, at the age of 40, Molotov was premier of the Soviet Union. (He would hold the position from 1930 until 1941, when Stalin decided to take it himself.) Molotov ran the agricultural five-year programs, which met considerable opposition. The plan involved "collectivization" of the peasantry. Individual peasant holdings were incorporated into collective farms. Stalin and Molotov made sure that those who opposed collectivization were wiped out.

The year 1935 was an important one in Molotov's future career. He started getting involved in foreign relations. The Soviet Union joined the League of Nations. By 1939 Molotov was commissar for foreign affairs. One of his first acts was to negotiate a non-aggression pact with Nazi Germany. The Soviet Union seized territory in eastern Europe. It began by dividing up Poland with the Nazis. Then, as Adolf Hitler (Number 1) took on western Europe, the Soviets gobbled up Estonia, Latvia, and Lithuania and invaded Finland.

In 1940, Molotov visited Berlin to talk about future possibilities with the Soviet Union's new ally. The Soviets wanted not only control of the Dardanelles, but influence in the Balkans and Finland. But Nazi Germany had its own interests to consider. It would not agree to such proposals.

From Ally to Enemy of Nazi Germany

In the spring of 1941, Molotov made a number of complaints about German maneuvers and troop buildup along the Soviet frontier. On June 22, 1941, the German ambassador handed Molotov what was essentially Hitler's declaration of war against the Soviet Union. For perhaps one of the few times in his professional life, the stone-faced Molotov expressed his genuine shock. "It is war," he blurted out to the German envoy. Then he asked, "Do you believe that we deserved that?"

Everything changed. Yesterday's ally was today's enemy. Yesterday's potential enemies were today's good and, hopefully, generous friends. Molotov now raced back and forth between Moscow and London for an alliance with Britain. After the attack on Pearl Harbor, he did the same with Washington to line up lend-lease aid.

Molotov was at all the major wartime meetings: Teheran, Yalta, Potsdam, and the San Francisco conference setting up the United Nations.

Shaping the Post-War World

As the war drew to a close, the Red Army moved through eastern Europe on the way to Berlin. The military presence soon reflected a political presence, and the Soviets were not about to give it up.

Molotov rejected the idea of participating in the Marshall Plan to rebuild Europe. He attacked the North Atlantic Treaty Organization and helped set up the Warsaw Pact in response.

During the war, Stalin's motto had been "not one step backward!" Molotov would take a similar position in what were loosely called "negotiations." Molotov would hang tough, talk tough, and often get what Stalin wanted by default.

In 1953, Stalin died. Molotov backed the idea of a committee taking over in Stalin's place, which worked for a while. When Nikita Khrushchev came to power in 1958, Molotov was shunted aside. He was expelled from the Communist Party in 1962 under the new de-Stalinization policy. He would not win reinstatement for more than 20 years.

Vyacheslav M. Molotov, Stalin's man of the hammer, died in 1986.

54 Semyon Timoshenko

Rebuilder of the Red Army

NATIONAL ARCHIVES

After the poor showing of the Red Army against Finland, Semyon Timoshenko saw the need for major reforms.

ollowing the Red Army purges of 1937 and 1938, Joseph Stalin's (Number 4) defense forces had been depleted of their officer corps. The danger to Soviet security became evident in the Russo-Finnish war of 1939–1940. The Soviets attacked Finland in November 1939 but were stopped cold and driven back. Stalin sent in Semyon Timoshenko, who broke the so-called Mannerheim Line to eke out a victory against tiny Finland. To Timoshenko, it was clear that the Red Army was not ready to fight a major war unless drastic steps were taken to revamp its training and tactics.

Semyon Timoshenko is the Soviet marshal who got the Red Army into shape by stressing mechanized warfare, insisting on more training in the field, and emphasizing the importance of the smallest army unit. His theory was that if the small unit was strong and unified, then the large unit would be strong as well. Of overriding importance, however, was the need to replace purged officers with trained, skillful leadership.

A Soldier in the Russian Revolution

Timoshenko was born in 1895 in Furmanka, imperial Russia. He was drafted into the czar's army during World War I and fought the Germans as a machine gunner. A hothead, he was imprisoned for striking a superior officer but was released after the Russian Revolution began in 1917.

The revolution set off a civil war in imperial Russia. On one side was the Red Army of revolutionaries. On the other side were the so-called "White Russians," who fought to restore the czar to his throne.

Timoshenko and his fellow soldiers killed their officers and joined the Red Army.

During the civil war, Timoshenko distinguished himself in battle. It is said that at one point he entered the dining area of a group of White Russian officers and told them to finish their dinner and proceed to the basement, where they were promptly shot.

That story may well be apocryphal. What is absolutely factual is that Timoshenko met a young Communist named Stalin while defending a city on the Volga River that would later be named Stalingrad. The two would become fast friends.

An Officer in the Red Army

In addition to fighting White Russian forces, Timoshenko fought various foreign groups trying to intervene in the Soviet takeover.

When those battles were completed, Timoshenko was sent to a whole range of military training institutes, each one preparing him for a higher level of responsibility.

In 1939, following the Nazi-Soviet pact, he was in charge of one of the Red Army groups attacking Poland from the east while the Nazis invaded from the west. The Red Army's opposition was minimal, but the campaign was hailed as a great victory.

A few months later, the Soviets invaded Finland. When the Russians were getting a terrible trouncing, Stalin sent in Timoshenko to take over. Under his new leadership, the Soviet force attacking Finland was successful. Timoshenko was now hailed as a hero for his work in Poland and Finland.

But Timoshenko was distressed by the poor showing in Finland. A brand new marshal, Timoshenko wondered what could be expected of the Red Army if it were up against a more powerful enemy when it struggled to defeat tiny Finland.

Marshal Timoshenko began putting the Red Army into fighting shape. He thought that both morale and discipline were important. The role for mechanized warfare had to be expanded. Appointed commissar of defense, he would later be credited by Stalin with rebuilding the Red Army from the ground up. Whether he did it all alone is open to conjecture, but his leadership role was essential in bringing about changes.

As the Soviet Union prepared for the struggle ahead, Timoshenko's words appeared throughout the Red Army ranks: "Don't ask what the numerical strength of the enemy is but ask where it is; then find and destroy it."

Battling Nazi Germany

On June 22, 1941, the Nazis attacked the Soviet Union. It took several days for the Russians to respond. Stalin, thunderstruck by the attack of his former ally, froze. He ordered that no counterattack be made without his final order. He simply could not believe that he had been double-crossed by Adolf Hitler (Number 1).

With the Nazis moving in on Moscow, Stalin put Timoshenko in charge of Russian forces defending the capital. Nearly 130 years earlier, Napoleon had taken Moscow and then had to retreat, but the Soviet capital was still a critical symbol in the war. A Nazi victory could crush morale among both soldiers and civilians. The city held.

Stalin then shifted Timoshenko south to defend the region of the Crimea. This time Timoshenko's troops could not hold, and the Germans swept into the area.

Timoshenko would be given a number of military assignments after this, but he never achieved the victories he had won earlier. Eventually, he was demoted and sent home to sit at a desk. This was never Timoshenko's strength. He was best as a field commander, but he could not get those assignments anymore. Other field marshals would come and go in Stalin's revolving door.

Marshal Semyon Timoshenko, the man credited by Stalin himself with having rebuilt the Red Army, died in 1970.

55 William L. Shirer

From Reporter to Historian

COLLIER

This is the railroad car in which Germany surrendered in 1918 to end World War I.
Twenty-two years later, Hitler had it brought back to Compiegne for the French surrender.
William L. Shirer's description of the scene is one of the memorable reporting events of the war.

It was the kind of tip that every reporter prays for, the one piece of advance information no one else knows. It would lead to what he would later call "the scoop of my life": "The armistice is to be signed at Compiegne." The French were about to surrender to Nazi Germany.

Shirer knew his history. Compiegne was the place where Germany had signed the armistice with the Allies at the end of World War I.

It was a warm day in June 1940 when Shirer first made his way to the tiny clearing in the forest at Compiegne. There was a huge war memorial there, commemorating the German surrender in 1918. Now there were also huge Nazi flags and an old railroad car. Shirer gasped. It was the same railroad car where the Germans had bowed to the French and signed the armistice in 1918.

Shirer watched the pageant unfold. He would describe what he saw to his radio audience in America: "I looked for the expression on Adolf Hitler's (Number 1) face.... I have seen that face many times at the great moments of his life. But today it is afire with scorn, anger, hate, revenge, triumph.... Suddenly, as though his face were not giving quite complete expression to his feelings, he throws his whole body into harmony with his mood.

He swiftly snaps his hands on his hips, arches his shoulders, plants his feet wide apart. It is a magnificent gesture of defiance, of burning contempt for this place now and all that it has stood for in the 22 years since it witnessed the humbling of the German Empire."

William L. Shirer was the reporter who became the historian of Nazi Germany. Reporters all write for tomorrow's historians. Shirer lived through the history, kept diaries, and then had access to the secret documents that emerged during the Nuremberg war crimes trials. Whatever book is published on Hitler or Nazi Germany, it will always be measured against Shirer's *The Rise and Fall of the Third Reich*.

Foreign Correspondent

Shirer was born in 1904 in Chicago. After graduating from college, he borrowed some money and made his way to Europe on a cattle boat. He visited England, Belgium, and France, and he got a job in Paris with the *Chicago Tribune*. His paper assigned him to stories all over central and western Europe. Shirer became the *Tribune's* chief correspondent in central Europe, headquartered in Vienna.

In 1931, he became Berlin correspondent for the Universal News Service. It was a critical time in German history. Ruinous inflation had virtually wiped out the middle class, unemployment was rampant, and political parties on the left and right were battling for power on the streets of Berlin. In January 1933, Hitler became chancellor. The following year, Shirer joined the Columbia Broadcasting System (CBS), which had offices in Vienna. Starting in 1937, Shirer began broadcasting regularly from different European cities as news broke. He reported from Vienna, London, Berlin, and Paris. As more CBS news reporters were added, his beat became Berlin.

Return to America and the McCarthy Era

Following his famous broadcast from Compiegne, the Nazi Propaganda Ministry began to look more closely at Shirer's scripts and news stories. Censors still remembered how Shirer had broken the story of the 1936 Olympics. He had written that the Nazis had taken down all the "No Dogs or Jews Allowed" signs in Berlin. It was true, of course, but it hurt the Nazi image. Finally the censorship became too difficult to handle, and late in 1940 Shirer returned to America.

In 1941, his *Berlin Diary* was published. It became an immediate best-seller. There was a great deal of interest in Nazi Germany, now a potential enemy. Not only did it put into print many of the stories he had broadcast from the German capital, but it included new material that Shirer could never have gotten through the Nazi censors.

From 1942 to 1948, Shirer was a columnist for the New York *Herald Tribune*. He also did commentary on CBS radio. In 1947 he was fired by CBS because one sponsor complained about some of his commentary. Shirer switched to the Mutual network for a few years.

But the era of McCarthyism had arrived. Senator Joseph McCarthy of Wisconsin crusaded not only against Communists but against "Communist sympathizers" in the media, the government, academia, and even the U.S. Army. Shirer, always frank and outspoken, found himself blacklisted over a period of five years. He made a living by doing "one-night stands," lecturing at colleges and universities.

An Opportunity to Write

This dark period in his life gave him the chance to examine his options. He decided to write a book on the history of Nazi Germany. *The Rise and Fall of the Third Reich* was published in 1960. This remarkable book was based not only on personal experience during years in Nazi Germany, but on a trove of captured Nazi documents. Shirer was in a position not only to read the documents but also to interpret them in terms of the personalities and policies involved. The book sold in the tens of millions, was widely translated, and became the first $10 book to make *The New York Times* best-seller list.

In 1969, Shirer published *The Collapse of the Third Republic* about the fall of France. It was far less successful, probably due to the fact that there was not that much interest in a book about French history. He also wrote several autobiographical accounts and a biography of Gandhi.

William L. Shirer died in 1993.

NATIONAL ARCHIVES

Gerd von Rundstedt annoyed Hitler because he told the Führer exactly what he thought. But Hitler recognized his military skill and called on von Rundstedt when needed.

The Führer's Bluntest General

When the Allies broke out of the Normandy beachhead in the summer of 1944, Wilhelm Keitel (Number 48) asked Gerd von Rundstedt what he thought should be done.

Von Rundstedt, with the blunt frankness that had made him famous, answered: "End the war! What else can you do?"

As soon as the word got back to Berlin, von Rundstedt was recalled home.

Von Rundstedt represents those traditional, non-political German officers who were obedient to authority. Their job, as they saw it, was to carry out the orders of the head of state, in this case—Adolf Hitler (Number 1). Such obedience was viewed by these officers as especially important in time of war.

Von Rundstedt's penchant for frankness put him in the position of being one of the generals whom Hitler trusted. The Führer might be temporarily angered at something von Rundstedt had said, but when the time came for putting a plan into operation, Hitler would often turn to von Rundstedt.

A Military Man

Gerd von Rundstedt was born in 1875 in Aschersleben, Germany. In World War I, he fought initially on the western front, but then was put into a staff position on the Russian front. After the war, he was given several important military commands, culminating with the Berlin military district.

After Hitler came to power in 1933, the German army went through a series of internal changes. Late in 1938, with the Munich crisis over the Sudetenland of Czechoslovakia at least temporarily resolved, Colonel General von Rundstedt retired.

The retirement lasted less than a year. Von Rundstedt was called back to lead the German army group south in the invasion of Poland. A year later, he headed a huge German force through the Ardennes to overwhelm France. After the French surrender, von Rundstedt was promoted to field marshal and assigned to Operation Sea Lion, the German plan to invade England. The invasion never came off, and the field marshal was given other assignments.

Fighting the Russian Front

Hitler now turned his attention to the east and the Soviet Union. Von Rundstedt, who had served on the Russian front in World War I, was given command of an army group for a new Russian invasion. Von Rundstedt, aware of the vast reaches of Russian territory, warned Hitler that the Soviet Union would not be the pushover that France had been. The Soviet campaign, he said, would not be a quick one.

Initially, the Germans made strong gains all along the huge front. An early winter stopped the drive and von Rundstedt wanted to pull back a bit to take good defensive positions in preparation for a new offensive the following spring. Hitler would not allow it. When von Rundstedt told Hitler to either accede to the field marshal's evaluation or get someone else, Hitler got someone else.

A Return to Europe to Face the Allies

Before 1941 was over, a bitterly cold Russian winter had set in. Equally important, America was in the war, courtesy of Japan, and Hitler had declared war on the United States. This opened the possibility of an Allied attack on the continent of Europe. Von Rundstedt found himself examining the hundreds of miles of French, Belgian, and Dutch coastline subject to invasion. Von Rundstedt and Erwin Rommel (Number 39) awaited the Allied assault.

D-Day would come on June 6, 1944. When the Allies broke out of the Normandy beachhead area, von Rundstedt made his famous remark that the only thing left to do was to end the war. The comment got back to Hitler, and von Rundstedt, once again, was sent packing.

Then came the bombshell, both figuratively and literally. Anti-Nazi German army officers, convinced that Hitler would end up destroying Germany, conspired to kill him. A bomb was set off inside one of Hitler's military headquarters. The Führer was wounded but survived the assassination attempt; a bloody purge of suspected plotters followed.

Hitler once again called on von Rundstedt, this time to set up a "court of honor" to judge the accused plotters. Two other German officers would preside as well: Keitel and Heinz Guderian (Number 12). The court discharged the accused officers from the army. This meant they could now be tried for treason by a civilian court. Many found guilty were placed on meat hooks and hanged with piano wire.

The Battle of the Bulge

In the fall of 1944, von Rundstedt was called in by Hitler to lead the single most daring offensive of the war. It was to be another offensive through the Ardennes, in what would become known as the Battle of the Bulge. The class of 1944—young German high school graduates who would ordinarily be used to replace the killed and wounded on the various German fronts—would be used to create a brand new army, trained by tough non-coms who would whip them into shape virtually overnight. Many would wear American uniforms, and some would drive American jeeps and even tanks. In mid-December, they would break through American lines and try to seize the port of Antwerp. The plan almost worked.

When it was all over, the Americans had prevailed. Antwerp was secure; Hitler's gamble had failed.

The American and German military cemeteries in Luxembourg mark the toll of that terrible battle. Most of the German dead were in their late teens.

By March 1945, von Rundstedt no longer had a command. He was taken prisoner a week before the German surrender and was held in custody for four years. No war crimes charges were ever brought against him.

Gerd von Rundstedt died in 1953.

57 Friedrich von Paulus

The Field Marshal and the Corporal

NATIONAL ARCHIVES

Friedrich von Paulus would become the first German field marshal to surrender. He surrendered at Stalingrad.

Propaganda chief Joseph Goebbels (Number 44) paced up and down his Berlin office. The plane from Stalingrad had landed a short time ago and the mailbags were on their way to his headquarters. It was clear that von Paulus was not going to hold out much longer. When the final German surrender came, Goebbels wanted to flood the world with ringing words of defiance and resolve from the letters of German troops at Stalingrad.

There was a knock at the door. His aides dragged in several sacks of mail from Stalingrad. It is not known how many letters—most of them addressed to mothers, wives, or sweethearts back home —Goebbels opened and read. But it was clearly enough for him to conclude that the letters were too bitter, defeatist, or—worst of all—anti-Nazi for propaganda purposes.

"Don't be bitter," one officer had written to his wife, "and do not suffer from my absence. I am not cowardly, only sad that I cannot give greater proof of my courage than to die for this useless, not to say criminal, cause."

Goebbels pondered the problem for a few minutes. The mail, of course, would not be delivered. It would be stored somewhere or destroyed. In the event of surrender, he would have Adolf Hitler (Number 1) pay a special tribute to the heroes who fought so gallantly for their Führer. That would do the trick.

The letters were shipped to a warehouse and forgotten. Years after the war, they were discovered and published.

Von Paulus represents those German generals who were hamstrung and overruled by their commander in chief, Adolf Hitler, who had risen all the way up to the rank of corporal during World War I.

The Battle of Stalingrad

Von Paulus was born in Breitenau, Germany, in 1890. He became an army officer and fought in World War I. Soon after Hitler came to power, an Armored Troops Command was established. Paulus became chief of staff to the unit in 1935.

After World War II broke out, von Paulus was involved in both the invasions of Poland and France. In 1940, he became chief operating officer of the German army. He was named head of the German 6th Army in early 1942.

The 6th Army drove deeper into Soviet territory than any German army ever. It began in the outskirts of Stalingrad and then drove into the city itself.

The Battle of Stalingrad was going on at the same time as actions raged all along the extensive Russian front. There was also fighting in North Africa. Von Paulus had to compete for reinforcements and supplies with German armies from Leningrad to the Caucasus and from Libya to Tunisia.

In short, the German army was overextended. Hitler was moving little pins around on his wall map, but all he was doing was robbing Peter to pay Paul or, in this case, robbing von Paulus to pay Erwin Rommel (Number 39).

Surrender to the Russians

On November 23, 1942, while he still had time and space to maneuver, von Paulus sent a message to Hitler:

> *"Ammunition and fuel are running short.... A timely and adequate replenishment is not possible.... I must forthwith withdraw all the divisions from Stalingrad itself and further considerable forces from the northern perimeter. In view of the situation, I request you to grant me complete freedom of action. Heil mein Führer!"*

Hitler, the former corporal, would not hear of it. Now that his armies had reached the Volga River, he wanted them to stay there. So Hitler promoted von Paulus to the rank of field marshal; every German officer knew that no field marshal had ever surrendered.

At Hitler's expressed order, the 6th Army dug in. They were digging their own graves; they had nothing left to fight with and no way out. On January 31, 1943, von Paulus surrendered 100,000 men.

Late in the summer of 1944, prisoner of war von Paulus began making propaganda broadcasts for the Soviets. He attacked both Hitler and the Nazi regime, urging German troops to surrender rather than die for Hitler. He stayed in the Soviet Union after the war ended. He later moved to and spent the rest of his life in East Germany, which was then under Soviet domination.

Friedrich von Paulus died in 1957.

58 Tomoyuki Yamashita

The Tiger of Malaya

COLLIER

Tomoyuki Yamashita took his troops through the Malayan jungles to take the British naval base of Singapore.

Before World War II began, the common military wisdom was that there were three fortified areas in the world that were absolutely impregnable: the Maginot Line in France, Singapore in the Far East, and Gibraltar, which guarded the entrance to the Mediterranean. Today, only Gibraltar remains on that list.

The Maginot Line and Singapore fell early in World War II. In 1940, German panzers smashed through Belgium and Holland and made an end run around the Maginot Line that forced France out of the war. Starting in December 1941, the Japanese made their way through Malayan jungles and took Singapore.

The Japanese general who led this stunning campaign was Tomoyuki Yamashita, who would thereafter be known to military historians as "The Tiger of Malaya."

Early Military Experience

Tomoyuki Yamashita was born in 1885 in Osugi Mara, Japan. He was graduated from the Hiroshima Military Academy and became a second lieutenant in the Japanese army. After World War I, he became a military attaché in Germany, Austria, and Switzerland. He taught at the War College, worked in the Military Affairs Bureau, and had several command positions.

In 1936, a group of young army officers attempted to overthrow the government and set up a military dictatorship. The coup attempt failed, and 17 of the officers were sentenced to death. Yamashita, who may have known of the plot, was never charged.

Japan unleashed war on China in 1937, and Yamashita took an active part in the invasion.

After war broke out in Europe, Yamashita was part of an official Japanese military team that was sent to observe German and Italian weapons and methods. Yamashita returned to Japan, greatly impressed by the German emphasis on air power and mechanized warfare. Agreeing with Isoruku Yamamoto (Number 6), he argued against Japan getting involved in a war with the United States. He felt that Japan did not yet have the military capability to do so. Nonetheless, Yamashita was ready to take on any military task he was given, and carry it out with great skill.

A new Japanese government under Hideki Tojo (Number 29) decided to go for broke in the Pacific. In December 1941, simultaneous attacks were launched against American, British, and Dutch bases.

An Unexpected Strategy to Take Singapore

Yamashita was confronted with one of the most challenging assignments of the war: to take the fortress of Singapore.

Yamashita examined the problem. The powerful British naval base was on an island off the tip of Malaya. There was a causeway to the island from Malaya. Huge fixed guns surrounded the island. The guns were excellent for protection against attacking enemy ships, but the huge fixed guns were ineffective against an invasion by foot soldiers from the Malayan mainland. Yamashita sent his 25th Army group into the jungles of Malaya.

The British believed the jungle to be virtually impenetrable by a modern army. But Yamashita knew that the Malayans were unhappy with their colonial status. Hypnotized by the Japanese motto of becoming part of a "Greater East Asia Co-Prosperity Sphere," the Malayans not only did not resist the Japanese, but they helped lead them through the jungle.

Yamashita's troops reached the bottom of the Malayan peninsula in mid-January 1942. The British promptly blew up the causeway and retreated to the island of Singapore itself.

Without air support or the protection of the major British warships *Repulse* and *Prince of Wales*, which the Japanese had sunk, the British waited for relief. Though some reinforcements did reach the island, they were too little and too late.

The Japanese landed forces on the island and seized the city's water supply. The situation was hopeless; the British surrendered to Yamashita on February 15, 1942.

Death in the Philippines

In July 1942, Yamashita was put in command in Manchuria. He was sent in July 1944 to command Japanese occupation forces in the Philippines. It was an assignment that would cost him his life.

In October 1944, the United States invaded Leyte, the beginning of the liberation of the Philippines. Yamashita kept his forces fighting in the islands until the end of the war.

Douglas MacArthur (Number 8) set up a military commission in the Philippines to try Yamashita for war crimes. During the recapture of the islands, some Japanese troops had committed atrocities. At his trial, Yamashita argued that in times of retreat, those in command often lose contact with individual units and that he had no knowledge of the atrocities taking place. Nevertheless, Yamashita was found guilty and was sentenced to death. But there were doubts raised about the legality of the military commission. The case went all the way to the U.S. Supreme Court, which ruled 6–2 against the Japanese general. He was hanged in February 1946.

Most military historians and legal scholars, including many Americans, believe that the Tiger of Malaya was innocent of the charges against him because he had no personal knowledge of the atrocities that had taken place.

Behind the North African Landings

COLLIER

Jean Darlan, shown here between Generals Dwight Eisenhower and Mark Clark, arranged a speedy cease-fire in French North Africa.

In the fall of 1942, Franklin D. Roosevelt (Number 2) sent Robert Murphy (Number 63) on a secret mission to French North Africa. The president instructed his trouble-shooter to make whatever political deal he felt was necessary to save American lives.

The United States and Great Britain were preparing to invade North Africa, which was then under the control of Vichy France. The reason for a deal was to limit, or eliminate altogether, any French resistance to the military landings.

The country called Vichy France had come about as a result of the French armistice agreement with Adolf Hitler (Number 1). Under its terms, northern and western France, including Paris, were to be occupied by the Nazis. Southern France, with its capital in Vichy, was not occupied and was considered neutral. It was led by Henri Petain (Number 27).

Relations between England and France, and the United States and France, were complicated. The United States had diplomatic relations with Vichy, but Britain did not. England had become a haven for the Free French, who, with Charles De Gaulle (Number 51), carried on the fight against Hitler.

Another complication was the role of the French fleet, anchored mainly at Toulon in southern France, but with units near Oran in North Africa.

Murphy met with key military and political people in North Africa. But he needed one major figure to issue an official order to cease fire once the landings were made. Admiral Jean Darlan, a Vichy official, happened to be in North Africa at the right time and was in a position to make the deal. As a reward, Darlan was named high commissioner of French North Africa.

Similar decisions would be made during the course of the war in areas of Italy and Germany taken over by the Allies.

Administering Occupied Territories

Darlan represents those men chosen to carry out important occupation roles. Among the factors to be considered were what jobs had to be filled and what experienced government officials were available to take them. That sounds a lot simpler than it was for several reasons.

First of all, the Fascists and Nazis had been in power so long that the pool of experienced administrators was apt to consist mostly of former Fascists or former Nazis. In North Africa, the pool might be largely—but not exclusively—Vichy French who had to work closely with the Nazis. Many Frenchmen who opted to fight Hitler had joined De Gaulle in London.

A second factor in selecting personnel was that each situation was unique in its own way. At the highest levels of government, political deals were sometimes required. Admiral Darlan's story is the story of the deal that secured French North Africa for the Allies.

Early Influence on French Naval Fleet

Jean Darlan was born in 1881 in Nerac, France. He was graduated from the French naval academy in 1902. The naval officer fought throughout World War I, from 1914 to 1918. In the years following the war, he rose rapidly in rank, becoming a rear admiral in 1929. During the next decade, he transformed the French navy into a modern fighting force. By 1937, he was commander of the entire French fleet.

A Question of Loyalty

War came in 1939. The following year, Hitler invaded France and crushed the nation within weeks. The defeated French land forces were demobilized, but a powerful French fleet, built largely by Darlan, remained. It was the kind of prize that might well tilt the balance to either side. Winston Churchill (Number 3) tried to convince the French fleet to either continue fighting on the side of Britain or else to sail to neutral ports in the Western hemisphere, out of reach of the Nazis. The French refused, and in the summer of 1940 there was a brief battle near Oran between British and French naval units. The French lost a ship and took heavy casualties; they left North African waters for Toulon. There they joined the rest of the fleet. Relations between the two former allies reached the breaking point.

The action gave the Nazis hopes that it might yet acquire the fleet. What the Führer did not know was that Darlan had secretly ordered naval commanders to scuttle their ships if it looked as if Hitler was about to seize them.

Negotiating North Africa

In the fall of 1942, French North Africa was firmly in Vichy control. By then, the United States was in the war. Britain and the United States wanted to occupy North Africa. If they did so, it would put pressure on Erwin Rommel's (Number 39) Africa Korps, which was menacing Suez. Amphibious landings would be made in North Africa, but casualties could be high. For the American forces, it was their first taste of battle in the European war.

Murphy and a military team held secret meetings with sympathetic French military and civil authorities. Darlan, however, just happened to be in North Africa a few weeks before the invasion. The sources differ on who approached whom on a deal, but the United States saw Darlan as the right man at the right time and in the right place. He had the authority to call a cease-fire. He also was influential in the disposition of the French fleet, then anchored in Toulon in southern France.

The deal was made and all went according to plan. Landings were made on the night of November 7–8, 1942. Three days later, Darlan called for a cease-fire. Shortly thereafter, he was named high commissioner of French North Africa.

The Nazis, in violation of the armistice, moved troops into Vichy France. As they did so, French naval officials scuttled the entire French fleet at Toulon, as Darlan had ordered many months earlier.

Controversy and Assassination

But America's deal with Darlan raised an outcry among the Free French under De Gaulle and among the British, who hated Darlan's affiliation with Vichy and the Nazis.

The furor would not last. On Christmas Eve 1942, Darlan was assassinated in Algiers by Ferdinand Bonnier de la Chapelle, a young zealot. Years after his death, a suppressed photo appeared in the newspapers showing Darlan and Dwight D. Eisenhower (Number 7), who appears to be giving orders to Darlan. Though the photo could not be published at the time it was taken, it did show that the United States exercised strict control over the man it had made high commissioner of French North Africa.

60 Frank Knox

From Rough Rider to Navy Boss

V.F.W.

Frank Knox, who had run against Roosevelt on the 1936 Republican ticket with Alf Landon, agreed to join FDR's cabinet in 1940.

I t was Teddy Roosevelt who urged, "Speak softly, but carry a big stick." He also saw the need for a powerful navy and sent the Great White Fleet around the world to demonstrate the power of the United States. So when Frank Knox, who was a close friend of Teddy, was nominated for secretary of the navy by Franklin D. Roosevelt (Number 2), it should have been no surprise.

But it was a shocker. Knox was not only a prominent Republican, but a strong opponent of the president on domestic issues. For him to join FDR's cabinet aroused a political uproar. Roosevelt, however, knew exactly what he was doing; not only was he putting the right man in charge of building up the navy, but he was making national defense a bipartisan issue.

The Fighting Editor

Frank Knox was born in 1874 in Boston and attended Alma College in Michigan. In 1898, he signed on with Teddy Roosevelt's Rough Riders and charged up San Juan Hill. The two men became close friends and political allies. Knox supported Roosevelt's presidential campaign.

Knox invested in several newspapers in different parts of the country. He was a fighting editor—literally: He once knocked out a saloon keeper during one of his newspaper crusades. His papers gave him the opportunity to exercise political clout. In 1910, the same year he bought the Manchester (New Hampshire) *Leader*, he was made chairman of the Republican Central Committee. Two years later, he backed Teddy Roosevelt for the Republican nomination. When his candidate failed to win, Knox urged him to run on the third party "Bull Moose" ticket. Teddy Roosevelt lost but split the Republican vote and helped elect Woodrow Wilson.

During Wilson's first term, the president had stated that America was "too proud to fight" in World War I. Knox attacked Wilson for the statement. When America entered the war, Knox volunteered, rising in the ranks from private to colonel in the field artillery.

Entering the Political Arena

Knox returned home to resume both journalism and politics. In 1928, he was made manager of all Hearst newspapers. Three years later, when the Chicago *Daily News* was up for sale, he bought it. After Franklin Roosevelt won election in 1932, Knox opposed the social programs of the New Deal, including social security and the Wagner Act's labor reforms.

In 1936 he ran for vice president on the Republican ticket with Alf Landon. That year, FDR carried every state except Maine and Vermont.

In 1937, after visiting the European dictatorships, Knox came home convinced that the United States had to build its defenses. When Japan sunk the U.S. Navy gunboat *Panay* in Chinese waters on December 12, 1937, Knox was outraged that more aggressive measures were not taken against the Japanese. He was alarmed by what he saw as an attempt by Nazi Germany to bring Nazism to the Western hemisphere. He started campaigning for a navy big enough to protect the nation in both oceans.

Before the outbreak of World War II, he was opposed to the United States getting involved in any European wars. But after Nazi Germany invaded the Low Countries, Knox pushed for rearmament.

When France fell and England stood alone, President Roosevelt called on two of the nation's most distinguished and respected Republicans to join his cabinet: Henry L. Stimson (Number 21) as secretary of war and Knox as secretary of the navy. Overnight the drive to stop Adolf Hitler (Number 1) became the policy of a coalition government.

Building a New Great White Fleet

For the rest of his life, Knox worked to get the navy into shape. There would be many difficult decisions and setbacks.

Britain needed destroyers to survive, and a deal was made to swap overage American destroyers for British naval bases in the Atlantic. Ships would be needed for lend-lease shipments. Nazi submarines had to be confronted and, if they sunk American ships, attacked.

The Japanese's successful attack on Pearl Harbor was the ultimate disaster for the U.S. Navy. Knox had to build the Pacific Fleet, adding many more carriers, battleships, cruisers, destroyers, and other naval vessels.

Knox had to negotiate with Henry J. Kaiser to build "Liberty Ships," merchant freighters built to ship war material overseas; Andrew Jackson Higgins (Number 69) to build landing craft; and hundreds of other contractors, large and small. The navy required torpedo boats, submarines, planes, bullets, shells, torpedoes, and a thousand other items that constitute a modern navy.

As secretary of the navy, Knox had to deal with Congress as well. When the ship *Normandy* was set ablaze in New York harbor soon after the United States entered the war, sabotage was suspected; Knox was ready to complain to Congress that he had asked specifically for funds to prevent sabotage. Because Congress did not appropriate the money, it was responsible, and not the U.S. Navy. Harry L. Hopkins (Number 22) explained to Knox why that was a bad idea. "Even if Congress does not act," Hopkins told him, "the secretary of the navy still has the responsibility."

Despite the many obstacles Knox faced, Teddy Roosevelt would have been astonished at what Knox had built: his own Great White Fleet.

Perhaps it was fitting for the war to end on a mighty battleship, the U.S.S. *Missouri*, in Tokyo Bay. But Knox was not alive to see it. He died in 1944, a year before the Germans and Japanese surrendered.

61 Josip Broz (Tito)

NATIONAL ARCHIVES

Tito led the most successful guerrilla campaign of the war, tying up huge German armies in Yugoslavia.

As German tanks rumbled into Yugoslavia, several war correspondents wondered how a small country peopled primarily by horses and carts could possibly hold up against Nazi armor. Associated Press journalist Robert St. John later quoted one of the reporters:

"...Serbia's a mountainous place.... This is not blitz country. These babies will lose the plains, but wait until they get the Nazis into the mountains. The Serbs know their mountains.... They can retire to the mountains of southern Serbia and fight there for a year....

"Did you ever see what these people live on? Black bread and onions. They've got enough flour and onions back in these mountains to feed an entire army for at least a year. Besides they'll eat their shoe leather before they'll give in to the Germans."

Ethnic Divisions in Yugoslavia

Two major ethnic groups in Yugoslavia, Serbs and Croatians, resisted the Germans. But traditional ethnic hatreds, as well as political differences with the Yugoslav government, split the two groups into warring factions.

The Croatian leader was Tito, a staunch Communist. The Serb leader was Draja Mikhailovich, who backed the royalist government of Yugoslav King Peter II. The king led a government-in-exile from London.

Tito's influence on the course of World War II and Yugoslavian history is twofold. First, his partisans engaged a dozen German divisions for four years. Those troops could have been used by the Germans elsewhere: against the Russians on the eastern front or against the Anglo-American armies on the western front.

Second, Tito was involved in an internal war within his own country. That war-within-a-war would have long-range implications for the future of the Balkans.

Leader of the Yugoslavian Communists

The man later known as Tito was born Josip Broz in 1891 in Croatia. During World War I, he was drafted into the army of Austria-Hungary; he was captured by the Russians and became a prisoner of war. When the war ended, the Austro-Hungarian Empire was split up into several countries, and Broz found himself in a newly created country called Yugoslavia.

He became a Communist, was imprisoned for his politics, and then worked in Moscow for a while. It was during the 1930s that he took the name Tito. During the Spanish Civil War, he recruited foreign volunteers to fight for the loyalist cause. He became head of the Yugoslav Communists.

The Fight against the Germans and within Yugoslavia

In April 1941, Adolf Hitler (Number 1) invaded Yugoslavia. Tito organized the partisans to fight a querrilla campaign against the Nazi occupiers. At the same time, a second querrilla group of Serbs under Mikhailovich, called Chetniks, was set up in Yugoslavia to fight the Germans.

For a brief time, the two groups managed, if not to work together, at least to keep out of each other's way. It did not last. The result was a civil war in the midst of the Nazi occupation. It was time for the exiled king to choose between them.

It was a difficult decision for the young king, sitting out the war in London. Peter knew very well that Tito had no love for the monarchy. But Britain and the United States urged the king to back him, based on the fact that his partisans were enormously successful in battling the Germans. The king had no real choice and grudgingly gave his support to Tito.

The king appointed Tito minister of war, and the partisan leader proceeded to liberate large areas of Yugoslavia. Mikhailovich, on the other hand, had stopped fighting the Nazis and was clashing with Tito's partisans.

The New Premier of Yugoslavia

In March 1945, Tito became premier of Yugoslavia. Two months later, Germany surrendered, and the European part of World War II was over.

Six months later, Tito's constituent assembly declared the country a republic, and King Peter II was out of a job.

With the war over, it was payback time for Mikhailovich. In 1946, the Chetnik leader was captured, put on trial, and executed for collaborating with the Nazis.

Joseph Stalin (Number 4) may have thought he had a new nation to dominate. But Tito did not like Stalin's brand of Communism. In 1948, the two Communist leaders officially split. Rumors circulated that Stalin was trying to have Tito assassinated. If so, the efforts never succeeded. Tito, Communist dictator of Yugoslavia, died in 1981, just days shy of his 90th birthday.

The Battle Continues

During his lifetime, Tito succeeded in holding together a polyglot country of many factions. With his death, however, the cracks in this artificial national foundation began to show. Years later, it would explode into terrible fratricide and bloodshed. In effect, the querrilla warfare of World War II would prove a precursor to "ethnic cleansing" and other terrible war crimes. It would lead to the breakup of Yugoslavia as one nation and the independence of several individual nations, each one free to pursue its own destiny.

upied by British April 1940

62 Maurice Gamelin

How France Lost the War

DISABLED AMERICAN VETERANS OF THE WORLD WAR

The Maginot Line was impregnable, especially if an enemy tried to attack it head on. Maurice Gamelin was surprised when the Germans decided to invade through Belgium instead.

It would be unfair to identify Maurice Gamelin as the one person who lost the war for France. Twice he had tried to stop Adolf Hitler (Number 1) in his tracks, and twice he was rebuffed by the French government.

In 1936, Hitler sent troops to occupy and fortify the Rhineland, which was contrary to the Treaty of Versailles. Gamelin urged the French government to allow him to go in and drive the Nazis out. At that point, the commander of the German military force was under secret orders to withdraw immediately if France moved against him. But the French government did nothing. It proved to the German general staff that bluffing could work.

In 1938, Gamelin urged Premier Daladier not to abandon Czechoslovakia at Munich and allow him to take the initiative against Hitler. Once again, the French government balked, and once again Hitler was strengthened at home as well as abroad.

But Gamelin, because of his command position in the French army, must share responsibility with fellow generals and politicians for the French debacle of May and June 1940.

A Prelude to War with Nazi Germany

Gamelin was born in 1872 in Paris. Descended from a military family, he was graduated in 1891 from St. Cyr, the French military academy, at the top of his class. He served as an infantry officer in Algeria. From 1906 to 1911, he served on the staff of General Joffre. In 1911, when Joffre was named commander in chief of the French army, Gamelin headed his group of advisors. When World War II came, Gamelin became Joffre's chief of staff.

Gamelin achieved fame in 1915 by stopping the Germans on the Marne. In the spring of 1917, Gamelin was assigned the 9th division, which distinguished itself in battle through the rest of the war.

Bolstering France's Defenses

With the war over, Gamelin was sent on special assignments to Brazil and Syria. He returned home and enjoyed a series of higher ranks and greater responsibilities. In 1931, he became chief of the general staff of the French army. At this time, he suspected that war between France and Germany was inevitable. In 1935, he succeeded Weygand as head of the French army. He became inspector general and assumed duties in the council of war, which was responsible for organization and training of the army.

Gamelin began to expand the mechanization of the army, but it would prove to be too little too late.

Gamelin supported a treaty with the Soviet Union. He also wanted to help the Loyalists in the Spanish Civil War, chase the Germans out of the Rhineland, and risk war with Nazi Germany over Czechoslovakia. A series of shaky French governments declined to take action.

The War Comes to Europe

The year 1939 was one of decision. France and Britain, awaiting a German strike somewhere in Europe, began discussing how to stand together against Hitler. Late in January of that year, Gamelin became chief of the general staff of national defense. When war came in September, Gamelin became commander in chief of all Allied armies.

His strategy was a simple one: Wait for the Germans to strike and then destroy them.

After the fall of Poland, there was lull in the fighting until the spring of 1940. Germany then attacked Belgium and Holland and moved into France. The German panzers swept through the Ardennes and cut off the British army around Dunkirk. The English, plus French and Belgian units, were evacuated back to Britain.

In panic, French civilians jammed up the roadways as Nazi forces moved deeper into French territory. With France exhausted and bleeding, Italy declared war on France and England and struck in the south of France.

This was an ironic twist of fate, for Gamelin had long scoffed at the military power of Fascist Italy. He had once made the observation: "If Italy should remain neutral, I should need five divisions to watch them. If she goes over to Hitler, I should need 10 divisions to beat her. But if Italy should join the Allies, I should need 15 divisions to help her." But it was the last nail in the coffin for France. Gamelin was out, replaced by Weygand. But France was forced to capitulate.

Analysis of Defeat

What went wrong? The military and political historians usually cite these as the main reasons for France's defeat:

1. Over-reliance on the Maginot Line.
2. Failure to fortify the region of the Ardennes.
3. Failure to build up adequate armor and airpower.
4. France's chaotic multiparty politics prevented a consistent government policy or timely action.
5. Presence in France of a "Fifth Column." This included prominent figures in both government and the military who were pro-German and spouted defeatism.
6. Failure of France to plan movements in consultation with her allies.

Three months after the surrender of France, Marshal Henri Petain (Number 27) had Gamelin arrested. He was charged, in effect, with losing the war. Gamelin thought the charges were ridiculous and refused to dignify them with a response. Gamelin may have assumed the military responsibility for overemphasizing the Maginot Line, not building up adequate armor and airpower, and ignoring the Ardennes. However, French politicians shared in those sins, plus others the military played no part in.

Gamelin was jailed, shipped to Nazi Germany to be held in a concentration camp, and then freed by American troops at the end of the war. Gamelin wrote his view of the war in his memoirs. He died in 1958.

63 Robert Murphy

A "Diplomat Among Warriors"

U.S. NAVY

In mid-October 1942, an American submarine silently surfaced off the coast of French North Africa. Robert Murphy and several army officers rowed to meet with French officials to discuss the coming invasion.

During the war, there were a number of novels about fictional agents who worked for the president, hobnobbing with the powerful and arranging top-secret deals. No fictional deeds came even close to the real exploits of Robert Murphy.

He called his autobiography *Diplomat Among Warriors* and concentrated on the events of World War II. His diplomatic achievements, however, began much earlier and ended much later.

Murphy's main influence during World War II involved his work with the Vichy government and French officials in North Africa. It would save countless American lives in Operation Torch, the invasion of French North Africa.

Charge d'Affaires in Vichy

Robert Murphy was born in Milwaukee, Wisconsin, in 1894. He graduated from George Washington University Law School in 1920 and joined the Foreign Service. His earliest posts were in Switzerland, Germany, and Spain. In 1930, he was sent to France, where he held increasingly important diplomatic positions through the next 11 years, beginning in Paris and ending in Vichy.

The years 1939 to 1941 were critical for France. War came in September 1939; France fell in June 1940, and that same year a new French government was set up in Vichy under Henri Petain (Number 27). Franklin D. Roosevelt (Number 2) now took one of the most extraordinary gambles of the war. Still neutral, and contrary to the policy of the British government, the United States decided to recognize the Vichy regime and work with it.

Murphy became charge d'affaires in Vichy. In September 1940, Murphy was called back to Washington to confer with President Roosevelt, who spoke of future operations in French North Africa, including possible occupation by the United States. Contacts had to be made; government and military officials had to be sounded out on where they stood politically.

One of the first projects Murphy accomplished was an arrangement for the United States to distribute food and clothing in French North Africa. This gave Murphy and a score of American "observers" an opportunity to meet and work with key French officials. These face-to-face arrangements would lay the groundwork for future North African operations when the United States entered the war.

Political Adviser to Eisenhower

After Pearl Harbor was attacked, the United States began planning for the first use of American forces in the European theater. Dwight D. Eisenhower (Number 7) was put in charge of the landings in French North Africa scheduled for November 1942. Two weeks before the landings, Murphy and a number of U.S. military officials, headed by General Mark Clark, landed in North Africa by submarine to arrange for French cooperation. When the invasion came, French resistance was relatively light.

When the invasion was over, General Clark held a press conference in which he appeared to take credit for the French cooperation. Murphy, who had been working on the project for two years, seethed. He got even in his memoirs by pointing out that Clark put on his staff as an assistant "not a professional soldier, but the motion picture producer Darryl Zanuck."

Murphy became Eisenhower's chief political adviser. Once North Africa was firmly in Allied hands, the next objective was Sicily and the mainland of Italy. Sicily was invaded early in July 1943. On July 25, Mussolini (Number 50) was removed from office. Murphy carried out secret negotiations with King Victor Emmanuel III, Badoglio (Number 74), and other major Italian political figures to bring about a surrender. Once again, Murphy worked behind the scenes to do the job. Italy was invaded by the Allies on September 3, and it surrendered on September 8, 1943.

Three months after D-Day in Normandy, Murphy was named Eisenhower's adviser on Germany. The diplomat was surprised that the American military was not particularly interested in reaching Berlin ahead of the Russians. Murphy speculated that there might well be heavy German resistance in the German capital, but that there were political advantages to be gained by the Western Allies getting there first. (Berlin was located in an area of Germany that was to be the Russian zone of occupation. Some military observers questioned the wisdom of spilling American blood on territory they were not going to be occupying anyway. The Russians reached Berlin first.)

Service after the War

After the war ended, among other tasks, Murphy worked closely with General Lucius Clay, who headed American occupation forces in West Germany. He served both Democratic and Republican presidents from Truman (Number 14) to Richard Nixon in many different capacities. For example, Murphy helped in carrying out the Marshall Plan in Europe, advised U.S. Ambassador Perle Mesta in Luxembourg and became U.S. ambassador to Belgium. He also negotiated the purchase of uranium ore from the Belgian Congo, became U.S. ambassador to Japan, played go-between in getting Japan and South Korea to work together, arranged a visit by Premier Khrushchev to the United States, and advised President Nixon on diplomatic appointments. One of his last tasks was to serve on the Foreign Intelligence Advisory Board.

One of the most extraordinary diplomats in American history, Robert Murphy died in 1978.

64 Karl Doenitz

Commander of the U-boats

Karl Doenitz (left) lost the Battle of the Atlantic. His U-boat crews ended the war with the highest casualty rate in the German armed forces.

If Adolf Hitler (Number 1) expected to win the war, he needed to stop the shipment of war materials headed first for England and later for the Soviet Union. The only way to accomplish this was by using "U-boats," submarines capable of sinking the merchant ships crossing the Atlantic from America.

The war between the merchant ships and the Nazi submarines would become known as the Battle of the Atlantic. Though other battles would become far better known—El Alamein, Stalingrad, Normandy, the Battle of the Bulge—none would be more important, because none of the other battles would have been won without the war materials brought by merchant ships. When Hitler lost the Battle of the Atlantic, he lost the war.

A Small U-boat Fleet Begins to Attack

Doenitz believed in the power of the U-boat, led the German U-boat fleet, built it, devastated Allied shipping, but ultimately suffered horrendous losses. The highest percentage of German casualties throughout its armed forces would be U-boat crewmen.

Karl Doenitz was born in 1891 in Berlin-Gruneau, Germany. He entered the German naval training school in 1910. When World War I broke out, he served first aboard a cruiser, then commanded a submarine. His sub sank several ships, but when it encountered mechanical difficulties, he was forced to surface and was captured.

When the war ended, Germany faced the prospect of vastly reduced armed forces. Specifically, the Treaty of Versailles forbade the German use of submarines. However, once Hitler came to power, an armaments buildup began and Doenitz was named commander of the small U-boat fleet. As with every other armed force in the world, there was competition among the top leadership for desired weaponry; Doenitz found himself last on the priority list. He lost out to planes, tanks, and ships. By September 1939, with war imminent, he could count fewer than 60 subs, many of them substandard (no pun intended).

Nevertheless, the available U-boats went into action. Not only were merchant ships sunk, but the British lost the aircraft carrier *Courageous* and the battleship *Royal Oak* in the first months of the war.

The Wolf-Pack Attacks

It was Doenitz who conceived the idea of the submarine "wolf-pack." When U-boats operated singly, Allied convoys could easily avoid them and protect vital materials. Doenitz arranged for packs of between eight and 20 submarines. When a convoy was spotted, German radio would contact a wolf-pack in the area. One of the subs would follow the convoy until nightfall. Then the other subs would join the shadowing sub at the site of the convoy, surface, and attack. The strategy proved quite effective.

When France fell in June 1940, submarine bases became available to the Nazis in the Bay of Biscay. Germany now occupied northern and western France. The Nazis could operate U-boats from right on the Atlantic. The U-boat fleet grew, and Allied losses mounted.

The year 1941 brought lend-lease, with war materials headed first for Great Britain and then for the Soviet Union. President Roosevelt (Number 2) wanted American merchant ships protected from U-boats and kept extending American naval patrols farther across the Atlantic. This inevitably led to the sinking of American ships by German U-boats. It also raised the possibility of America being drawn into the war, as it had been pulled into World War I.

Following Japan's attack on Pearl Harbor and the German declaration of war against the United States, U-boat activity increased dramatically. Hundreds of Allied ships were sunk.

German Submarine Warfare Is Defeated

The tide turned during 1943. The British code-breakers began to uncover the location of U-boat wolf-packs. The Royal Air Force and U.S. Army Air Force bombed the subs as they were assembling. New radar devices tracked subs at sea. New naval ships called corvettes proved more than a match for the Nazi U-boats.

By the beginning of 1944, the Battle of the Atlantic was just about over, and the Allies had won. The Germans estimated that they had sunk more than 2,200 ships, but it had cost them nearly 800 submarines and 32,000 seamen. Although some U-boats did go out from time to time, German submarine warfare had virtually come to an end.

At German shipyards, workers toiled furiously on newly designed "snorkel" submarines. These were much faster than the old ones and could recharge their batteries without surfacing. As with the jet aircraft, these new superweapons could not be manufactured in time to save Hitler.

Hitler's Successor

Doenitz found himself commander in chief of a German navy that had almost ceased to exist. Thousands of sailors with nothing to do were put into army uniforms and sent off to fight on the Russian front.

As the war drew to a close, the Führer brooded over who would succeed him. Hitler planned to commit suicide, but who could he trust to take over the leadership of Germany? He discounted someone from the army because of the July 20, 1944 officers' plot to kill him. He could not count on the air force because he felt Hermann Goering (Number 43) had tried to betray him. So Hitler turned to the navy—and Karl Doenitz.

Negotiating Germany's Surrender

The admiral of the German navy officially took over as chief of state on May 1, 1945, the day after Hitler's suicide.

Doenitz tried to negotiate a surrender with the Western Allies only, hoping to continue to fight the Soviets. This offer was refused, and Doenitz ordered that the necessary steps be taken for complete capitulation on all fronts. The new head of state also halted the destruction of German infrastructure and fired the Nazi officials in the government hierarchy.

Following the unconditional surrender, Doenitz was one of the Germans arrested and put on trial at Nuremberg. He was found guilty of crimes against peace and was sentenced to 10 years imprisonment.

After his release, Doenitz had plenty of time to write his memoirs. He died in 1980 at the age of 89.

65 Heinrich Himmler

The Führer's Hit Man

CORBIS

Heinrich Himmler (far left) and the Führer enjoy the sights of Paris.

As the infamous Charles Manson was, Heinrich Himmler was a serial killer who sent others to murder. He was a Nazi who took real pride in his work. Adolf Hitler (Number 1) told him who had to die, and Himmler made sure that the right killers were on hand with the appropriate murder weapons. Sometimes they needed machine guns, sometimes poison gas, sometimes piano wire. What the Führer wanted, the Führer got.

A Cold-Blooded Mass Murderer

One of the most chilling statements ever made by a mass murderer was delivered by Himmler in October 1943. Addressing a group of Reichsleiters and Gauleiters—Nazi officials—he confided to them:

This is one of the things that is easily said: "The Jewish people are going to be exterminated," that's what every [Nazi] Party member says.... And then they all come along, the 80 million worthy Germans, and each one has his one decent Jew [that he wants to save]. Of course, the others are swine, but this one, he is a first-rate Jew. Of all those who talk like that, not one has seen it [a mass extermination] happen, not one has had to go through with it. Most of you men know what it is like to see 100 corpses, side by side, or 500 or 1,000. To have stood fast through this and—except for cases of human weakness—to have stayed decent, that has made us hard. This is an unwritten and never-to-be-written page of glory in our history....We can say that we have carried out this most difficult of tasks in a spirit of love for our people. And we have suffered no harm to our inner being, our soul, our character.

Himmler was referring specifically to the role of his SS, the elite guards of the Nazi Party, in carrying out the Holocaust program.

What kind of miscreant could conceive and condone the mass murder of men, women, children, and infants?

A Leader of Assassins

Heinrich Himmler was born in 1900 in a town just outside Munich, Germany. After World War I, he joined the Nazi Party, dabbling in politics while running a chicken farm.

In 1929, Himmler was made head of the SS, Hitler's elite guard, which was dubbed "blackshirts." Initially a small group, it was destined to carry out the Führer's assassinations of individuals and large groups of people. By January 1933, when Hitler came to power, the blackshirts had grown to more than 50,000. The following year, Himmler was also made head of the Gestapo, the German secret police.

In 1934, Himmler and his SS were key figures in what was known as the Blood Purge: the assassination, ordered by Hitler, of the hierarchy of the SA, Hitler's private army. It meant the slaughter of old comrades, but neither Himmler nor his men flinched from the executions.

Himmler's power and prestige continued to expand. When war came in 1939, he was in charge of 39 divisions of Waffen-SS troops. Highly trained and disciplined, they were kept apart from the regular German army. Hitler wanted the separation because he believed that some of his army officers opposed him.

The Waffen-SS fought in a number of major battles of the war, but its most important task was implementing the Final Solution, the slaughter of Jews and other "subhumans."

There were also foreign units of the Waffen-SS, including volunteers from the Ukraine, Latvia, Yugoslavia, Estonia, Russia, Holland, Hungary, France, Belgium, and Scandinavia. Virtually every nationality conquered by the Germans was represented—except Poles. Hitler's hatred and contempt for Poland was deep and abiding.

Himmler Seeks to Save Himself

Following the unsuccessful plot by German officers to kill Hitler, Himmler was put in charge of rounding up the conspirators and their families. He spoke of cleansing the tainted blood from Germany. There were initial accounts of mass executions of not just close family members of the conspirators, but mistresses, aunts, uncles, nieces, nephews, and even distant cousins, although historians disagree over whether this policy of mass reprisal was actually carried out.

Shortly thereafter, the SS chief was put in charge of what was called a People's Army. The "army" consisted of old men and young boys: Though it sounded good for propaganda purposes, it had no guns, ammunition, or training. It was strictly for propaganda purposes to bolster morale.

In mid-April 1945, as Nazi Germany crumbled, Himmler tried to negotiate with the Western Allies through Sweden. Hitler was furious at such treason. Under threat of arrest, Himmler tried to lose himself in the flow of German refugees moving westward.

The war ended on May 8, 1945. Two weeks later, a disguised Himmler was stopped at a British checkpoint. Held for questioning, he committed suicide by biting into a poison capsule.

Though the SS and Waffen-SS would be labeled as criminal organizations by the Nuremberg War Crimes Tribunal, most of the criminals were never brought to justice. Both the Soviet Union and the Western Allies wanted Germany on their side in any possible future conflict between East and West.

The Great Appeaser?

NATIONAL ARCHIVES

Prime Minister Neville Chamberlain, left, with Neville Henderson, British ambassador to Germany. The prime minister's hopes for peace with Germany ended with the invasion of Poland.

"I believe it is peace in our time." The British prime minister addressed the relieved crowds in front of 10 Downing Street. He had come back from a conference in Munich, Germany, where he had agreed to hand over a portion of Czechoslovakia to Adolf Hitler (Number 1) without the prior consent of the Czech government. It was a great victory for the Führer, who had won a battle without firing a shot.

Neville Chamberlain's name would forever be associated with the word "appeasement," although historians still debate the fairness of that label.

Chamberlain was the British statesman who tried to pacify Hitler. When that failed, he girded for battle and took England to war.

On the Eve of War

Neville Chamberlain was born in Birmingham, England, in 1869. The son of British politician Joseph Chamberlain, Neville served on the Birmingham city council and as lord mayor before entering national politics. He won a seat in Parliament in 1918. As leader of the Conservative Party, he served as chancellor of the exchequer for several years. In 1937, he succeeded Stanley Baldwin as prime minister.

It was a difficult time—not just in Europe, but all over the world. There was a great depression, with massive unemployment, starvation, and social unrest. In short, it was a time ripe for the rise of demagogues and dictators. On the continent of Europe, Adolf Hitler was saber-rattling, and the danger of a new European war was very real.

The Surrender of Czechoslovakia

In 1938, Hitler demanded that the Sudetenland, an important part of Czechoslovakia, be turned over to Nazi Germany. A meeting was held in Munich to discuss the crisis. Present were Hitler, Chamberlain, Benito Mussolini (Number 50) of Italy, and Eduard Daladier of France. Ironically, England and France had no legal authority to act on behalf of Czechoslovakia, which was not allowed to particpate.

On September 30, 1938, the deal was struck. Chamberlain and Daladier, representing the two Western democracies, acquiesced to Hitler's demands. The Czechs had been sold out.

What were Chamberlain's options? England was clearly unprepared for war. Even if he defied Hitler, there was no way to save Czechoslovakia. By submitting to what seemed to be inevitable, he gave England and France time to build their defenses in preparation for the showdown that lay ahead.

Was it possible that Hitler could have been bluffed into doing nothing? Doubtful. Hitler had gambled in the past and had won. Why would he stop now?

Chamberlain publicly declared that the Munich agreement meant peace. Privately, he expected the worst.

An Ultimatum...and War

Early in 1939, Hitler occupied all of Czechoslovakia. England would soon have to take a stand. It came on September 1, 1939, when Germany invaded Poland. Chamberlain gave Hitler an ultimatum: Withdraw or face war. Hitler refused to retreat. Two days later, Britain and France declared war on Nazi Germany. The day of appeasement was over.

After defeating Poland, Hitler turned toward western Europe, invading Norway and Denmark. This served two purposes: It secured his access to Swedish iron and it protected his northern flank. British attempts to dislodge the Germans were disastrous. Chamberlain took the blame and resigned in May 1940. He was succeeded by Winston Churchill (Number 3).

His spirit broken, an embittered Chamberlain died in November 1940.

67 Anthony McAuliffe

Crisis at Bastogne

The Battle of the Bulge hinged on holding the critical road center at Bastogne. Anthony McAuliffe and his men held until they were relieved by Patton.

One of the most famous quotations of the war, and certainly the briefest, is attributed to Brigadier General Anthony McAuliffe during the Battle of the Bulge. On December 21, 1944, under siege in Bastogne, he was ordered to surrender by the German army.

McAuliffe is said to have given the one-word reply "nuts!" Upon delivering the message to the German commander, an American colonel was asked what it meant. He replied, "It means 'Go to hell!'"

Some crusty old army veterans, however, insist that what the general really said was "balls!" Those were far more innocent days, and it is conceivable that army public relations people may have concluded that "nuts!" would get across the idea of defiance and be more apt to make page one of family newspapers back home. In any event, the "nuts" quote is now official history.

From West Point to Normandy

McAuliffe is notable not for his words, but for his deeds. By holding out until his force was relieved by George S. Patton (Number 11), McAuliffe delayed the Nazi offensive long enough for reinforcements to arrive and subdue the Germans.

McAuliffe was born in 1898 in Washington, D.C. He was graduated from West Point in 1919. Although he missed out serving in World War I, he made up for it in World War II.

When the war broke out in Europe in 1939, he was sent to the army's War College. Then he was involved in investigating new war equipment, such as the jeep and the bazooka. When America entered the war, he headed the artillery section of the 101st Airborne Division.

McAuliffe broke his back in a practice parachute jump before the Normandy invasion, but he recovered in time to jump into France with his men on D-Day. As the newly appointed deputy division commander of the 101st, McAuliffe coordinated the final assault on Catenton, Normandy.

McAuliffe took part in the aborted Market-Garden operation in Holland in September 1944. The plan involved American glider troops and British ground forces. The 101st and 82nd Airborne Divisions were used in the assault by air and reached their objectives: the bridges at Eindhoven and Nijmegen. British forces achieved nearly all of their objectives. But at Arnhem, they faced fierce resistance and held only one end of the bridge targeted for seizure. British troops held out as long as possible but could not be relieved and were forced to surrender. It was a bitter defeat for the Allies, but the worst was yet to come.

A Surprise German Offensive

Three months after Market-Garden came a powerful new threat. On December 16, 1944, the Germans began a surprise offensive through the Ardennes section of Belgium. It was the beginning of the Battle of the Bulge.

McAuliffe, now in overall command of the 101st Airborne, was in a training camp in France, pulling his outfit together. Many of the men were brand-new replacements, in training for only a week. Asked if his men were ready for action, McAuliffe, knowing how critical the situation was, answered in the affirmative. He knew they would not be ready until February 1st at the earliest, but there was no time to spare. The entire force was trucked to Bastogne a few days after the German offensive began.

When they arrived in Bastogne, McAuliffe was shown a map of the town and all the roads leading away from it. The general had been told to use his own judgment on how long to stay in place. McAuliffe decided to hold it until relieved. It would not be easy, but Bastogne was the plug in the dike.

McAuliffe set up defensive positions in and around the town of Bastogne. The Germans attacked first from one area, then from another. The weather was foul, with snow and heavily overcast skies. American air power could not be used to help the Bastogne defenders.

The 101st Airborne, along with troops from other American divisions, kept fighting against overwhelming odds and waited for relief.

On December 21, 1944, came the German demand for surrender, which was summarily rejected by McAuliffe.

Several days later, with clear weather and the U.S. Air Force in full support, Patton's army broke through to relieve Bastogne. The Battle of the Bulge had not yet run its course, but it had been contained.

Questioned at a press conference following the battle, McAuliffe mildly protested the news reports that his outfit had been "encircled" by the Nazis. The general explained that the 101st Airborne Division had been sent to Bastogne to hold up the German advance.

In January 1945, McAuliffe was promoted to major general and was given command of the 103rd Infantry Division.

After the war, he commanded U.S. Army units in Europe. Following his retirement from the army, he became a corporate executive. He died in 1975.

68 Gustav Krupp/Alfred Krupp

The Family Business

QUARRIE

This is one of the Krupp manufacturing plants. In this and similar installations,
the Krupps manufactured their guns and tanks and built their submarines and battleships

In the year 1811, Friedrich Krupp set up a small iron and steel works in Essen, Germany. The company that began as a producer of iron and steel products for civilian use would become the largest and most influential arms dynasty in the world. It would take Germany from spectacular rise to utter devastation. Beginning in 1812 with the development of powerful new bayonets, the generations of Krupps to follow would go on to develop superior muskets, cannons, artillery, tanks, battleships, and submarines.

Between 1866 and 1945, Germany fought four major wars using arms fashioned by Krupp: the war against Austria in 1866, then France (1870–71), and then the two World Wars of the 20th century.

A Family Tradition

Gustav and Alfred Krupp were father and son. Gustav financed Adolf Hitler's (Number 1) dictatorship and headed the Krupp Works for many years, including the first half of World War II. His son, Alfred, was a corporate officer and headed the company in the last half of the war.

When the war ended, first Gustav and then Alfred were charged with crimes against humanity. The Krupps were put into the dock not for making better quality steel, but for using slave labor under inhuman conditions to do so. Other German industrialists had done their bit for the Reich by designing gas chambers, crematoria with elevators for easy disposal of corpses, and poison gas pellets for the extermination of "large animals."

Gustav von Bohlen und Halbach was born in 1870, the year of the Franco-Prussian War. Krupp weapons proved crucial in the Prussian victory over France. Gustav would grow up to marry Bertha Krupp, become head of the Krupp empire, and add Krupp to his name.

Their son Alfred was born in 1907. When Alfred was only 2 years old, the Krupps were working on a super cannon. Called "Big Bertha" in honor of Gustav's wife and Alfred's mother, it would be used in World War I.

The war ended in German defeat. Under the terms of the Treaty of Versailles, German war production was strictly limited. The Krupp Works, however, continued to produce weapons. This was done in secret simply by disguising products as being for agricultural or other civilian use.

Joining the Nazi Fold

The period of the 1920s was one of economic slump, ruinous inflation, and political unrest. Though the Krupps favored right-wing political parties, they were wary of Hitler and his National Socialists at first for two major reasons. First, the Nazi program originally favored the nationalization of German industry. Second, Hitler was viewed as a questionable character who could not be trusted.

By 1932, things had changed. The Nazis had given up the idea of nationalizing industry. The real turning point was the election of 1932, when the Nazis lost 35 seats and the Communists gained 19. The Nazis were on the brink of bankruptcy. But the Communist gain so scared the industrialists of Germany that they turned to Hitler and the Nazis.

Lucrative Profits of War

It was after Hitler came to power that Gustav Krupp met him for the first time, when he and other industrialists were invited to a meeting with the Führer. After the new chancellor had made his pitch for their financial support, Gustav Krupp was the first to stand up and pledge a million marks. The industrialists, Krupp in the lead, had signed on. With the chancellorship and a fat new bankroll in his pocket, the Führer was free to unleash his reign of terror.

Krupp would be rewarded for his enthusiasm. He became part of Hitler's rearmament program, and his company profited handsomely.

During World War II, the Krupps would not only have lucrative contracts, but also an estimated 100,000 slave laborers who worked without pay. The combination added up to enormous profits for the company.

Representing the German Arms Industry at Nuremberg

When the war was finally over, two dozen top Nazis were charged at Nuremberg with war crimes. Three would never stand trial: Robert Ley committed suicide, Martin Bormann disappeared during the Battle of Berlin, and Gustav Krupp was ruled too sick to stand trial (the press reported he was suffering from "senile softening of the brain").

The victorious Allies believed that the German arms industry should be represented in the dock. In 1947, Alfred Krupp and 11 other Krupp directors were put on trial. Alfred was found guilty, along with his colleagues. He was convicted of plundering countries occupied by the Nazis and using slave labor under inhuman conditions and sentenced to 12 years imprisonment.

Alfred Krupp served a total of six years and was then released. His property rights were restored. Officially, he was ordered to sell some of the Krupp holdings, but he never did so. The Krupps were back in business.

Death would bring an end to the empire. Gustav died in 1950 and Alfred in 1967. In 1968, the Krupp firm became a publicly owned corporation. The Krupp family business was no more.

69 Andrew Jackson Higgins

Eureka!

COLLIER

Amphibious landing craft produced by Andrew Jackson Higgins made possible the Marine landings in the Pacific and the Army landings in North Africa and Europe.

In the late 1930s, a boat builder in New Orleans came up with a new craft that he called the "Eureka." It was a 36-foot-long motorboat, with a bow shaped like a spoonbill and a propeller in a tunnel within the hull. What made it truly remarkable was that it could go from the water onto the beach without damaging the craft. The navies of three countries became interested in the new craft: the United States, Great Britain, and Finland.

"Eureka" would become the prototype for amphibious landing craft that would become better known as Higgins boats, named for the man who designed and produced them.

U.S. Industry Supplies the Allies

Andrew Jackson Higgins represents American industry, which supplied the United States, the Soviet Union, China, France, and other Allied powers with the weapons needed to win the war. American workers turned out ships, planes, tanks, guns, jeeps, uniforms, and thousands of other items needed to support the war effort. During the war, many American factories maintained three shifts a day, seven days a week. Historians may argue many aspects of World War II, from strategy to heroes, but there is universal agreement among scholars worldwide that U.S. industry was a major, if not *the* major, factor in the Allied victory.

Higgins was born in 1886 in Columbus, Nebraska. As is the case with all tycoons, there are legends of his youthful business acumen and ability to deal with adversity.

One story is that at the age of 12, he built a boat in his basement. When the boat was finished, he discovered that it was too big to go through any available door or window. Young Higgins solved the problem by removing some bricks at a convenient location, easing out the boat, and then re-bricking.

Though his interest in boats began in his boyhood, he got into the boat business almost by accident. He worked in the lumber business and set up his own lumber mills in Mississippi and Alabama. In order to export lumber overseas, he set up a company in New Orleans. The business required many boats, and Higgins first bought, and then built, the boats he needed, including schooners and brigantines.

Building a Better Boat

In 1930, he set up Higgins Industries, Inc., which produced all types of motorized boats, tugs, and barges. Higgins turned his attention to boats that could solve problems, such as the special needs of oil riggers and farmers who had to navigate in shallow waters. One of his most unusual designs was a boat for use in shallow waterways and swamps. Propellers were always getting fouled or stuck. The problem-solver came up with a propeller that was built in a protective tunnel so that it would not be damaged in shallow areas.

What followed next was inevitable: a boat that would not only operate well in shallow waters, but actually climb up onto the beaches. Higgins, a student of Greek, might very well have exclaimed "Eureka!" at the discovery and decided to give the new craft that name. The Higgins boat would revolutionize amphibious warfare.

Winning Wars and Breaking Rules

When the war came, Higgins produced dozens of other pieces of war equipment, including motor torpedo boats, landing craft, patrol boats, tank carriers, anti-submarine boats, torpedo tubes, power gun turrets, communication devices, and mechanical steering devices.

Higgins attempted to land a contract for the building of Liberty Ships, which were merchant freighters used for the shipment of war material overseas. It fell through when a shortage of steel developed. Some Higgins supporters claim that other industrialists, afraid of competition after the war, ganged up on him and cut off his supply. The namesake of Andrew Jackson insisted on taking his case to the president. Higgins ended up with other contracts, including one for helicopters.

Higgins knew when to break the rules and when to stick to them. In addition to women, he hired a large percentage of African American workers and insisted on paying them the same wages as white workers. Within his factories and his worker housing, however, they were kept separated. It was Higgins's own version of "separate but equal," considered quite radical for where and when it took place: the Deep South in the early 1940s.

Isoruku Yamamoto (Number 6), the man who planned the attack on Pearl Harbor, was strongly opposed to Japan getting involved in a war against the United States. The American industrial might, he said, would crush Japan in the long run. It was men such as Higgins that the Japanese admiral had in mind.

Andrew Jackson Higgins died in 1952.

70 Edward R. Murrow

"This...is London."

COLLIER

Edward R. Murrow's radio reports from London brought
to America the sounds of air raid sirens and falling bombs.

W hen Harry L. Hopkins (Number 22) first arrived in London early in
1941, he was there as the personal emissary of President Roosevelt
(Number 2). With FDR now reelected for a third term, the U.S. government was moving forward as quickly as possible to support the British fight against Adolf Hitler (Number 1).

The first person Hopkins met with upon his arrival was neither the British prime minister nor the American ambassador. It was Edward R. Murrow.

It was Murrow's voice that the American people were listening to over the radio, telling
them what was happening in bomb-ravaged London.

As Americans listened, they could hear in the background the sound of air-raid sirens,
followed by the thump-thump of bombs hitting their targets.

"This," a quiet voice would say, "is London."

A New Way of Covering the News

Hopkins knew that Murrow had an enormous impact on public opinion in America.
Since the war had begun in September 1939, the tide had begun to shift from extreme isolationism to sympathy for Britain. At the very least, the United States was building up its
defenses; it had even instituted a peacetime draft.

In those pre-television days, Murrow was one of the few journalists whose voice was
recognizable to millions over the radio. He had more than an audience; he had a following.

Edward R. Murrow was born in 1908 in Greeensboro, North Carolina. He grew up in the state of Washington and graduated from Washington State University, where he studied political science, speech, and dramatics. He went to work for the Columbia Broadcasting System (CBS) in 1935, covering talks and special events.

When war threatened in Europe, he went to London and began assembling a group of news reporters to cover events in London, Paris, Rome, Berlin, and wherever else news was breaking. This new way of presenting the news via radio won an instant group of listeners who did not want to have to wait for tomorrow's newspaper for fast-breaking news.

From Radio Journalist to Television Pioneer

Once the United States was in the war, Murrow would try to cover events on the spot. He would either record his description of what was happening or take notes and broadcast his story as soon as he got back to the studio. In addition to his London broadcasts during the blitz, his most famous stories were descriptions of bombing raids over Berlin and the dropping of parachutists into Holland during Operation Market-Garden, as well as his vivid account of the liberation of a Nazi concentration camp.

After the war, Murrow returned to the United States to discover the new medium of television. He embraced it as his own with extraordinary success. His *See It Now* news documentaries were stunning examples of what television was capable of doing to educate and enlighten. Some of the most famous programs included reports of migrant farm laborers, the link between smoking and deadly diseases, and, most famous of all, his report on Senator Joseph R. McCarthy of Wisconsin. The latter program has been credited with helping to bring down McCarthy, who was later condemned by the U.S. Senate.

But Murrow's daring television was too much for CBS executives. The programs were not only controversial, leading to the loss of advertisers, but expensive to produce. Television was in the entertainment and advertising business.

Murrow found himself assigned to different kinds of programming. He became host of a series called *Person to Person*, in which he interviewed such celebrities as Marilyn Monroe "at home." He seemed to take it like a good sport, but the new assignment must have stuck in his craw. The message could not be clearer: Slowly, he was being eased out.

In 1961, Murrow went to work for the new Kennedy administration as director of the U.S. Information Agency. But government was not really his thing. He resigned the job in 1964 and died a year later.

A Voice of the American Conscience

Murrow had been a reporter during the Golden Age of both radio and television, long before ratings became the only thing that counted.

Some historians of the media have called Murrow "objective." That is nonsense. If he had a strong point of view on a subject, whether about Nazis, or migrant workers, or demagogues, he let his audience know it.

That could be the reason Hopkins stopped in to see Murrow that first day in London. He might very well have heard Murrow's broadcast to America on New Year's Eve, December 31, 1940:

> *Most of you are probably preparing to welcome the new year. May you have a pleasant evening. You will have no dawn raid, as we shall probably have if the weather is right. You may walk this night in the light. Your families are not scattered by the winds of war.... You have not been promised blood and toil and tears and sweat, and yet it is the opinion of nearly every informed observer over here that the decision you make will overshadow all else during this year that opened a few hours ago in London.*

Murrow was reaching out for the conscience of America, as he would do on radio and television for years to come, until the age of ratings.

The Little Guy's War

Ernie Pyle's newspaper accounts of the war changed the focus from the generals at headquarters to the G.I.s in the foxholes.

Ie Shima is a tiny, 10-mile-square island in the Pacific, west of the much larger island of Okinawa. During the war, Okinawa was invaded by the United States because of its four-airstrip airport.

To guarantee the security of Okinawa, the tiny islands around it had to be cleared of all enemy forces.

On April 18, 1945, a Japanese machine gunner was spraying bullets in a wide arc across advancing American troops. When someone cried out in pain, the Japanese soldier probably believed that he had hit an enemy soldier. He never knew that he had killed a non-combatant, a reporter named Ernie Pyle.

A Battlefield Correspondent

This was nothing new. In every war, and especially in World War II, many non-combatants died. Pyle, of all people, would have understood that. He wrote about the little guy's war and realized that when hot lead is traveling through the air, innocent people are going to get hit.

Pyle is notable not because of how he died, but rather how he lived, how he did his job, and how he brought the news of the war to the people back home.

Pyle was one of many thousands of war correspondents covering the war for audiences on different sides. Some had jobs that took them close to the decision-makers at war departments in capital cities; others covered the war from the generals' headquarters behind the lines, where top officers outlined the strategy of future offensives.

Then there were correspondents such as Ernie Pyle, who covered the war from the battlefield, whether on land, on the sea, or in the air. Hundreds died, as Pyle did, to get the story.

Reporting the G.I.'s War

Ernie Pyle was born near Dana, Indiana, in 1900. A writer for the Scripps-Howard newspapers, Pyle traveled all over America and wrote mostly about little-known people trying to cope with life's indignities the best way they knew how. It proved to be a very popular approach, and Pyle became a columnist. When war broke out, Pyle was sent by his newspaper syndicate to London to cover the German air raids on the British capital.

After the United States entered the war, Pyle insisted on covering the war from the point of view of the combat infantryman, the pilot, the anti-aircraft gunner, the airplane mechanic. His subjects were rarely anonymous. He would give not just the name of the soldier, but also his hometown address and sometimes a bit about the family back home.

In short, Ernie Pyle turned the general's war into the G.I.'s war. It was no longer a vast multitude struggling to get off the Normandy beaches; it was Hy Haas from the Bronx, backing his vehicle into the water to take out a German pillbox with an anti-aircraft gun. It was no longer a casualty list; it was a group of infantrymen saying farewell to their dead Captain Henry Waskow, who was from Texas.

Tributes to a Buddy

Pyle's wartime correspondence would win him the Pulitzer Prize. He would publish two books with collections of his columns, *Here Is Your War* and *Brave Men*.

Hollywood produced the movie *The Story of G.I. Joe*, a fictionalized account of how Pyle covered the war, ending with a dramatization of Pyle's famous account of the death of an American infantry captain.

Ernie Pyle is buried in the military cemetery near Pearl Harbor. He is there not as a correspondent of World War II, but as a veteran of World War I. He served in the army toward the end of that "war to end all wars."

Following Pyle's death, he received many tributes, from President Truman (Number 14) to General Eisenhower (Number 7). Perhaps the greatest tribute was a marker set up on Ie Shima by American infantrymen: "At this spot the 77th Infantry Division lost a buddy, Ernie Pyle, 18 April 1945."

Up Front

Bill Mauldin's cartoon heroes, Willie and Joe, depicted the war with grim humor.

There is nothing funny about men at war. Nothing humorous about screeching artillery shells, or mud, or grime, or rats, or fatigue, or the prospect of violent death. It takes a very special insight, not to mention talent, to convert painful situations into a kind of gallows humor or an occasion for comic relief.

No matter what label is put on his work, the World War II cartoons of Bill Mauldin were unique. By showing reality, they raised the morale of American fighting men. He made them laugh out loud at the troubles and foibles of America's citizen army.

Bill Mauldin was the G.I.'s own editorial cartoonist. His cartoon appeared as a single panel drawing under the title *Up Front*, featuring Willie and Joe. The two G.I.s just tried their best to cope and stay alive in the battle for Europe.

His characters were almost always disheveled and unshaven, often tired to exhaustion, but always painfully aware of the reality of their violent world.

Bringing Home to Civilians the G.I.'s War

Bill Mauldin was born in 1921 in Mountain Park, New Mexico. During World War II, he was attached to the 45th Infantry Division in Italy, France, and Germany. His work appeared in the army newspaper *Stars and Stripes*, as well as in civilian newspapers back home.

Mauldin's heroes were the foot soldiers, the dogfaces, and the infantrymen. He could poke fun at officers: "What a magnificent view! Is there one for the unlisted men?"

With tongue planted firmly in cheek, he could poke fun at how the different branches handled rotation and tours of duty: "You have completed your 50th combat patrol. Congratulations. We'll put you on mortars awhile."

He could even find some grim humor in those who spotted enemy targets: A G.I., in his foxhole, speaks into his walkie-talkie as a German tank looms just above his head. "Able Fox Five to Able Fox. I got a target but ya gotta be patient."

Mauldin even took on George S. Patton (Number 11), who didn't like the way Mauldin's soldiers were depicted. The general tried to get Mauldin to give his characters a shave and clean them up. Not only did Mauldin go right on doing what he had been doing, but he drew a cartoon or two on the special dress and grooming rules of Patton's 3rd Army.

In 1945, he was awarded the Pulitzer Prize for *Up Front*. That same year, he published a book of his cartoons along with appropriate commentary. He brought home to American civilians the kind of war their young men were facing. Though the humor did not have the same impact on civilians, it did give them some idea of what war looked like—and felt like—on the battlefield.

After the war, Mauldin returned home to do cartoons on veterans returning to private life. He also drew editorial cartoons on national and international issues for several newspapers.

73 Breckinridge Long

Silent Partner of the Holocaust?

COLLIER

Breckinridge Long had a well-appointed office here at the U.S. State Department building in Washington. His orders went to U.S. consular officials all over the world—sometimes with tragic results.

He never loaded a Jew onto a cattle car, never made a selection at the Auschwitz train platform, never poured deadly Zyklon B crystals down into a gas chamber, and never performed a diabolical medical experiment on a human guinea pig at Ravensbruck.

He never machine-gunned Jews lined up at the edge of a huge burial pit, burned down a synagogue after the congregants had been locked inside, or in any way personally killed or maimed a single Jew.

Nevertheless, many believe Breckinridge Long was responsible for the deaths of untold thousands of Jews who were trapped in Europe during the Holocaust. And he did it all not from Gestapo headquarters in Berlin, but from his office at the U.S. State Department in Washington, D.C.

The Right Political Connections

Breckinridge Long was born in St. Louis in 1881. He graduated from St. Louis Law School and then went on to get his master's degree from Princeton. There he was a student of Woodrow Wilson. Long backed Wilson in his run for the White House and was awarded the post of assistant secretary of state.

During this time, he became friendly with Franklin D. Roosevelt (Number 2), then the assistant secretary of the navy.

Later, Long supported Roosevelt in his campaign to become governor of New York. In 1932, he supported Roosevelt again in his race for the presidency.

The president appointed him ambassador to Fascist Italy. When Benito Mussolini (Number 50) invaded Ethiopia, there was talk of an international oil embargo against Italy. Long fought successfully against the embargo, arguing it would trigger a European war. In 1936 he was recalled as ambassador, either because of ill health or because he had praised the Italian victory in Ethiopia.

In 1940, Long became assistant secretary of state in charge of the division on immigration and visas.

Rationalizing a Tough Immigration Policy

As Long saw it, his job was to keep Jewish refugees out of the United States. He may have believed that he was reflecting the will of the American people. The fact is that public opinion polls during the late 1930s and early 1940s generally opposed the admission of European Jews to the United States. Long also had the ear of the president, telling him that German agents would be swarming into the United States in the guise of Jewish refugees. The president gave him his approval to continue his tough visa policy.

So it was easy for Long to rationalize his policy, if he ever felt the need to justify it. Apparently he never had the slightest remorse or twinge of conscience. He carried out the visa policy with great efficiency.

In appearances before congressional committees, he would cite statistics designed to distort the truth and mislead Congress into believing that many more Jewish refugees had been allowed to enter the country than had actually done so.

To prevent the rescue of Jews required a combination of bureaucratic red tape, deferred decisions, and general procrastination. Worst of all was the policy of tight deadlines. If the applicant failed to meet a deadline with newly required information, he had to start the entire process all over again.

It all added up to a cruel joke on helpless, desperate people trying to save their lives.

Creating a Bureaucratic Maze

Here is how Long officially put his policy into operation. In the summer of 1940, Long sent the following memo to State Department officials James Dunn and Adolf Berle, Jr.:

> *We can delay and effectively stop for a temporary period of indefinite length the number of immigrants into the United States. We could do this by simply advising our consulates to put every obstacle in the way and to require additional evidence and to resort to various administrative devices which would postpone and postpone and postpone the granting of the visas.*

Long would find other reasons to bar European Jews. He expressed the fear that some might be German agents trying to get into the United States to do mischief. Then there was the idea that if any Jews had left relatives behind in Germany, they might be subject to blackmail by the Germans. Under this latter theory, only an *entire* family could be considered for entry, not just part of a family.

As a result, only a fraction of available emergency visas for Jews was ever used.

Time Runs out for Many Refugees

What happened to those Jews who never made it through the bureaucratic maze created by Long? Some of them may have survived. The vast majority undoubtedly met their ends in the death camps of eastern Europe. Years later, Americans who had volunteered to be sponsors told of how, during the war, they had received letter after letter from those they had hoped to save. The refugees told of constant visits to American consular offices to give whatever additional information was requested to get the precious visas. They did this until time ran out—just as Long knew it would.

The government of the United States was not in unanimous agreement on this issue. The State Department and Treasury Department were at odds over the policy. Treasury supported and State contested admitting Jewish refugees. The State Department, however, with its specific responsibility for immigration and visa policy, clearly held the upper hand and set the official guidelines.

When Under-Secretary of State Sumner Welles resigned, Long was considered in line for the post. Instead it went to Edward Stettinius, Jr. Long's biases had become known, and there was strong opposition to any promotion for him.

Long went into private practice and died in 1958.

Author's Note: The Long memo to consular officials calling for deliberate delays in issuing visas is from *The Politics of Rescue*, by Henry L. Feingold. Long's misleading Congressional testimony is discussed in an essay by Dwight Macdonald in *Memoirs of a Revolutionist*. Long's close working relationship with Roosevelt, especially regarding Jewish matters, may be found in *The War Diary of Breckinridge Long*, edited by Fred L. Israel. A very brief but pointed reference to Long's anti-Semitism by historian Doris Kearns Goodwin appears in her book, *No Ordinary Time*. See the bibliography for complete publication information on these works.

Surrendering Italy

DOUBLEDAY, DORAN & COMPANY, INC

Addis Ababa was the site of one of Pietro Badoglio's greatest victories. Because of this triumph, he was given the title Duke of Addis Ababa. Here is what the Ethiopian capital looked like after its conquest.

Late in July 1943, following the ouster of Benito Mussolini (Number 50) as dictator of Italy, King Victor Emmanuel III sought a new premier. He wanted someone who had the confidence of the country and would unite it in a time of disaster and uncertainty. Italy had been invaded. The Western Allies had already taken over most of Sicily, and an invasion of the Italian mainland appeared to be imminent.

A Military Hero

Pietro Badoglio was given the reins of government in Italy following the overthrow of the Fascist dictator. Badoglio was a perfect choice: a war hero dating back nearly half a century who had been given many honors by his country through the years. It would be his responsibility to get Italy out of the war and, hopefully, bring order back to a shattered economy. It did not work out that way. Italy would become a battleground with two competing Italian governments and with Italians fighting each other. It would become the only country in World War II to declare war—at different times—on both the Allies and the Germans.

Pietro Badoglio was born in 1871 in Grazzano Montferrato in the province of Piedmont. He attended a military school in Turin and became a sublieutenant of artillery. He entered the War College and joined the Royal Army Corps.

From 1895 to 1896, he fought in the East African campaign, but the Italian army was badly beaten in its war against Eritrea. In 1912, Badoglio's troops' victory over Turkey gained Libya for Italy and a reputation for Badoglio.

During World War I, Italy was allied with Britain, France, and the United States. Badoglio became chief of staff in the Sixth Army Corps. His campaigns against Austria-Hungary were legendary, and he was promoted to general. Defeated at Caporetto in 1917, he scored a smashing victory at Vitotorio Veneto in October 1918. This led to an allied armistice with Austria-Hungary. With the war over, Badoglio was made chief of the general staff and a senator for life.

The Fascist Party Takes Power

The year 1922 was a critical one for Italy: Mussolini marched on Rome and took over as dictator of Italy. Badoglio had wanted to use the army to put down the uprising, but the king refused Badoglio's request and Mussolini firmly established himself in power.

To keep Badoglio off his back, the Duce sent him off as an ambassador in South America. When the Duce thought it was safe, he brought Badoglio home and made him once again chief of the general staff. One honor followed another. Badoglio became a field marshal, was knighted, and became governor of Libya.

In the mid-1930s, Mussolini planned to conquer Ethiopia. Badoglio opposed the idea, but when Italian forces suffered a series of humiliating defeats, Badoglio was sent in to crush the African nation. He did so and became Viceroy of Abyssinia (the name Mussolini gave to Ethiopia). Later, the title Duke of Addis Ababa was conferred on him.

During the Spanish Civil War, Badoglio was apparently behind the scenes in mapping strategy for Francisco Franco (Number 75).

By now, Badoglio was getting on in years. He enjoyed talking strategy and tactics with his old allies from World War I. He and French General Maurice Gamelin (Number 62) would spend hours discussing the merits of troops holding their position versus moving on the attack.

New Loyalties as War Erupts

That kind of camaraderie came to an end when Adolf Hitler (Number 1) invaded Poland in September 1939. Mussolini had been pressured by Hitler to enter the war with him. As Galeazzo Ciano (Number 80) was, Marshal Badoglio was opposed to having Italy enter the war. Both believed that the country was not prepared to fight.

In June 1940, Mussolini insisted on getting into a war that seemed to be almost over. Britain had evacuated its forces from Dunkirk, and France was on the verge of surrender. Italy invaded southern France and prepared to win some territory quickly and easily. Feeling his oats, Mussolini foolishly decided to annex Greece. The Italians were badly mauled, and the Germans had to send an army in to save the day for Mussolini.

Approaching age 70, Badoglio decided it was time to retire; he did so in December 1940.

Three years later, the old marshal would take on the most difficult task of his career. Late in July 1943, with Mussolini out of power, the king called on Badoglio to become the new premier and to head the armed forces.

Badoglio's job was clear: Get Italy out of the war. He personally negotiated an armistice with Dwight D. Eisenhower (Number 7). The plan was to have American forces move in and occupy Rome upon the surrender. But German forces moved in quickly to reinforce Rome, and an imprisoned Mussolini was freed by German commandos. A rival Italian government was set up in northern Italy under Mussolini. With Nazi Germany occupying Italy and firing on Italian citizens, the Badoglio government declared war on Germany.

The Badoglio mission to bring peace to Italy had failed. The Italian peninsula became a battleground between the Allies and Germany, and Italians fought each other. When Rome was finally liberated in June 1944, Badoglio resigned as premier and King Victor Emmanuel III gave up the throne. The Allies established a new government, but the fighting in Italy would go on until the end of the war.

Marshal Pietro Badoglio died in 1956.

75 Francisco Franco

Prelude to a World War

NATIONAL ARCHIVES

Francisco Franco overthrew the government of Spain in the Spanish Civil War.
It would be a dress rehearsal for the world war to follow.

The Spanish Civil War was, in every respect, a prelude—perhaps *the* prelude—to World War II.

To begin with, it started in 1936 and ended in March 1939. World War II was launched in Europe in September 1939.

Secondly, it lined up the potential adversaries: Germany and Italy backed Franco; the Soviet Union and France backed the Spanish Republic. Though the United States took no side in the Spanish Civil War, American volunteers formed the Abraham Lincoln Brigade to fight for the Spanish Republic.

Finally, new weapons and tactics were used in the Spanish Civil War, allowing the military to field-test them. The dive-bombing of cities, the war on civilian populations, and the concept of total war would be lessons learned in Spain and then perfected in the World War of 1939–45.

Francisco Franco is the man who unleashed the civil war in Spain, laying the groundwork for the worldwide conflict to come.

Depression Devastates a New Republic

Francisco Franco was born in 1892 in El Ferrol, Spain. He graduated from the Toledo Military Academy. As a young officer, he helped put down an uprising in Morocco.

In 1931, Spain voted against the monarchy of King Alfonso, who fled the country with his family. A republic was established and a socialist government was put in place. Franco, a monarchist, disapproved of the change in government. He assessed the situation very carefully and bided his time.

The Great Depression that swept the world in the early 1930s devastated the Spanish economy. In 1934, a general strike was called throughout the country. Spain, along with other countries, appeared on the verge of economic collapse. Some members of the military attempted to revolt and restore the monarchy, but the coup failed. The country split into two camps: On one side were the monarchists and big landowners and on the other side were trade unionists and those who supported the republic.

A Brutal Civil War

Early in 1936, the combined left-wing Popular Front was elected; riots in the streets followed. General Franco, then stationed in the Canary Islands, made his move.

On July 17, 1936, Spanish military officers issued a call to overthrow the republican government. Franco took command of the anti-government forces in Morocco and invaded the Spanish mainland. The Spanish Civil War was underway.

There is no war more brutal than a civil war, pitting neighbor against neighbor and sometimes brother against brother. Worse, in a civil war each side believes that it has been betrayed by the other side, and the ensuing conflict is filled with death.

Fascism Comes to Spain

When the Spanish Civil War ended in March 1939, more than a million Spaniards had been killed and the country lay in ruins. Franco set up a ruthless Fascist dictatorship. Tens of thousands of Loyalist soldiers were imprisoned for years to come. Spain was devastated, physically, socially, and psychologically; both the land and the people were exhausted. So when Adolf Hitler (Number 1) asked Franco to get involved in the war against England, France, and later Russia, he hesitated.

Historians do not agree on exactly what Hitler promised or what Franco wanted. This much is certain: Franco not only refused to attack Gibraltar on his own, but he would not agree to having German troops go through Spanish territory to attack Gibraltar. However, Franco did send a division to fight against the Soviet Union. When the war ended, there was some discussion among the victorious Allies about overthrowing Franco's regime. Winston Churchill (Number 3) would not hear of it. He knew that Franco had denied Hitler taking out Gibraltar.

In 1969, Franco and the Spanish parliament designated Prince Juan Carlos, son of the former king, as future king and head of state. Following Franco's death in 1975, Juan Carlos became king. Today, Spain has a constitutional monarchy.

Picasso's Mural

Preparing for his legacy, Franco had a magnificent monument built in his own honor—a modern-day pharaoh spending the meager resources of an impoverished people for reasons of personal vanity. It is Franco's monument to himself.

There is another monument to Franco. It is not as big or as fancy, but far more famous. It is a mural by Pablo Picasso called *Guernica*. In 1937, this ancient Spanish city was devastated by Franco's bombers. Picasso, outraged by the destruction of the city and its inhabitants, painted this abstract view of horror in tones of gray and black. People and animals are strewn about the landscape in the throes of agony. From the heavens, an eye looks down in horror.

Picasso's mural is Franco's true legacy.

76 Harold Alexander

Ike's First Choice

NATIONAL ARCHIVES

Harold Alexander, at right, was one of England's best field commanders.
Eisenhower had wanted him to be deputy commander in Europe, but Churchill chose Montgomery.

When Dwight D. Eisenhower (Number 7) was chosen supreme commander for the invasion of Europe, it was clear that an Englishman had to be picked for the deputy spot in the Anglo-American coalition. Ike preferred Harold Alexander, who possessed a strong reputation among the military for both skill and judgment. The two men had worked together in the Tunisian campaign, where Alexander had served as Ike's deputy. They had known and liked each other and, even more importantly, had gained each other's respect professionally. But the partnership was not to be. The British chose Bernard Montgomery (Number 37), the popular hero of El Alamein. That decision would later strain the Anglo-American coalition during the most trying days of the war.

Wide-Ranging Military Experience

Harold Alexander was one of the outstanding commanders of the war, a thoroughgoing military professional with experience in the Battle of France, the evacuation at Dunkirk, the defense of Britain, and the fighting in Burma, El Alamein, Tunisia, Sicily, and Italy. He performed his job brilliantly, whether on the attack or on the defensive.

Born in 1891 in London and graduated from Sandhurst in 1911, Alexander spent the better part of World War I fighting in France. He was wounded and decorated several times. By the time the war ended, Alexander was an acting brigadier. He took part in military operations to help Poland and the Baltic states retain their newly won freedom and he served with the occupation army in Turkey. He then went on to attend the Staff College and the Imperial Defense College.

In the early 1930s, Alexander led British forces in India. By the late 1930s, he had won promotion to major general. When World War II came, he commanded a segment of the British Expeditionary Force in France. When the German breakthrough drove British forces to the port of Dunkirk, Alexander was placed in charge of the rearguard defense unit, the group that keeps fighting until everyone else is evacuated. Normally the rearguard is left behind to be captured, but Alexander was able to evacuate the overwhelming majority of his men.

From Defending England to Invading North Africa

With Adolf Hitler (Number 1) threatening an invasion of Britain, Alexander was given command of the defense of a large part of the English coast. In June 1941, when the Führer turned on the Soviet Union, the threat of a Nazi invasion was clearly over.

War erupted in the Pacific in December 1941, with Japan striking out simultaneously against American, British, and Dutch territories. Alexander was sent to Burma to stave off the Japanese. He held them off as long as possible, then retreated with Joseph W. Stilwell (Number 83) into India.

In the spring of 1942, Alexander was assigned to be the deputy commander under Eisenhower for the coming invasion of French North Africa. It was important that the overall commander of the operation be American; two years earlier, the British Fleet had attacked French ships in Oran, and friction was still strong between the two former allies.

To Egypt, Italy, and the End of Conflict

Three months before the North Africa invasion, Alexander was given a new assignment. He was to become Near East commander, headquartered in Cairo. With North Africa about to be invaded, it was important that Erwin Rommel (Number 39) be kept at bay in Egypt.

Alexander arrived at his new post about the same time that his subordinate, Montgomery, was assuming command of the 8th Army. Much of the planning to stop Rommel and take the offensive was done by Alexander and carried out by Montgomery. The Africa Korps was stopped at El Alamein, and the Germans were driven out of Africa.

After working with Eisenhower on the Tunisian campaign, Alexander led both British and American forces in Sicily and Italy. The latter campaign was a long, brutal series of battles up the "boot" of Italy, whose mountains provided perfect defensive positions for the Nazis. The German army would surrender in Italy just days short of the official end of the European war on V-E Day, May 8, 1945.

After the war, the field marshal became governor general of Canada and, later on, minister of defense in Winston Churchill's (Number 3) cabinet. Viscount Alexander died in 1969.

77 Albert Speer

The Slave Master

NATIONAL ARCHIVES

Albert Speer, at right, began his career with Hitler as the Nazis' chief architect.
By the end of the war, he was their chief slave master.

Late in 1945, when two dozen Nazis went on trial in Nuremberg, some foreign observers were surprised by the presence in the dock of Albert Speer. An architect, the builder of the Reichstag, a war criminal? How could that be?

A Program of Extermination through Work

Deputy Prosecutor Thomas J. Dodd stood before the International Military Tribunal and made the case:

> [T]he defendant Speer, as Reichsminister of the Central Planning Board, bears responsibility for the determination of the numbers of foreign slaves required by the German war machine, was responsible for the decision to recruit by force, and for the use under brutal, inhumane and degrading conditions of foreign civilians and prisoners of war in the manufacture of armaments and munitions, the construction of fortifications, and in active military operations....

We say this system of hatred, savagery and denial of individual rights, which the conspirators erected into a philosophy of government within Germany...followed the Nazi armies as they swept over Europe—the Jews of the occupied countries suffered the same fate as the Jews of Germany, and foreign laborers became the serfs of the "master race" and they were deported and enslaved by the millions.

Many of the deported and enslaved laborers joined the victims of the concentration camps, where they were literally worked to death in the course of the Nazi program of extermination through work.

The Führer's Architect

How does an architect turn into a slave master?

Albert Speer was born in 1905 in Manheim, Germany. He became an architect following in the footsteps of both his father and grandfather. Speer was graduated from the Munich Institute of Technology in 1924. The following year he studied at the Institute of Technology, Berlin-Charlottenburg.

The young architect's life changed in 1933 when he met Adolf Hitler (Number 1). The two became friendly and Speer became the in-house Nazi architect. He designed the new Reichstag building and staged key Nazi Party events for the camera of Leni Riefenstal, cinematographer for the world's first infomercials.

But Speer must have had stars in his eyes when he was asked by Hitler to design a brand new capital for the Führer's forthcoming world empire. It was to be called Germania. Unfortunately, the war intervened. At first, Hitler believed that the construction could proceed, but the war made that clearly impossible. Speer was flattered at the honor. Architectural critics who saw the plans after the war were less than enthusiastic, labeling the work more grandiose than grand and no better than mediocre. But Speer was dazzled by the commission, and he was ready to do anything that was asked of him by his Führer.

Worker Shortage Leads to Slave Labor

In 1943, Speer was put in charge of war production, labor mobilization, and central planning. There were not enough German workers to meet production goals, so Speer turned to the use of foreign slave labor. As the war went on, factory construction became more and more reconstruction, as Allied bombers pulverized the German industrial centers. Despite the multiple problems that he faced, Speer, using slave labor, kept production going for his Führer.

Speer's major stumbling block was palace politics. Heinrich Himmler (Number 65), for example, had his own slave labor program for his own special projects. There was competition not only for materials and labor, but also, and most importantly, for Hitler's ear. The longer the war dragged on, the more vicious the political intrigue.

Disagreements with Hitler

One of the most controversial debates that raged in Berlin was how far Germany should go in asking loyal Nazis to make major sacrifices, such as giving up slave labor house servants. Speer, who needed the slave labor to fulfill production quotas, found himself on the wrong side of the argument. Hitler hated the idea of depriving the master race of their due.

A more serious difference of opinion involved Hitler's scorched earth policy. As the war wound down, the Führer ordered Speer to destroy German infrastructure: dams, bridges, power plants, water systems, telephone lines, railroads, shipyards, and factories. Speer knew that Germany would need these when the war was over. He would not carry out the order himself and discouraged others from doing so.

Accepting Responsibility for Crimes

At Nuremberg, Speer insisted that he knew nothing of the mass extermination program. He admitted to knowing about the concentration camps where slave labor produced war materials under terrible working conditions, but he denied knowledge of the death camps.

Despite this denial, Speer was ready to take responsibility. He told the tribunal, "This trial is necessary. There is a common responsibility for such horrible crimes in an authoritarian system."

Convicted at Nuremberg for using forced slave labor, Speer was sentenced to 20 years imprisonment. He served the full term, was released in 1966, and published his memoirs, which he had been working on secretly while still in prison.

Albert Speer, the architect turned slave master, died in 1981.

78 Eleanor Roosevelt/ Madame Chiang Kai-shek/Queen Elizabeth

The Feminine Mystique

Eleanor Roosevelt and Madame Chiang Kai-shek (left photo)—along with Queen Elizabeth—symbolized the role of women in the war. All three supported their husbands the best way they knew how.

Traditionally, women did not actively participate in wars. The exceptions are so rare that they are famous: Joan of Arc, Molly Pitcher, Florence Nightingale, and Mata Hari are well known for playing varied roles in four separate conflicts. Respectively, one led an army, one was a revolutionary fighter, one a wartime nurse, and one a military spy. However, until World War II, the roles of women were to keep the home fires burning and preserve civilization to the extent possible.

Women Join the War Effort

During World War II, women poured into the defense plants. "Rosie the Riveter" assembled the planes and tanks, launched the ships, and mixed the explosives. Women nursed the wounded in combat, drove the generals in staff cars, and harvested the crops. They served in the armed forces as WACS, WAVES, SPARS, and Women Marines. In Europe and Asia, women even fought as guerrillas and spied on the enemy.

They were one thing more: anonymous.

There were exceptions. Eleanor Roosevelt, Madame Chiang Kai-shek, and Queen Elizabeth were the wives of famous wartime leaders who shared certain values of all other wartime women. All believed deeply in their countries and the righteousness of their cause.

The influence of women was difficult to measure during a time of great land and sea battles. But after the war, women's accomplishments would shape the lives of all women forever. These three famous women and all their sisters would create and mold a brand-new feminine mystique.

A Champion of Human Rights

Eleanor Roosevelt, the niece of President Theodore Roosevelt, was born in New York City in 1884. She married her distant cousin, Franklin D. Roosevelt (Number 2), in 1905. When he developed polio in August 1921, she urged him to continue a political career. Following his election to the presidency in 1933, she became the eyes and ears of the paralyzed president, visiting Depression-torn communities of the poorly fed, ill-housed, and unemployed. All were in need of assistance, and she campaigned on their behalf.

Her concern for human rights intensified when the war broke out in Europe. Mrs. Roosevelt lobbied for the admission of refugees fleeing oppression. She concerned herself with the future of "young colored people."

In January 1944, she wrote to her friend Joseph P. Lash: "I must say I worry about the future.... It really is discouraging because the Christian spirit seems so un-Christlike!" Years later, she would take these human rights issues to the United Nations for action.

During the war, the first lady visited army and navy bases in the British Isles, Australia, the South Pacific, and all parts of the United States. She was a one-person morale booster both at home and abroad.

After the death of her husband, she was called upon by President Harry S Truman (Number 14) to serve as a delegate to the United Nations. There she championed and won adoption of the Universal Declaration of Human Rights. It was the crowning achievement of her career as a humanitarian. Eleanor Roosevelt died in 1962.

A Call for Action Against Japan

Madame Chiang Kai-shek was born in Shanghai, China, in 1898. A member of the distinguished Soong family, she was educated in the United States. One of her sisters married Sun Yat-sen, an early leader of modern China. Madame Chiang's husband, Chiang Kai-shek (Number 87), was the key military and political leader of China during the war.

Madame Chiang carried the fight for action against Japan, well aware that the United States was concerned with defeating Adolf Hitler (Number 1) first, rather than Japan.

In February of 1943, Madame Chiang addressed Congress to plead for action in the Far East:

> *"Let us not forget that the longer Japan is left in undisputed possession of these [conquered] resources, the stronger she must become. Each passing day takes more toll in lives of both Americans and Chinese."*

However, the decision to beat Germany first was unchanged. The United States would turn to the Far East only after victory in Europe was won. When it did, the war would end with the atomic bomb.

After the war, the Chinese Communists took over mainland China, and the Chiangs fled to Taiwan and established a new base of power. Following the death of her husband in 1975, Madame Chiang moved permanently to the United States.

A Symbol of British Courage

Queen Elizabeth was born in Scotland in 1900. She was the wife of King George VI (Number 95) and is the mother of Queen Elizabeth II. She became queen when her brother-in-law, Edward VIII, abdicated the throne in order to marry Wallis Simpson, an American divorcee.

Despite the dangers of the German *blitzkrieg*, Queen Elizabeth would not consider leaving England.

Following a bombing attack on Buckingham Palace in 1940, a journalist asked about the possibility of sending her children, Princess Elizabeth and Princess Margaret Rose, to safety in Canada. The queen replied, "The children will not leave unless I do. I shall not leave unless their father does, and the King will not leave the country in any circumstances whatsoever."

Her words rang throughout Britain. Despite thousands of civilian bombing victims, the English faced up to the German bombardment with dignity, courage, and determination.

79 Lavrenti Beria

Scorched Earth and Non-Persons

COLLIER

Lavrenti Beria scorched the earth and locked up Stalin's enemies.

Lavrenti Beria's expertise was in two areas: leaving scorched earth and transforming enemies of the state into "non-persons."

Destroying the Enemy's Conquest

Unlike Adolf Hitler (Number 1), Napoleon took Moscow. But when French forces moved into the city, they found smoking ruins and ashes. The Russians had burned the city to the ground before they evacuated. Napoleon had won and lost. His long retreat from Moscow followed.

Joseph Stalin (Number 4) had learned from history and he put Beria in charge of the scorched earth policy.

Beria's major job during World War II was to make sure that nothing of any possible value to the enemy was left behind. Whatever territories or cities the Nazis conquered in the Soviet Union were destroyed: factories, buildings, power plants, railroad lines, motor vehicles, airports, harbors, bridges, tunnels, and general infrastructure. Often crops were burned in the fields and farm structures were put to the torch. Even farm animals became part of the scorched earth.

In short, advancing Nazi troops would find nothing but blackened earth as they moved into the Soviet Union.

Creating Non-Persons

Throughout most of his career, Beria was in charge of obliterating counterrevolutionaries by turning them into "non-persons"; Soviet dissidents disappeared without a trace. Sometimes prominent enemies of the state were given public "trials," but most often they were promptly shot or sent off to Siberian labor camps.

Second only to Stalin, Beria was the most feared individual in the Soviet Union. He headed the dreaded secret police, a monstrous presence that protected the Soviet dictatorship from any form of dissent or criticism.

Beria was one of the five Russians responsible for conducting the war against Hitler. The group included Stalin, Vyacheslav Molotov (Number 53), and Communist Party officials Georgi Malenkov and Kliment Voroshilov. Beria had significant responsibilities: scorched earth, the secret police, espionage, and discouraging Red Army retreats.

A Bolshevik Becomes Head of the Secret Police

Lavrenti Beria was born in Abkhasia, imperial Russia, in 1899. He was graduated from the Polytechnic Institute of Baku in 1919. While there he studied architecture and construction and formed a student Marxist group.

When the Russian Revolution erupted in 1917, he became a Bolshevik. He attempted a revolt against the rival Menshevik political group in Russian Georgia. He was arrested, imprisoned, and deported to Azerbaijon.

Back among his fellow Bolsheviks, Beria assumed a position that would identify him for the rest of his life. He became deputy chairman of a government agency called the Cheka. It was his first taste of life in the secret police. The Cheka not only caught and prosecuted accused offenders, but it judged them as well.

Beria had found his niche. From this point on, although the titles and geographic areas might change, Beria was in the secret police. Through the years, the agency names would change: the OGPU, the NKVD, the NKGB, and the KGB; the locations would vary from Azerbaijon, to Soviet Georgia, to the entire Soviet Union. His assignment might involve the use of secret agents, espionage, or counterespionage. His sphere of responsibility might be designated as internal security, or internal affairs, or state security, and his position would be called director, chairman, vice commissar, or commissar. The work, however, was basically the same. If someone's behavior was questionable, or if Stalin *thought* it was inappropriate, that was enough for imprisonment and sometimes execution.

Subduing the Opposition

The early Soviet Union was subjected to numerous attempted revolutions. Beria's job was to put down such rebellions, and he did so with great cruelty. During one uprising in

Georgia, the dissidents were treated so harshly that a visiting British labor group protested. During the 1930s, there were show trials in Moscow. Government officials, and later, Red Army officers were tried for treason and shot.

Sometimes those who had taken part in the purges were purged in turn. There is a famous underground joke whispered by the Russians at those times:

Three prisoners find themselves in the same jail cell. The first prisoner asks the second, "Why are *you* here?" He answers, "I supported Popov. What about *you*?" The second answers, "I was *against* Popov." Both then turn to the third prisoner and ask why he is there. He answers, "I'm Popov."

The work of the secret police was not, however, confined to the Soviet Union. The murder of Stalin's arch-enemy, Leon Trotsky, was carried out by a Soviet agent in Mexico City on April 20, 1940. Trotsky was hit over the head with a mountaineer's pickax and died.

Wartime Espionage

Hitler's attack on the Soviet Union in 1941 added to Beria's duties, including increased espionage and counterespionage. Through a spy in Tokyo, he learned that Japan would not attack the Soviet Union in the Far East, but would move against Dutch, British, and American bases in the Pacific. This information allowed Stalin to pull many of his troops out of Siberia and use them in the war against Hitler.

Beria's agents in the United States stole the secrets of the atomic bomb, and Beria was charged with running the Soviet project to build atomic weapons.

The man in charge of internal security was given the task of making sure that the Nazis would find only scorched earth in any Russian territory they occupied. He used specially trained units behind Soviet lines to ensure that Soviet troops did not retreat unless Stalin wanted them to do so.

After the victory over Nazi Germany, the power and outreach of Stalin and Beria went far beyond the Soviet borders, as Soviet espionage was extended throughout the globe.

After the War, a Non-Person

In 1953, Stalin died. Within the Soviet hierarchy, those who hated and feared Beria made their move. He was arrested, tried, and shot several months after Stalin's death.

Late that year, an American professor leaving Russia was stopped by a Soviet customs official. The professor was carrying Volume 2 of the *Great Soviet Encyclopedia*, the volume marked "B." The official took a razor blade and carefully cut out five pages of the encyclopedia, and then gave the professor five replacement pages. The five pages removed contained a laudatory account of the life of Lavrenti Beria. The new pages had material on a little-known hydroelectric plant and an expanded section on the Bering Sea.

Lavrenti Beria had become a "non-person."

80 Galeazzo Ciano

Mussolini's Heir Apparent

As Foreign Minister of Italy, Count Galeazzo Ciano (left of Hitler) had many occasions to meet with Hitler.

There were five condemned men in all: Galeazzo Ciano and four others. Each was tied to a chair, their backs to five separate firing squads consisting of six men, three kneeling in the front, and three others standing behind them. Ciano struggled briefly and tried to turn around to face his executioners. On the order to fire, shots rang out simultaneously from 30 rifles. Most of the chairs, including Ciano's, fell to the ground with their bound captives, and any man still alive was finished off with pistol shots to the head. Benito Mussolini's (Number 50) son-in-law, foreign minister, and original choice as il Duce's successor, was no more. Mussolini himself had sealed Ciano's fate.

An Ambivalent Fascist

Count Galeazzo Ciano was one of the major diplomats in Europe, both prior to and during the war. He was born in 1903 in Leghorn, Italy. His father had been an early supporter of Mussolini. Young Galeazzo shifted back and forth in his enthusiasm for Mussolini's Fascism. As a young teenager, he was a supporter; a few years later he became a critic. Still later, as a young man, he was a fervent admirer of Mussolini and his ideas for Italy.

Several years after Mussolini seized power in Rome, Ciano was graduated from the University of Rome with a law degree. He wrote about books and the theater for the official Fascist newspaper.

In 1925, Ciano took exams for the diplomatic service. He won appointments to successive posts in South America, China, and the Vatican.

In 1930, Ciano married Edda Mussolini, daughter of the Italian dictator. He became an immediate favorite of the Duce.

A Perceptive Foreign Minister

Ciano took part in the Italian war on Ethiopia. He led a bombing squadron over that underdeveloped African nation and dropped the first bombs. Ethiopia was conquered by the force of Italian arms.

Ciano became Mussolini's consul general in Shanghai. Later he would serve as president of a League of Nations commission investigating the Japanese bombing of that city.

In 1935, Count Ciano was appointed minister for press and propaganda. The following year, he became foreign minister of Italy, a position he held until mid-1943. Throughout much of this period, Ciano was portrayed in the press as a playboy. However true that might have been, his diaries and private papers show him to have had a firm grasp of international issues and perceptive views of the major political leaders of the time.

He took part in negotiating some of Italy's most important pacts and treaties, particularly the one with Nazi Germany establishing the Axis. The Rome-Berlin Axis was formed on October 25, 1936, and was formalized on May 22, 1939.

In mid-August 1939, Ciano told Adolf Hitler (Number 1) that an invasion of Poland would lead to a general European war. In September, when Poland was attacked by the Nazis, Ciano flatly opposed Italy's entry into the war. He told Mussolini that the country was simply not ready.

Mussolini would wait until France was on the verge of surrender in June 1940 to enter the war on the side of Hitler. At that time, it looked as if the Nazis had already won the war. But Italy soon discovered that the fighting had just begun and would require resources it did not have. Italian troops were bloodied on the Russian front and in North Africa. When Italy invaded Greece, Hitler had to send in German troops to bail out Mussolini's forces.

Executed for Treason

In the summer of 1943, Sicily was invaded by the British and Americans. Several weeks later, the Fascist Grand Council voted to overthrow Mussolini. Ciano voted with the majority against his father-in-law. That summer, a new government was established that began peace negotiations with the Allies.

Ciano was in trouble with the new Italian government. Fearing arrest, he decided to leave Italy. He apparently considered two havens: Spain and Nazi Germany. Because he could not arrange for Spain, he flew to Germany. It was a mistake; Hitler imprisoned him.

In September 1943, the Italian mainland was invaded and Italy surrendered. Mussolini, meanwhile, had been imprisoned by the new Italian government. He was freed by Hitler's commandos and set up as a puppet ruler in northern Italy.

Count Ciano was transported to northern Italy, where he was tried for treason by Mussolini's court.

Convicted and sentenced to death, the count had tried, unsuccessfully, to obtain poison so that he could take his own life. He was executed by a firing squad in the specified manner for the crime of treason: shot in the back. He and the four other condemned traitors were executed at Scalzi prison, Verona, on January 11, 1944.

If the count's end was brutal, Mussolini's was savage. Fifteen months later, as Hitler awaited his fate in a besieged Berlin bunker, the Duce was captured by Italian partisans in northern Italy. He was shot by a firing squad and hung up by his heels in Milan for the mob to vent their rage on his battered body.

Humiliation at Munich

DOUBLEDAY, DORAN & COMPANY, INC.

Eduard Benes, president of Czechoslovakia, had an army at his command. However, he could not fight off Nazi Germany alone. England and France had sold him out at Munich.

The two Czech diplomats had been sitting alone in the small room since 2 o'clock in the afternoon; it was now 7 p.m. For five hours they had been expecting to be called into the conference room next door. There, four men were making decisions about the fate of Czechoslovakia. It was September 29, 1938, in Munich, Germany.

The four men were among the most powerful in Europe at the time: Adolf Hitler (Number 1) of Nazi Germany, Neville Chamberlain (Number 66) of Great Britain, Benito Mussolini (Number 50) of Italy, and Eduard Daladier of France.

Betrayal at Munich

The Czech diplomats were never called in. At 7 p.m., the door opened and a member of the British delegation came out to tell them that all had been decided.

Decided? But what were the decisions? Hitler had been making territorial demands on Czechoslovakia for years, and Britain and France had always been protective of Czech interests.

Now decisions had been made about Czechoslovakia without the presence of the Czechs. The diplomats pressed for details, but they would have to wait. Three hours later, they were handed a map of Czechoslovakia. Certain areas had been marked off; these areas would be handed over to Nazi Germany.

The stunned Czechs would report to their president, Eduard Benes. It was truly a bitter pill for him. Benes had been one of those responsible for the founding of the new nation of Czechoslovakia following World War I. It originally had been a part of the Austro-Hungarian Empire.

Now, in 1938, after less than 20 years of independence, the small democracy was being sliced up, and its allies were participating in the carving.

Eduard Benes represents a small country that was abandoned and humiliated in order to appease Hitler. The Munich conference convinced Hitler that the Western democracies would not stand up against him. Hitler was wrong; resistance and war would come a year later.

Czechoslovakia Becomes Hitler's Prime Target

Benes was born in 1884 in Bohemia, then part of Austria-Hungary. After World War I, the Treaty of Versailles divided that empire into a number of states, and Benes had helped create Czechoslovakia. In 1935, Benes became president at the same time that troubles began with Hitler.

The Führer had cast greedy eyes on Czech territory for years. The following year, Nazi propaganda chief Joseph Goebbels (Number 44) accused Czechoslovakia of harboring Soviet planes and pilots within its borders. It was a serious charge, and Benes ordered that the Czech-German border fortifications be strengthened. The propaganda was stepped up in 1937 when Czechoslovakia was accused of mistreating ethnic Germans.

In February 1938, Hitler gave a speech in which he promised he would protect the Germans in Czechoslovakia. The Czechs responded that they would defend themselves. The following month, European geography changed. Hitler annexed Austria, and Czechoslovakia now found itself hemmed in on three sides by the new German borders.

When German troops massed on the Czech borders, Benes mobilized 100,000 men. Britain and France stood strongly behind the Czechs and the crisis appeared to ease politically, if not militarily. The German army began reinforcing its border with France and called for a buildup of airpower.

The Crisis Escalates

A more dangerous crisis developed in the summer of 1938. Nazi Germany said it planned to hold "maneuvers," requiring the activation of 750,000 reservists. Britain and France responded by calling up their reserves.

The crisis continued to escalate: more threats by Hitler and more reserves activated by Britain and France. By mid-September 1938, war seemed imminent. A meeting in Berchtesgaden had failed to achieve a settlement. Hitler then called for a meeting at the highest levels to take place in Munich. The top leaders of Germany, Italy, Britain, and France would attend. At first, Hitler flatly refused to have any Czechs invited. Then he relented, as long as the Czechs would not take part in any discussions, but instead be available in another room for any consultation. The consultation never took place.

It was there in Munich that the four political figures met and gave away a piece of Czech territory, destroying its sovereignty.

The Sacrifice of a Country

Why did the British and the French submit to Hitler's demands? Part of the reason was that their countries were not yet ready for war. The sacrifice of Czechoslovakia, however, was particularly cruel. Theoretically, Czechoslovakia could have refused to accept the deal and fought all alone. It would have had to face a civil war internally (with German ethnics) and Hitler's panzers externally. It would have lost.

After the Munich conference, Benes resigned and left for Britain. He knew that Hitler would be back for more. Sure enough, five months later, the Nazis occupied all of Czechoslovakia.

When World War II broke out, Benes established a provisional government for Czechoslovakia in London. When the Red Army drove the Nazis out of Czechoslovakia, Benes returned to take part in a coalition government with the Communists. He resigned in 1948 and died several months later.

Betrayal and Death

JOHN MURRAY

Wladyslaw Sikorski, at right, is welcomed to London by King George VI and Queen Elizabeth. Sikorski would head the Polish government-in-exile.

The story of Wladyslaw Sikorski during World War II is basically the story of Poland: one of betrayal and death.

Sikorski was a Polish general and statesman who dreamed of using a Polish army alongside the Red Army to drive the Nazis out of Poland. That was the dream. The reality was a Polish army without guns, without ammunition, and short on rations. Reality was rotting corpses of Polish army officers buried in mass graves in the Katyn forest. Reality was a suspicious plane crash that killed Sikorski near Gibraltar. It was not the first time that Poland had been betrayed during World War II, and it would not be the last.

A Nation Struggles with Its Independence

Sikorski was born in Tuszow, Poland, in 1881. A professional soldier, he saw action both in World War I and the Russian-Polish engagement of 1920. The latter campaign led to the expulsion of the Bolsheviks from Poland. It was the period after the Treaty of Versailles had been signed, and Poland was struggling with its newly won freedom. The transition from Russian dominance to independent nation did not come smoothly.

Following the assassination of Poland's president in 1922, Sikorski, then chief of the general staff, was asked to form a new government. He became minister of the interior and proclaimed martial law in Warsaw. After a few years, his government resigned, but Sikorski became minister of war in the new cabinet.

Sikorski retired from the army in 1926. He took the time to write about military matters—the Russian-Polish campaign of 1920 and a book *Future War*, which was widely acclaimed by military strategists.

An Impossible Collaboration with the Russians

Poland was invaded on two fronts in September 1939. Nazi Germany attacked from the west and the Soviet Union from the east. Poland was partitioned between the two countries. The invasion of Poland officially began World War II in Europe.

A Polish government-in-exile was established, first in France and then in England. Sikorski became its premier.

In June 1941, Adolf Hitler (Number 1) attacked the Soviet Union. Two months later, the Polish government in London made an arrangement with the Soviets to create a Polish army on Soviet soil to fight the Germans. Polish General Wladyslaw Anders, captured by the Soviets after their invasion of Poland, was released from a Soviet prison to set up the new army.

From this point, the history is unclear. According to the Soviets, a Polish army was organized but was never sent into battle, and eventually it left the country through Iran.

According to the Poles, their army was shortchanged on everything, from weapons to rations. What was worse, Anders, who was raising his army from Polish prisoners of war, had heard reports of Polish war prisoners being murdered by the Soviets.

The collaboration was obviously not going to work. The Polish army did leave the Soviet Union. It would become part of the British 8th Army and fight, with distinction, in Italy.

The Discovery in the Katyn Forest

But the story of executed prisoners troubled the Polish government back in London. Was it true? In April 1943, Nazi Propaganda Minister Joseph Goebbels (Number 44) announced the discovery of mass graves in the Katyn forest of Poland. According to the Nazis, who had occupied the area after driving out the Russians, thousands of Polish army officers had been shot in the back of the head by the Russians and buried in the Katyn forest. The massacre was said to have taken place in 1940, when the Soviets still occupied the area.

Sikorski asked the Russians for an explanation. The Soviets were shocked, *shocked* that an ally could ask such a question. Of course it was the Nazis who did things like this.

Sikorski was furious. In his heart, he felt that the Soviets were probably respon-sible. But at that point in the war, he did not want to disrupt what was a shaky alliance, at best, between the Western Allies and the Soviet Union. What was important was to continue the war against Hitler and restore freedom to Poland. A Polish request for an investigation by the International Red Cross was withdrawn.

But the Katyn forest massacre was a wound that would not heal. The bad blood between the Soviets and Poles in London would have both short-range and long-range implications.

Assassination and Final Betrayal

On July 4, 1943, Sikorski's plane, taking off from a runway near Gibraltar, crashed. Many years later there were rumors that the team of Burgess, Maclean, and Philby (Englishmen who had become notorious Soviet spies) had a hand in the assassination of Sikorski, though details were never disclosed.

Joseph Stalin (Number 4) virtually ignored the Poles in London, setting up his own puppet government. When the war was over, the Soviet Union ended up with a big piece of Poland; Poland was given part of Germany in return. The betrayal was complete. It would be years before Poland was truly free and independent.

As for the mystery of Katyn forest, it was solved officially in April 1995 when a Rus-sian spokesman named A. Krayushkin revealed at a press conference in Smolensk that the Soviet secret police had been responsible for carrying out the killings. In all, he said, more than 20,000 Polish officers and men, all prisoners of war, had been executed.

Sikorski's death remains a mystery to this day.

83 Joseph W. Stilwell

The Mission That Failed

NATIONAL ARCHIVES

This happy picture of Joseph W. Stilwell with Chiang Kai-shek and Madame Chiang is deceptive. The relationship was strained because Stilwell believed that reforms were badly needed in Chiang's regime.

T here is an old saying that truth is the first casualty of war. That may well be so when military realities clash with civilian expectations. But the military must always deal with accurate intelligence information and face harsh truth. One cannot win a battle or a war wearing blinders.

Convincing a Reluctant Enemy

The epitome of plain talking during World War II was Joseph W. Stilwell. Dubbed "Vinegar Joe" for his blunt, sometimes acidic, comments, the general was given one of the toughest assignments of the war: how to deal with an ally who was reluctant to fight.

Stilwell's mission was to go to China and confer with Chiang Kai-shek (Number 87), find out how to get the Chinese army into fighting shape, and then mount a military campaign against the Japanese. Stilwell believed this could be done by a critical look at the problems confronting Chiang's army and regime. But when truth butted up against political considerations, politics usually won.

Multiple Assignments to China

Joseph W. Stilwell was born in 1883 in Florida. He graduated from West Point in 1904 and was initially stationed in the Philippines. He taught foreign languages and coached sports at West Point.

Shortly after China's Manchu Dynasty collapsed in 1911, Stilwell was assigned to China.

In 1917, after the United States entered World War I, he was sent to France, where he distinguished himself as an intelligence officer during the Saint Mihiel campaign.

When the war ended, Stilwell was reassigned to China. It would be the first of three such tours over the next two decades, during which he would witness many social, economic, and political changes in that country.

Throughout the 19th century, parts of China had been occupied by the major European powers. Post-Manchu China was struggling from both internal and external pressures—local warlords at home and aggression from abroad.

In 1931, Japan had occupied Chinese Manchuria. Six years later, Japan began a war of conquest on the Chinese mainland, but it was only after Pearl Harbor was attacked that the United States began providing military assistance to China.

However, once in the war, the United States still focused on defeating Adolf Hitler (Number 1) in Europe.

The China-Burma-India Theater

Early in the war, Stilwell headed two different infantry units. George Marshall (Number 5) tapped him for the invasion of North Africa. The U.S. Army chief of staff was trying out his field commanders for eventual service in the invasion of Europe. Stilwell might well have been another George S. Patton (Number 11), Omar Bradley (Number 33), or even Dwight D. Eisenhower (Number 7).

Fate intervened. Another American general had been slated to look into the China-Burma-India theater of operations, especially the status of the Chinese army. When that general withdrew from the assignment, Stilwell was assigned the job. It was not going to be easy. Because America's emphasis was on Europe, that theater received many of the supplies and reinforcements that might have been earmarked for the Pacific.

In March 1942, Stilwell was put in charge of all American forces in China, Burma, and India. May of that year brought defeat in Burma. Addressing a press conference in India, Stilwell, never one to mince words, said, "I claim we got a hell of a beating and it's humiliating as hell." A year later, he would return to Burma to avenge the disaster.

An Impossible Assignment

Stilwell's chief mission lay ahead: to get Chiang Kai-shek and the Chinese army to take a more active part in the war against Japan. The assignment became agonizing for a man of Stilwell's integrity and temperament. From Stilwell's papers and diaries, it is plain that the American general despised Generalissimo Chiang and his regime. To his personal abhorrence, Stilwell found that the Chinese army in particular was a cesspool of corruption. What was worse, Stilwell believed that Chiang was reluctant to fight the Japanese because he feared that the Chinese Communists would take over the country.

Stilwell had the highest regard for the individual Chinese soldier, but he felt that too many of China's army leaders were thieves, swindlers, and smugglers, getting rich on the blood of their troops. Some Chinese officers overstated the size of their forces to get pay allotments for nonexistent troops; others used transport for smuggling purposes, left their sick and wounded soldiers behind, or sold lend-lease material to the enemy.

The China problem was politically loaded, not just in Chungking, China, but in Washington, D.C. There, a China lobby worked overtime to send more war material to China and push for more reinforcements.

Stilwell tried several approaches. He was Chiang's chief of staff, but Chiang would not let him operate. He was put in charge of lend-lease distribution, but this did not sit at all well with Chiang and his generals, who were violently offended by the appearance of distrust.

A Failed Mission

The politics, especially back in the States, could not be overcome. There, the powerful China lobby worked overtime to have Stilwell recalled. They succeeded in October 1944. There are news photos of Stilwell being decorated by Chiang before he left China. Stilwell could not have looked more solemn. The mission had failed.

Stilwell ended the war in command of U.S. forces on Okinawa. After the war, he became head of the Western Defense Command in the United States.

Joseph W. Stilwell died in 1946.

84 Jonathan Wainwright

Last Message from Corregidor

NATIONAL ARCHIVES

After more than three years in Japanese captivity, a gaunt Jonathan Wainwright, at right, is embraced by his former commander, Douglas MacArthur.

It was May 6, 1942, on the island of Corregidor in Manila Bay. The island was under Japanese siege. Deep inside one of the tunnels, a young radio operator pounded out his message on the radio key, transmitting the story of the island's final hours. He had been told to keep his transmission going, that a message was being prepared.

The radio operator kept the line open by describing the terrible pounding of Japanese siege guns, the wounded American soldiers filling up the tunnels, the soldiers destroying their weapons and bawling like babies, and the affection of the men for their commanding general, Jonathan Wainwright.

Courage and Decency in the War's Darkest Days

Finally, after many hours, the message he had been waiting for was handed to him. It was from Wainwright to the president of the United States.

It began, "With broken heart and head bowed in sadness but not in shame I report to your excellency that today I must arrange terms for the surrender of the fortified islands of Manila Bay...."

Then the transmission stopped abruptly. Apparently the Japanese had managed to cut off the communications link. In any case, it would be years before the rest of that message would become known.

Jonathan Wainwright is a symbol of courage and decency during the darkest days of the war in the Pacific.

Assuming Command of the Philippines

Wainwright was born in 1883 in Walla Walla, Washington. He graduated from West Point in 1906 and served in the Philippines. During World War I, he rose to the rank of lieutenant colonel as chief of staff in two different army units, the 82nd Division and the Third Army. During the 1930s, he held posts in Fort Myer, Virginia, and San Antonio, Texas. In 1940, he was sent to the Philippines, where he served under Douglas MacArthur (Number 8). The following year, the Japanese attacked Pearl Harbor and invaded the Philippines.

In March 1942, MacArthur was ordered to Australia, and Wainwright, now a lieutenant general, assumed command of all American forces throughout the Philippine Islands.

The main force of American and Filipino troops was on the Bataan peninsula on the main island of Luzon. The Bataan garrison was under the command of Major General Edward King, Jr. The defenders of Bataan ran out of both food and ammunition. After eating all the dogs and mules, they had turned to eating monkeys. When Japanese forces came within artillery range of the American field hospitals, King, fearing a slaughter, surrendered Bataan. The decision was made on his own, without consulting Wainwright.

Wainwright continued to fight from Corregidor island, but when the Japanese established a foothold on the island, the Allies were doomed. Before the capitulation, Wainwright officially transferred command to other officers on the other islands of the Philippines. The Japanese would not agree and wanted him to surrender the entire Philippines.

Wainwright faced a terrible dilemma. His men on Corregidor were already disarmed, but the Japanese told him that if he did not surrender the entire Philippines, they would resume the fighting. That would have meant a massacre of the garrison. Reluctantly, he announced the surrender of the Philippines and, on the express order of the Japanese, went on radio to command all American forces to lay down their arms throughout the islands. MacArthur was furious, telling George Marshall (Number 5) that Wainwright must have lost his senses.

Wainwright spent more than three years in a Japanese prisoner-of-war camp, sharing the privations of his men.

As the surrender of Japan was being choreographed, Marshall suggested to MacArthur that Wainwright attend the ceremonies. The gaunt figure, his clothes hanging on an emaciated frame, was there on the U.S.S. *Missouri* to bear witness, along with British General Arthur Percival, who had surrendered Singapore to the Japanese.

Honoring a Hero

With the war over, Wainwright's complete message to President Roosevelt (Number 2) was made public for the first time. It was one of the documents of American history that was displayed on the "Freedom Train" on its trip around the country after the war. This is how Wainwright's message ended:

> *There is a limit of human endurance and that limit has long since been passed. Without prospect of relief I feel it is my duty to my country and to my gallant troops to end this useless effusion of blood and human sacrifice.*
>
> *If you agree, Mr. President, please say to the nation that my troops and I have accomplished all that is humanly possible and that we have upheld the best traditions of the United States Army.*
>
> *May God bless and preserve you and guide you and the nation in the effort to ultimate victory.*
>
> *With profound regret and with continued pride in my gallant troops I go to meet the Japanese commander. Goodbye, Mr. President.*

Following the fall of Corregidor, Marshall had wanted Wainwright to receive the Congressional Medal of Honor, but MacArthur had opposed it. Now, Marshall proceeded to honor the hero of Corregidor.

Jonathan Wainwright died in 1953.

The Sullivan Brothers/
The Four Chaplains

On Brotherhood

NATIONAL ARCHIVES   U.S. NAVY

On the left, he five Sullivan brothers lived together, enlisted together, became shipmates together, and died together. On the right, the doomed troop transport *Dorchester*, four chaplains gave up their lifejackets to those who had none, linked arms, and went down with the ship.

D eath is the essence of war. When it comes to warriors, death is usually accepted by those who mourn. It is the supreme sacrifice, above and beyond the call of duty. It is patriotism and courage, and all the stuff that Fourth-of-July speeches are made of.

Some deaths, however, come about under such extraordinary circumstances that they touch the very heart and soul of a people and a nation. These are two such examples: five brothers named Sullivan, and four chaplains on a doomed troop transport who made a fateful decision.

The Sullivan Brothers

Gunner's mate 2/c George, Coxswain Francis, Seaman 2/c Joseph, Seaman 2/c Madison, and Seaman 2/c Albert Sullivan were born in Waterloo, Iowa. At the time of their deaths, they ranged in age from 20 to 29.

After a friend of theirs was killed at Pearl Harbor, the five brothers enlisted together, requesting that they be permitted to serve on the same ship.

All five were stationed on the light cruiser *Juneau*. In November 1942, the ship was torpedoed near Savo Island during the naval battle off Guadalcanal. The five brothers perished. Following that tragedy, the U.S. Navy established a new policy to keep close relatives from serving together on the same warship.

In September 1943, the U.S. Navy christened a new destroyer *The Sullivans*, in honor of the brothers' memory; it saw action in the invasion of Okinawa.

The Ultimate Sacrifice

In wartime, death comes swiftly and unexpectedly. In some cases, however, death comes through choosing to save others. The American troop transport the *Dorchester* was in the North Atlantic heading for Greenland when it was hit by a torpedo in 1943. Those soldiers on board prepared to abandon ship.

The *Dorchester* did not hold lifejackets for all the passengers. Protestant chaplains Clark Poling and George Fox, Catholic chaplain John Washington, and Jewish chaplain Alexander Goode gave theirs up to other soldiers. Then the four army lieutenants linked arms and went down with the sinking ship.

●●●

The accounts of the deaths of the Sullivan brothers and the *Dorchester's* courageous chaplains galvanized the nation. All America grieved with the Sullivan family and marveled at the beneficent action of the four chaplains. These were the ultimate statements of brotherhood and sacrifice. At a critical time in the war, these accounts inspired patriotism and spurred efforts to carry on the fight to final victory.

86 Charles Lindbergh, Jr.

QUARRIE

The America First Committee, which opposed entry into the war, had many prominent members. Charles A. Lindbergh, Jr., was a national hero and one of those members.

He had been an authentic American hero, the first man to fly solo across the Atlantic. He had seen for himself what kind of air force the Nazis had built up in Germany. Now he was saying that Adolf Hitler (Number 1) was far too powerful and that America should stay out of this European war.

How could anyone fail to trust this clean-cut, shy, intelligent young man? He was the perfect poster boy for the America First Committee. He was eager to be used, and they used him.

Charles A. Lindbergh, Jr. represents those well-organized isolationists who fought against American involvement in World War II.

A Tragic Hero

Charles A. Lindbergh, Jr. was born in 1902 in Detroit, Michigan. As a boy, he was fascinated by flying. He took flying lessons and joined the Missouri National Guard as a pilot, then earned money flying the U.S. mail. In 1927, Lindbergh became the first person to fly solo across the Atlantic. When he landed outside Paris, he was mobbed by French crowds. Overnight he became an international hero.

Lindbergh married the poetess Anne Morrow on May 27, 1929. Tragedy struck three years later, when their infant son was kidnapped and murdered in 1932. It was, at the time, the crime of the century, and the media exploitation was savage. Following the trial and the conviction of the kidnapper, Bruno Hauptmann, the Lindberghs moved to England.

Refuge in Europe

The Lindberghs toured Europe, making several visits to Nazi Germany. There Hermann Goering (Number 43) presented him with a medal.

The U.S. military attaché in Berlin asked Lindbergh to take a close look at German military airpower. The Nazis obliged, taking the famous aviator on a tour and carefully arranging for German military aircraft to fly repeatedly from one field to another. Lindbergh was seeing many of the same planes over and over again, and, decieved by the tactic, he reported a huge Nazi air force. Later he would comment, "The German air fleet is more supreme in air than the British fleet at sea."

In mid-September 1938, he reported that Germany intended "to extend her influence still further to the east within the next year." He added: "There would be nothing gained by a military attempt on the part of France and England to stop the German movement toward the east. The opportunity to do this was lost several years ago when German policies went unopposed."

It was part truth and part propaganda, but the conclusion could have come right from the German Propaganda Ministry: The Nazis are invincible, so why try?

His viewpoint might have been näivete, or even genuine belief on Lindbergh's part, but the fact was that he was parroting the official Nazi line.

A Spokesperson for Isolationism

When war broke out in 1939, there was intense opposition to any U.S. involvement. The American isolationist movement was strong and heavily financed. An organization called the America First Committee was founded in September 1940 by a group of business executives and political leaders. In a short time, it boasted more than 800,000 members.

Lindbergh made speeches throughout the country, urging America to stay out of the war. Tagging along with the America First supporters were members of the American Communist Party, who often chanted, "The Yanks are *not* coming!" Because of the Nazi-Soviet pact, the two organizations were strange bedfellows, equally against the United States getting in the war.

Lindbergh, who was embarrassed by the Communist support, was genuinely relieved when Hitler attacked the Soviet Union in June 1941. The Communists would soon have a new slogan: "A Second Front Now!"

The climax of the aviator's campaign came in a rally in Des Moines, Iowa, on September 11, 1941. At that time, Lindbergh said: "The three most important groups who have been pressing this country toward war are the British, the Jewish, and the Roosevelt administration." Once again, it was the line straight from Berlin: that the war was one big Jewish plot. Lindbergh was denounced on all sides.

A Civilian Volunteer during the War

After the attack on Pearl Harbor, the America First Committee faded away. Lindbergh volunteered to fight in the Army Air Corps, but his request was denied. Instead, he flew missions in the Pacific as a civilian volunteer. From all indications, his service was carried out with both courage and dedication.

After the war, he consulted with aircraft manufacturers as well as military and naval officials. Charles A. Lindbergh died in 1974.

The Agony of China

SIMON AND SCHUSTER

Chiang Kai-shek had been fighting a losing battle against the Japanese for years. Now, with the United States in the war, he hoped for the military assistance needed to drive out the enemy.

Every government, democratic or otherwise, must protect its people. If it cannot protect them, it must be in a position to retaliate against those who would abuse its citizens. If it cannot do that, it loses its legitimacy.

For eight years, from 1937 to 1945, the Republic of China was at war with Japanese invaders, but the brutality of the Japanese against the Chinese population went unpunished by China's government throughout the war. It was an agony that crept into the very soul of the Chinese. Even today it remains a part of the national consciousness.

A Government under Siege from All Sides

Chiang Kai-shek was the head of the Chinese government during the Japanese atrocities. He could not—some historians say *would* not—do very much to retaliate. There were a number of reasons for his inadequacy. He had mainly an untrained army, few modern weapons, and no understanding of modern warfare. More importantly, he was virtually surrounded by perceived danger and uncertainty. It was not just the Japanese at his front; it was the Chinese Communists at his back; it was individual warlords throughout the provinces. He could not protect his people, and he could not punish their tormentors.

Perhaps Chiang Kai-shek could have influenced the course of the war more significantly, considering that China was not only at war longer than any other country, but had the greatest population and suffered the most casualties. Yet Chiang's influence during the war was relatively minor.

A Military Career

Chiang Kai-shek was born in 1887 in the village of Chikou in the Chinese province of Chekiaang. After a poverty-stricken boyhood, he joined the provincial army and the military became his career. He was sent to Tokyo to study at the Military State College. Following graduation, he spent some time in the Japanese army. While in Japan, he met Sun Yat-sen, a Chinese visionary seeking the end of China's Manchu dynasty.

In 1911, a revolution overthrew the Chinese emperor. There was a struggle for power. Sun Yat-sen emerged as the major Chinese leader, but various warlords held on to power in local provinces. Chiang was one of Sun's closest supporters.

In 1925, when Sun died, Chiang became commander of the Nationalist Army. He attempted to clear out the warlords and unify the country, and he received the backing of the Soviet Union for this task.

Cooperation with the Communists, however, did not last, because they wanted economic and social changes that Chiang opposed. Chinese Communists, forced out of the government, called on their supporters to make the "Long March" to northern China, where they could regroup and plot their return. In 1936, Chiang was kidnapped by the Chinese Communists but released a few weeks later. No one knows why.

War Comes Early to China

As far as China is concerned, World War II began in 1937, when Japan invaded China. Though Chiang and the Chinese Communists talked about a united front against Japan, neither one trusted the other.

The Japanese moved quickly, occupying the port of Shanghai and then moving against the capital city of Nanking.

The city fell in December 1937, and the agony of the Chinese people began: Unarmed men were rounded up and machine-gunned, women were raped, babies were bayoneted. The Chinese casualties ran not in the tens of thousands, but in the hundreds of thousands.

The story of Nanking made the newspapers at the time. So horrifying were the reports that some people abroad may have shrugged off the story as propaganda.

Chiang Kai-shek moved his government to Chungking to establish a new capital. But he could not punish the enemy. Nor could he protect his people when Japanese troops occupied other Chinese cities. The Japanese acted with complete impunity, and the Chinese people knew it.

Limited Aid from Allies as War Goes on

Chiang asked the United States and the Western European democracies for military weapons to fight off the Japanese. Some of the European countries provided weapons, but once the war came to Europe that was no longer possible. Some help came from the United States, but America had neutrality laws that made it difficult to provide help for the Chinese military. Supplies were supposedly earmarked for civilian needs only.

Late in 1941, when war between Japan and the United States threatened, the "Flying Tigers" came to Chiang's aid. These were American volunteers flying American planes. Chiang was finally getting some real military support. Once Pearl Harbor was bombed, Chiang felt that his time had come to drive out the Japanese. But the United States and England had taken a "Europe: first" approach: China would get plenty of war materials, but full-scale war against Japan would come only after Adolf Hitler (Number 1) was defeated.

The charming and sophisticated Madame Chiang Kai-shek (Number 78) came to the United States to lobby for immediate action in Asia. She addressed Congress but was unsuccessful in changing American military strategy. She did, however, set in motion what became known as the "China lobby," a group of congressmen, scholars, media people, and others who campaigned on behalf of China. The lobby was active during and long after the war.

Joseph W. Stilwell (Number 83) was sent to China to evaluate military actions against Japan. In his view, the regime was corrupt: Chiang was not capable of taking on the Japanese in any major way, and he was unwilling to let Stilwell do it. The war continued, and Chiang was kept supplied via truck over the Burma Road or via plane "over the Hump" (the Himalayan mountains). The Sino-Japanese war went on, but it did not have a high priority for the Allies.

Civil War and the Fall of a Government

When World War II ended, Chiang faced civil war. The Chinese Communists, supported by the Soviets, moved against Chiang. George Marshall (Number 5) was sent by President Truman (Number 14) to negotiate an end to the civil war, but after a temporary pause, the fighting resumed.

Chiang's government could not be saved. Chiang took the remains of his army and civilian supporters and established himself on the island of Taiwan. As of this writing, there are still "two Chinas."

Chiang Kai-shek died in 1975.

88 Tadeusz Bor-Komorowski

Leader of an Underground Army

QUARRIE

As the Red Army arrived at the gates of Warsaw, Tadeusz Bor-Komorowski called for an uprising to help the Russians battle the Nazi occupiers. The Red Army held off its attack on the city, until Warsaw looked like this and the underground army was destroyed.

In July 1944, General Bor heard the words he had been waiting for. The Red Army was nearing Nazi-held Warsaw, and the Russian radio was urging the Poles to rise up and crush the German tyrants. On August 1, as leader of the Polish Home Army, Bor gave the order to begin an uprising. After five years of Nazi occupation, the liberation of Warsaw was at hand, and the Poles would help the Russians drive out the hated occupiers.

Poles began firing on German troops throughout the city. It was the perfect time for the Red Army to enter Warsaw. Then a strange thing happened to the advancing Russian army. It stopped at the Vistula River and did...nothing.

Leading the Resistance Movement

The military leader of the Warsaw uprising was born in Poland as Tadeusz Komorowski in 1895. Following the end of World War I, Poland, which had been a part of Imperial Russia, became an independent nation. Komorowski joined the Polish Army and rose to the rank of colonel. In 1939, Nazi Germany and the Soviet Union invaded Poland and divided up the country.

With the Polish army disbanded, Komorowski became part of the resistance movement in Nazi-occupied Poland. He took the pseudonym "Bor." After that, he was known as Bor-Komorowski, General Bor, or just plain Bor. He bided his time, slowly building up his people's army.

Abandoned by the Red Army

With the Russian army poised to move into Warsaw, General Bor's little army began the uprising. The Germans were caught off guard by the ferocity of the Polish assault and brought in heavy artillery and dive bombers to put down the rebellion.

Meanwhile, the Red Army just sat and waited. It soon became obvious that Joseph Stalin (Number 4) was not interested in the survival of a true Polish army, no matter how amateur and ill-equipped. The question was no longer when or if Stalin would help Bor and his fighters. The issue was whether he would allow the Western Allies to do so.

Western Allies Withhold Aid

Back in London, the Polish government-in-exile was putting pressure on Winston Churchill (Number 3) to have the British and Americans supply the Polish Home Army with food and weapons. The official Soviet position was that it did not want to get involved in the "adventure."

Churchill tried to get Stalin to agree to allow the Western Allies to fly over Warsaw, drop supplies, and then use Soviet airfields to refuel before the long flight back. Stalin refused.

The British prime minister prepared a message to Stalin in which he threatened to cut off all military aid to the Soviets if they did not allow the use of Russian airfields to aid the Polish resistance. The message was never sent. Churchill, angry and frustrated by a situation beyond his control, might have been blowing off steam. The Poles never got aid.

The Warsaw Uprising

Two months after the uprising began, it ended with the surrender of General Bor. An estimated 60,000 Poles lost their lives in the uprising, the vast majority of them civilians.

What happened in Warsaw in late 1944 was similar to the uprising in the Warsaw Ghetto in the spring of 1943. The leader at that time was Mordecai Anielewicz (Number 97). There again, people who had an opportunity to help the underdog stood by and did nothing.

During the Warsaw Ghetto uprising, the world paid little attention to what was going on. Polish life beyond the Ghetto went on as usual. Except for a few weapons provided by the Polish underground groups, the Jews fought with the handful of weapons at their command.

During the uprising in the city of Warsaw, however, the world was very much aware of what was happening. Churchill's attempt to supply arms to the Poles failed and the Russians waited until the battle was over to move into Warsaw.

Upon his surrender, General Bor was sent to a concentration camp. He was freed by victorious Allied armies.

After the war, Bor was part of the Polish government-in-exile in London. He then worked for a Polish relief agency. He died in 1966.

89 Claus von Stauffenberg

The Plot That Failed

COLLIER

Claus von Stauffenberg placed a bomb in Hitler's headquarters, but the Führer escaped death.

It was called the "Wolf's Lair." Located in Rastenburg, the headquarters was one of Adolf Hitler's (Number 1) meeting places, where he could confer with his key military leaders.

This time the meeting was called for 12:30 p.m. on July 20, 1944. The officers assembled, Hitler arrived, and Colonel von Stauffenberg greeted the Nazi dictator. Shortly after the session started, the colonel excused himself to make a phone call. He placed his briefcase on the floor next to Hitler and left the room. He had 10 minutes to get out before the bomb exploded.

Von Stauffenberg, well outside the building, saw the explosion. Hitler had to be dead, he thought, but he was wrong. An officer had moved the briefcase because it was in the way, and the Führer had survived. He would wreak terrible vengeance on the conspirators.

Nazi Opponents Powerless against the Führer

Claus von Stauffenberg appears here representing those Germans who secretly opposed Hitler. Some of those in the anti-Nazi movement were military officers, some were in the government, and some were civilians. Their opposition to Hitler's policies could not be expressed publicly. There was, of course, no other political party or opposing political leader, nor was there an alternative to the Nazi-controlled press and radio.

The opposition to Hitler was not only small in numbers, but impotent in its ability to bring about change. As time went on, it became clear that as long as Hitler lived, he would continue to exercise absolute power over Germany. The only way to remove him from power was to kill him and have his Nazi henchmen rounded up and stripped of their power. Only one group in the underground could do that: the army. That was the rationale of the plotters.

Over the years, several attempts had been made to kill Hitler. All had failed. Once it was a last-minute change in Hitler's schedule; another time it was a bomb that failed to detonate. But on July 20, 1944, von Stauffenberg would make sure the bomb would be there when Hitler was; he would deliver it personally.

Plotting to Kill Hitler

Count Claus von Stauffenberg was born in 1907 in Upper Franconia, Germany. A member of a distinguished military family, he became a military cadet, attended the War Academy, and then was hand-picked for the German General Staff.

When World War II came, he fought in Poland, France, and the Soviet Union. In North Africa, he was severely wounded by a strafing plane. He lost his left eye and right arm and suffered other serious injuries.

During his recuperation, von Stauffenberg had a lot of time to think. Back on the Russian front, he had seen and heard of terrible atrocities committed against the civilian population. After some reflection, the young count concluded that Hitler was the anti-Christ and decided that the Nazi dictator must be killed.

There had been small underground units in Germany for years. The colonel joined a group of army officers who also hated Hitler, and soon the plot to kill the Führer was set in motion. The code name for the plot was "Valkyrie," which is ironic, because Valkyrie was also the name of a plan by the Nazis to put down any possible rebellion by foreign slave laborers inside Germany.

The Valkyrie assassination plot included the killing of Hitler and possibly some of his top aides and the overthrow of the Nazi regime. This could only be carried out by army units under the command of key German generals.

Execution for the Plotters

Following the explosion at Wolf's Lair, von Stauffenberg flew off to Berlin. Even as he was on route, word had gotten to Berlin of the attempted assassination. Joseph Goebbels (Number 44) immediately announced that Hitler was alive and that the conspiracy had been crushed.

Von Stauffenberg and some of the other officers were shot that night; they were the lucky ones. Others would later be put on trial and sentenced to particularly brutal deaths: They were strangled with piano wire and hung up on meat hooks. Their death throes were filmed with the intention of having the films shown at military academies as a lesson for anyone thinking of betraying the Führer. The one time it was shown, horrified cadets ran from the screening room. The film was never shown publicly again.

Some historians claim that Hitler would watch the film alone or sometimes show it to guests. Other historians dispute that.

In any case, the film disappeared after the war.

90 Anne Frank

Keeping a Diary

ANDREW MOORE

In a secret annex of this factory building in Amsterdam, Anne Frank hid from the Nazis. She was discovered and never survived the war—but her diary did.

A nne Frank's life was so brief. She never reached the age of 16.

That is not much time to live, and hardly time enough to have influenced anybody about anything.

During the war, anonymous Jews died by the millions. Their only identification was a tattooed number on the arm. When the concentration camps were liberated, their bodies were stacked up like cordwood, ready for cremation.

Anne Frank, however, gave a human face to six million anonymous corpses.

Hiding from the Nazi Threat

Born in 1929 in Frankfort on Main, Germany, Anne Frank's family moved to Amsterdam when Adolf Hitler (Number 1) came to power. There, Anne, her older sister, and her parents began a new life. Then the Nazis invaded Holland. As danger neared, the Franks arranged to hide out in a "secret annex" behind a warehouse building in Amsterdam. Four other Jews joined them, including a boy a little older than Anne.

They were discovered after living there for two years. Except for Anne's father, Otto, all perished. Anne died of typhus in the Bergen-Belsen concentration camp in 1945.

Humanity Amid Brutality

Anne's is not a unique story. It was typical of probably tens of thousands of Jews who tried to hide, were discovered or betrayed, taken away, and killed outright or allowed to die of starvation, disease, or exposure or as the result of medical experiments on their bodies.

What made Anne special is that she kept a diary during the years in hiding. She told her diary what was going on in the hiding place, what people said and did and argued over. It sounds quite ordinary, but under the circumstances, it is actually quite extraordinary. The adolescent girl becomes a young woman, gets her first kiss, and talks of hopes and dreams that she will never realize.

What shines through in her words is a humanity that defies the shadow of impending brutality and death.

A Legacy of Hope

The diary she left behind in the secret annex would be published in many languages after the war ended. Plays, motion pictures, and television documentaries have been written and made about Anne and her life. Her work is studied in literature classes, in history courses, in Holocaust curricula, and in interfaith gatherings around the world.

Her best-known diary entry reads: "It's really a wonder that I haven't dropped all my ideals, because they seem so absurd and impossible to carry out. Yet I keep them, because in spite of everything I still believe that people are really good at heart."

So powerful has been her message of human dignity and human decency that some of those who deny that the Holocaust ever happened have scoffed at the idea that she ever wrote the diary. They have been proven wrong, in court.

As a Jew, she was a threat to Hitler and his Third Reich, so she had to die. But long after names including Adolf Eichmann (Number 91), Breckenridge Long (Number 73), and even Hitler have turned to dust and faded from human memory, her name—and her diary—will live on.

91 Adolf Eichmann

"Terribly and Terrifyingly Normal"

COLLIER

The man in the bulletproof glass booth is Adolf Eichmann.
He is on trial in Jerusalem for carrying out the Holocaust. He will be found guilty and hanged.

The Nazis who carried out Adolf Hitler's (Number 1) sentence of death against the Jews of Europe have been described in many ways: murderous, sadistic, twisted, bloodthirsty, barbaric, cruel, bestial, and savage. But the most unusual description was the one offered by Hannah Arendt, who covered the trial of Adolf Eichmann in Jerusalem in 1961 for *The New Yorker*.

Eichmann stood accused of being the individual in charge of carrying out the Final Solution for Hitler. Today it is known as the Holocaust, the slaughter of 6,000,000 European Jews.

Israeli prosecutor Gideon Hausner, Arendt wrote in her book *Eichmann in Jerusalem*, "wanted to try the most abnormal monster the world had ever seen.... It would have been very comforting indeed to believe that Eichmann was a monster....The trouble with Eichmann was precisely that so many were like him, and that many were neither perverted nor sadistic, that they were, and still are, terribly and terrifyingly normal."

Directing the Extermination

Eichmann was one of those "terrifyingly normal" Germans who rounded up the Jews, ran the trains to the death camps, developed the poison gas, designed the crematoria, tattooed the numbers on the inmates, kept the records, and shipped the gold taken from Jewish teeth to Swiss banks. In addition to common thugs, Eichmann had a lot of help from "ordinary" people.

Under his direction, the trains ran on time to the death camps. The gas chambers and crematoria worked overtime with the usual German efficiency.

The Final Solution Is Initiated

Adolf Eichmann was born in 1906 in Solingen, Germany. Growing up in Austria, he was apparently taunted as a child for looking Jewish. When he grew up, he joined the Austrian Nazi Party. Once Hitler annexed Austria, Eichmann found himself welcomed into the Nazi bureaucracy dealing with Jewish affairs. Before the war broke out, he even had the opportunity to visit Palestine and meet with the Grand Mufti of Jerusalem. It was his first visit to Jerusalem, but it was destined not be his last.

On January 20, 1942, Eichmann co-chaired a conference at Wannsee, a suburb of Berlin. He and Reinhard Heydrich (Number 25) told the 13 assembled bureaucrats of the plans for a "Final Solution" of the Jewish problem in Europe. Those Jews strong enough to work would be slave laborers; the others would be exterminated. The slave laborers would eventually be killed as well, so that there would be no Jewish survivors.

Heydrich was originally supposed to head the project, but he was assassinated several months later and Eichmann was put in charge.

An Attempt to Barter the Hungarian Jews

Eichmann and his bureaucrats did their work well. By August 1944, he could report to Heinrich Himmler (Number 65) that four million Jews had been killed in the death camps and another two million had died in other ways, including mass shootings. The report at that time might have been somewhat exaggerated by Eichmann, but by war's end the total had reached six million.

In the spring of 1944, the long-awaited Allied landings in Europe were imminent. It was Hitler's worst nightmare: a two-front war, with the Russians to the east and the Americans and British to the west. Eichmann came to Hungarian Jewish leaders with an unusual offer. The Germans, he said, needed winterized trucks, to be used only on the Russian front. If the Allies would furnish those trucks, he would free Hungarian Jews instead of sending them to the extermination camps.

Eichmann sent the Hungarian leaders to Palestine by way of Turkey with the proposal, which would then be transmitted to Allied leaders. To sweeten the deal,

Eichmann even offered to ship several hundred Jewish children to freedom before the delivery of a single truck, just to demonstrate "good faith."

No such deal was possible, as Eichmann was in the very process of sending Hungarian Jews to the death camps—the same people he said he wanted to swap. The Allies saw the idea for what it was: a cynical attempt to convince the paranoid Joseph Stalin (Number 4) that the Western Allies were out to double-cross him and make a deal with Hitler. Stalin might then conclude his own deal with Hitler, stop the fighting in the east, and allow Hitler to turn his full attention to the forthcoming western front. The deal never got off the ground. Once the invasion came and the second front was established, the Germans were doomed and forced to surrender.

Escape to Argentina and Final Retribution

After the war, Eichmann was detained but escaped to Argentina. It was a haven for escaped Nazis, and Eichmann lived and worked there for 14 years under an assumed name. In 1960, he was seized by Israeli agents, who brought him to Israel to stand trial. The trial took place from April to August 1961.

Eichmann's defense was that he was only carrying out orders. Interrogated by the Israelis, Eichmann said: "The Final Solution itself—I mean the special mission given to Heydrich...the extermination of the Jews, was not provided for by Reich law. It was a Führer's Order...and Himmler and Heydrich and Pohl, the head of Administration and Supply—each had his own part in the implementation of this Führer's Order. According to the then prevailing interpretation, which no one questioned, the Führer's orders had the force of law."

Eichmann would claim in his defense that he harbored no hatred toward Jews. But during his Nazi heyday he had once said, "I will leap laughing into my grave" knowing he was responsible for killing millions of Jews.

He had no chance to do so. In 1962 he was hanged for crimes against the Jewish people. His body was cremated, and the ashes were flung into the Mediterranean.

92 Robert Jackson

Judgment at Nuremberg

NATIONAL ARCHIVES

The top Nazis go on trial at Nuremberg for war crimes and crimes against humanity. Associate Justice Robert Jackson of the U. S. Supreme Court will be a major prosecutor.

O n November 21, 1945, some six months after the war had ended in Europe, a member of the U.S. Supreme Court stood up in a courtroom in Nuremberg, Germany.

Back home, Robert H. Jackson would have been seated as an associate justice. Here, however, he was chief U.S. prosecutor, outlining the case for the International Military Tribunal, a group of judges from four different nations.

Trying Crimes against Humanity

This prosecutorial role was of far greater significance than any other legal assignment he had ever participated in. On trial were two dozen German political and military officials charged with a series of war crimes. (Twenty-two would be prosecuted; one of the accused 24 would commit suicide shortly after the trial began, and a second would have his case postponed because of illness.)

The defendants were once among the most powerful men in the world. They were Adolf Hitler's (Number 1) men, carrying out his program for world domination. The crimes committed were so horrifying and of such magnitude that the defendants could not excuse themselves by saying they were only obeying orders. Now these tired old men sat in the prisoners' dock, headphones over their ears, listening to the translation of the proceedings.

"The wrongs which we seek to condemn and punish," said Jackson to the tribunal, "have been so calculated, so malignant, and so devastating that civilization cannot tolerate their being ignored because it cannot survive their being repeated."

This was not a case of victors trying the vanquished. If so, the defendants would have been punished at once. Legal procedures were established for rules of evidence, for selection of judges and prosecutors, and for the availability of defense attorneys. Most of the evidence would come from Nazi documents, many signed by individual defendants. The Third Reich had been meticulous in keeping records about such things as orders, reports, and statistics.

The trial was not about revenge, but about justice.

Guilty of Their Crimes against Humanity

Chief prosecutor Jackson represents those who served the International Military Tribunal. The Nuremberg trials served as a warning. Future conspirators, plotters, and accomplices of those who commit war crimes and crimes against humanity would face the wrath of the international community.

The chief presiding judge of the International Military Tribunal was Lord Justice Geoffrey Lawrence of Great Britain. Other judges included Francis J. Biddle of the United States, Professor Henri Donnedieu de Vabre of France, and Major General I.T. Nikitchenko of the Soviet Union. It was their job to weigh the evidence, decide guilt or innocence, and pronounce sentence. At least three out of four votes were required for a guilty verdict.

Of the 22 defendants, 19 would be found guilty. Of these, 12 would be sentenced to death and seven to prison. Three would be acquitted.

Hermann Goering (Number 43) was sentenced to death, but took poison the day he was to be executed. Among those hanged were Joachim von Ribbentrop (Number 52), Wilhelm Keitel (Number 48), Alfred Rosenberg, and Alfred Jodl (Number 46). Among the imprisoned: Albert Speer (Number 77) and Karl Doenitz (Number 64).

A Distinguished Career

Jackson was born in Spring Creek, Pennsylvania, in 1892. Beginning his professional career as a corporation counsel, he went on to become a government attorney for New York governor—and future president—Franklin D. Roosevelt (Number 2). In Washington, he rose from solicitor general to attorney general and finally, in 1941, to associate justice of the Supreme Court. When the war ended in 1945, he was chosen one of the war crimes prosecutors. The trial of the top Nazis concluded in October 1946.

Robert H. Jackson returned to the Supreme Court in Washington, where he served until his death in 1954.

93 Henry Morgenthau, Jr.

A Plan for Germany

What should be done about Germany once the war ended?
Henry Morgenthau, Jr., secretary of the treasury, had a plan.

In September 1944, following a conference in Quebec, Franklin D. Roosevelt (Number 2) and Winston Churchill (Number 3) issued a communiqué on the meeting. One sentence stunned the world: "The Allies were looking forward to converting Germany into a country primarily agricultural and pastoral in character."

The statement reflected a plan that had been approved at the conference: the Morgenthau Plan. It was intended to destroy the industrial base of Germany in the future, thus making it impossible for the country to start another war. Author of the plan was Henry Morgenthau, Jr., the U.S. secretary of the treasury.

The Force behind the War Bond Effort

Henry Morgenthau, Jr., was born in New York City in 1891. His father had served as ambassador to Turkey in the Wilson administration during World War I.

Young Morgenthau owned a large farm several miles from the Hyde Park estate of Franklin Roosevelt. He became friends with Roosevelt, backing him both for governor of New York and for president. In 1934, he became FDR's secretary of the treasury.

During the war, Morgenthau vigorously pushed for Americans to purchase savings bonds, later called War Bonds, to keep down inflation. The program was an enormous success, with sales of more than $200 billion worth of bonds.

Eliminating the German Threat to World Peace

Roosevelt encouraged his advisors to speak out on issues not necessarily in their bailiwicks. Morgenthau did so with great relish, especially on issues of foreign policy. Staff members in his Treasury Department strongly opposed the State Department's immigration policy on Jewish refugees. His department had a radio program called "The Treasury Hour," which, even before Pearl Harbor, actively supported Roosevelt's anti-Axis initiatives.

Morgenthau's single most important foreign policy venture was a document called the "Program to Prevent Germany Starting World War III." The idea was to deindustrialize Germany so it would no longer be a threat to the peace of the world.

Following the statement after the Quebec conference, the roof caved in, and all of the criticism did not come from Berlin.

A Controversial Plan

At the time, the Western Allies were in France preparing to invade Germany. Hitler had survived an assassination attempt by his own generals, and his government appeared shaky, at best. For Nazi propaganda purposes, the plan could not have come at a better time.

Propaganda chief Joseph Goebbels (Number 44) seized the opportunity, screaming that the plan meant that the Germans must go on fighting until the bitter end.

The Morgenthau Plan aroused great controversy in the United States, as well. There was concern about what would happen in Europe after the war. Would the Soviet Union emerge as the dominant power? If so, wouldn't a strong Germany be better than a weak Germany, acting as a buffer to western Europe?

The plan was shelved, never again to be seriously considered.

Following Roosevelt's death in April 1945, Harry S Truman (Number 14) was sworn in as president. Three months later, with the occupation of Germany underway, Truman asked for Morgenthau's resignation. By so doing, the new president made his position on post-war Germany quite clear.

Morgenthau died in 1967.

Architect of the United Nations

COLLIER

The United Nations was established at the San Francisco conference in 1945.
Cordell Hull, architect of the U.N., would win the Nobel Peace Prize for his efforts.

He holds the record for having been secretary of state longer than any other individual—nearly 12 years. That record will probably stand, because Cordell Hull held the position during most of the administration of Franklin D. Roosevelt (Number 2). FDR was the only man to be elected more than twice, and under the current Constitution, he is the only one who ever will be.

The great irony is that Roosevelt was really his own wartime secretary of state. The president pretty much did his own negotiating and foreign policy decision-making. Hull's expertise was in Latin American relations and reciprocal trade agreements.

Hull, however, does hold the distinction of being the chief architect of the United Nations international organization, one who was involved deeply in its planning and creation. It would win him the Nobel Peace Prize.

Secretary of State in Name Only

Cordell Hull was born in Pickett County, Tennessee, in 1871. He graduated from the Cumberland Law School in 1891 and was admitted to the bar. He served in the state legislature for six years, fought in the Spanish-American War, and became a judge. He served in the House of Representatives before election to the U.S. Senate in 1931. In the House, he had worked on the new federal income tax program.

In 1933, newly elected President Roosevelt named him secretary of state. In the early years of the Roosevelt administration, Hull was mainly concerned with international trade and Latin America. When war came, some key duties of secretary of state would be co-opted by the president.

An Opportunity to Act the Part

Hull had his chance to play the outraged secretary of state on December 7, 1941. Having broken the Japanese code, the United States knew that the Japanese were sending a message to be delivered precisely at 1 p.m. Washington time. The message, to be delivered personally to the secretary of state, was to break off any further negotiations with the United States. War was imminent. (It was clear that something was being planned by the Japanese to coincide with 1 p.m. Washington time. It turned out to be the time of the Japanese attack on Pearl Harbor.)

The Japanese envoys came to Hull's office late. They had been instructed to have no lower-level staff person type the message. It had to be done by one of the top members of the embassy staff, someone who was not a skilled typist. Hull kept the envoys waiting, then received them and pretended to read a message that he already knew about. Hull had a chance to express his outrage, characterizing the document as filled with "falsehoods and distortions." The envoys were then dismissed.

A Call for an International Organization

It was one of the few times during the war that Hull had a chance to speak out as secretary of state. Throughout the war, either Roosevelt or his confidante, Harry L. Hopkins (Number 22), carried out the crucial negotiations with allies and neutrals. It was Hopkins, for example, who attended the major wartime conferences with the president.

Hull's great wartime triumph was the United Nations, although FDR must be credited with the name. It came about in January 1942, when those nations fighting the Axis powers declared they would not sign a separate peace. In the original draft of the declaration, the Allied Powers were identified as the "Associated Powers." The president did not care for the nomenclature, crossed it out, and substituted "United Nations." The name stuck not only throughout the war, but to the present day.

The idea for a post-war successor to the League of Nations emerged in the fall of 1943 in Moscow. The United States, Britain, and Russia called for the creation of an international organization to keep the peace.

A Significant Achievement

Then Hull took over. In the summer of 1944, representatives of 39 nations met at the Dumbarton Oaks estate in the Georgetown area of Washington, D.C. The participating nations considered the idea of a post-war international organization.

The Dumbarton Oaks conference agreed on the basic structure of the future organization: a General Assembly representing all member nations, a Security Council where the major powers dominated by virtue of their right to veto, a Secretariat, and an International Court of Justice. The conference also dealt with issues beyond war and peace. It dealt with the social and economic issues that often bring about armed conflict.

Hull was well aware of the need for bipartisan support in the future, and he made sure that Republicans were represented in the American delegation and that they took an active part in the discussions.

Late in 1944, with his greatest work virtually achieved, Hull resigned as secretary of state. He was then 73 years old.

The United Nations Is Established

The founding conference of the United Nations was held in San Francisco beginning on April 25, 1945. The 50 nations represented were determined that there should never be another world war.

Roosevelt died just two weeks before the conference was scheduled to begin. But because of the momentum of Dumbarton Oaks, and the planning by Hull and his staff, the work could go forward with ease. The framework of the U.N. had been solidly built. By the end of June 1945, the attending delegates voted to set up the United Nations. Each country would now have to have its government ratify membership in the international body.

In 1945, Cordell Hull won the Nobel Peace Prize for his work in helping to establish the U.N. Hull died in 1955.

Crowned Heads, Royal Symbols

NATIONAL ARCHIVES   SIMON AND SCHUSTER   NATIONAL ARCHIVES

George VI of Great Britain, Christian X of Denmark, and Leopold III of Belgium (left to right) were among the crowned heads of Europe during the war. Each king's leadership defined his respective place in history.

The early part of the 20th century was not a kind one for the crowned heads of Europe. After World War I, three of the most powerful rulers were gone: Kaiser Wilhelm II of Germany had fled to exile in the Netherlands; Czar Nicholas II of Imperial Russia had been murdered by the Bolsheviks; and Francis Joseph, both Emperor of Austria and King of Hungary, died 10 days after the armistice. There were no successors.

By the time of World War II, the crowned heads generally reigned rather than ruled. But they also served as symbols to their people.

Symbolic Royalty

The three kings in this chapter came to symbolize something different in the eyes of their countrymen. One was a symbol of determination in a time of national danger. One shared the fate of his people in a time of defeat and occupation by a brutal enemy. The last was pilloried for caving in to Nazi pressure and leaving his allies exposed and vulnerable.

An Inspiration to the Battered British People

George VI, King of Great Britain, Northern Ireland, and the Dominions, was born in 1895 in London.

He was never really expected to become the sovereign. But when Edward VIII abdicated in 1937 to marry Wallis Simpson, he was crowned king. His brother, Edward VIII, had the personality, style, and bearing to be king. George was shy, stammered, and was uncomfortable with the pomp and circumstance. Two years later, as war threatened, he and his wife visited the United States. The highlight of the trip was eating hot dogs with President and Eleanor Roosevelt (Number 2 and 78, respectively) at Hyde Park. It made history, for it was the first visit by a reigning British monarch to the United States. It also made friends for Britain in America, friends England would soon need.

When war came, Britain was pounded by German bombs and, later, rockets. But George VI, his wife, Queen Elizabeth (Number 78), and daughters Elizabeth and Margaret Rose, constantly made the rounds of wartorn London to boost morale in the face of national danger.

The royal family insisted on painting a line in the royal bathtub indicating the maximum depth of the water to be used. This was to conserve water. The English cheered when they saw the newspaper photo of Princess Elizabeth, the future queen, changing the tire of an army vehicle.

After the landings on D-Day, both Winston Churchill (Number 3) and George VI wanted to step foot on the shores of France. It may be apocryphal, but the story is that they did, and that Dwight D. Eisenhower (Number 7) himself accompanied them.

In 1952, seven years after the end of the war, George VI died, a symbol of wartime courage and resolution during England's darkest hour.

Saving the Jews of Denmark

Christian X was born in 1870; he became King of Denmark in 1912. When his country was occupied by the Nazis in 1940, Christian X stayed with his people during the occupation. He continued to ride out on his horse each morning, drawing crowds of adoring Danes. He refused to be a puppet monarch under Nazi control and kept the Danes united as a people.

Many historians believe that Christian X set the example for his people, which is why Denmark, of all the conquered countries of Europe, conspired to save its Jews. They found out when the Nazis planned to round up Jews, arranged to warn them in advance, put them in trucks and cars, drove them down to the docks, had fishing boats ready to receive them, and transported them to safety in neutral Sweden.

One of the legends about Christian X is that he said he would wear the first yellow Star of David if the Nazis required Danish Jews to wear it. He did not have to. His people knew what to do—and did it. An estimated 90 percent of Danish Jews survived the war thanks to the Danish people.

Christian X died in 1947.

A Quick Surrender of Belgium

Leopold III was born in 1901; he became king in 1934 after the death of his father.

When Germany attacked in 1940, Leopold took over as commander of the armed forces. Against the advice of his government, he surrendered very quickly. This allowed Nazi panzers to swarm into the heart of France before the British and French could form new defensive positions. In fact, the Germans moved so quickly that the British Expeditionary Forces were hemmed in around the port of Dunkirk.

The British were forced to withdraw by sea, and the French surrendered. Both British and French military and political leaders were bitter about Leopold's hasty surrender. They felt even a little bit more time could have enabled them to stave off what turned out to be a disaster for the Western Allies.

Both during and after the war, the people of Belgium were divided over the action of their king. Some even believed that he had made some kind of deal with Hitler in exchange for some favored role in a future German-dominated Europe, although this was never proven. After the war, following a major political struggle, Leopold III abdicated in favor of his son; he died in 1983.

The End of Royalty

These were three kings who influenced their people, and the war, in very different ways.

Long after the war, King Farouk of Egypt predicted, "Soon, there will only be five kings left in the world: the King of England and the four kings in a deck of playing cards." Many kings disappeared after World War I and more disappeared after World War II, especially from the Balkans.

As the 21st century unfolds, will there still be a place for crowned heads and royal symbols?

96 Haile Selassie

The Plea That Failed

COLLIER

Emperor Haile Selassie of Ethiopia pleads at the League of Nations for international action against Fascist Italy.

NORTH SEA
GREAT DENMARK
BRITAIN
NETHER-
LANDS
London

I t was June 30, 1936. In Geneva, the League of Nations was meeting in the Assembly Hall. The chair recognized Haile Selassie. As he reached the microphone, Italian journalists began hissing, booing, and hooting at the emperor of Ethiopia. It was a historic moment, for the future of the League as an effective agency to promote peace was at stake.

Italian Aggression against Ethiopia

Haile Selassie made an early plea for the security of a small nation that was the victim of aggression. With great dignity, the emperor made his plea before an organization dedicated to preserving the peace of the world.

Haile Selassie was born in Ethiopia in 1892 and took the throne in 1930. In 1934, a military clash occurred on the border between two African states: Ethiopia and Italian Somaliland. Italy wanted reparations arising out of the incident, and Ethiopia called for an investigation into what had happened.

Early in October 1935, Benito Mussolini (Number 50) invaded Ethiopia. The League declared that Italy was the aggressor and voted for sanctions, which would later be lifted.

In March 1936, the Italians conducted all-out war against Ethiopia, using both bombing planes and poison gas. Soon, Italy occupied all of Ethiopia. The African nation became part of what was called Italian East Africa. The emperor had fled to England, but he had not given up.

Abandoned to the Aggressor

On June 30, 1936, Haile Selassie decided to appear before the League of Nations in person. The Italian journalists who were heckling him were escorted from the chamber, and the emperor delivered his plea:

I...am here today to claim that justice which is due to my people and the assistance promised to it eight months ago when 50 nations asserted that aggression had been committed. None other than they can address the appeal of the Ethiopian people to 50 nations.... Given that I am setting a precedent, that I am the first head of a state to address the Assembly, it is surely without precedent that a people, the victim of an iniquitous war, now stands in danger of being abandoned to the aggressor....

I assert that the problem submitted to the Assembly today is a much wider one than the removal of sanctions. It is not merely a settlement of Italian aggression. It is collective. It is the very existence of the League of Nations.... In a word, it is international morality that is at stake....

Representatives of the world, I have come to Geneva to discharge in your minds the most painful of the duties of a head of state. What reply shall I take to my people?...

It is us today. It will be you tomorrow.

A Prophecy Fulfilled

The prophecy proved all too accurate. The major powers, first Italy's supporters and later Italy's critics, recognized the new African map drawn by Benito Mussolini.

The League of Nations had faltered. It would never again be seen as anything but a sophisticated debating society.

The Ethiopian emperor lived in exile in Britain. After World War II broke out, his country was liberated by the British in 1941.

In 1974, Selassie was overthrown in a military coup; he died in 1975.

He Fought Back

Pre-war Warsaw boasted a thriving Jewish community. Following the German Occupation, Hitler ordered that the Jewish community be crammed into a walled ghetto in the city. When the ghetto was ordered destroyed, Mordecai Anielewicz led the fight against the Nazis.

A common misconception about the Holocaust is that Jews went like sheep to the slaughter. It is true that some did line up naked in front of huge burial pits, waiting to be machine-gunned. Others stepped off the cattle cars at Auschwitz and walked into the gas chambers without resistance. There were many Jews, however, who fought back. With all the desperation of the condemned, they faced the powerful Nazi war machine and resisted their tormenters.

Defying Nazi Persecution

One of the first to do so was Mordecai Anielewicz, the young commander of the Warsaw ghetto fighters organization. He represents Jewish ghetto fighters and partisans. They carried out revolts in ghettos and death camps; they fought a guerrilla campaign against the German army in the mountains and forests of Europe.

Mordecai Anielewicz was born in 1919 in Warsaw. He was 20 when the Nazis invaded Poland in 1939. Anielewicz left the doomed Polish capital for eastern Poland, which was soon occupied by the Soviet army. He was imprisoned by the Russians, released, and returned to Nazi-occupied Warsaw.

In the fall of 1940, the Nazis established a ghetto, a walled-off segregated area, in the heart of Warsaw. All Polish Jews in the city were required to live behind the ghetto walls. Suspicious and fearful of what the Nazis had in mind for the Jewish community, Anielewicz began to organize small self-defense groups.

There were about 360,000 Jews in Warsaw at that time. Additional Jews were relocated from other parts of Poland until half a million were crammed together under the most deplorable conditions. They were underfed, inadequately housed, ill-clothed, and lacking in the most basic medical facilities. By July 1942, an estimated 85,000 Jews had died of starvation and disease. Then the Nazis began to "deport" Jews from the ghetto.

Anielewicz and his small band of resisters had heard reports from underground sources of Nazis massacring Russian Jews following the German invasion of the Soviet Union. What would be the fate of the deported Polish Jews? By January 1943, the answer became abundantly clear. More than 300,000 Jews from the Warsaw Ghetto had been shipped to a place called Treblinka for extermination. The Jewish commander organized for resistance.

And so, when the Nazis came early in 1943 for further deportations, the tiny Jewish force struck back. Shots were fired, Nazis were killed, and the deportation stopped, temporarily.

The Warsaw Ghetto Uprising

Word got back to Berlin. The following month, Henrich Himmler (Number 65) ordered that the Warsaw ghetto be destroyed. He wrote that "we must achieve the disappearance from sight of the living space for 500,000 sub-humans that has existed up to now, but could never be suitable for Germans."

The end was approaching. Mordecai Anielewicz began rounding up whatever weapons he could. Bunkers were built in key areas of the ghetto. Nearly 60 revolvers were obtained for the more than 700 volunteer fighters.

On April 19, 1943, the Nazis entered the ghetto to begin the final mass deportations. An estimated 60,000 men, women, and children were scheduled for removal.

The Nazis were greeted with gunfire, grenades, and "Molotov cocktails" (bottles of flammable liquid set ablaze).

The Nazis brought in reinforcements, including tanks, and a fierce battle took place. On May 8, Anielewicz and a hundred of his followers were trapped in their headquarters bunker on Mila Street. When they refused to surrender, the Nazis threw gas canisters inside. Anielewicz and his fighters chose to die rather than surrender to the Nazis.

Even without their leader, the defenders of the ghetto continued to resist for another eight days.

On May 16, 1943, General Juergen Stroop, in command of the German forces, advised Berlin of his "glorious" victory: "The former Jewish quarter of Warsaw is no longer in existence."

A Fierce Resistance

With all the firepower at its command, including tanks and artillery, the mighty German army had taken four weeks to defeat a group of Jewish civilians with 60 handguns. It had taken the German army less time to defeat far more sophisticated enemies, including Belgium, Holland, and Norway.

The sacrifice of Mordecai Anielewicz and his resistance fighters in the Warsaw Ghetto took place in a virtual vacuum from the rest of the world, including Warsaw itself. Even as artillery fired and flames rose up over the ghetto, life outside the ghetto walls went on. An amusement park located just outside the ghetto continued operating, its carousel spinning to the merry sound of music.

A Wish Fulfilled

In a letter written to a friend four days into the battle, Anielewicz said: "Perhaps we will see one another again. The most important thing is that my life's dream has come true. Jewish self-defense in the ghetto has been realized. Jewish retaliation and resistance has become a fact....I have been witness to the heroic battle of the Jewish fighters."

The brave young commander was only 24.

98 Joseph P. Kennedy

A Controversial Ambassador

NATIONAL ARCHIVES

U. S. Ambassador to Great Britain Joseph P. Kennedy believed that Britain would lose the war—and made his views known.

Lyndon Johnson liked to tell the story of what happened when he was a young Congressman. It was late in 1940, and Johnson was sitting in the Oval Office opposite Franklin D. Roosevelt (Number 2). The president was on the phone with Joseph P. Kennedy, the American ambassador to Great Britain.

Speaking in as cordial a manner as he could muster, President Roosevelt told Kennedy how he was looking forward to seeing him soon in Washington. At this point, according to Johnson, Roosevelt looked at Johnson, grinned, and slid his finger across his throat. Kennedy was going to get the axe.

Early Business Success

Joseph P. Kennedy was one of the most disastrous appointees of Roosevelt's presidency. The patriarch of what was to become the Kennedy dynasty was quite simply the wrong ambassador serving in the wrong country at the wrong time in history. There was a danger that he could be misunderstood—both by America's allies and its enemies. Britain might be led to believe that America was selling her out. Adolf Hitler

(Number 1) might think he was free to do as he chose, without any interference from the United States.

Joseph P. Kennedy was born in 1888 in Boston. The son of a local politician, he extended his influence by marrying the daughter of Boston Mayor John Francis ("Honey Fitz") Fitzgerald.

Kennedy was successful as a banker, financier, businessman, and Hollywood mogul. He was so successful in the legal liquor business that some sources speculate that he might have been a bootlegger during Prohibition.

Kennedy backed Roosevelt in 1932 and became the first chairman of the Securities and Exchange Commission.

Late in 1937, he was appointed Ambassador to Great Britain. Although his nine beautiful children were popular subjects for photographs, London was less than idyllic and Kennedy faced political challenges.

In the summer of 1938, Kennedy commented to a Nazi diplomat in London that he understood the German policy on Jews, but said that the same thing could be accomplished without "such a lot of noise." The diplomat notified Berlin of the conversation. How was that information evaluated, considering that it came from an official American source?

During the fall of 1938, England and France appeased Hitler and awarded him part of Czechoslovakia without him having to fire a shot. But in September 1939, following the invasion of Poland, the two Western democracies declared war on Nazi Germany.

Ill-Chosen Words

Roosevelt recognized the danger of Nazism and looked for ways to support the Western democracies. Ambassador Kennedy in London saw things differently. He thought that Hitler was going to win the war and said so in public and private. At one point, he said, "Democracy is finished in England."

The British were furious. It was bad enough that American isolationists back in America were saying things like that. However, the American ambassador saying such things in London? He further infuriated the British by arguing that Britain should pay in advance for any war materials from the United States.

Finally, a British official presented Roosevelt with a summary of Kennedy's statements. It was clear to Roosevelt that the ambassador had to be removed; he was called back to Washington and allowed to "resign."

After the war, Kennedy began preparing his sons for public service. All three surviving sons would become U.S. senators. John Fitzgerald Kennedy would become president but would fall to an assassin's bullet in 1963. Five years later, Robert Kennedy would suffer that same fate.

Joseph P. Kennedy spent his final years paralyzed following a stroke. He died in 1969.

99 Paul Reynaud

A Voice in the Wilderness

COLLIER

Paul Reynaud wanted to continue the fight against Hitler.

For years he had cried out his warnings in the French chamber of deputies. France, he said, could not rely solely on that huge, fixed fortification known as the Maginot Line. France, he continued, had to modernize its army with armored divisions; it could not afford to appease dictators.

For years, the French politicians would not listen. When they finally did, it was too late.

A Bitter Surrender

On June 10, 1940, a bitter, depressed, and defiant Paul Reynaud, now premier, weighed the choices available to him. Only a week before, the last British troops had been evacuated from Dunkirk. That very day, Benito Mussolini (Number 50) had suddenly declared war on France, invading from the south.

Premier Reynaud had begged Franklin D. Roosevelt (Number 2) to fill the sky with planes and save France, but the president explained that only Congress could declare war, a then-unlikely possibility.

The French premier then sent a message to Washington, indicating his intentions: "Today the enemy is almost at the gates of Paris. We shall fight in front of Paris, we shall fight behind Paris, we shall close ourselves in North Africa to continue the fight...."

Reynaud was crying in the wilderness again. The French would not fight for Paris; they would not take the French fleet to North Africa to carry on the fight. They would surrender.

A Warning Unheeded

Paul Reynaud was a prophet who would not be believed. He was born in 1878 in Barcelonnette, France. He studied law at the Sorbonne and entered politics, serving 10 years as a member of the Chamber of Deputies (1914–1924). Once defeated, he returned to the chamber in 1928 and remained there until 1940, when France ceased to exist as an independent state. That dozen years would prove to be one of France's most critical periods since the Napoleonic era.

From the 1920s to the 1930s, France's closest neighbors—Italy, Germany, and Spain—had succumbed to fascist dictators. France's traditional ally, Russia, was under the brutal despotism of the Soviet state. Could it be relied on in a crisis?

As a deputy, Reynaud had looked nervously over the Maginot Line at what the Führer was doing. Britain had introduced tanks in World War I, and now armies around the world were examining the potential of armored warfare. France's own Charles De Gaulle (Number 51) had written a new book on armored warfare. Shouldn't this be something the French army should be examining? The old generals smiled. We have the Maginot Line, they pointed out. It is impregnable. Reynaud's impassioned speeches in the chamber of deputies were of no avail.

A Time of Unrest and Upheaval

France was no better off politically or socially than it was militarily. A wide range of disparate groups fractured the body politic. The 1930s was a time of economic dislocation in France as well as the rest of the world. There were riots in the streets and, for a brief time, a popular front of Radical Socialists, Socialists, and Communists was in power. It did not last. There were also pro-Nazi groups and "defeatists" who wanted to do business with Adolf Hitler (Number 1).

Through all of this, Reynaud served in a number of cabinet posts in different governments. He was always there, sounding his warnings and urging policy changes before it was too late.

France had several opportunities to stop Hitler. Reynaud had failed to move France to action. When the Nazis occupied the Rhineland, the German commander was under secret orders to withdraw immediately if France moved against him; France did nothing.

In 1938, the then-Premier Eduard Daladier and Prime Minister Neville Chamberlain (Number 66) appeased Hitler at Munich and surrendered part of Czechoslovakia.

In September 1939, when the Nazis invaded Poland, Daladier did declare war on Nazi Germany. France even began to move troops across the German border but then, for reasons unknown, abruptly withdrew them.

The Reynaud Government Falls

In March 1940, Reynaud succeeded Daladier as premier of France. It was too late for many things. Two months later, Nazi forces made an end run around the Maginot Line and through Belgium. The Germans cut off the British Expeditionary Force and headed for Paris.

Premier Reynaud's appeal to Roosevelt had failed, but he wanted to continue the war against Hitler. However, on June 16, Reynaud's government fell, and Henri Petain (Number 27) became premier, moving for an armistice with the Germans. It was signed on June 22, 1940.

Petain would run a puppet government in France. He would have Reynaud arrested for allegedly mishandling government funds. Reynaud spent several years in a Nazi prison camp.

After the war, Reynaud won election to the chamber of deputies. And, once again, he was free to speak his mind.

Paul Reynaud died in 1966.

100 Pope Pius XII

The Sound of Silence

NATIONAL ARCHIVES
Pope Pius XII holds an audience in Rome.

There is a famous apocryphal story about Pope Pius XII. It deals with an incident that supposedly took place during a wartime Big Three conference. Franklin D. Roosevelt (Number 2), Winston Churchill (Number 3), and Joseph Stalin (Number 4) were meeting, and a particularly sensitive issue came up. Either Roosevelt or Churchill asked Stalin, "But what will the Pope say?"

"The *Pope*?" Stalin is said to have responded. "How many divisions does *he* have?"

Silence Implies Consent

In terms of military divisions, the Pope, of course, had none. But those who followed his guidance on matters of faith and morals numbered 400–500 million.

His influence could have had an impact on the Holocaust. The genocide of the Jews was carried out with remarkable ease. It was accepted by world leaders who chose to look away; Pope Pius XII was one of them. The pontiff had enormous influence, which he chose not to use.

Scholars have uncovered statements showing that he was distressed by the plight of the Jews in Europe, but the only thing he could do about it was to offer prayers on their behalf.

Those statements of sorrow were relatively few and far between. Pope Pius XII could have been more outspoken, more specific on what could be done, and far more proactive when specific situations occurred, literally, in his own backyard. When 3,000 Jews were rounded up in Rome, they were loaded in trucks to transport them to their deaths. The vehicles deliberately drove alongside the Vatican so that the Nazi guards accompanying the Jews could get a look at the Vatican firsthand. That sad convoy drove virtually under the windows of the pontiff. His silence was deafening.

A Voice of Dissent

By contrast, the record of his predecessor, Pope Pius XI, is striking. Pius XI made his position on the persecution of Jews crystal clear. In September 1938, as Nazi Germany prepared to move from discrimination to extermination, Pius XI said: "Anti-Semitism is...a movement in which we, as Christians, cannot have any part whatever.... Spiritually, we are Semites."

Pius XI was in the process of having the Church prepare an encyclical on anti-Semitism, but he died before it could be promulgated. With the ascent of Pius XII to the head of the Roman Catholic Church, the encyclical proposal was scrapped.

The Excuse of Neutrality

Some Vatican scholars insist that Pius XII did many things to alleviate the suffering of Jews during the Holocaust, but those records have not yet been shared. The Vatican was, of course, neutral during the war, and such actions might have questioned that neutrality. But certainly such neutrality applied to the armed combatants, not the slaughter of innocent, unarmed civilians.

It is said that Pius XII was afraid that Catholics might be put in danger if he spoke out. Yet individual Catholics, including laymen, priests, nuns, and church leaders as exhalted as cardinals, defied the Nazis by hiding Jews, protecting them, and helping them escape. Many Catholics died in concentration camps and gas chambers for practicing the basic tenets of their faith.

Perhaps the major criticism of Pius XII is that his silence might have been interpreted as tacit acceptance of the genocide.

A Concordat with Germany

The man who would become Pope Pius XII was born in Rome Eugenio Pacelli in 1876. His family had been involved in Vatican affairs for centuries. He obtained a doctorate in canon law and theology. Ordained in 1899, he rose quickly in the church hierarchy, serving in diplomatic posts in Germany, first in Bavaria, then Munich, and finally Berlin.

He returned to Rome in 1929 to become an archbishop and then a cardinal. In 1930, he became secretary of state.

In July 1933, he negotiated a concordat, a treaty between the papacy and Nazi Germany. The concordat was of great importance, not only for Germany but for the world. It legitimized the regime of Adolf Hitler (Number 1).

In the concordat, certain privileges were extended to the Catholic clergy and to Catholic schools in Germany. Church law was recognized for German Catholics. The Catholic political party in the Reichstag was dissolved. Catholic organizations and Catholic newspapers would no longer engage in social or political action.

In the mid-1930s, Cardinal Pacelli, as secretary of state, travelled abroad. He visited the United States, crisscrossed the country, and lunched with President Roosevelt.

Accession to the Papacy

Following the death of Pius XI in 1939, Rome looked for a new pontiff in a time of growing international crisis. Cardinal Pacelli, secretary of state, was chosen. His international experience was seen as extremely important for the years ahead. Pope Pius XII was elected in March 1939. By September, there would be war.

Pope Pius XII died in 1958, his papacy a subject of controversy to this day.

Appendix A

Honorable, Dishonorable, and Special Mentions

Some of the honorable mentions below include men who fought on the Axis side. They are cited here purely for the influence they exerted during the war. The dishonorable mentions include traitors to their countries and war criminals. The special mentions speak for themselves.

Honorable Mentions

Military and Naval Officers

Claude Auchinleck, Werner von Blomberg, Walther von Brauchitsch, Lewis Brereton, Claire Chennault, Mark Clark, Andrew Cunningham, W. Scott Cunningham, Thomas Farrell, Franz Halder, Gotthard Heinrici, Adolf Heusinger, Courtney Hodges, Hastings Ismay, Albert Kesselring, Edward P. King, Jr., William Leahy, Willis Lee, Jr., Curtis LeMay, Lesley McNair, Marc Mitscher, Alexander Patch, Frank Schofield, William H. Simpson, Walter Bedell Smith, Carl Spaatz, Harold R. Stark, Alexander Vandegrift, Archibald Wavell, Maxime Weygand, and Orde Wingate.

The Bureaucracy

Clement Attlee, William Beaverbrook, Alexander Cadogan, Eduard Daladier, Elmer Davis, James V. Forrestal, Fumimaro Konoye, Nikita Khrushchev, Mao Tse-tung, Hjalmar Schacht, and King Victor Emmanuel III.

Diplomats

William C. Bullitt, Joseph E. Davies, Anthony Eden, Howard Elting, Jr., Joseph C. Grew, Yosuke Matsuoka, Kichisaburo Nomura, Friedrich von der Schulenburg, Paul Henri Spaak, Edward R. Stettinius, Jr., Hans Thomsen, Shigenori Togo, Andrei Vishinsky, and Raoul Wallenberg.

The Front Line

John Bulkeley, Alexander Drabik, William Dyess, Chaplain Howell M. Forgy, James M. Gavin, Howard Gilmore, Daniel Inouye, Leon Johnson, Colin P. Kelly, Jr., Audie Murphy, Matthew Ridgeway, Irving Strobing, Maxwell Taylor, and Paul Tibbetts, Jr.

Intelligence Officials and Spies

Wilhelm Canaris, Allen Dulles, Reinhard Gehlen, Alvin Kramer, Kanji Ogawa, Richard Sorge, and F.W. Winterbotham.

Scientists

Niels Bohr, Enrico Fermi, and Edward Teller.

The Media

Margaret Bourke-White, David Breger, Walter Duranty, John Gunther, Marion Hargrove, John Hersey, Frank Hewlett, Ralph Ingersoll, Edward Kennedy (A.P. correspondent), Arthur Krock, Chesly Manly, Drew Pearson, Robert Sherrod, Merriman Smith, Robert St. John, I.F. Stone, Dorothy Thompson, and Walter Winchell.

Historians and Biographers

Stephen E. Ambrose, Charles A. Beard, Thomas Buell, Edward Crankshaw, Martin Gilbert, Doris Kearns Goodwin, William Langer, Forrest Pogue, Cornelius Ryan, Robert E. Sherwood, A.J.P. Taylor, John Toland, H.R. Trevor-Roper, Barbara Tuchman, and Alexander Werth.

Other Individuals

Bob Hope, Henry J. Kaiser, Pastor Martin Niemoeller, Eduard Schulte, Oscar Schindler, Alexander P. de Seversky, and Wendell Willkie.

Dishonorable Mentions

Klaus Barbie, Rose D'Aquino (Tokyo Rose), Hans Frank, Mildred Gillars (Axis Sally), Rudolf Hess, Rudolf Hoess, William Joyce (Lord Haw-Haw), Ernst Kaltenbrunner, Tyler Kent, Pierre Laval, Robert Ley, Josef Mengele, Kim Philby, Ezra Pound, Vikdun Quisling, Alfred Rosenberg, Artur Seyss-Inquart, and Julius Streicher.

Special Mentions

To three men who are doing their best to see to it that the men and women of World War II are never forgotten: Robert Dole, Steven Spielberg, and Tom Hanks.

Appendix B

Chronology of World War II

1931
Sept. 18: Japanese invade Manchuria.

1933
Jan. 30: Adolf Hitler becomes chancellor of Germany.

1935
September: Nuremberg Laws limit rights of German Jews.
October: Italy invades Ethiopia.

1936
March: Hitler sends troops to occupy the Rhineland.
May 9: Ethiopia annexed by Italy.
July: Franco sets off Spanish Civil War.
Oct. 25: Rome-Berlin Pact signed.

1937
July: Japanese invade China.

1938
Sept. 30: Munich agreement. Hitler is awarded the Sudetenland in Czechoslovakia.
Nov. 9–10: Pogroms rock Germany and Austria on "Crystal Night," the night of broken glass. Jews are killed, beaten, and imprisoned. Synagogues and businesses are set ablaze.

1939
Mar. 14: Germany occupies all of Czechoslovakia.
Apr. 7: Italy invades Albania.
Aug. 23: Nazi-Soviet Pact signed in Moscow.
Sept. 1: Germany invades Poland.
Sept. 3: England and France declare war on Germany.
Sept. 5: United States proclaims neutrality.
Sept. 17: Soviet Union invades Poland.
Sept. 28: Poland partitioned between Germany and U.S.S.R.
Nov. 30: Soviets invade Finland.

1940

Apr. 9: Germany invades Denmark and Norway.

May 10: Germany invades Belgium, Holland, and Luxembourg; Churchill becomes prime minister in Great Britain.

May 12: Nazis invade France.

May 16: Germans break through at Sedan.

May 26–June 4: Evacuation of British Expeditionary Force from Dunkirk.

May 28: Leopold III surrenders Belgium.

June 10: Italy declares war on France and Britain.

June 14: Nazis enter Paris.

June 15–16: Soviets occupy Estonia, Latvia, and Lithuania.

June 20: Roosevelt appoints Republicans Stimson and Knox to cabinet.

June 22: Armistice between France and Germany signed at Compiegne.

July 3: British attack French fleet near Oran, North Africa.

July 10: Germans begin air blitz on Britain.

Aug. 17: Nazis institute a blockade around Britain.

September: America First Committee organized in the United States.

Sept. 2: United States swaps destroyers for British naval bases in Western Hemisphere.

Sept. 16: Congress passes Selective Service Act.

Sept. 27: Rome-Berlin-Tokyo military pact signed.

Oct. 28: Italy invades Greece.

Nov. 14: Nazis raid Coventry.

Dec. 17: Roosevelt suggests lend-lease approach.

1941

Jan. 6: Roosevelt proclaims Four Freedoms.

Mar. 11: Lend-lease signed into law.

Mar. 30: Germans counterattack in North Africa.

Apr. 6: Germany invades Yugoslavia and Greece.

May 10: Hess parachutes into Scotland to propose plan for peace.

May 27: Nazi battleship *Bismarck* sunk.

June 22: Nazi Germany invades Soviet Union.

June 24: FDR backs aid for U.S.S.R.

July 24: United States assails Japanese move into French Indo-China.

Aug. 14: Roosevelt and Churchill announce Atlantic Charter after meeting at sea.

Aug. 21: Nazis begin siege of Leningrad.

Sept. 19: Germans take Kiev.

Oct. 11: Hideki Tojo becomes new premier of Japan.

Nov. 27: U.S. commanders at Hawaii, the Philippines, the Canal Zone, and the Presidio warned that war with Japan appears imminent.

Dec. 7: Japanese attack Pearl Harbor.

Dec. 8: U.S. Congress votes for war against Japan; Luzon invaded by Japan.

Dec. 10: British ships *Repulse* and *Prince of Wales* sunk by Japanese.

Dec. 11: Guam surrenders; Germany and Italy declare war on the United States, which responds in kind.

Dec. 23: Wake Island falls.

Dec. 25: Hong Kong falls.

1942

Jan. 1: Twenty-six countries form United Nations to fight Axis.

Jan. 2: Manila falls.

Jan. 10: Japanese invade Dutch East Indies.

Jan. 20: Wannsee conference in Germany lays out plans for the "Final Solution of the Jewish Problem"; the Holocaust begins.

Jan. 26: American troops arrive in Northern Ireland.

Feb. 15: Singapore falls.

Feb. 20: Americans of Japanese descent on West Coast sent to relocation camps.

Mar. 17: MacArthur arrives in Australia.

Apr. 9: Bataan falls.

Apr. 18: Doolittle raiders bomb Tokyo.

May 4–8: Battle of Coral Sea.

May 6: Corregidor falls.

May 30: First 1,000-plane raid by RAF on Cologne.

June 3–6: Battle of Midway.

June 7: Japan occupies two Aleutian islands.

June 13: U.S. creates O.S.S. (Office of Strategic Services) for intelligence work.

June 21: Germans take Tobruk.

June 25: Eisenhower commands U.S. forces in European theater.

Aug. 7: Marines land on Guadalcanal.

Aug. 19: British-Canadian force raids Dieppe, France.

Oct. 26: Naval battle at Santa Cruz in the Solomons.

Nov. 2: British win North African battle at El Alamein.

Nov. 7: United States and Britain land in French North Africa.

Nov. 11: Nazis occupy all of France.

Nov. 13–15: Naval battle off Solomons.

Nov. 19: Russians begin counterattack at Stalingrad.

Nov. 27: French scuttle their fleet at Toulon.

Dec. 24: Darlan assassinated in Algiers.

1943

Jan. 14–24: Casablanca conference between Roosevelt and Churchill.

Jan. 23: British take Tripoli.

Feb. 2: Nazis surrender at Stalingrad.

Feb. 6: Eisenhower heads U.S. forces in North Africa.

Feb. 25: U.S. forces beaten at Kasserine Pass, Tunisia.

May 12: Germans surrender in Tunisia.

July 9: Sicily invaded by Allies.

July 24: Hamburg hit by saturation bombing.

July 25: Mussolini ousted in Italy.

Aug. 15: Aleutian island of Kiska retaken by United States.

Sept. 3: Italy invaded by Allies.

Sept. 8: Italy surrenders.

Sept. 9: Allies land at Salerno, Italy.

Oct. 13: Italy declares war on Nazi Germany.

Nov. 20–24: Tarawa taken by Marines.

Nov. 22–26: Cairo conference with Roosevelt, Churchill, and Chiang Kai-shek.

Nov. 28–Dec. 1: Teheran conference with Roosevelt, Churchill, and Stalin.

Dec. 24: Roosevelt names Eisenhower to command invasion of Europe.

1944

Jan. 22: U.S. troops land at Anzio, Italy.

Apr. 10: Russians take Odessa.

June 4: Rome falls to the Allies.

June 6: D-Day as Allies land at Normandy.

June 13: Nazi V-1 "buzz-bombs" fall on London.

June 19: Battle of Philippine Sea.

July 3: Russians take Minsk.

July 20: Plot to kill Hitler fails.

July 25: St. Lo breakthrough from Normandy beachhead.

Aug. 15: Allies invade southern France.

Aug. 21–Sept. 28: Dumbarton Oaks conference lays groundwork for United Nations international organization.

Aug. 25: Paris falls to the Allies.

Sept. 3: British take Brussels.

Sept. 8: Nazi V-2 rockets land on London.

Sept. 17: "Operation Market-Garden" landings in Holland.

Oct. 20: United States invades Philippines.

Oct. 21: Aachen, Germany falls to United States.

Oct. 23–26: Battle of Leyte Gulf.

Nov. 7: Roosevelt wins fourth term.

Nov. 24: Superfortress raid Tokyo.

Dec. 16: Battle of the Bulge begins.

Dec. 26: Bastogne relieved by Patton's army.

1945

Jan. 9: United States invades Luzon.

Jan. 17: Soviets take Warsaw.

Feb. 3: Americans take Manila.

Feb. 4–11: Roosevelt, Churchill, and Stalin meet at Yalta.

Feb. 13: Dresden bombed.

Feb. 19–Mar. 16: Marines take Iwo Jima.

Mar. 7: U.S. Army seizes Remagen bridge on the Rhine.

Apr. 1–June 21: Battle of Okinawa.

Apr. 12: Roosevelt dies.

Apr. 13: Buchenwald concentrate camp liberated; Vienna falls to Russians.

Apr. 25: Americans and Russians link up at Torgau.

Apr. 28: Mussolini executed by partisans in northern Italy.

Apr. 29: German armies give up in northern Italy.

Apr. 30: Hitler commits suicide in Berlin.

May 1: Doenitz heads German government.

May 2: Berlin surrenders to Russians.

May 7: Germany surrenders unconditionally at Reims.

May 8: V-E Day.

June 26: United Nations Charter signed in San Francisco.

July 16: First atomic bomb tested at Alamogordo, New Mexico.

July 17–Aug. 2: Truman, Churchill, and Stalin meet at Potsdam. In middle of meeting, Churchill is replaced by Attlee.

July 26: Japan warned of complete destruction.

Aug. 6: Atomic bomb dropped on Hiroshima.

Aug. 8: Soviets declare war on Japan; Atomic bomb dropped on Nagasaki.

Aug. 14: Japan agrees to surrender.

Sept. 2: V-J Day. Formal surrender of Japan on the U.S.S. *Missouri* in Tokyo bay.

Nov. 20: International Military Tribunal opens in Nuremberg for war crimes trials.

Nationalities of the World War II 100

BELGIUM

Leopold III (95)

CANADA

Stephenson, William (23)

CHINA

Chiang Kai-shek (87)
Chiang Kai-shek, Madame (78)

CZECHOSLOVAKIA

Benes, Eduard (81)

DENMARK

Christian X (95)

ETHIOPIA

Selassie, Haile (96)

FRANCE

Darlan, Jean (59)
De Gaulle, Charles (51)
Gamelin, Maurice (62)
Petain, Henri (27)
Reynaud, Paul (99)

GERMANY

Braun, Wernher von (31)
Doenitz, Karl (64)
Eichmann, Adolf (91)
Frank, Anne (90)
Goebbels, Joseph (44)
Goering, Hermann (43)

Guderian, Heinz (12)
Heydrich, Reinhard (25)
Himmler, Heinrich (65)
Hitler, Adolf (1)
Jodl, Alfred (46)
Keitel, Wilhelm (48)
Krupp, Alfred (68)
Krupp [von Bohlen und Halbach], Gustav (68)
von Paulus, Friedrich (57)
von Ribbentrop, Joachim (52)
Rommel, Erwin (39)
von Rundstedt, Gerd (56)
Speer, Albert (77)
von Stauffenberg, Claus (89)

ITALY

Badoglio, Pietro (74)
Ciano, Galeazzo (80)
Mussolini, Benito (50)

JAPAN

Hirohito, Emperor (49)
Homma, Masaharu (45)
Kurita, Takeo (38)
Tojo, Hideki (29)
Yamamoto, Isoruku (6)
Yamashita, Tomoyuki (58)

POLAND

Anielewicz, Mordecai (97)
Bor-Komorowski, Tadeusz (88)
Sikorski, Wladyslaw (82)

SPAIN

Franco, Francisco (75)

UNION OF SOVIET SOCIALIST REPUBLICS

Beria, Lavrenti (79)
Chuikov, Vasily (42)
Molotov, Vyacheslav M. (53)
Rokossovsky, Konstantin (47)
Stalin, Joseph (4)
Timoshenko, Semyon (54)
Zhukov, Georgi (17)

UNITED KINGDOM

Alexander, Harold (76)
Bader, Douglas (10)
Brooke, Alan (28)
Chamberlain, Neville (66)
Churchill, Winston S. (3)
Elizabeth, Queen (78)
George VI (95)
Harris, Arthur (34)
Menzies, Stewart (15)
Montgomery, Bernard (37)
Ramsay, Bertram (16)

UNITED STATES

Arnold, Henry H. (41)
Bradley, Omar (33)
Donovan, William J. (24)
Doolittle, Jimmy (9)
Einstein, Albert (13)
Eisenhower, Dwight D. (7)
Four Chaplains, The (85)
Friedman, William (40)
Groves, Leslie R. (32)
Halsey, William F., Jr. (26)
Higgins, Andrew Jackson (69)

Hopkins, Harry L. (22)
Hull, Cordell (94)
Jackson, Robert (92)
Kennedy, Joseph P. (98)
Kimmel, Husband E. (19)
King, Ernest J. (20)
Kinkaid, Thomas (35)
Knox, Frank (60)
Lindbergh, Charles, Jr. (86)
Long, Breckinridge (73)
MacArthur, Douglas (8)
Marshall, George C. (5)
Mauldin, Bill (72)
McAuliffe, Anthony (67)
Morgenthau, Henry, Jr. (93)
Murphy, Robert (63)
Murrow, Edward R. (70)
Nimitz, Chester (18)
Oppenheimer, J. Robert (30)
Patton, George S., Jr. (11)
Pyle, Ernie (71)
Roosevelt, Eleanor (78)
Roosevelt, Franklin D. (2)
Shirer, William L. (55)
Short, Walter (19)
Sprague, C.A.F. (36)
Stilwell, Joseph W. (83)
Stimson, Henry L. (21)
Sullivan Brothers, The (85)
Truman, Harry S (14)
Wainwright, Jonathan (84)

VATICAN CITY

Pius XII, Pope (100)

YUGOSLAVIA

Broz, Josip (Tito) (61)

Allen, Thomas B. and Norman Polmar. *Code-Name Downfall: The Secret Plan to Invade Japan—and Why Truman Dropped the Bomb*. New York: Simon & Schuster, 1995.

Ambrose, Stephen E. *Citizen Soldiers*. New York: Simon & Schuster, 1997.

Andreas-Friedrich, Ruth. *Berlin Underground*. New York: Henry Holt, 1947.

Arendt, Hannah. *Eichmann in Jerusalem: The Banality of Evil*. New York: Viking Press, 1963.

Astor, Gerald. *A Blood-Dimmed Tide: The Battle of the Bulge by the Men Who Fought It*. New York: Donald I. Fine, Inc., 1992.

——. *June 6, 1944: The Voices of D-Day*. New York: St. Martin's Press, 1994.

Baldwin, Hanson. *Battles Lost and Won*. New York: Konecky & Konecky, 1966.

Baumont, Maurice. *The Origins of the Second World War*. Translated by Simone de Couvreur Ferguson. New Haven: Yale University Press, 1978.

Beard, Charles A. *President Roosevelt and the Coming of the War 1941: A Study in Appearances and Realities*. New Haven, Conn.: Yale University Press, 1948.

Blum, John Morton. *From the Morgenthau Diaries: Years of Urgency, 1938–1941*. Boston: Houghton Mifflin, 1965.

——. *Roosevelt and Morgenthau: A Revision and Condensation of the Morgenthau Diaries*. Boston: Houghton Mifflin, 1970.

Boatner III, Mark M. *Biographical Dictionary of World War II*. Novato, Calif.: Presidio Press, 1999.

Boelcke, Willi A., ed. *The Secret Conferences of Dr. Goebbels: The Nazi Propaganda War 1939–43*. Translated from the German by Ewald Osers. New York: E.P. Dutton, 1970.

Boesch, Paul. *Road to Huertgen: Forest in Hell*. Houston: Gulf Publishing Co., 1962.

Bradley, Omar N. *A Soldier's Story*. New York: Henry Holt & Co., 1951.

Brereton, Lewis H. *The Brereton Diaries*. New York: William Morrow and Co., 1946.

Brissaud, Andre. *Canaris: The Biography of Admiral Canaris, Chief of German Military Intelligence of the Second World War*. Translated and edited by Ian Colvin. New York: Grosset & Dunlap, 1974.

Buell, Thomas B. *Master of Sea Power: A Biography of Fleet Admiral Ernest J. King*. Boston: Little, Brown, and Co., 1980.

Butcher, Harry C. *My Three Years with Eisenhower*. New York: Simon and Schuster, 1946.

Cadogan, Alexander. *Diaries of Sir Alexander Cadogan*. London, 1971.

Chaney, Jr., Otto Preston. *Zhukov*. Norman, Okla.: University of Oklahoma Press, 1971.

Chang, Iris. *The Rape of Nanking: The Forgotten Holocaust of World War II*. New York: Basic Books, 1997.

Charman, Terry. *The German Home Front, 1939–45*. New York: Philosophical Library, 1989.

Churchill, Winston S. *The Second World War: The Gathering Storm*. Boston: Houghton Mifflin, 1948.

——. *The Second World War: Their Finest Hour*. Boston: Houghton Mifflin, 1949.

Churchill, Winston S. *The Second World War: The Grand Alliance*. Boston: Houghton Mifflin, 1950.

——. *The Second World War: Triumph and Tragedy*. Boston: Houghton Mifflin, 1953.

——. *Great Destiny*. New York: Putnam, 1962.

Ciano, Count Galeazzo. *Ciano's Hidden Diary, 1937–1938*. Garden City, N.Y.: Doubleday, 1945.

Ciano, Edda Mussolini. *My Truth*. As told to Albert T. Zarca. Translated from the French by Eileen Finletter. New York: William Morrow and Co., 1976.

Clark, Mark. *Calculated Risk*. London: George G. Harrap & Co., Ltd., 1951.

Clark, Ronald. *The Man Who Broke Purple: The Life of Colonel William F. Friedman*. Boston: Little, Brown, and Co., 1977.

Cole, Wayne S. *Roosevelt & the Isolationists*. Lincoln, Nebr.: University of Nebraska Press, 1983.

Collins, Larry and Dominique Lapierre. *Is Paris Burning?* New York: Simon & Schuster, 1965.

Cook, Haruko Taya and Theodore F. Cook, eds. *Japan at War: An Oral History*. New York: The New Press, 1992.

Cornwell, John. *Hitler's Pope: The Secret History of Pius XII*. New York: Viking Penguin, 1999.

Costello, John. *Days of Infamy*. New York: Pocket Books, 1994.

Craig, William. *Enemy at the Gates: The Battle for Stalingrad*. New York: Reader's Digest Press/ E.P. Dutton, 1973.

Crankshaw, Edward. *Khrushchev: A Career*. New York: Viking Press, 1966.

Cunningham, W. Scott, with Lydel Sims. *Wake Island Command*. Boston: Little, Brown, and Co., 1961.

De Gaulle, Charles. *Memoires de Guerre*. 3 vols., Paris, 1954.

Del Boca, Angelo. *The Ethiopian War, 1935–1941*. Translated by P. D. Cummins. Chicago: University of Chicago Press, 1969.

Divine, A.D. *Dunkirk*. A. Watkins, Inc., 1948.

Documents on German Foreign Policy. Series D. Washington, D.C.: U.S. Government Printing Office, 1949.

Dulles, Allen. *The Secret Surrender*. New York: Harper & Row, 1966.

Dyess, William. *The Dyess Story*. New York: G.P. Putnam's Sons, 1944.

Eisenhower, Dwight D. *Crusade in Europe*. Garden City, N.Y.: Doubleday & Co., 1948.

Farago, Ladislas. *The Broken Seal: The Story of "Operation Magic" and the Pearl Harbor Disaster*. New York: Random House, 1967.

Feingold, Henry L. *The Politics of Rescue: The Roosevelt Administration and the Holocaust, 1938–1945*. New Brunswick, N.J.: Rutgers University Press, 1970.

Field, Jr., James A. "Admiral Yamamoto," in *U.S. Naval Institute Proceedings*, Annapolis, Md.: October 1949.

Findling, John E. *Dictionary of American Diplomatic History*. Westport, Conn.: Greenwood Press, 1980.

Fleming, Peter. *Operation Sea Lion: The projected invasion of England in 1940—An account of the German preparations and the British Countermeasures*. New York: Simon and Schuster, 1957.

Foreign Relations of the United States, 1940. Vol. I. Washington D.C.: U.S Government Printing Office.

Forsberg, Franklin S., ed. *Yank—The GI Story of the War.* New York: Duell, Sloan & Pearce, 1947.

Frank, Anne. *The Diary of a Young Girl.* Garden City, N.Y.: Doubleday & Co, 1952.

Fredborg, Arvid. *Behind the Steel Wall.* London: Harrap, 1944.

Freiden, Seymour and William Richardson, eds. *The Fatal Decisions.* New York: William Sloane Associates, 1956.

Galante, Pierre with Eugene Silianoff. *Operation Valkyrie: The German Generals' Plot Against Hitler.* Translated from the French by Mark Howson and Cary Ryan. New York: Harper & Row, 1981.

Gamelin, Maurice. *Servir.* 3 vols. Paris: 1947.

Gavin, James M. *On to Berlin: Battles of an Airborne Commander, 1943–1946.* New York: Viking Press, 1978.

Geddes, Donald Porter, ed. *Franklin Delano Roosevelt: A Memorial.* New York: Pocket Books, 1945.

Gehlen, Reinhard. *The Service: The Memoirs of General Reinhard Gehlen.* Translated by David Irving. New York: World Publishing, 1972.

Gilbert, Martin. *The Second World War: A Complete History.* New York: Henry Holt & Co., 1989.

——. *The Day the War Ended: May 8, 1945—Victory in Europe.* New York: Henry Holt & Co., 1995.

Goodwin, Doris Kearns. *No Ordinary Time: Franklin and Eleanor Roosevelt: The Home Front in World War II.* New York: Simon & Schuster, 1994.

Grew, Joseph C. *Turbulent Era.* 2 vols. Boston: Houghton Mifflin, 1952.

——. *Ten Years in Japan.* Boston: Houghton Mifflin, 1944.

Grose, Peter. *Gentleman Spy: The Life of Allen Dulles.* Boston: Houghton Mifflin Co., 1994.

Groves, Leslie R. *Now It Can Be Told: The Story of the Manhattan Project.* New York: Harper & Row, 1962.

Guderian, Heinz. *Panzer Leader.* Translated by Constantine Fitzgibbon. New York: E.P. Dutton, 1952.

Gunther, John. *Inside Europe.* New York: Harper & Brothers, 1940.

Hamilton, Nigel. *Master of the Battlefield: Monty's War Years, 1942-1944.* New York: McGraw-Hill Book Co., 1983.

Hart, B.H. Liddell. *The German Generals Talk.* New York: William Morrow & Co., 1948.

Hassett, William D. *Off the Record with F.D.R.: 1942–1945.* New Brunswick, N.J.: Rutgers University Press, 1958.

Henson, Maria Rosa. *Comfort Woman: Slave of Destiny.* Philippines: Philippine Center for Investigative Journalism, 1996.

Hersey, John. *Men on Bataan.* New York: Knopf, 1942.

——. *Hiroshima: A New Edition with a Final Chapter Written 40 Years After the Explosion.* New York: Vintage Books, 1989.

Hicks, George. *The Comfort Women: Japan's Brutal Regime of Enforced Prostitution in the Second World War.* New York: W.W. Norton, 1994.

Hodgson, Godfrey. *The Colonel: The Life and Ways of Henry Stimson.* New York: Alfred A. Knopf, 1990.

Ingersoll, Ralph. *The Battle Is the Pay-Off.* New York: Harcourt, Brace & Co., 1943.

——. *Top Secret.* New York: Harcourt, Brace & Co., 1946.

Inoguchi, Rikihei and Tadashi Nakajima. *The Divine Wind.* Annapolis, Md.: U.S. Naval Institute, 1958.

Ismay, Hastings. *The Memoirs of General Lord Ismay.* New York: Viking Press, 1960.

Israel, Fred L., ed. *The War Diary of Breckinridge Long: Selections from the Years 1939–1944.* Lincoln, Nebr.: University of Nebraska Press, 1966.

Kahn, David. *Hitler's Spies: German Military Intelligence During World War II.* New York: Macmillan, 1978.

Kendrick, Alexander. *Prime Time: The Life of Edward R. Murrow.* Boston: Little, Brown, and Co., 1969.

Kersaudy, Francois. *Churchill and De Gaulle.* New York: Atheneum, 1982.

Khrushchev, Nikita S. *Khrushchev Remembers.* Translated and edited by Strobe Talbott. Boston: Little, Brown, and Co., 1970.

Kimball, Warren F., ed. *Churchill & Roosevelt: The Complete Correspondence, Volume III, February 1944–April 1945.* Princeton, N.J.: Princeton University Press, 1984.

Kimmel, Husband E. *Admiral Kimmel's Story.* Chicago: Henry Regnery Co., 1955.

Landstrom, Russell, ed. *The Associated Press News Annual, 1945.* New York: Rinehart & Co., 1946.

Langer, Howard J. "The Impact of Personality on History: An Interview with William L. Shirer" in *Social Education.* Washington, D.C.: National Council for the Social Studies, 1983.

——, ed. *The History of the Holocaust: A Chronology of Quotations.* Northvale, N.J.: Jason Aronson, Inc., 1997.

——, ed. *World War II: An Encyclopedia of Quotations.* Westport, Conn.: Greenwood Press, 1999.

——, ed. *Encyclopedia of World History.* Boston: Houghton Mifflin Co., 1948.

——. *Our Vichy Gamble.* New York: Alfred A. Knopf, 1947.

Lash, Joseph P. *Love, Eleanor: Eleanor Roosevelt and Her Friends.* Garden City, N.Y.: Doubleday & Co., 1984.

Lichtenstein, Nelson and Eleanora Schoenebaum, eds. *Political Profiles: The Kennedy Years.* New York: Facts On File, Inc., 1976.

Litoff, Judy Barrett and David C. Smith, eds. *Since You Went Away: World War II Letters from American Women on the Home Front.* New York: Oxford University Press, 1991.

MacArthur, Douglas. *Reminiscences.* New York: McGraw-Hill, 1964.

MacDonald, Callum. *The Killing of Obergruppenfuehrer Reinhard Heydrich.* New York: The Free Press, 1989.

Macdonald, Dwight. *Memoirs of a Revolutionist: Essays in Political Criticism.* New York: Farrar, Straus and Cudahy, 1957.

Manchester, William. *American Caesar: Douglas MacArthur, 1880–1964.* Boston: Little, Brown, and Co., 1968.

——. *The Arms of Krupp, 1587–1968.* Boston: Little, Brown & Co., 1968.

Mauldin, Bill. *Up Front.* New York: Henry Holt & Co., 1945.

McNeal, Robert H. *Stalin: Man and Ruler.* New York: New York University Press, 1988.

Michelmore, Peter. *The Swift Years: The Robert Oppenheimer Story.* New York: Dodd, Mead & Co., 1969.

Morison, Samuel Eliot. *Victory in the Pacific.* Boston: Little, Brown, 1960.

Morton, Louis. *The Fall of the Philippines.* Office of the Chief of Military History, Department of the Army. Washington, D.C.: U.S. Government Printing Office, 1953.

Moseley, Ray. *Mussolini's Shadow: The Double Life of Count Galeazzo Ciano.* New Haven, Conn.: Yale University Press, 1999.

Murphy, Robert. *Diplomat Among Warriors.* Garden City, N.Y.: Doubleday & Co., Inc., 1964.

Nichols, David, ed. *Ernie's War: The Best of Ernie Pyle's World War II Dispatches.* New York: Random House, 1986.

Office of United States Chief of Counsel for Prosecution of Axis Criminality. *Nazi Conspiracy and Aggression.* Washington, D.C.: U.S. Government Printing Office, 1946.

Overy, Richard. *Why the Allies Won.* New York: W.W. Norton & Co., 1995.

Patton, George S. *War As I Knew It.* Boston: Houghton Mifflin, 1947.

Pershing, John J. *My Experiences in the World War.* New York: Frederick A. Stokes and Co., 1931.

Philby, Kim. *My Silent War.* New York: Grove Press, 1968.

Pogue, Forest C. *George C. Marshall: Ordeal and Hope, 1939–1942.* New York: Viking, 1966.

——. *George C. Marshall: Organizer of Victory, 1943–1945.* New York: Viking, 1973.

Preston, Paul. *Franco: A Biography.* New York: Basic Books, 1994.

Pyle, Ernie. *Brave Men.* New York: Henry Holt, 1944.

Radzinsky, Edvard. *Stalin.* Translated by H.T. Willetts. New York: Doubleday, 1996.

Reid, Warren R., ed. *Public Papers of the Presidents of the United States: Harry S Truman, 1945.* Washington, D.C.: U.S. Government Printing Office, 1961.

Robertson, Terence. *Dieppe: The Shame and the Glory.* Boston: Atlantic Monthly Press/Little, Brown, and Company, 1962.

Romanus, Charles, and Riley Sunderland. *Stilwell's Mission to China.* Washington, D.C.: Department of the Army, Historical Division, 1953.

Rooney, Andy. *My War.* New York: Random House, 1995.

Roosevelt, Elliott. *As He Saw It.* New York: Duell, Sloan and Pearce, 1946.

Rosenman, Samuel I. *Working with Roosevelt.* New York: Harper, 1952.

Rothfels, Hans. *The German Opposition to Hitler.* Revised ed. Chicago: Henry Regnery Company, 1962. Translated by Lawrence Wilson.

———. *The Bombing of Germany*. Translated by Edward Fitzgerald. New York: Holt, Rinehart and Winston, 1962.

Ryan, Cornelius. *A Bridge Too Far*. New York: Simon & Schuster, 1974.

———. The Longest Day: June 6, 1944. New York: Simon & Schuster, 1959.

———. The Last Battle, New York: Simon & Schuster, 1966.

Schapsmeier, Edward L. and Frederick H. Schapsmeier. *Political Parties and Civic Action Groups*. Westport, Conn.: Greenwood Press, 1981.

Schmidt, Paul. *Hitler's Interpreter*. New York: MacMillan, 1951.

Schneider, Franz and Charles Gullans, eds. and trans. *Last Letters from Stalingrad*. New York: William Morrow, 1962.

Sereny, Gitta. *Albert Speer: His Battle With Truth*. New York: Alfred A. Knopf, 1995.

Seversky, Alexander P. de. *Victory Through Air Power*. New York: Simon and Schuster, 1942.

Sherrod, Robert. *Tarawa*. New York: Duell, Sloan and Pearce, 1944.

Sherwood, Robert E. *Roosevelt and Hopkins*. New York: Harper & Brothers, 1948.

Shirer, William L. *Berlin Diary*. New York: Alfred A. Knopf, 1941.

———. *The Rise and Fall of the Third Reich*. New York: Simon & Schuster, 1960.

———. *The Collapse of the Third Republic: An Inquiry into the Fall of France in 1940*. New York: Simon & Schuster, 1969.

Snyder, Louis L. *Historical Guide to World War II*. Westport, Conn.: Greenwood Press, 1982.

Slater, Elinor and Robert Slater. *Great Jewish Men*. Middle Village, N.Y.: Jonathan David Publishers, Inc., 10996.

Speer, Albert. *Infiltration*. Translated by Joachim Neugroschel. New York: Macmillan, 1981.

Stevenson, William. *A Man Called Intrepid: The Secret War*. New York: Harcourt Brace Jovanovich, 1976.

Stimson, Henry L. and McGeorge Bundy. *On Active Service in Peace and War*. New York: Harper & Brothers, 1948.

St. John, Robert. *From the Land of Silent People*. Garden City, N.Y.: Doubleday, Doran, 1942.

Stone, I.F. *The War Years 1939–1945*. Boston: Little, Brown and Co., 1988.

Stuhlinger, Ernst, and Frederick Ordway III, *Wernher von Braun: Crusader for Space*. Malabar, Flor.: Krieger Publishing Co., 1994.

Taylor, A.J.P. *The Origins of the Second World War*. New York: Fawcett, 1961.

Taylor, Lawrence. *A Trial of Generals: Homma, Yamashita, MacArthur*. South Bend, Ind.: Icarus Press, 1981.

Terkel, Studs. *The Good War*. New York: Pantheon Books, 1984.

Toland, John. *The Rising Sun*. New York: Random House, 1970.

———. *The Last 100 Days*. New York: Random House, 1966.

Trevor-Roper, H.R. *The Last Days of Hitler*. New York: Macmillan, 1947.

———. *Final Entries 1945: The Diaries of Joseph Goebbels*. Translated by Richard Barry. New York: G.P. Putnam's Sons, 1978.

Tuchman, Barbara W. *Stilwell and the American Experience in China: 1911–45*. New York: Macmillan, 1970.

Vassiltchikov, Marie. *Berlin Diaries, 1940–1945*. New York: Alfred A. Knopf, 1987.

von der Grun, Max. *Howl Like the Wolves: Growing Up in Nazi Germany*. New York: William Morrow, 1980.

von Mellenthin, F.W. *Panzer Battles: A Study of the Employment of Armor in the Second World War*. Translated by H. Betzler. Norman, Okla.: University of Oklahoma Press, 1956.

von Studnitz, Hans-Georg. *While Berlin Burns*. London: Weidenfeld & Nicholson, 1963.

Warlimont, Walter. *Inside Hitler's Headquarters, 1939–45*. Translated from the German by R.H. Barry. Novato, Calif.: Presidio Press, 1964.

Watts, Franklin, ed. *Voices of History 1943*. New York: Gramercy Publishing Co., 1944.

Werth, Alexander. *Russia at War: 1941–1945*. New York: E.P. Dutton & Co., 1964.

Weygand, Maxime. *Rappele au Service*. Paris: 1950.

White, W.L. *They Were Expendable*. New York: Harcourt, Brace & World, 1942.

Willkie, Wendell L. *One World*. New York: Simon and Schuster, 1943.

Winterbotham, F.W. *The Ultra Secret*. New York: Harper & Row, 1974.

Yamazaki, James N. with Louis B. Fleming. *Children of the Atomic Bomb: An American Physician's Memoir of Nagasaki, Hiroshima, and the Marshall Islands*. Durham, N.C.: Duke University Press, 1995.

Young, Desmond. *Rommel: The Desert Fox*. New York: Harper, 1950.

Young, Peter, ed. *The World Almanac Book of World War II*. New York: World Almanac Publications, 1981.

——. *Medal of Honor Recipients 1863–1978*. Prepared by the Committee on Veterans Affairs, United States Senate, 1979.

——. *Peace and War: United States Foreign Policy, 1931–1941*. Washington, D.C.: U.S. Government Printing Co., 1943.

——. *The Best from Yank: The Army Weekly*. Selected by the editors of *Yank*. New York: E.P. Dutton & Co., Inc., 1945.

Index of Names

Index of Subjects

About the Author

H oward J. Langer is an author, journalist, and public speaker. A graduate of Brooklyn College and the Columbia University Graduate School of Journalism, he has been a newspaper reporter, magazine and textbook editor, and publications director for national organizations.

His books include *World War II: An Encyclopedia of Quotations, The History of the Holocaust: A Chronology of Quotations, American Indian Quotations, The American Revolution, Who Puts the Print on the Page?* and *Directory of Speakers.* A forthcoming work is *America in Quotations: A Kaleidoscopic View of American History.*

His recorded interviews with famous world figures are in the Smithsonian/Folkways collection. They include Eleanor Roosevelt, Sir Edmund Hillary, and Justice William O. Douglas, among others.

He and his wife, Florence, live in New City, New York.